The Macdonalds of Cedar Park

An Ordinary Family in Extraordinary Times

The Manhattan Project Facilities – 1942-1946

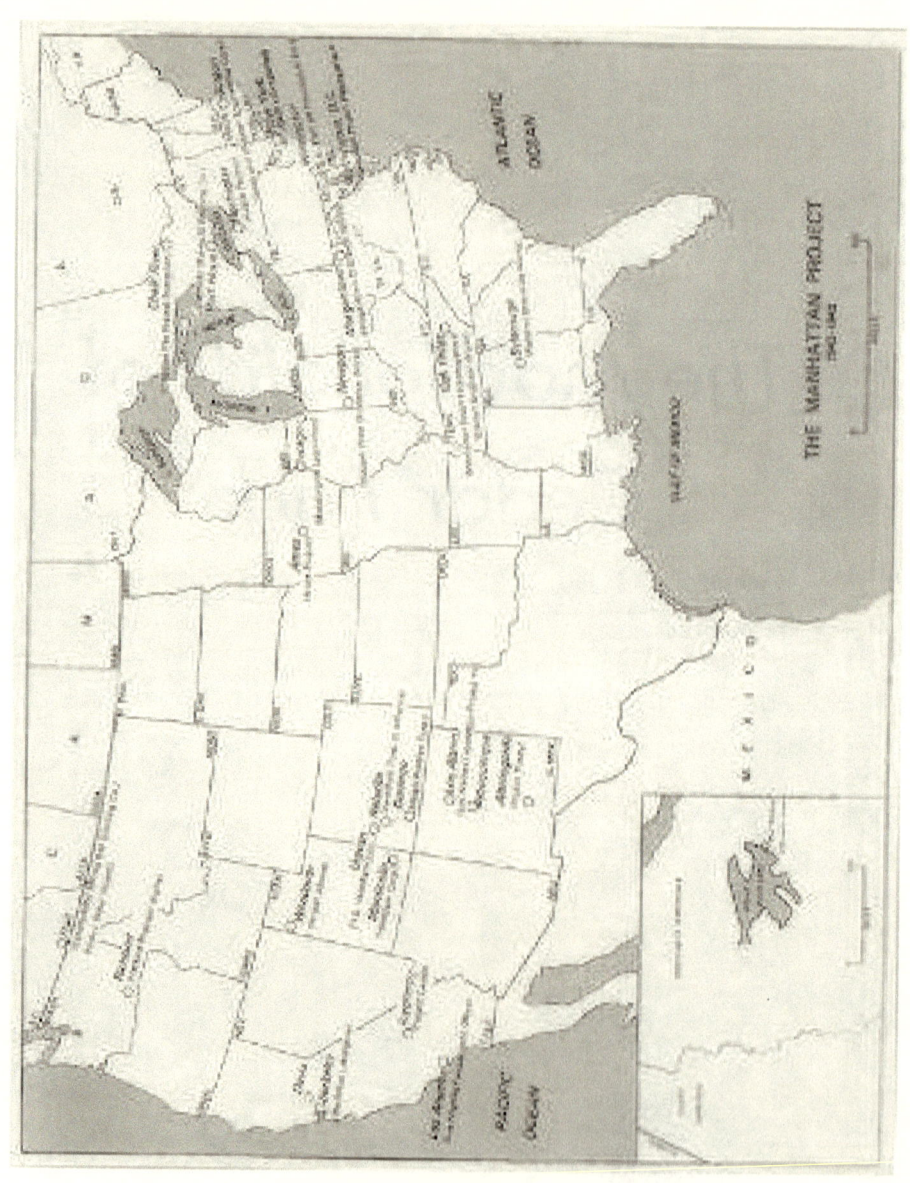

The Macdonalds of Cedar Park

An Ordinary Family in Extraordinary Times

A.E. MACDONALD

Skye Lewis Books

Text Copyright © 2025 Anne E. Macdonald
Published by Skye Lewis Books
ISBN:978-0-9983818-1-7

Cover Design by Peter Selig, Peter Selig Cover Designs
Cover Photo Credits:
Colorado Snowsports Museum (soldiers)
James Edward Westcott, courtesy of the National Archives (calutron operator)
Author Photo by Raj Das, ED Photos

Manhattan Project Facilities 1942-1946 map can be found a Department of Energy, Manhattan Project History, Resources, Maps and Jones, Vincent C., *Manhattan, the Army and the atomic bomb*, 1985
10th Mountain Division battalion locations during the Spring Offensive map can be found at the Denver Public Library, Special Collections and Archives, 10th Mountain Division Resource Center

DEDICATION

For my grandparents, Bertha and Mac, my uncle, Sonny, and my father, Ig, without whom there would be no story

PART ONE: 1941

ONE

BERTHA OBSERVED her family at the dining table. Her husband, Mac, was headed into Boston for his Saturday half-day at Stone and Webster Engineering. Their two sons, Sonny, 18 and a college freshman, and Ig, 12, were preparing for a day of skiing in Epping, New Hampshire. A dusting of snow, no more than an inch, had fallen overnight in Melrose, Massachusetts. Fresh snow in December was like manna from heaven for those inclined to ski. If there was an inch in Melrose, Massachusetts, how much more would there be an hour north?

"Sorry to be so late," Mrs. Brown said as she bustled around the dining room, placing plates of eggs, bacon, and toast in front of each person.

"Eat up, Ig. Eggs are good for you," Bertha said. "And don't feed the dog your breakfast."

"How come we have so many eggs?" Ig asked.

Mrs. Brown put more bacon on his plate. She knew how to get him to eat eggs.

"You need to eat too," Mrs. Brown said to Bertha.

"Ginny, get out from under that table," Mrs. Brown said. Ginny, their boxer, obeyed Mrs. Brown, her head hanging low.

"More coffee, Mrs. Mac?" Mrs. Brown asked.

"Yes, thank you, Mrs. Brown," Bertha replied before yelling out to her two sons, who had left the dining room table to prepare for their day of skiing.

"When does Hooker arrive?" Mac asked.

"Should be here any minute," Sonny said. "He's picking up Tiny and Web on the way."

"He said to be ready so we can pick up Charlie and get on the road ahead of the crowd," Ig said.

"Were you going to let Ginger out?" Mac asked.

"Can't you do it?" Sonny asked.

"We didn't want to chase her," Ig shrugged.

Bertha heard Mac mutter about his children's ability to care for 'their' dog. The boys had been attentive when the dog first arrived. Now he and Bertha were taking care of Ginny, their reddish brown boxer.

"Don't forget, there are sandwiches in the icebox for you," Bertha called out.

"More coffee, Mr. Mac?" Mrs. Brown asked, coffee pot in hand.

"No, thank you. I should get ready, too." Mac pushed his plate aside. "I'll be home for dinner. It would be great if we could have beans and franks. I'll take the car today," Mac said, the train whistle sounding in the distance. It was good that they lived a four-minute walk from the train station. But on Saturdays, when he worked a half-day, Mac preferred to drive.

"Have a good day, Mr. Mac," Mrs. Brown said.

"See you Monday, Mrs. Brown," Mac replied.

With Mac heading into work, the boys chasing snow for the day, and her mother, Gran, with her sister, Mabel, for a few weeks, she had a day to herself. With time to kill before meeting the Club Ladies for lunch and some Christmas shopping, Bertha enjoyed the sun shining through the bow window in the dining room, warm coffee, and the newspaper at hand. She felt lucky to have a nice, efficient, caring housekeeper and cook. Mrs. Brown came in the mornings Monday through Saturday to make breakfast, clean the house, do some shopping, and help prepare for dinner. She headed home to Mattapan by train each noon to care for her growing family. The thought that Mrs. Brown might no longer be able to take care of them niggled at the back of her mind. She usually pushed these thoughts away, but today, they floated to the top.

"How are you?" Bertha asked.

"It's crazy out there these days. I had to walk to the train. My son and daughter-in-law took extra shifts at the factory, so I had the baby all night. Then Mr. Brown had lots of calls for the taxi, so he was on the road when I left."

"Where's the baby now?" Bertha asked.

"My daughter-in-law came home."

"That's good."

"It seems like we went from no work to too much work," Mrs. Brown said, shaking her head, picking up the empty plates left behind by Mac and the boys.

After the long depression, they enjoyed stable, dependable work. Stone and Webster Engineering had taken Mac back on board after a decade away at other jobs. They appreciated Mac's drafting, fabricating, production, and testing skills, and he became involved in more projects. He frequently traveled to Pittsfield and Springfield, Massachusetts factories for work, and often wrote reports into the night at home. The boys were in good schools; they had a good life even as the threat of war hung over their heads.

Bertha turned her attention back to the newspaper. She hated to admit her mother was right. Hitler's march across Europe, first Poland, then Norway and Denmark, followed by France, and then the Battle of Britain, had been steady and relentless. The United States was neutral, according to the Neutrality Act, but could sell goods to Europe. They thought this would help England and France, but France had fallen, and England seemed to be holding on by a thread. Gran couldn't get over the idea that Charles Church, where she had been baptized in Plymouth, England, had been destroyed in an attack by the Nazis. President Roosevelt signed the new Lend-Lease Act, and the United States' ability to provide goods to other countries was no longer limited to cash transactions.

"Do you think there'll be war?" Mrs. Brown asked, returning to check on Bertha's coffee and her plate, which she had only picked at.

"I hope not. Although we seem to be providing many goods to the war effort overseas." To herself, she admitted the war was getting too close for comfort.

"All this activity has been good for my family. My daughter's husband got a promotion at the General Electric plant in Lynn, and my oldest boy got a job at the shipyard in Quincy," Mrs. Brown said.

"How's your youngest?"

"He's heading to Howard University in the summer, as soon as he graduates."

"That's wonderful. What is he planning to study?"

"Engineering. Mr. Mac put in a nice word for him."

"Mr. Mac is good at that," Bertha said. Mac had taught math and drafting at a trade school for three years before being hired by Stone and Webster for the first time. He helped students who strived to improve themselves, regardless of their color, religion, or economic background. "Possibly he can help with an internship or job after graduation."

"That's a nice offer but Stone and Webster Engineering only hires black folks as custodians."

Bertha nodded. "Mr. Mac knows all sorts of people in all sorts of businesses, he may still be able to provide some guidance." Mrs. Brown smiled but Bertha saw the skepticism in her eyes.

TWO

MAC CHECKED himself out in the mirror by the front door. His dark hair was beginning to thin, but nothing serious; a bit of gray at the temples made him look distinguished. He put on his suit jacket, buttoned his warmest overcoat, adjusted his hat, and checked out how he looked in the mirror by the front door. He heard a car pull into the driveway on the side of the house, horn beeping. Making his way through the living room, dining room, and to the back door, he stepped out and made a slashing motion across his throat. Ginger slipped out behind him and headed for her favorite tree.

"You'll wake the neighbors," Mac said as Hooker unrolled the driver's window. Mac nodded as Tiny got out of the car to keep an eye on Ginger.

"Right," Hooker said, getting out of the car and shaking Mac's hand. "Are we still on for Monday?"

"Of course," Mac replied. Web helped Sonny load their skis onto the rack on top of the car while Ig put their boots and polls in the trunk.

"Will you have any more building projects soon?"

"Not until steel becomes more available. Everything's tied up in government contracts right now."

"This Lend-Lease work is really changing things, isn't it," Hooker said. Mac nodded and grabbed Ginny's collar so Tiny could get back in the car. "It doesn't seem like the steel restrictions will loosen soon." Steel was tied to the factory work to support the war in Europe, and it certainly didn't seem like the war was ending.

Mac nodded again. "Anyone else going with you today?"

"We're picking up Charlie. We'll meet with the rest of the ski team and the Saugus boys in Epping. We'll be back in time for dinner," Hooker replied.

"Why Epping?" Ig asked.

"Maybe get a run or two in before it all melts," Hooker replied.

"We'd better get moving. The Holcombs' light went on, which means he'll be out to yell at us," Sonny said.

"Please tell the Holcombs I'm sorry for the noise." Hooker got in the driver's seat, put the car in gear, backed out of the driveway, and headed out.

"I'm sure they've reported the noise to someone already." Mac put a leash on Ginger for a walk, waving to Holcomb, who was glaring from his front step. Holcomb went out of his way to point out what was wrong with everyone and everything in 'his' neighborhood. As Mac passed the Ramsdells, Ken Ramsdell was on his porch and asked if they would take the train together. Mac invited him to drive into town with him. Back at the house, he found Bertha at the dining room table. Ginny sniffed around her seat for crumbs.

"I've given her a quick walk," Mac said. "I'm giving Ken a ride in."

"That's nice, particularly since they live so close."

"And Ken hardly ever complains about noise."

"Very true," Bertha smiled. "Do you think there'll be any snow skiing?"

"I doubt it, but it will keep them out of your hair for the day, and we can hear about their adventures at dinner. Give me a call before you leave, I'll give you a ride home. I hope the ladies don't talk about me too much."

"You went to high school with them, too; what do you think?" Mac winced, kissed Bertha, and headed out the door again.

Mac was grateful that Stone and Webster Engineering had come calling when one of the steel-framed homes he designed and built in 1937 was featured in the Boston newspapers. They offered him a drafting job, but he quickly advanced to inspector. As much as he liked the adventure of owning his own business, the steady income, varied projects, and responsibility appealed to his family provider side. This job enabled them to purchase a house in a better neighborhood in a good town with a good school system and regular train service to Boston.

He never admitted to Bertha that he missed creating steel frame houses with his father-in-law, the old construction pro, as his advisor and Hooker as his best employee. Telling Hooker that he had no work coming up, he felt almost as bad as when he had been forced to let everyone go before closing the Pittsburgh Test Labs' Boston Office in 1934, after seven years as General Manager. It was one of the hardest things he had ever done. The other was burying Bobby Bruce, their middle son, who died from scarlet fever, and admitting Bert to a psychiatric hospital for observation after the funeral. The National Dairy Council contract came along at a time when he didn't know where his next job would come from; they had all moved to Chicago. When they moved back to Melrose, he started steel framing work for a large contractor.

"Penny for your thoughts," Ken said.

"Oh, sorry, I was thinking about work," Mac replied.

"And what's in store for us next?"

"I was thinking about the reports I need to finish for Monday. Are you moving to a new project?"

"It's just a rumor I heard about something local coming in."

"That's interesting. I haven't heard anything."

"That's because you're on the road more than in the office."

"Lots of inspection work. What's the new project about?"

"Not sure, I thought you might know."

Mac laughed. He traveled too much to hear the office gossip. It was good that new projects were in the offing.

THREE

BERTHA REVIEWED the gray dress that fit her trim figure perfectly. Strands of gray were beginning to creep into her wavy blond hair, which she pulled back in a chignon. She paid particular attention to how she looked when she met with the club ladies, her group of high school friends that had started meeting when they were sophomores in 1915 and continued to meet 26 years later.

Mrs. Brown gave Ginger a bone, which Ginger took to her favorite spot under the piano in the front room, where the sun would keep her warm. Ginger knew the bone meant she would be spending the day at home. Bertha said goodbye to Mrs. Brown and headed down the front steps and down the street to the train station. Looking at her watch, she calculated that getting an earlier train allowed her some time to herself to Christmas shop before meeting Johnny, Alice, the twins Edith and Ethel, and Millie for lunch. Maybe even time for a quick stop at a bookstore, too. Bertha loved literature, and she wanted to ger her Christmas book list to Mac so that she got something she wanted to read rather than something a sales clerk recommended to him.

The sun had turned the snow on the street into a slippery slush. Treading cautiously on the downhill portion of North Cedar Park, she arrived at the bustle of rushing cars covering the once-white snow banks with muddy dark brown slush. Cars splashed through the dirty potholes, covered windshields, and blocked drivers' views while simultaneously soaking pedestrians on the sidewalk with the slush. Honking horns and fists waving in the air proclaimed the anger of both drivers and pedestrians. There's nothing like the first snow of the season. Spying an opening in traffic and a cleared spot on the opposite sidewalk, she made her way across Vinton without getting too splashed. Hurrying down the street and onto the shoveled path through the park, she put the sounds of cars splashing and people yelling behind her. She arrived at the train station out of breath.

"Mrs. Macdonald, what a surprise to see you here," Mrs. Holcomb said as Bertha impatiently waited for the train. Mrs. Holcomb worked at a department store downtown.

"Good morning. How are you?"

"I was woken up by the car horn this morning. Jimmy said that Mr. Hooker was taking the boys skiing. All that activity and noise for so little snow. The streets are so dry now that I don't need these galoshes," Mrs. Holcomb said, looking at her feet.

"Bob Hooker wants to drive up to look over the ski slope he's been running the past few winters. It was nice of him to take the boys along for an outing."

"I would never let Jimmy wander with Mr. Hooker and Mr. Benedict. They seem a little loose if you know what I mean," Mrs. Holcomb said. She knew Hooker had a reputation with women. Still, he was an excellent instructor and a dedicated skier, and he made sure Ig paid attention on the ski jump and didn't daydream into another accident. Web coached the high school ski team, taught English, and had recently married. Sonny's friends Elaine and Nancy said that all the high school girls dreamed about Mr. Benedict, but he kept his students working hard both in class and on the slopes. Still, rumors traveled fast and tended to stick.

"Does Jimmy like to ski?" Bertha asked. She wondered if Jimmy was allowed to breathe.

"Jimmy says it's fun, but his studies come first," Mrs. Holcomb replied.

"Are you talking about my husband?" Gertie asked, joining Bertha and Mrs. Holcomb. Mrs. Holcomb's face showed a tinge of pink.

"Yes, Mrs. Holcomb was talking about skiing," Bertha said.

"Ah, there are my friends now," Mrs. Holcomb said, raising a hand and waving to a group further down the track. "Wonderful to see you."

"Nice to see you, too," Bertha said as she watched Mrs. Holcomb weave in and out of the growing train crowd. She sometimes felt bad that they kept Jimmy so sheltered. Sonny thought Jimmy was a know-it-all in school, which didn't surprise her. But she also wondered if Mrs. Holcomb had friends.

The train pulled in, and Bertha and Gertie boarded the car for the 15-minute ride to Boston's North Station.

"Who is that?" Gertie asked, as Mrs. Holcomb took a seat in the same car.

"My neighbor has lots of opinions of what others should and shouldn't do."

"She has quite an opinion of Web," Gertie huffed. She and Web had been married for six months.

"I think she's commenting more on Bob Hooker's reputation."

"Does she know him?"

"That's a good question. He does seem to get around. But that's catty of me. So, are you working today?"

"Yes, today's my last day in the office. I've started to show."

"Oh, how exciting. When's the baby due?"

"In May. I can't wait."

They chatted away and soon found themselves at North Station. Gertie headed to work and Bertha headed downtown to shop and then meet her friends for lunch.

FOUR

IG GRINNED as Hooker pulled onto Route 1, picked up speed, and the six of them headed north to New Hampshire. He was eleven years old, and he was going skiing with the older guys, the really good skiers. This was something he could brag about to his friends. Web rode shotgun with Ig stuffed between them in the front seat. Tiny was in the back seat with Sonny and Charlie. He pulled some beers out of the bag at his feet and handed them around. Ig put his hand out for one but Hooker shook his head and the beer disappeared into the back seat.

He had known these guys all his life, well, since he was four when they had moved to Melrose and the Hookers, the McWades, and the Benedicts were their neighbors and friends. Hooker had always fascinated Ig because he was 35, close to Dad's age, unmarried, of average height, and had a firm, compact build, and had a girl on his arm at any event. Hooker told everyone how he learned to ski as a boy, skied for Harvard, and now taught skiing for the Melrose recreation department at the ski tow and ski jump they had built at the Mt. Hood recreation area. He also ran the local outing club. Mom said Hooker needed to grow up someday, and Dad said he was a smart guy who didn't want to settle down.

Hooker liked his independence and spent as much time skiing as possible. He founded the outing club to teach young men and women to ski safely and to attract customers to his weekend ski area in Epping. Ski trains ran from Boston to Epping, and the ski area was a short walk from the depot. Hooker and Tiny said it was the way skiing should be. Ski down, hike, or herringbone back up the slope and ski down again. No tow ropes or other mechanical devices. He and the professor who owned the land split the proceeds from the weekend. When he wasn't skiing, he worked on engineering projects, including some of Mac's building projects.

Tiny and Web were both 24. Tiny was short and lithe, and loved skiing as fast as possible with the wind and sun on his face, every worry slipping away. He joined the Civilian Conservation Corps after high school graduation in 1935, since college wasn't a part of his plans, and enjoyed living and working outdoors, cutting ski slopes somewhere in New Hampshire for a year or two before taking a sales job, at which he excelled. He was one of Hooker's ski instructors on the weekends.

Web, also 24, six feet tall, blond, and blue-eyed, was the best-looking of the bunch. He possessed an effortless grace in skiing, English, carpentry, and with everyone he met. He was a good skier, a better friend, and lacked musical talent, unlike his musician parents and sister. His friends envied his good looks and ease with girls.

Mom thought the world of Web, and Ig had to admit that he was hard to dislike. Web had studied English in college, taught High School English and carpentry, coached the nascent Melrose High School ski team, which had included Sonny and his friend Charlie, and skied as much as possible, to the chagrin of his wife, Gertie.

The minimal snow was disappearing in the bright sunshine, and the grass showed when they arrived in Epping. Hooker pulled over, followed by some other cars of skiers, including the guys from Saugus who also skied at Mt. Hood. After a quick consultation, they agreed to head further up the road to North Conway and see how the snow looked at Cranmore and Cannon since they were already halfway there. Several of them, including Hooker, wanted to show off their skills and see if Hannes Schneider had room for them in his new ski school. As they bumped along, Ig wondered what time they would get home, but didn't say anything. This was an adventure, and he was just a passenger. He was amazed at the number of people driving with skis on their cars. He had no idea that so many people would be skiing. After Epping, some people seemed to turn back toward home rather than look for another ski area.

"Ig, we'll stop and rent some skis for you and then head to the mountain for a ski lesson."

"I have skis," Ig said.

"They're old and too short for you. Let's try you on something that's the right size," Hooker replied.

"Can we get some lunch?"

"We'll make sure you get some food," Hooker replied.

Ig nodded. It never hurt to have another lesson, and from what everyone was saying, this ski area was a lot larger than Mount Hood. Hooker pulled up to a one-story red building with skis on the roof. The six of them piled out of the car as a second car of boys from Saugus pulled up behind them.

"Any idea where we're staying?" One of them asked.

"The old farmhouse on the way to Cranmore. You know, the one we stayed at before."

"Right, we'll see you there. Happy skiing." At least we have a place to sleep, Ig thought. Mom and Dad probably thought he was sleeping at home tonight.

"OK, Ig, let's get you some skis."

"I thought you told Dad we'd be home tonight."

"Right," Hooker replied. "Sonny, call your father at the office. He said he was working on reports today, and let them know we're staying overnight." Sonny reluctantly headed for the pay phone. Ig grinned; he liked anyone who told his older brother what to do.

A bunch of girls passed them as they headed for the door of the ski shop.

"He's cute," one of the girls said, pointing at Ig. They all giggled.

"So, ladies, you up for some skiing this weekend?" Web asked, turning on all his considerable charm.

"We are. Where are you skiing?"

"Cranmore," Hooker replied as he and Ig headed inside, shooting Web a look. Sonny, Charlie, and Tiny were smiling and nodding as if they had all lost the ability to speak. Web glared at Hooker. Ig figured it had something to do with Web and Gertie getting married soon.

"Same here. Maybe we'll see you on the slopes," the girl replied.

"Looking forward to it," Web replied, with a dashing tilt of his head towards the girl doing the talking. "Check us out."

The girls waved goodbye.

"Aren't you married? I seem to remember being an usher at your wedding," Tiny asked, knowing full well that Web was, indeed, married. He had been an usher at the wedding.

"I'm looking out for you and Hooker," Web replied.

"In that case, you should have asked them where they were staying," Tiny said.

"All in good time, my friend," Web replied.

Inside, Hooker steered Ig towards the ski racks.

"What size?" A voice said.

"I don't know," Ig replied. "I've grown a lot."

"Let's see," he heard the guy say as he stood skis up next to Ig to check on height. After a few tries, they agreed on a pair of skis. Then they found him a pair of low, toe-clip boots and selected poles. Ig pulled out money and got some change back, which he stuffed in his pocket. He'd count it later. They were told to have the skis back no later than 9 pm on Sunday; Ig said they would be back much sooner because they had to be home. Hooker rolled his eyes. Ig wondered what his parents would think of all this.

At Cranmore, Tiny took off to ski alone, fast and straight, communing with the world around him. Web, Sonny, and Charlie headed up the slope to practice in the soft powder before the bright sun turned it to ice. Ig allowed Hooker to tell him how to put on skis and do some basic snowplowing.

Some girls joined in, and then others, and soon Hooker had an impromptu class going that attracted the attention of the instructors. When an instructor stopped by to ask him what he was doing, Hooker explained that Ig was a student of his in Melrose, and this was his first time on a larger mountain. There was some giggling, and Ig noticed that the other ski instructors did not seem appreciative of his efforts. Hooker took Ig up his first tow rope, and the two of them skied down the main slope that ended at the ski school, followed by a group of hangers-on.

At the bottom, Hooker had a brief conversation with Hannes Schneider. While they were chatting, Minnie Dole, the National Ski Patrol founder, said he'd like to chat with Hooker, Web, and Tiny. Hooker invited Dole to stop by the farmhouse later, and Dole agreed.

FIVE

BERTHA STOPPED at her favorite bookstore on Washington Street and purchased Between the Acts by Virginia Woolf. She would set it aside as a Christmas gift for one of the Club Ladies. She, along with Johnny, Millie, Alice, Arlene, and the twins, Edith and Ethel, had founded the Club Ladies in their junior year of high school. They had seen each other through weddings, marriage, work, children, elderly parents, and moves across the country and back. Over the years, the group had grown quite large, but the core members, except for Arlene, who had moved to Chicago, were having lunch to celebrate their 26th anniversary.

For the 18 months she, Mac, and the boys had lived outside of Chicago, she and Arlene had gotten quite close, but now she was back in Melrose, and they were back to being Christmas card friends. They exchanged letters about the book choice each month, but the content became increasingly less personal. Arlene may be the recipient of the book she had just purchased.

Bertha left the bookstore and rushed to the Jordan Marsh department store cafe. Millie, an executive secretary at Stone and Webster, had arrived and was seated and waiting for them. Her lunchtime was precious, and Bertha felt a little guilty for running late. She envied Millie for working, meeting new people, and participating in dynamic projects; she knew that her life had not been easy as a widow raising her boy alone. Johnny, the unmarried school teacher in the group, arrived on her heels. She preferred Johnny to her given name, Selena. The twins, Edith and Ethel, the serenest people she knew, never a hair out of place or a bad word for anyone, arrived together. Alice was the last to arrive, breathless and full of gossip.

"Bertie," Alice used Bertha's high school nickname, "That woman is waving to you. Isn't that Mrs. Wills, wife of Royal Barry Wills, the well-known architect? I didn't know you and Mrs. Wills were such good friends," Alice said.

"Sonny and her son Charlie are good friends," Bertha replied. "They are skiing together today. That's the extent of our acquaintance."

"Frank would be excited to meet Mr. Wills. There are so many things they could do together. Mr. Wills must be an important resource for Mac in his career," Alice said.

Bertha winced. She had known Alice most of her life, but Alice liked to name-drop and gather acquaintances that might turn into business for her husband, Frank, another Somerville High School classmate.

"I believe Mac and Mr. Wills have a working relationship," Bertha replied, uncomfortable with Alice fishing for an introduction.

"Well, then, we should all get together sometime. Maybe you can introduce us at your next party."

"What does everyone think of Evil Under the Sun?" Johnny asked, changing the topic. "I enjoyed it."

"Christie is not one of my favorite authors," Bertha replied. "And I'm not sure about this new detective, Hercule Poirot. He seems a bit prissy. The plot was interesting, but not great literature."

"I think it's well written," Millie said. "I agree that it's not great literature. I'm looking forward to our next book."

"Oh, let's not hash out this book. We can discuss it next week at our Christmas party. What is everyone wearing?" Alice would rather gossip than talk about books.

Bertha was enjoying the lively discussions. Alice hadn't deterred them from talking about books as well as party clothes, politics, their children and the sense that war was looming. Millie announced that she had to return to work. Alice's husband, Frank, was picking her up, and she left with Millie. The twins still had more Christmas shopping to do, so they headed off together, leaving Bertha and Johnny to organize the money everyone had contributed, ensure the bill was paid, and tip the waitress.

"Where are you off to next?" Johnny asked Bertha.

"I'm picking up some coats I had put on layaway for the boys. Ig is getting taller every month and outgrowing everything. Sonny wants a new coat to look good for the girls on campus."

"What happened to Nancy?"

"Oh, she was playing the field, and Sonny found out. They still talk and occasionally go out but seem less serious about one another."

"What do you mean by playing the field?"

"Ig caught her kissing someone near the docks at Brant Rock."

"And he told Sonny?"

"No, he took Sonny and Ginny for a walk on the beach, and they found Nancy at the same spot, kissing another guy."

"I don't know about kids these days. They are certainly bold. By the way, my mother wants to know if you would like to use the cottage for a week in June?"

"That would be great. Now that Mabel's sold her cottage, I've been fishing around for ideas of what to do. Tell your mother we accept."

"I'll let her know. Are you catching a ride home with Mac, or would you like a ride?"

"I'm meeting Mac after I get the coats."

Johnny accompanied Bertha on her rounds and did some shopping of her own before they headed to Mac's office together since Johnny had parked on Franklin Street, too. As they approached the front door of the building, they saw Millie greeting a man also waiting at the door and watched as the two of them kissed.

"Well, well, who might this be?" Johnny said, catching up to Millie and the mystery man wearing a naval uniform. Bertha trailed a step or two behind with her packages.

Millie promptly turned pink, the color rising from her chin to her forehead, and smiled weakly at her two friends. The tall, distinguished naval officer turned, smiled, and offered his hand.

"Bert, Johnny, this is Commander Jones. Commander, these are two old friends of mine," Millie said.

"I'm Bertha Macdonald, Bert has been a nickname since childhood," Bertha said.

"And I'm Selena Wilson. My brother called me Johnny when I was little because he wanted a brother, not a sister, and Johnny it has been ever since. I like it better than Selena."

"Lovely to meet you both. Millie, we should be on our way." Commander Jones whisked Millie into a waiting car.

"And here I am, in case anyone's interested," Mac said as Bertha and Johnny watched the car pull away. "I see you've met the Commander."

"How long have you known?"

"I met him a few minutes before you."

"A likely story. Well, I need to get home. I'm babysitting tonight," Johnny said.

"Babysitting? For whom," Bertha replied. "All your nieces and nephews are too old."

"Joanne has a boy coming over, and I promised to keep an eye on the two of them while the rest of the family scampers off to the movies."

"The poor boy," Mac said.

Johnny laughed, got into her car, and headed for home, where she lived with her mother, brother, brother's wife, and nieces and nephews, at least those who were still home.

Mac took Bertha's parcels and put them in the back seat. He had no briefcase, which meant he wouldn't be working on any reports the rest of the weekend. It also meant he would go into the office on Monday morning and not travel.

"Are the boys home?"

"Sonny called to say there wasn't any snow in Epping, so they continued to North Conway. They'll stay overnight and drive home tomorrow. Mabel called to say she's dropping your mother off with us."

"I wondered how long she and Mabel would last together."

"Where did you and the girls have lunch?"

"At the Jordan Marsh cafe. We talked about the book we're reading, Johnny's students, our children — the usual stuff."

"Someday, you'll have to tell me what they say about me," Mac said.

"You should be more concerned about what I say about you."

They laughed and chatted on the drive home. Ramsdell had taken the train rather than wait. The snow and slush were now gone, and the streets were dry. Ginger greeted them at the door, tail wagging. Mac grabbed Ginger's leash, and they headed out for a walk. Gran roused herself from a nap in her chair while Mabel played solitaire at the dining room table.

"The boys called. They're staying overnight," Mabel said.

"Did you bring dinner?" Gran asked.

"Yes, I have franks in the icebox, baked beans, and brown bread."

"I'm not that hungry. I'll scrounge something up in the kitchen. The two of you should go out together. You don't need me tagging along."

"What about me?" Mabel asked.

"You can stay with me," Gran replied.

Mabel looked at their mother. "If I had known that, I would have gone to Ro's and had dinner with my grandchildren."

"Why don't you stay overnight?" Bertha asked her older sister.

"It's been a busy couple of weeks," Mabel said, looking at her mother. "And I promised Ro I'd watch the kids tomorrow morning, so I'll head to his house. I'm sure they'll have something for me to eat." Mabel gathered her things.

"There's a letter from your brother on the table," Gran said. Mabel paused to wait to hear about the letter.

"Willis?"

"No, Don."

"Did you read it?"

"No, it's addressed to you."

Bertha picked up the letter. It had no return address and was postmarked from Washington, DC. If he and Martha were back from Norway, they hadn't let anyone know.

"We should call tomorrow," Bertha said. It was her attempt at distracting her mother from the fact that. Don, her youngest, the promised one, the West Point grad, seemed never to have time for his mother.

"Put your coat on. We're driving up to Essex for some fried clams," Mac said, returning with Ginger. "The Ramsdells are joining us."

"Oh, in that case, I'll go too," Gran said.

"I thought you weren't hungry?" Mabel asked.

"I'm hungry for seafood," Gran replied, getting her coat and hat on and heading for the car.

"Well, then, I'll be on my way," Mabel said, picking up her things and heading for her car.

Ginger followed them to the kitchen, looking at them expectantly.

"Of course, you can come too," Mac said. Ginger wagged her tail and started to drool.

Bertha shook her head and made up the rear. The odds they would find fried clams in December were slim, but it would be a nice ride up the coast.

SIX

SKIING ENDED when the sun set. They packed up their things and drove to the converted ski lodge down a dark road. Ig followed the guys into a large, brightly lit farmhouse that sat on a hill. A snowball fight was taking place outside and inside were lots of people yelling over the noise. Cigarette smoke, stale beer, and burnt popcorn greeted them. Those were the smells Ig could identify. The guys yelled greetings to those inside, trooped upstairs, and looked for spaces to sleep for the night. The bedrooms were littered with mattresses and a few beds. It was a communal space that provided a place to sleep for anyone who wanted to ski and stay overnight but wasn't going to spring for a hotel or motel.

Hooker found an empty room, and they dropped their things onto various mattresses to claim their space. None of them had brought much for a change of clothes, so they left coats, gloves, and scarves. They trooped downstairs, where food was strewn around the dining room table and any free surface in the living room. Ig headed for the kitchen. He grabbed a sandwich and a beer from the refrigerator. Hooker took the beer from him and handed him a glass of milk, noting that growing boys needed milk.

Ig sat at the dining room table to eat and observe everything. It was the guys' farmhouse, he had heard, and some girls had stopped by for the party. He wondered how some guys would get up and ski in the morning if they kept drinking beer. Sonny chatted up a girl in the living room, and Ig couldn't wait to tell Nancy. Sonny needed someone else, not a girl who kissed everyone she met. He may not have kissed a girl yet, but he didn't like what Nancy was doing, even if she was experimenting. He saw Charlie join a group of guys and girls in a snowball fight outside. They seemed to be having a great time. Of course, Charlie had a girlfriend. They had been going together since first grade, according to his mother.

He watched as Minnie Dole entered the house and drew Hooker's attention. Hooker, Web, and Tiny were ski patrol members, something Sonny and Charlie wanted to be someday. Ig was surprised when Minnie took a seat across the dining room table.

"That sandwich looks good. Does your mother know you're here?"

"She knows I'm in North Conway, I think," Ig said with a smile.

"You looked good out there on the slope today. Been skiing for long?"

"A couple of years," Ig replied.

"You're from Melrose, right?" Minnie asked.

Ig nodded.

"Ever tried the ski jump there?"

"Of course," Ig said, which he had. "I love it."

Dole laughed. "Of course you do. Are you planning to join the ski team when you get to high school?"

Ig scrunched up his face. "I don't know. My brother likes it. Sometimes I need to do my own thing."

"Good answer," Dole replied. "Everyone needs to find their way."

Hooker, Web and Tiny, and some other guys Ig didn't know took seats at the dining room table. Hooker suggested that Ig leave, but Minnie said he should stick around and listen. Sonny continued chatting with the girl in the living room, oblivious to everything around him. Charlie wandered through to the kitchen for another beer, with some girls trailing behind him.

After exchanging a few pleasantries with the men seated around the table, Dole turned serious. The Army was creating a new unit, the 87th Mountain Infantry Battalion, which was being activated at Fort Lewis, Washington. As a consultant and founder of the National Ski Patrol, he was actively looking for volunteers to join the ranks of this nascent unit. He talked about how the Finnish troops, trained in winter warfare, had kept the Nazi invasion at bay two years earlier. How the Germans could hold the high country in the Alps with their well-trained troops, but the United States had not yet developed similar mountain and skiing troops.

"Hooker and Tiny, you both volunteered to help train some troops at Lake Placid last year. What do you think?"

"We're not at war, and we aren't going to war," Dick, one of the others at the table, said. "I don't see any reason to join something that will never happen."

"I don't know about that," Hooker said, evenly, almost kindly. "We are creating more and more jobs and factories to provide supplies to Europe. I think it's just a matter of time."

"I agree with Ken," Dave said. "I think we're jumping the gun."

"I'm in," Tiny said, looking at Dole, no hesitation in his voice or manner.

"Much appreciated, Tiny," Dole replied with a smile. "This effort might seem a bit premature given that we aren't directly at war, but having trained troops ahead of any action is always smart planning."

"If you don't mind, I'd like to think about this and get back to you on Monday," Hooker said, more serious than Ig could ever remember seeing him.

"Of course, Hooker," Dole replied. "How about you, Web?"

"Well, as much as I'd like to join you, I'm not ready to stop teaching partway through the semester. Plus, Gertie and I are expecting our first child this spring. I will stay out for now."

"Congratulations," Dole said. "I'm happy for you both."

"Jesus Christ, Web, when were you going to tell us?" Sonny asked.

"On the way home," Web replied.

As his head drifted onto the table and his eyes closed, Ig thought this was the most exciting day he had ever had. He and Gran were fascinated with the war in Europe and listened to the radio reports whenever Mom wasn't around. Mom said the war would never affect them, and they were listening too closely to the radio. He and Gran were pretty sure that wasn't true.

SEVEN

THE SIX of them rattled down Route 1 late Sunday morning. Sonny and Tiny were in the front seat with Hooker, while Ig, Charlie, and Web were relegated to the back. Ig leaned against Web. As far as anyone could tell, he was asleep.

"If you're worried about Dad, don't be," Sonny said. "I can smooth things."

"I know your Dad," Hooker said. "He'll have something to say."

"Tell him about the offer. He'll understand," Web replied. "Mr. Mac's a good guy."

"What can he do? I'm a college freshman. I'm my own man," Sonny said.

"Ig is 12. Your parents won't be happy," Tiny said.

"I'm awake," Ig said. "I'm resting my eyes."

"What will you tell your parents?" Hooker asked, looking at Ig in the rearview mirror.

"I met Hannes Schneider, Toni Matt, and Minnie Dole, and I had a great time skiing on a big mountain."

"And what will you say if they ask about drinking beer?"

"I had some beer."

"And how many beers did you have?"

"So many I lost count."

"You say that, and I'll pound you," Sonny swung around, hand curled into a fist. Ig cringed and smirked out of his brother's reach as Web put his hand on Sonny's shoulder.

"This won't solve anything."

Sonny slumped in the front seat, arms crossed. Why had they brought his little brother anyway? Oh yeah, someone needed to keep an eye on

Ig while Mom met with her friends and Dad worked. Gran wasn't home with them, so it fell to him. They had headed out to ski in Epping for the day. Then Hooker had said they should drive to North Conway and check things out. Then Dad had agreed they should stay overnight and drive home in daylight but hadn't sounded pleased. He would have a word or two with his parents about babysitting.

"Looks like we will all be home for Sunday dinner," Web said.

Hooker turned off Route 1. The Saugus boys in the car behind beeped the horn to let them know they were turning for home. He dropped Charlie off first, then Web, then swung to the Macdonald's on Cedar Park.

"Are you coming in?" Sonny asked.

"I think I should explain," Hooker replied.

EIGHT

MAC WAS at the back door as soon as he heard the car pull up, Ginger following along to greet everyone. Bertha and Gran were in the kitchen preparing Sunday dinner.

"Nice of you to get them home," Mac said to Hooker as Sonny and Ig got out of the car and gathered their things to bring into the house.

Hooker winced at the sarcasm. "We skied yesterday and early this morning," Hooker replied.

"That's good," Bertha said, taking Ginger inside.

"Why don't you two get settled inside? I want to chat with Hooker," Mac said, leaning against Hooker's car. Sonny gave his father a look. Mac didn't respond and Sonny followed Ig into the house with their skis and boots.

"I apologize for keeping the boys out so long. I got caught up trying to impress Hannes Schneider and didn't think about how you and Mrs. Mac would react."

"It won't happen again, will it?"

"No, sir."

"I like you, Bob, but there are limits to what I'm willing to tolerate. You have to respect that I'm their father."

"Understood," Hooker paused for a moment. "You know I appreciate all your help, and I want your boys to be the best skiers and men they can be."

"So do I."

"Are we still on for lunch tomorrow? I want to talk with about an offer Minnie Dole made to join the new 87th Mountain Infantry regiment," Hooker said. Mac liked chatting with Hooker and providing advice when asked.

"And you're going to take it?"

"I think so, but I want to consider it first. And talk to my mother and sister."

"What about Tiny and Web?"

"I'm signed up already," Tiny said from the back seat, smiling.

"Sort of a continuation of your CCC work," Mac said. Tiny nodded.

"I'm teaching, and Gertie and I are expecting this spring," Web said. "That's exactly what I told him."

"Congratulations, Web. Mrs. Mac told me the good news last night" Mac said. Web nodded. Nothing much stayed a secret in this town.

"Lunch tomorrow?" Hooker asked.

"Of course. We'll discuss things, especially after I talk to Ig."

Hooker smiled, Web laughed, and Tiny shook his head.

"There you are," Mac said as he walked into the living room where Sonny was sitting on the couch and Ig was fiddling with the radio dial, trying to tune in one of his shows.

"Hey, Dad."

"So, Ig, how much beer did you have?"

"I'm sure they had no beer at all. They are both too young," Bertha said, coming out of the kitchen with a roast beef on a platter, and a dishtowel over her shoulder. Gran followed with mashed potatoes.

"Dinner's ready, take your seats," Bertha said.

"Sorry, we weren't here for dinner last night," Sonny said, smiling his most charming. "And to help with the dishes."

"No dishes last night. We drove up to Essex for some fried clams," Gran said. "How was the skiing?"

Sonny scowled. He loved fried seafood.

"Fun. I met Hannes Schneider and Minnie Dole. Hooker said he was my instructor. I was supposed to act like I'd never skied before," Ig replied.

"Bet that wasn't too hard, squirt," Sonny said.

"I'm a good skier, Minnie Dole said so. It was fun, and the girls were pretty."

"What girls?" Bertha asked.

"The ones on the bunny slope. They thought Hooker was great and that Web was so handsome. One of them said I was cute."

"That is something," Mac said, with a twinkle in his eye.

"Where did you stay?"

"At the farmhouse," Sonny said.

"There were a lot of guys there," Ig said. "I slept on a mattress on the floor."

"And was there beer?"

"Oh, yeah, and milk."

"And did you have any beer?"

"One when Hooker wasn't looking," Ig replied. "He made me drink milk when he caught me." Sonny pushed him from behind to remind him to say nothing that would get them both in trouble.

"I'd hate to think you had more than that," Mac said before Bertha could say anything.

"Where was Sonny?" Bertha asked.

"He was talking to some girls," Ig said. Sonny punched him from the side. "Some of them stopped by, but they were staying somewhere else. At the girls' farmhouse, I guess."

Mac looked at Bertha to see her reaction. She didn't look happy but she wasn't yelling either. Maybe a good sign that she was letting the boys grow up. Just then, the radio show was interrupted for a news bulletin.

"The Japanese have attacked Pearl Harbor." They looked at one another in astonishment. "Listen in to this report that has been received."

"I am speaking from the roof of the Advertiser Publishing Company Building. We have witnessed this morning the distant view a brief full battle of Pearl Harbor and the severe bombing of Pearl Harbor by enemy planes, undoubtedly Japanese. The city of Honolulu has also been attacked and considerable damage done. This battle has been going on for nearly three hours. One of the bombs dropped within fifty feet of KTU tower. It is no joke. It is a real war. The public of

Honolulu has been advised to keep in their homes and away from the Army and Navy. There has been serious fighting going on in the air and in the sea. The heavy shooting seems to be . . . . We cannot estimate just how much damage has been done, but it has been a very severe attack. The Navy and Army appear now to have the air and the sea under control."

"Pearl Harbor. That's where Don was stationed when I visited him," Gran said.

"That's in Hawaii. Why would the Japanese attack us?" Ig asked, his hands dripping water all over the dining room rug from the glass he just knocked over.

"It's a mistake. They must have attacked someplace else," Bertha replied. "The Japanese would never attack us."

"But they just did," Sonny said.

"Shush, both of you. We need to listen," Mac said.

"I told you we were at war," Gran said, absently scratching Ginger behind the ears.

"No, we're not," Bertha replied, putting her head in her hands.

"Not officially," Mac said, his pipe in one hand, looking like he was trying to solve a problem.

"Stop it. I can't believe you are talking about war," Bertha yelled. "Turn off that radio and sit down to dinner."

They all looked at her in astonishment, then took their seats at the table, the radio still playing the same report. A ringing phone broke the silence. It was Bertha's older brother, Willis, calling to find out if they had heard about the attack on Pearl Harbor. And now Guam and the Philippines.

"Are we at war?" Ig asked. "That Minnie guy seemed to think so."

"There already is a war," Gran replied.

"Right, sorry, Gran. I meant, will we be in the war?"

"I hope not," Bertha replied.

Mac turned off the radio, and they said grace for the first time in a long time before eating dinner. The table was silent throughout the meal, and then the boys picked up the plates and dishes and took them into the kitchen. Sonny returned with the cake Gran had made, and Ig with the serving utensils. Mac took dessert plates from the dining room hutch and served cake and coffee.

"Why don't you boys go get changed. Did you take showers this morning?" Bertha asked.

Sonny and Ig trooped upstairs to wash up and change. They heard some scuffling at the top of the stairs but it didn't appear to be anything serious.

"It looks like the boys had a grand time," Gran said.

"What did you say about not getting into trouble?" Mac asked Bertha.

"I can't believe Hooker would allow them to drink."

Gran studied her tea, not looking at either of them, but Mac could see she was suppressing a smile.

"Hooker, Tiny, and Web are nice, responsible boys," Bertha said.

"They are grown men, not boys. Ig won't soon forget this weekend," Mac said.

"Say no next time," Bertha said. Mac turned the radio back on and ignored her.

Sonny and Ig returned downstairs and took their seats for dinner. The radio remained on, and they heard the reports about Pearl Harbor being repeated over and over again. The broadcaster described the horror of ships burning and sinking in Battleship Row. Of the horror of seeing men floating, blackened, or on fire, presumably dead men in the water, with others trying to swim away from the sinking, burning ships. Then, he announced more attacks on Guam and the Philippines. A deliberate, all-out attack on the United States.

Dinner was a solemn affair. Mac noticed that Bertha barely ate anything. After dinner, the boys did the dishes and then joined their parents in the living room to continue listening to the day's reports.

In the evening, President Roosevelt made a radio address to the nation.

"Good evening, ladies and gentlemen, I am speaking to you tonight at a very serious moment in our history. The Cabinet is convening and the leaders in Congress are meeting with the President. The State Department and Army and Navy officials have been with the President all afternoon. In fact, the Japanese ambassador was talking to the president at the very time that Japan's airships were bombing our citizens in Hawaii and the Philippines and sinking one of our transports loaded with lumber on its way to Hawaii.

By tomorrow morning the members of Congress will have a full report and be ready for action.

In the meantime, we the people are already prepared for action. For months now the knowledge that something of this kind might happen has been hanging over our heads and yet it seemed impossible to believe, impossible to drop the everyday things of life and feel that there was only one thing which was important - preparation to meet an enemy no matter where he struck. That is all over now and there is no more uncertainty.

We know what we have to face and we know that we are ready to face it.

I should like to say just a word to the women in the country tonight. I have a boy at sea on a destroyer, for all I know he may be on his way to the Pacific. Two of my children are in coast cities on the Pacific. Many of you all over the country have boys in the services who will now be called upon to go into action. You have friends and families in what has suddenly become a danger zone. You cannot escape anxiety. You cannot escape a clutch of fear at your heart and yet I hope that the certainty of what we have to meet will make you rise above these fears.

We must go about our daily business more determined than ever to do the ordinary things as well as we can and when we find a way to do anything more in our communities to help others, to build morale, to give a feeling of security, we must do it. Whatever is asked of us I am sure we can accomplish it. We are the free and unconquerable people of the United States of America.

To the young people of the nation, I must speak a word tonight. You are going to have a great opportunity. There will be high moments in which your strength and your ability will be tested. I have faith in you. I feel as though I was standing upon a rock and that rock is my faith in my fellow citizens.

Now we will go back to the program we had arranged…"

"If we do declare war, I'll enlist," Sonny said.

"Bet you were going to flunk out anyway," Ig replied.

"No one is going to do anything just yet," Mac replied, more calmly than he felt.

NINE

MAC WAS up early before there was even a hint of sunrise on the Monday morning after the bombing of Pearl Harbor. Sleep had eluded him, so he decided to clear his mind by taking Ginger for a walk. It wasn't official yet, but Mac couldn't see any way around it—they would be going to war. He wasn't worried about Ig, but he was concerned about what war would mean for Sonny, now 17, and himself, turning 45 in March.

He and Sonny had been exempted from the two previous selective service registrations, because those had focused on men ages 21 to 35 - like Hooker, Tiny, and Web. Tiny had already made his decision to join the ski troops. Hooker would most likely do the same thing. Web's decision was more challenging.

Mac found Ginger waiting patiently at the bottom of the stairs, hoping someone would take her out, and Sonny and Ig glued to the radio. He turned off the radio and suggested they all take Ginger for a walk.

"Dad, what do you think will happen next?" Sonny asked.

"I suspect we'll go to war," he replied.

"Will you go?" Ig asked.

"I'm not sure they'll want someone as old as me," Mac replied, ruffling his youngest's hair.

He had decided to push for the Navy if he was called up. It's where he was heading when WWI ended. His engineering skills and experience would be highly sought after, more so than when he registered for the draft in June 1918 after his sophomore year at Tufts ended. Back then, all the male students drilled on the Tufts College green between classes.

During the summer of 1918, he worked as a surveyor, his first real job in his field. He returned to Tufts to teach basic drafting classes in the fall. Armistice was declared on November 11, a week before his date to report to the navy as a draftsman, and too late to start classes that semester. He decided to become a two-year man and to continue working as a surveyor and teacher, both good jobs. He could return to school if things didn't work out. His old friend, Mel Pride, a high school and college classmate, was now a naval officer somewhere near Pearl Harbor. He would pick up some newspapers to see if Mel was among the wounded or dead. At least Bertha's brother, Don, was no longer at Pearl Harbor.

Ginger explored all the scents on the street, in the bushes, in the grass, around the fire plugs, and on the sidewalk. There was little that Ginger wouldn't investigate.

"I'll go," Sonny said with the assuredness of the invincible. He was too young to understand that going off doesn't mean you return a hero or the same person you were when you left.

"I wanted to go to war in '17. I told my mother I wanted to be useful, I wanted to join the Army Air Corps like your Uncle Willis, to fly a plane, shoot the enemy, become a hero, and marry your mother. Your grandmother was against it. I was her last remaining family member and she didn't know what she would do if I didn't come home," Mac said. "A lot of boys didn't come home."

"Yeah, but you didn't go did you?" Sonny said, not trying to hide his sarcasm.

"I lacked the one thing the Army Air Corps demanded, perfect vision," Mac replied. "But I had skills that the navy wanted, in particular drafting."

"So what happened?" Ig asked.

"The war ended a week before I was to report for duty," Mac said.

"What would Granny Macdonald have done if you didn't come home?" Sonny asked.

"She would go back to Maine and stay with her mother, brothers, sister, nieces, nephews, and many, many cousins if something happened to me."

"Yeah, I didn't think it would happen, but I miss her stories," Sonny said.

The Great War had been deadly, and this war, he felt, sure to be fought on too many fronts, by too many countries, would be deadlier. They had already seen what Hitler and Hirohito were willing to do to other countries. He doubted this war would end in 19 months, like the last one. Now he understood his mother's worries for him when he was 20.

Outside Garniss Market, several people were waiting for the newspaper delivery truck, nickels ready, to pick up the latest news. The day was young, and a lot could and probably would happen by the time the afternoon newspapers were out. He pulled out a dime and grabbed two papers, one for the train and the other for Bertha. He told the boys to leave the paper for their mother, not take it to school.

"Mom won't need it. The other papers will be delivered soon," Ig said.

"How will you be getting to school today?" Mac asked Sonny.

"Bill's driving a bunch of us to campus around 11. It's a reading day and we're hunkering in the library until it closes."

"Be sure to tell your mother when you plan to be home. She'll be anxious today."

Sonny nodded.

"In case anyone wants to know, I'll be walking to school at the regular time," Ig said.

"Thank you," Mac said. "If you are running late for any reason, call and let your mother know."

"I'm 12," Ig said as if that explained everything. But he nodded, which was a good sign.

"And Sonny, don't sign anything until we've had a chance to talk. The official age to join any service is 21."

"It's my life, you know. I'm a good skier, they might make an exception for me."

"I know, but it would be good to talk first." Sonny gave him a look that said a great deal about his choices. Everyone's blood was running high.

When they returned, Mrs. Brown had oatmeal, eggs, bacon, and toast ready.

"It's about time you got back. I wouldn't want all this food to go to waste," Mrs. Brown said, smiling, pouring coffee for Bertha and tea for Gran. The radio was on again, but at a low enough volume not to interfere with the conversation.

"It's going to be quite a day," Mac said.

"It is indeed," Mrs. Brown replied, returning to the kitchen with Ginger trailing behind to see what treats he might find. Mac ate quickly while everyone perused the paper.

"I don't see Mel's name anywhere," Bertha said. "That's a relief."

"He's a cat with nine lives," Mac replied, getting up from the table. He patted Ginger, who had returned to the table for more scrounging, kissed Bertha, nodded to the boys, put on his overcoat and hat, checked himself in the mirror, and headed for the train, one paper tucked under his arm; the remainder were distributed across the dining room table.

PART TWO: 1942

TEN

IN JANUARY, the newspapers started reporting on American deaths from German attacks on American ships carrying equipment and food to England. These stories appeared beside the stories of American fatalities and heroism at Pearl Harbor.

Newspapers, including local newspapers, featured articles and instructions on air raid testing and blackouts. Every home was expected to know these instructions and prepare for each test. February was the shortest month of the year, but it seemed like the longest. The household limit of five tires per car, including four on the car and one additional tire, was monitored by a tire ration board that had the authority to search houses and property for extra tires, and inspect every car when a new tire was requested. Every neighborhood had air raid wardens, and some local citizens seemed to take pleasure in inspecting their neighbors.

All tin cans had to be separated from the trash, flattened, and left for special pickups. Tin toothpaste tubes had to be turned in to get a new one. Cooking grease was collected for the war effort, generally in tin coffee cans.

Restrictions were placed on new cars as automobile factories were being converted to war work. It was unfortunate that Mac hadn't turned in their old jalopy sooner. Mac seemed to find every rock and pothole on his travels.

ELEVEN

"A FINE for too many car tires. That's absurd," Bertha said as Mrs. Brown poured coffee for everyone except Gran, who had her teapot by her cup.

"That's what it says here," Ig replied. "We're supposed to put any extra tires out to be picked up."

"Eat your breakfast," Bertha took the paper from Ig and read the article. The weeks after Pearl Harbor were the usual rush of holiday activities, shopping, parties, cards from friends and family, and gift-giving. The United States officially declared war against Japan on December 8, and against Germany and Italy on December 11, 1941. The newspapers largely avoided mentioning the war, instead providing updates on the missing and deceased. One dreary concession to the war was the request not to use Christmas lights, either inside or outside homes. Main Street had no Christmas lights.

The Club Ladies exchanged books and talked about the war. Millie announced that her son had survived the bombing of Pearl Harbor, bringing the war much closer to home. Johnny wanted to ask about the naval commander they had seen Millie with, but declined to do so after that announcement. Bertha sent a book to Arlene along with a Christmas card and learned from Arlene's card that her oldest, already 21, had joined the Army.

Mac worked longer hours traveling to vendors to review work for contracts in progress, and scope out replacement parts for the ships that survived the Japanese attacks. New contracts were coming in requesting design modifications for ships about to be built. There were rumors at work that the Army was clamoring for attention. Stone and Webster engineers and draftsmen attempted to keep pace with current needs while evaluating new projects they were being approached to handle.

"In case anyone is wondering, I'm taking the train to the office today," Mac said, folding up the paper he had been reading. Four newspapers were delivered daily, two in the morning and two in the evening, along with the Melrose Free Press and the occasional Somerville paper.

"You're not traveling?" Bertha asked. "Will you be home for dinner?"

"I'm not sure what time I'll be home," Mac replied. "I'll call and let you know."

Bertha was worried. Mac was rarely home for dinner these days and traveled a lot, often at a moment's notice. She had been so wrapped up in the war and the holidays, the boys, the household, Mrs. Brown, and her shortened schedule that she hadn't focused enough on Mac. He had come home around 10 pm the night before and fallen asleep almost immediately.

"Would you pick up the Ski Annual at Asa Osborne's today?" Sonny yawned.

"How nice of you to grace us with your presence this morning," Mac said.

"I needed to catch up on my rest," Sonny said. He kissed his mother on the cheek as she continued reading.

"Can you believe this? Everyone is supposed to turn in every extra tire they have. How can they do this to us? People need their extra tires," Bertha said.

Gran snorted as she sipped her tea and handed Ginger pieces of bacon under the table.

"We need the rubber for the war," Mac replied.

"That doesn't mean people should have to turn in something they already paid for."

"Maybe it will save us a few cents on the war," Sonny said as he took his place at the dining room table. "Hey, Pops, can I use the car today since you're not traveling I'm driving the guys to school today. At least I am if I can have the car."

"Yes, be back for dinner," Mac said.

"Ah, Pops, I have some plans," Sonny replied.

"I bet you're going to take Nancy out," Ig said, a sly grin on his face.

"Shut up, runt, you're not too big to pound, you know." Sonny shot him a look that said that he would find Ig later.

"Ig, get ready for school. First, it was no Christmas lights on Main Street, and now it's tires. What's next?" Bertha said.

"Ig, time to go," Mac said. He was standing at the door, ready to leave. "We can walk together."

"Have a good day, dear."

"Don't forget the Ski Annual."

"There's a civil defense test on Saturday," Ig said.

"Where did you hear that?" Bertha asked.

"On the radio," Ig replied.

"We have to reduce your radio time," Bertha said.

"I'll be home for dinner tonight. Nothing much should keep me. Do we have errands to do?" Mac said as he and Ig headed out the door.

"Grocery shopping would be good," Bertha replied. "Mrs. Brown hasn't had time for that lately."

"Don't forget the Ski Annual," Sonny called out.

"If I have time," Mac replied.

TWELVE

MAC AND Ig headed down Cedar Park toward the train station. The joke in Melrose is that all the men emptied the town by taking the morning trains to Boston and filled up the town when they returned home around 5 pm. It was a small town with three train stations built to take advantage of the commute. One of the reasons for moving to Melrose was the easy access to the train station, and the other was the quality of the schools. Ken Ramsdell and Mrs. Holcomb were among the neighbors heading to the train. The group of commuters was large enough that they stopped traffic on Vinton Street to cross and then spread apart again as they headed for the train. They could hear the whistle at the Highlands stop, so they knew the inbound train would arrive in a few minutes.

Mac said goodbye to Ig and watched as he joined some friends walking toward the school on Main Street. Mac was glad Bertha had gotten him a new coat, but it looked short, and Ig's pants needed to be altered so they would cover his ankles. The boy had had another growth spurt. He was now as tall as Sonny.

Mac and Ramsdall sat together on the train, taking seats facing one another while Mrs. Holcomb continued through the car to sit with her friends at the other end. They typically spread out and read their papers, ignoring the passengers getting on in the hopes that they would move on to other empty seats. As the train pulled into Malden, the crowds filled almost every seat. Mac wondered if folks were on the early train because they couldn't sleep. In the past few weeks, it seemed like people were heading into work early more frequently.

"Mr. Macdonald, Mr. Ramsdell, mind if I join you?" Betty, a young clerk at Stone and Webster Engineering, was hovering in the aisle while others pushed and shoved to get by. He stood to let her into the seat near the window. Ramsdell nodded and continued reading.

"My gallant neighbors," Mrs. Holcomb said, and her friends tittered.

"Is everything ok?" he asked.

Betty burst into tears. He handed her his handkerchief to dry her eyes.

"It's Al, he's going to join the navy today."

"What did your dad say?"

"You know how obstinate he can be, especially when Dad tells him not to do something. He and Dad had such an awful row this morning that I'm on pins and needles." Mac wasn't sure he remembered young Al as being obstinate or disagreeing with his father, but it had been a long time since he had seen them together.

"I guess I should pull myself together. It won't look good if I go to work with my face all red and puffy."

"So Betty, remind me, did your father serve in the Great War?"

Mac knew the answer, but he wanted to see how Mrs. Holcomb would use this opportunity to tell the neighborhood and Bertha how he had made a girl cry on the train.

"Will Al stop by to see you, do you think?"

"I hope so. It would be nice to talk to him without Dad yelling."

"Let me know if Al wants to chat."

"Thanks, Mr. Macdonald; it's nice to talk with someone who's fatherly and isn't yelling. What will your sons do?" Betty asked. Her snuffles slowed.

"Sonny isn't old enough to register yet. You have to be 21, and he's 18, and Ig is 12," Mac replied.

When the train pulled into North Station, Ramsdall grabbed his things and headed for the door quickly so he wouldn't get caught in the crowd, saying he'd see Mac at the office. Mac would have joined him, but he decided to walk Betty to the office as a favor to her grandfather, his first employer. They walked through the station, down Canal Street, across Haymarket Square, then up Congress to Devonshire Street. Newspaper hawkers were on every corner, yelling all kinds of headlines, including a few that weren't in the papers.

Mac smiled and nodded to Mrs. Holcomb, who turned up Washington Street while he and Betty continued down Congress Street to the Stone and Webster building on Franklin Street.

THIRTEEN

"HEY, POPS, it says in the paper that you have to register for the Selective Service. You missed this cut-off by three weeks. Isn't that a hoot?" Ig greeted Mac, who arrived at the dining room table early on a February morning, followed by Sonny, to find Ig reading the paper while Bertha and Gran were chatting about the news.

"Sorry to be so late," Mrs. Brown said as she bustled around the dining room, placing plates of eggs, bacon, and toast in front of each person. She gave Ig a look that told him she expected a clean plate.

"Eat up, Ig. Eggs are good for you," Bertha said, settling into her place. "And, don't feed the dog your breakfast."

"We won't be getting so many eggs soon, right?" Ig asked. Rumors of food shortages had begun.

"Mrs. R, anything you would like this morning?" Mrs. Brown asked Gran.

"More tea wouldn't go amiss."

"Would you like that here or up in your room?"

"Upstairs is fine," Gran replied.

Mrs. Brown hustled back into the kitchen.

"You have to register too, Sonny," Ig said. "But not until June."

"Yeah, but I'm young. They'll want me," Sonny replied.

"You seem to think my engineering skills aren't needed," Mac said.

"You're funny, Dad," Ig said. "I think it's exciting. Do you think I'll have to register to serve before this is all done?"

"I certainly hope not," Bertha replied. She saw a smile on Mac's face. The boys did make him laugh, which was good to see.

"We'll have this done and all wrapped up in a year, don't you worry," Sonny said.

"I don't think the war will be over so soon. Look at how long it's been going on in Europe, and England," Gran said, as she got up and headed upstairs

Bertha looked at her mother. She struggled to admit that her mother had been right about the war.

"What classes do you have today?" Mac asked Sonny.

"Mechanical Engineering with old man Crowder. Boy, is he tough."

"Yeah, I bet he is."

"You know him?"

"He was in my class."

"Good thing he doesn't know who I am," Sonny replied.

"How do you figure that?" Mac asked.

"It's not like you don't have the same name," Ig said.

"He's never said anything about knowing you. I thought he was tough on me because I'm such a wise ass."

"Language," Bertha said, ignoring the plate of food in front of her as she read the paper.

"Sorry," Sonny said automatically.

"Gran doesn't seem as spry these past few days. Is she ok?" Mac asked Bertha.

"I'm not sure. She has a doctor's appointment today; her breathing has been bothering me."

Bertha watched as Ig looked from one parent to another. She knew he was wondering about his grandmother's health.

"Wow, look at the time, I better be getting to school," Ig said, getting up from the table, picking up his things.

"He's like a little old man," said Sonny. "He's going to be just like you, Dad."

Ig smiled. "That's exactly who I want to be."

FOURTEEN

IT WAS a raw and cold walk from North Station to the office on a dark February morning. Mac stepped off the stairs and joined the stream of folks exiting the elevator on his floor. As they streamed through the lobby to the time clock to punch in, the receptionist, whom the young women and men not so affectionately called the "old battle-axe," looked at the clock and made notes. She monitored all the comings and goings on the floor, even though they all used time cards. He cued up to punch his time card, noting that much like the train, there was a lot of activity taking place on the floor early on a Friday morning.

After he punched in, Millie, the executive secretary for one of the senior project engineers, and his and Bertha's old school friend, called him over.

"You have a message from your wife," she said, pointing to one of the messages on her desk while writing up notes on her stenographer's pad.

"Thank you," Mac said as she continued making notes.

"Be ready; they want to see you this morning," Millie said.

"Who?"

Millie nodded at the manager's office without lifting her head from her task. Mac nodded and was about to turn toward his desk when he heard his name.

"Mac, would you join us?" the manager asked. It wasn't a request he could ignore.

"Of course," Mac said. Stepping into the manager's office, he was surprised to see two senior engineers, men he did not interact with regularly, and Ken Ramsdell. Mac closed the door behind him and took a seat.

"Mac, we're impressed with the relationships you've cultivated with your vendors and your knowledge of metals, particularly steel." Mac assumed they were talking about his article on structural steel for the American Society of Civil Engineers, but it would be nice if they mentioned it directly.

"Thank you." He knew he had good vendor relationships, but he appreciated the recognition.

"Things are heating up with some new war-related projects, and we have been asked to help with some work at a factory in Beverly. We're taking over a contract from the National Board of Standards."

Mac nodded. "What is the project?"

"We don't have all the details. That's where you and Ramsdell come in. We're heading up to Beverly tomorrow morning to learn more. We want to know that we can count on you and your relationship skills with difficult clients."

"Of course, you can count on me." It's all he could offer since they weren't providing details.

All three men looked at him expectantly. They seemed to want something from him, but he had no idea what it was. Finally, they nodded. He'd been holding his breath. There was a tension in the air that he couldn't place.

"This is top-secret work. Work that you can't discuss with anyone."

"Except for the vendor, and Ken, of course."

The manager looked at the senior engineers and nodded in response. "The more specific requirements that have yet to be refined, and the work needs to be completed on time and on budget."

"So this is more of an exploratory meeting with the vendor to determine the requirements and find the best way forward," Mac chose his words carefully. He struggled with starting work when the entire problem was not yet defined.

"That's correct, except that we can't extend the deadline."

"I will do my best."

"Your abilities will be appreciated, along with your discretion. You'll be working with a team that includes Dr. Alexander, Captain Ruhoff, an Army engineer, and various scientists," his manager said. "There will be weekly reports."

There were always weekly reports.

"What does Dr. Alexander do?" Mac asked. This was different than the work he was usually assigned.

The three men in the room exchanged glances before one answered.

"Brilliant man. Changes his mind daily. Once you've met him and learned a little about what he wants to do, you'll help us develop blueprints, get approval, and build the plant."

"How quickly does all this need to be done? It sounds like it would take more than a year?"

"It should, but we need to be up and running in about five months," his boss said.

Mac paused. Even if the designs were outlined and drafted on time, he doubted they could build a factory that quickly.

"What should I do to prepare for this meeting?"

"Clean up whatever's on your desk today. Your current work is being reassigned."

Mac nodded. This new project seemed intriguing. New projects tended to be a rush for the first few days, then slowed as the team realized they needed more time.

"Should I suggest my replacement?" Mac asked.

"We'll have the current project manager figure that out. We want you and Ramsdell focused on the current project."

Mac nodded. There was a bright young man he wanted to suggest, someone he suspected the project manager would overlook because of his youth, but it sounded like a replacement decision had been made.

"We'll meet you in Beverly at nine tomorrow morning. Would you drive up yourself and meet us there? You may need to stay longer than we will be staying. You'll enjoy meeting Dr. Alexander. He's fascinating."

Mac thanked them again and stood to leave the office.

"Before I forget, you'll move to a new space today."

"Today? I have those reports to finish up today."

"They're waiting for you at the new office now."

Mac nodded. He wanted to ask who 'they' were, how his replacement for the current project had been selected, and what his new role was in this new project.

Millie was waiting for him as he left the office.

"Now that's out of the way, here's your new timecard, and here's the new office assignment." She handed him the timecard and a slip of paper indicating where he should be going. "You should pack what you need now and get over there quickly. They are waiting for you. And don't forget to call Bert."

"How long have you known about this?" Mac asked quietly.

"Since about six this morning. They asked me to come in early."

Mac looked at the clock. It was 8:30 am. It used to be that hardly anything new happened on Fridays.

FIFTEEN

SONNY WALKED to the Tufts Engineering building. The main campus was located at the top of the hill, but Engineering was situated at the bottom, near the parking lot. After he dropped off his mechanical engineering paper, he would trudge up the hill to his English class. His father had the best intentions, insisting that he pursue engineering—a degree that would provide a good job and stability, a future with opportunities and certainty. If he had a choice, he would choose to study English.

Dad loved engineering and had worked hard to afford Tufts after his father died when he was a high school senior. And engineering had been good to Dad, providing him with jobs even at the height of the Depression. He wondered what it would be like to study English. What if he studied English and became a teacher like Web rather than an engineer? He could support himself, but Nancy drained him of all the money he made cleaning rail cars for the Boston and Maine railroad. She was a challenge. Dad left engineering school after his second year because he expected to be drafted into the military. Would he be drafted after two years, too? The similarity was uncanny.

He greeted everyone he saw as he walked through the double doors into the engineering building and headed to his professor's office. He handed his finished paper to the secretary and bowed with a Shakespearean flourish. The paper was some of his best prose, handed in a day early. Hopefully, he would get some credit for that.

"Mr. Macdonald, are you looking for some extra points?" Professor Crowder said. Sonny turned in surprise, the noisy hallway had covered the sound of his professor's arrival.

"Yes, sir. I mean no, sir," Sonny stumbled over his words. "I mean yes, I'm turning it in early, and, no, sir, I'm not looking for extra points."

"You should be. Your work has been pedestrian, at best. However, your grammar and sentence structure are impeccable. I think your father did better."

Professor Crowder strode into his office, closing the door to his inner sanctum without looking back. Sonny flushed brilliant crimson. He wanted to storm into the professor's office and give him a piece of his mind. How dare he refer to his father like that? Frustrated, Sonny headed into the cooler air in the hallway.

"Don't let him get to you. Your father is brilliant," Professor Bergman, an emeritus professor who maintained an office in the engineering building, said.

Sonny turned and looked at the old, retired professor with curiosity and surprise.

"Crowder has resented your father since I picked your father over him as my teaching assistant their sophomore year."

"I see," Sonny replied, unsure how to respond to the old man. His father had talked about Professor Bergman, but Sonny had never spoken to him.

"Jealousy and ambition, the two edges of the same knife, are a constant," Bergman said.

College was rife with both. "Thank you. I'll tell Dad I ran into you."

"Please tell your father to call me sometime this week. He and I need to talk."

"Of course," Sonny said, unsure what the old man needed to chat about. "It's been nice talking to you."

"Don't forget to tell your father to call me," Bergman said.

"I will; I mean, I won't forget," Sonny said.

He headed out of the engineering building and across the street to walk up the long set of stairs to the upper campus. He strolled across to Jumbo, the gigantic stuffed elephant, and rubbed his trunk for luck—a campus tradition, like rubbing John Harvard's toe on Harvard's campus.

Of course, John Harvard's statue was brass and Jumbo was a taxidermied elephant, but the idea was the same.

"Hey, Sonny, you wishing for an A?" yelled one of his classmates.

"It's as good as anything else," he yelled. What, he wondered to himself, did he want?

SIXTEEN

MAC AND Ramsdell arrived at the small factory building in downtown Beverly at 9 am on Saturday. While waiting for everyone else, they assessed the existing building, a small factory, and the large empty lot next to it, where they assumed the expanded factory would be built. Mac wondered if this project was worth the effort, and if it was, whether the deadlines could be met, and eight months to build a factory that does what it's supposed to do, and which wasn't known yet, seemed both aggressive and foolhardy.

As they returned to the front of the building, they found several other cars parked and waiting. In short order, a man and a woman arrived, unlocked the doors, and invited them into the building. The man and woman were Dr. and Mrs. Alexander. Dr. Alexander was the President of Metal Hydrides, and his wife, Mrs. Alexander, was the secretary. The Vice President, the eminent chemist Thayer Lindsley, joined them in the small conference room.

The others joining them were a young captain from the Army Corps of Engineers, two scientists from the Massachusetts Institute of Technology and one from the University of Chicago, and the three senior engineers from Stone and Webster Mac and Ramsdell had met with the previous day. Mac was surprised to also see Millie; he thought she would be at the Club Ladies' luncheon and book talk. Millie smiled at him and sat, getting her steno pad out to record the meeting.

Dr. Alexander had a brilliant vision for creating metals in various forms, mainly powder, that scientists could use for their experiments. To realize this vision, Dr. Alexander needed assistance in constructing a building to support his work.

"Mac, as a part of this project, Dr. Alexander will be creating powdered uranium to be used in experiments at Columbia University," the most senior of the Stone and Webster engineers spoke directly about the project's goals, which was helpful. "As a part of this project, we will need to have vacuum valves that can handle the volatility of the uranium."

Mac nodded.

"That's why we asked you to join us today. You have a strong relationship with the two companies we hope to involve in this project, Chapman and Badger. Ken, we asked you here today to work on the construction of the new building needed for this process."

"Is there a name for this project?" Mac asked.

"It's the trialloy project," the Army engineer replied.

"Isn't that confusing? Trialloy is a whole different process?" Ken asked.

"It's a code name. It should confuse anyone who hears about the project. This is part of a top-secret project. We're looking to misdirect anyone who might come across the name."

Everyone in the room nodded.

As the discussions progressed, Mac gained a better understanding of the functional requirements for the building that would help get the products available as fast as possible. The project was war-related, and their work was shrouded in secrets. Mac felt that this project needed to be fleshed out to be successful. He was informed that there was a strict schedule to meet, highlighting the urgency of the project and the need for efficient coordination.

Mac's primary assignment was assessing the strength and controls of the vacuum valves. Ken's role was to ensure the designs and plans were completed and that all the necessary subcontractors were in place. Everyone's role was to ensure that Dr. Alexander didn't change his mind, with the ultimate goal of having the factory in production by October or November at the latest. All subcontractors, except the valve vendors, were to be local. They discussed the issues around splitting the vendors between those known to Stone and Webster and those who were local and small. Everyone favored the split plan, making it difficult for Ken to proceed.

Over the next several months, Mac reminded himself that he had been led into this project wearing blinders. Stone and Webster assembled a team of engineers and draftsmen comprising recent graduates with no prior experience, alongside seasoned engineers and draftsmen who had acquired knowledge and skills but were not as up-to-date on current standards as the newly graduated. Mac did his best to smooth the way for all parties, but the ever-mercurial Dr. Alexander changed plans weekly. Captain Runoff was learning his roles in process development and government oversight of the project. Parts were ordered in the hope they wouldn't need to be changed, and then they were changed. He spent more time than he felt necessary recalculating what was required of the valves to make the process work. It made for a volatile combination, exacerbated by the fact that team members were constantly changing as other projects took precedence. They were stumbling around in the dark.

When the authorizing agency, which changed from the National Bureau of Standards to the Office of Scientific Research and Development, a newly created agency under the direction of his old math instructor from Tufts, Dr. Vannevar Bush, pointed out that the products needed to be available or they would move on to other vendors, they came to a workable, if far from perfect, understanding.

SEVENTEEN

BERTHA GOT off the bus on Somerville's Highland Avenue, her and Mac's hometown, a bustling industrial city carved out of Charlestown in 1842, on the last Saturday in February. Funny, she remembered that detail. Somerville was in a constant building boom in her youth, but had now settled into itself. She was heading to a Club Ladies' meeting at Alice's home. She corrected herself; it was Alice and Frank's home now, but had been Alice's parents' home when they were in school.

She walked past the Somerville library, where she and Johnny's sister, Eileen, had spent many happy hours reading and dissecting books. She carried a copy of Evil Under the Sun by Agatha Christie. Christie was not one of her favorite authors, but was popular with the group. Eileen would agree with her, but Eileen lived only in her memory since her sudden death four years earlier. She missed Eileen's beautiful operatic voice, exquisite taste, and wide-ranging discussions about books, art, theatre, and social sciences. These were things she loved but didn't get from a husband who worked all the time, although he did bring home all the latest books for her to read, and two sons who were intelligent and articulate but not inclined to discuss the intricate complexities of writers and plots.

Next was the high school, where she and Mac, Johnny, Alice, Frank, and the twins had graduated in 1916. Their class had been broken into two sections, and she and Mac were in the afternoon section, otherwise known as 16 B. Mac had been closer to her younger brother Don, who was two years behind them in the class of '18, so they had a nodding acquaintance. Don, Mac, and her older sister, Mary, hated her tendency to bury her nose in books. They loved musicals and acting, particularly anything Gilbert and Sullivan, which she considered painful. Sadly, Mary, who had been sickly most of her life, was also gone.

Don had frequently brought Mac around, and Mac, being an only child, had soaked up the experience of being part of a larger family. Don took credit for getting the two of them together. The death of Mac's father during their senior year caused her to look at Mac more closely, observing how he hid the shock and hurt of losing his father.

"Howdy, stranger," Johnny said, walking quickly behind her. "Did you take the bus?"

"Yes. Working?" Bertha asked.

"I was catching up on paperwork before walking over," Johnny replied.

"How are your students this year?"

"I can't believe we were ever that young and foolish."

"We were brilliant. There was no one like us."

"I agree there was no one like us. I'm not so sure of the brilliant part anymore," Johnny laughed.

"How are Tommy and Martha?"

"She's bemoaning her children going off to college and not living at home while Tommy's planning to rent out their rooms." Johnny had lived at home in the old Victorian she now resided in with her family, commuting to Boston University to earn her teaching degree. She had returned to teach at Somerville High School.

"Have you ever thought of getting an apartment of your own?"

"And leave my poor mother alone with my brother and his wife? Hell, yes." Johnny said.

At the corner, she and Johnny stopped to admire the facades of the string of homes on the opposite side of the street, some small and some very grand. They were heading to the grandest house. One they had visited frequently in High School.

"Remind me," Johnny said. "Which houses did your father build?"

"He built the smaller house next door for Alice's grandmother when she couldn't stand living with Alice's parents any longer."

"She should have kicked them out," Johnny said.

"People didn't do that back then. Besides, the grandmother got a new home and continued enjoying her rose garden behind the big house."

"Which Alice and Frank tore out for a lawn. Are you ready for the gauntlet?"

Bertha laughed. "How bad do you think it will be?"

"I hope Alice doesn't go on about how women in the workplace tempt their husbands."

"Does she have any idea how uncomfortable she makes everyone feel?"

"She assumes we don't know anything about Frank leaving her for his secretary and returning when things didn't work out."

"Maybe we can grill Millie about the commander?" Bertha said. "I can't believe that she didn't tell us about him."

"Millie won't be joining us today," Johnny said.

"Oh?"

"Her son's joined the navy, and he's heading out next week. She wants to spend time with him."

"I hope he comes home," Bertha replied with a shiver. "I can't believe he's old enough."

"He's 24 now. Millie was the first to get married, right out of High School."

Bertha and Johnny crossed the street, walked up the two granite front steps, crossed the gracious front porch, and entered the house. Bertha paused to take in the curved staircase in the front hall that led to the second floor.

"You must remember when your father worked on the stairs," Alice said, greeting them in the front hall.

"Yes, of course," Bertha said. "And the house next door, too."

Alice walked them through the house to the glassed-in sun room at the back that had once overlooked the rose garden. They enjoyed a light lunch of finger sandwiches, lemonade, coffee, and tea, followed by a discussion of Evil Under the Sun.

Alice reminded them that their 27th anniversary was approaching, and they wanted to do something special this summer. For their 25th, they had gone to New York City. The group discussed the merits of doing something special, but ultimately, they reached no conclusions. The next book they were reading was announced—The Keys of the Kingdom by A. J. Cronin. Bertha was excited that it wasn't Agatha Christie, and they would meet at Ethel's home in Winchester.

It was dark when Frank popped his head in to say that Mac had called to say he would pick up Bertha on his way home.

"Didn't he drive you here?" Alice asked.

"He had a meeting in Beverly for work," Bertha replied.

"Are you sure Mac was working?"

"Yes, Alice, I'm sure," Bertha replied, frustrated to be addressing this topic of husbands and work again.

"You never know what they are up to when they're not home," Alice replied. Frank blushed.

Bertha could see Johnny rolling her eyes. The group disbanded, and everyone gathered their belongings. Frank opened the front door to find Mac, hand raised, ready to knock.

"Good to see you, old man," Frank said jovially, shaking Mac's hand.

"Good to see everyone," Mac replied to the chorus of greetings from their former schoolmates. Ig was standing behind him in the shadows. "And who's this handsome young man?" Alice asked.

"My security," Mac replied. "I picked him up on my way here."

"Good to see you, Mrs. Sunderland," Ig said.

Mac offered Johnny a ride while the others jumped into their cars or rides. Johnny joined Bertha in the back seat.

"Bert, I should have bet you she would get that in," Johnny said, laughing.

"You know my bet is five cents," Bertha replied.

"You're so cheap!" Johnny exclaimed.

"What are you two talking about?" Mac asked.

"Alice has a bee in her bonnet about whether or not you were working," Bertha said.

"I work every Saturday," Mac said wearily.

"Once Frank said you were picking Bertha up, she warned everyone about the perils of men working late and secretaries," Johnny said.

"Me? I admire the female form, but that doesn't mean I'm having an affair," Mac replied. "Besides, I don't have a secretary."

"You admire the female form?" Bertha exaggerated her surprise. Mac ignored her, as he always did when she acted horrified at his fascination with girlie pictures and bawdy houses.

"How many women would want to date a man who works until 10 pm every night and prefers his home to the city lights and enticements?" Johnny said. "Did you see how Frank blushed?"

"Very funny. Besides, Bertha doesn't seem to mind my schedule. And my boys appreciate my being home infrequently to provide my fatherly guidance."

Ig laughed. Having just turned 13, he had been exposed to his father's humor long enough to understand the joke.

"I'm glad you were there, Ig. If you hadn't been, Alice would be talking for months." Tears of laughter rolled down Johnny's face as she hopped out of the car. "As always, spending time with you has been a pleasure."

After dropping Johnny off, they headed to Tufts to pick up Sonny, who had spent the day studying at the library. Since their birthdays were so close, they were going out for dinner to celebrate Ig's 13th and Mac's 45th. While Mac would have preferred his traditional beans, franks, and brown bread for dinner, Ig insisted on going to a restaurant, and Bertha and Sonny had agreed without hesitation.

EIGHTEEN

"MOM, THE street lights went out," Ig yelled. "I'll grab the blankets."

Bertha turned out the lights downstairs. She and Ig covered the front hall, living room, and dining room windows with the gathered blankets. Bertha was heading to the kitchen, and Ig was heading upstairs when there was a knock on the door. Ig flipped off the kitchen light while Bertha went upstairs to check on Gran and make sure all the lights were out and the windows shaded.

"Hello, young Master Macdonald," said Mr. Holcomb, their neighborhood air warden. He wore his air warden hat, carried a clipboard, and tapped his foot with a look of disapproval on his face. "As you can see, we are having a blackout drill."

"We heard the siren and saw the street lights go out," Ig replied. "The lights are out, and blankets are over the window. I was about to block the kitchen window when you arrived."

"Why can I see light around the bedroom window?" Holcomb stood on the covered front porch and looked up as if they could see through the porch roof.

"You can't see a bedroom light from here," Ig replied. Mr. Holcomb's eyes narrowed. "Let's step into the front yard and check."

Mr. Holcomb huffed but followed Ig down the front stairs onto the front lawn to look at the second floor. No light was seeping out of the upstairs windows. Ig turned to look at other homes in the neighborhood and noticed more than a few upstairs lights blinking off. They must be the first home that Mr. Holcomb visited.

"There's no light coming through those windows," Bertha said, joining them on the front lawn.

"I see a glow around the window frame there," Mr. Holcomb said.

"I don't see anything," Bertha said. By this time, Ginger had joined them on the front lawn. The four of them stared at the darkened second-story and attic windows. "I covered those windows myself."

Bertha watched Mr. Holcomb take a step back and look over his shoulder to see how other homes were faring.

"Is Mr. Macdonald here?" Mr. Holcomb huffed.

"Dad's traveling on business," Ig replied. "Should be home later tonight. I'm the man of the house until he gets home."

"That's what he's doing with his gas rations," Holcomb said sarcastically.

"Of course he is," Bertha replied. The sharpness in her voice caused both Ig and Mr. Holcomb to jump. "What is this all about, Mr. Holcomb?"

"The Gilchrists haven't blocked any of the lights on the second floor. Why don't you check on them?" Ig said.

"Mind your manners, young man," Mr. Holcomb said.

"You have checked on our home quite enough, Mr. Holcomb. I'm happy to have you move on and check other homes," Bertha said.

"Because I'm checking on you," Mr. Holcomb replied.

Neighbors were out and about checking their windows and wondering what was happening. Mrs. Ramsdell, the other air warden for their neighborhood, started across the street.

"I mean, I'm checking on your home. I'll take each home in order." Mr. Holcomb looked at Mrs. Ramsdell and the Gilchrist's house nervously. Mrs. Ramsdell turned and headed for the Gilchrists, where elderly Mrs. Gilchrist might have missed the siren.

"Douglas, please go and check on your grandmother."

"No need, I'm right here," Gran called from the front porch, in a voice stronger than Ig had heard in recent months. Ginger walked up the porch stairs and stood next to Gran.

"Everything alright there, Mrs. Macdonald? Ken called to say they would be late tonight. All cars and trains are to stop and turn off their lights, too."

"We're fine. Mr. Holcomb demonstrated how little light comes through the windows when they are blocked. As compared to the Gilchrists across the way."

"How dare you! I can report you to the authorities." Holcomb flushed with anger.

"What authorities?" Ig asked.

"The air raid board, of course. I'll be watching you," Mr. Holcomb said as he stomped across the street. "You haven't heard the last of me."

"I wonder what he has against your father?" Bertha asked.

"He's trying to figure out who his wife is having an affair with," Mrs. Ramsdell said. Then she continued down the street.

Ig's ears perked up at the word affair as his mother pushed him towards the door. "That's some gossip."

"You are not to say a word about this to your father; he has enough to worry about," his mother said, shaking her finger at him to make her point.

"Why not?"

"Because I said so."

Ig looked at her quizzically. The all-clear signal sounded, and they went inside to take the blankets off the window.

"Is Dad having an affair with Mrs. Holcomb?"

"You know he can't stand her."

"What in the world is wrong with that man?" Gran asked. "Spreading rumors like that about his wife."

"Everything ok?" Sonny asked as he came in the front door. "We had to wait on the train with all the lights out and pull the shades down until we got the all-clear signal, even though we were in the station."

"Everything's fine," Ig heard his mother say. He couldn't wait to tell Sonny what had happened. "Why don't you help Gran take the blankets off the windows upstairs?"

Sonny bounded up the stairs, and she turned to Ig and said, "Let me tell him the story first."

Ig realized that his mother knew he'd never keep it a secret. That was a nugget to store away for another day.

NINETEEN

As she walked home from the downtown stores, Bertha observed that clouds were replacing the beautiful, sunny morning. Mrs. Brown could no longer do the shopping for her, and Bertha was worried she would no longer work at all. Mrs. Brown's family life had gotten even more hectic and she could only come three mornings a week to cook and clean. Bertha could take care of the shopping, mending, and ironing.

In bad weather, she relied on Sonny or Mac to drive her to her errands. When they drove her, they implored her to start driving again. They knew why she had stopped driving. She walked into the house with her packages to find Mac already home.

"You're home early," Bertha said.

"I'm taking Ginny for a walk," Mac said, leash in hand. Ginger was immediately at his side, ready to go.

"I walked her this morning," Bertha said.

"Wasn't Ig supposed to do that?" Mac asked. He patted Ginger on her sides as she watched the street activity.

"I was up early," Bertha said.

"So everyone could see you out and about after the events of the other night?" Mac asked.

Bertha's eyes narrowed suspiciously. "What do you mean?"

"Rumors are all over the neighborhood. Gossip says that the Holcombs and Gilchrists are the offended parties. At least that's what I've heard," Mac smiled at Bertha. "And Ken and I are off doing nefarious things."

"Since when do you listen to neighborhood gossip? What are you up to?" Bertha crossed her arms and tapped her foot as Ig pushed past his mother to join his father. "I wish you would get ready that quickly on a school morning," Bertha said to Ig.

"I do better on Saturday afternoons," Ig said, grinning from ear to ear.

"Ramsdell is coming with us," Sonny said to his father as he passed his mother with his coat and hat on. "He's already outside with some others."

"I thought you two had lots of homework to do. No disturbing you until dinner."

"This isn't disturbing, it's a break," Sonny replied.

"Are you going to harass the Holcombs?" Bertha asked. Gran lowered the gas flame under the baked beans while failing to suppress a grin.

"We might run into them on our walk," Mac replied. Bertha could see the corner of his lips turning up. She had filled him in on the black-out drill and Mr. Holcomb.

"We'll be the neighborhood laughingstock." She appreciated Mac coming to her defense, but worried the neighbors might think they were harassing the Holcombs.

"If we're going to be a laughingstock, I don't want to miss a minute of it," Ig said.

"Maybe I should come along too."

"No, that would ruin the whole effect," Mac said.

Her men and her baby girl, Ginger, headed out the door. How dare they think she needed defending. She wanted to throw something at them, but that wouldn't be dignified, and she'd have to pick it up. How dare Mr. Holcomb threaten action, making her feel uncomfortable in her home? Holcomb's insinuation that Mac was having an affair while attempting to embarrass her made her angry again. She understood Mac's desire to address Holcomb's offensive behavior, but she hoped that would be one-on-one. With her sons and Ramsdell going along, there would be an audience and another round of gossip. If they had left Ginger, she might have taken a walk to spy on the goings-on.

"They have good intentions, no matter how childish they act," Gran said as she poured hot water into the tea kettle. "Why don't we have some tea and then see what's happening?"

Her mother, the quiet agitator. There had been random comments from neighbors, a pitying look or two at the grocery store, and some expressions of sympathy to see what dirt they could get from her, and so far, she had held her head high and refused to give in. Gran put a cozy over the teapot to let it steep, and they headed out to see what was happening. They ran into Mrs. Ramsdell and some neighbors heading in the same direction.

"So you've heard?" Mrs. Ramsdell asked.

Bertha paused. There were so many things that the question could refer to that she wasn't sure how to respond.

"I guess you haven't. The ward committee voted to replace Mr. Holcomb as the air raid warden for this area," Mrs. Ramsdell continued.

"Who is replacing him?"

"I am," Mrs. Ramsdell replied, a twinkle in her eye and a smile tugging at her lips. This would add some punch to today's confrontation.

"About time," Gran said.

"What brought this about?"

"Too many complaints about Holcomb and his attitude," Mrs. Ramsdell said. "You aren't the only ones he decided to act out his grievances on."

"I know you'll do a good job. I'm surprised they didn't pick you at the start," Gran said.

"Thanks, Mrs. R."

A small crowed had convened outside the Holcombs' house, including Mr. and Mrs. Holcomb, Jimmy Holcomb, Mac, Ramsdell, old Mrs. Gilchrist, Sonny, and Ig holding Ginny's leash. Mrs. Ramsdell asked to speak to Holcomb alone. Holcomb noted that anything they had to say, they could say in front of the group. Mrs. Ramsdell informed everyone that neighbors had raised some concerns about the air raid test. After discussing the complaints, they agreed to appoint Mrs. Ramsdell as the air raid warden. She concluded by saying she welcomed Mr. Holcomb's help with any review. She suggested that everyone head home.

Bertha watched Mr. and Mrs. Holcomb retreat into their home, followed by old Mrs. Gilchrist and Mrs. Ramsdell, and the other ward members entering the house.

"What a bust," Ig said.

"No, it wasn't," Bertha replied.

"I wanted to see a fight."

"You did see a fight," Bertha replied. Ig looked at her quizzically.

"Holcomb had it coming," Gran said.

TWENTY

IT WAS Good Friday in April, and the warm weather, longer days, and the promise of spring skiing in Tuckerman's Ravine were calling to them. With Hooker and Tiny already gone, and Web about to be a father any day, and having received his draft notice, it was Sonny and Charlie who drove up to the White Mountains, picking up some beer on the way up. Sunday was Easter, so they had Saturday to ski before heading home early Sunday morning to spend Easter with their families.

Their conversation revolved around the war, work, school, girls, and which branch of service they wanted to join. Every guy they knew was weighing the pros and cons of the different branches of service. For Sonny, it was the mountain troops who were looking to expand their roster of trained skiers and mountain climbers. Charlie wanted the Air Corps, like Web.

The sun was low in the sky, and the lights were on in the farmhouse. No one was yelling from the front door, no one was jumping off the roof into the snowbanks, no girls were being enticed to join the party, and no beer bottles littered the front lawn. Sonny made a mental correction; no one threw beer bottles out now that everything was recycled. Inside, they found a roomful of guys who appeared to be looking anywhere but at each other.

"It's a wake in here," Sonny said, standing with his hands on his hips at the door to the living room. "You guys are moping around like you lost your best friend.

"It is a wake," someone said quietly. Someone started sobbing.

"What happened?"

"Ted and Hank were behind us; we'd already reached the bottom. It was awful; you could see the wall of snow behind them. They couldn't outrun it. It was like the snow picked them up and pushed them over."

Sonny was stunned. He had skied with Ted and Hank many times. They were just acquaintances, but still, they were ski buddies.

"Jesus Christ," Charlie said, bowing his head.

"It could just as easily have been me." Sonny wasn't sure who had said it. He was thinking the same thing. If he and Charlie had arrived earlier, they would have skied the Tuck. Would it have taken them over the edge into a deep crevice? What would his parents think if it had been him?

"What about their families? Has anyone let them know?" Sonny asked.

"Yeah, we called. They'll be up in the morning but there's nothing to be done until it melts."

"My god. They're leaving the bodies there," Charlie said.

"Have to. No way to get in right now."

No wonder it was so quiet. No one knew what to think or what they could do, but no one was ready to go home.

"Minnie Dole said there'll be a group going up to bring the bodies down if they can reach the bodies, in June. He's looking for anyone who wants a recommendation from the ski patrol."

"A recommendation for what?" Someone asked.

"For the new ski troops."

"I thought they were mountain troops?" Sonny asked.

"They're both."

Dole entered the house and stood next to Sonny and Charlie, who were still standing by the doorway to the living room.

"It'll be more of a rock climbing effort but safer than trying anything now," Dole said. "Is there anyone here who wants to volunteer?"

Dole's voice was soothing. No one was happy leaving the bodies of two of their friends in the Tuck.

"For the climb or the ski troops?" Charlie asked.

"Either, but for now, I'm looking for volunteers to bring down the bodies after the snow melts," Dole replied.

"I'll do it. They would do the same for me." Sonny heard himself say.

"Thanks, Sonny, much appreciated," Dole said.

A couple of other guys also volunteered. Charlie hung back. He liked to ski, but he wanted to take to the skies in a plane, not on skis.

"It doesn't look like you have any food here. Why don't I buy you dinner in town?" Dole said.

The guys slowly roused themselves, piled into several cars, and headed into town.

"What is needed to get into the ski troops?" Sonny asked once they were seated.

"Three recommendations, one from the Ski Patrol, and the ability to ski," Dole said.

"The Tuck is pretty scary stuff. Do you think you can handle it?" One wise guy said. The laughter briefly ignited the overall somber mood.

"I can, but I'm not sure you could." The comment made Sonny's blood boil. Once his anger was triggered, he couldn't shut up. He told the guy exactly what he thought of anyone who wasn't skilled enough and not a good enough friend to bring a friend home. Charlie had to drag him off the guy and put him in a booth as far away as possible to cool down.

TWENTY-ONE

THEY WALKED to church and back home again on Easter Sunday. Bertha was relieved to see that Sonny was on the porch with Ginger, waiting for them to return. They would be together for Sunday dinner, and Mac wouldn't mouth off an 'I told you so' while she and her mother got Sunday dinner on the table.

"Look what the cat dragged in," Ig said to Sonny.

"Aren't you funny," Sonny replied, grinning from ear to ear.

"Why didn't you join us at church?" Mac asked.

"Ginny needed a walk, didn't you, girl?" Sonny responded while rubbing Ginny's belly. Ginny's tail wagged. She loved it when they talked about her and rubbed her belly at the same time.

"What did they talk about at Sunday school?" Sonny asked Ig.

Ig shrugged and sat on the porch step. "Boring stuff."

"And how was the skiing?" Gran asked.

"Thank you, Gran. The skiing was ok. We skied at Cranmore, the Tuck was closed." Sonny took his grandmother's arm to help her up the steep front stairs. Bertha and Mac followed, with Ig and Ginger bringing up the rear.

"How are your classes?" Mac asked.

"Oh, fine. You know how it is." Sonny was non-committal. Bertha could tell he was depressed.

"I was chosen to assist Professor Gilchrist as his teaching assistant during my freshman year. Any prospects like that for you?"

"No one could calculate on a slide rule to the 6th degree like you, or so all my professors say," said Sonny.

"That's not what got me a teaching assistant position."

"Good, steady, hard work and applying yourself," Sonny replied, making it sound like drudgery.

Bertha could see Mac considering another lecture. His lectures hadn't improved Sonny's grades.

"Ig, are you going to the party at the Gorschack girl's house on Saturday?" Bertha asked to distract from the conversation between Sonny and Mac.

"Oh, Mom, you know I don't like her or parties. I'm a more serious soul."

"She seems like a nice enough young lady. Maybe she would make a good friend or a study partner. I understand she's at the top of your class," Bertha replied. Mac looked at Bertha over the newspaper. She saw that he was suppressing a laugh.

"I'm second in the class, you know."

"We know," Mac replied.

"That's going to change, squirt," Sonny said.

"No, it's not. I'm never going to like her."

"I meant studying. You won't always be brilliant."

Bertha decided not to linger on her thoughts about how much sleep, if any, her son had gotten or how much beer he and his friends had drunk. She was about to say no radio until after dinner when she saw Mac hand Ig part of the paper and suggest he read. Ig muttered but took the paper and slouched on the couch. She entered the kitchen in time to help Gran right the dangerously tilting roast platter she had taken out of the icebox.

"I suspect you will want to warm this for dinner," Gran said once they had the platter safely on the kitchen table. As much as she wished her mother wouldn't go to such lengths to try to observe the cold Sunday supper tradition she had grown up with, she didn't want to criticize her for helping. Her parents had strictly adhered to the Presbyterian Sabbath rules, which included no cooking, no work of any sort —no reading, not even the Bible, no card games, no running, and no playing —while she was growing up. Mac's mother kept a more traditional New England Sunday tradition of church service followed by a large meal. Mac had preferred his mother's way of doing things, and she had to admit, she did, too.

"I think Mac and the boys would like their meat a little warm," Bertha replied. The potatoes had been set in the oven on low to roast before they headed out for church, and the green beans and carrots were ready to be boiled.

Dinner was served promptly at 1 pm. Sonny had cleared his books and set the table without being asked. Ig had somehow wormed his way over to the radio and was listening with his ear to the speaker, keeping the sound low. Bertha suspected that he had turned it on as soon as she was out of sight. Ginger was lying next to him, listening intently, the volume low enough for her ears. Mac peered over the top of the paper with a look that was more like a shrug as if he was saying 'I did what I could do, but...'

"Ig, turn off the radio and wash your hands."

"Ah, Mom, can't we leave it on? It's the best part," Ig said.

"It can't always be the best part when I ask you to turn it off."

"It usually is," Ig muttered. He reluctantly turned off the radio.

"And do not put your finger in any part of that cake, including the frosting," she said as she heard his footsteps pause on the way to the sink. She placed a salad in each of the settings.

"What if the frosting is on the plate?" Sonny asked. Her boys observed very fine rules about frosting; anything on the plate was free for tasting.

"Even if it's on the plate," Bertha replied clearly, in case Ig took his brother seriously. It would be quite an accomplishment if the cake made it to the table without being touched by either boy. The salad was followed by the warm roast, already carved, accompanied by Yorkshire pudding, roasted potatoes, green beans, and carrots.

"Eat all your carrots, Ig," Bertha said.

"Why can't we have raw carrots? I hate them cooked."

"Hate is a strong word. Use dislike instead," Bertha replied automatically.

"Jeez, kid, you'll never grow big and strong if you don't eat all your vegetables." Sonny enjoyed all food, except peanut butter, and he loved vegetables. Ig was the pickiest eater she had ever seen, pickier than herself, but he loved peanut butter.

"Should we place a bet on how long it will be before you fall asleep?" Mac asked Sonny.

"You'd probably win," Sonny said with a yawn.

"Why was the Tuck closed?" Bertha asked.

Sonny paused. "Two guys were pushed over into a crevice by an avalanche."

"What! That's horrible. What happened?"

Sonny filled them in on what he knew had happened and the plans to bring the bodies down in June. The parents had arrived on Saturday, but there wasn't much to be done.

After dinner, Gran settled into her rocking chair with her darning basket, and Bertha settled into her chair with her knitting to contemplate what had happened to Sonny over the weekend. Mac smoked his pipe while he fiddled with the radio, attempting to find a clear signal. Ginger sat patiently beside Mac, waiting to be scratched behind the ears. Sonny and Ig laughed and splashed water as they washed the dishes. She would check on the thoroughness of their work once they were done. Mrs. Brown had cleaning and laundry to do in the morning, not redoing the Sunday dishes. Assuming Mrs. Brown didn't call to say she couldn't make it on Monday.

TWENTY-TWO

MAC HAD been lying in bed in the dark, contemplating various problems about how best to compress the powdered uranium cubes in a manner that wouldn't cause them to ignite. When the phone rang, he leapt out of bed and ran down the stairs before it woke the whole house. He'd contemplated installing a second phone line upstairs until he learned that all homes were restricted to one phone line per home and no new installations were being made. Restrictions were beginning to pile up, and some of them were starting to irritate him.

He grabbed the phone and answered in a low voice. Dr. Alexander let him know there had been a small fire in the drying room once the melting and casting of 'trialloy,' the code name for uranium, which still caused confusion, but seemed to make everyone happier than saying uranium. They agreed to meet as soon as possible to brainstorm ideas before the 10 am meeting with the larger team. He then called Ramsdell to inform him of the problem. Ramsdell agreed to drive up with Mac.

When he hung up the phone, Ginger was next to him, waiting patiently to be taken out. Bertha was heading for the kitchen with Gran following. Sonny came down the stairs, already dressed, and took Ginger for a walk. He headed upstairs to shower, dress, and wake Ig. It was a quick start to Monday morning. He had hoped to chat with Mrs. Brown when she arrived later this morning, but he'd have to leave that to Bertha.

TWENTY-THREE

BERTHA WAS reading the local newspapers, encouraging residents to grow victory gardens. Articles started to appear in March, and by early April, they were more frequent. More than one newspaper article mentioned that it was a great way to obtain fresh food that wasn't rationed. It wasn't too late, the Grange said in a different article, to get started. And if you didn't have a yard that could accommodate a garden, there were plots of land that could be had all over Melrose for growing food. There were ads for compost from farms as far away as Haverhill and southern New Hampshire, offering delivery to Melrose. Canned vegetables weren't rationed, but everyone believed they would be hard to find.

Mac had left early to visit Metal Hydrides after a frantic phone call in the early morning. Based on what she overheard on the phone, she couldn't quite tell if there had been a fire or not. Mrs. Brown was running late, something that was happening more frequently, but she assured Bertha she would be there as soon as possible. Ig had left for school, and Sonny had decided to take the train to school to get an early start on his next paper in the library.

Bertha looked out at the side yard of their home. Once the sun cleared the trees, it received the most sun. Their house was on a corner and faced north. The yard was on the east side of the house, while the west side had the driveway and trees. The front was too short and steep to use. She hoped the side yard didn't get too much sun.

"What do you think of having a victory garden?" Bertha asked her mother, who was heating water for another pot of tea.

"I think it's wise if we want vegetables," Gran replied.

Mrs. Brown hustled in the back door and took over the tea-making, asking Gran to wait in the dining room; she needed to talk to them both. Gran dutifully took her seat and waited patiently. Ginger went into the kitchen to see if there might be more food for her to gather. She was quickly shooed out and took her place underneath the dining room table. She brought tea and coffee to the dining room table and took a seat.

"As you may have noticed, I've been coming more erratically of late," Mrs. Brown said.

Bertha had always been impressed with Mrs. Brown's perfect diction. It was hard to believe this woman had only a 5th-grade education before she started working.

"Yes, we have noticed," Bertha replied. Mrs. Brown nodded.

"I'm afraid I have to give my notice."

"We've been expecting that," Bertha said.

"My husband took a job at the naval yard. There's so much work now, we want to take advantage of the opportunities. We'll be moving to Quincy, and the commute isn't reasonable. Plus, I'll be taking care of the baby and probably other babies while folks work multiple shifts."

Bertha was sad to see Mrs. Brown leave, but she understood. She and Gran had been getting breakfast together for a couple of weeks now.

"We will be sad to see you leave," Bertha said. Gran put her hand over Mrs. Brown's folded hands and bowed her head.

"I know, it's hard for me too."

"Are you leaving right away?" Gran asked.

"I'm staying until noon. I'll get the beds organized and sheets washed and hung. Then I'll be on my way. If you want someone new, the best thing to do is call the agency. I'm not sure you'll get someone regular like me, but there should be some help. I'll leave my new phone number if you have any questions."

"Thank you," Bertha said. She meant that from the bottom of her heart. She would miss Mrs. Brown, but she had been anticipating this conversation.

Mrs. Brown headed upstairs to strip the beds and wash the sheets. Bertha sighed and returned to the victory garden articles. Gran had a garden wherever they lived, except for Belmont, where there was no land. During the last war, she and her sisters, Mabel and Mary, lived at home and helped with the garden. Well, she and her niece, her sister Sue's daughter Dorothy, helped out. Mabel, who worked full-time as a restaurant hostess to support her two children, and Mary, who worked as a bookkeeper at the curb exchange, helped out when they were home. Gran was now 79, Mabel lived in Hudson, Dorothy had succumbed to the 1918 flu, Mary had passed away four years previously, and Mrs. Brown would no longer be helping them. Sonny and Ig would be her helpers.

"What do you think we should grow?"

"Lettuce is always good. Carrots, peas, and beans can be eaten, preserved, or put in stews."

Bertha nodded. The Grange encouraged growing tomatoes, at least 12 plants per household. They could do more than that in their yard.

"What does Uncle Owen keep in his garden?" Her mother's half-brother enjoyed gardening.

"Beatrice keeps the garden. Uncle Owen isn't home enough to take care of anything. He likes his grapes, though. They grow tomatoes, cucumbers, and some flowers. I'm not sure what else."

"They have a grape arbor, don't they?"

"Bea makes grape jelly every year. Are you thinking of a grape arbor in the yard?"

"I don't think it would work in our yard. Let's grow things we will eat."

"I eat grapes," her mother said, preparing to take her tea to the living room to listen to the radio.

"I'm thinking more about what we eat," Bertha replied.

"You mean food Mac and the boys will eat," Gran said, and Bertha nodded.

Bertha thought about what she wanted to grow for a few more days before calling Aunt Beatrice to chat about her garden and grape arbor. Then, she attended classes at the Grange on what to have in a victory garden.

With information from Aunt Beatrice and the Melrose Grange, seeds provided by the Grange, and compost delivered from a farm in Haverhill, she was ready to start on her victory garden. She started seeds indoors. Sonny and Ig dug up the yard and spread the compost. She planted the seedlings and hoped to have fresh vegetables for the summer with leftovers for canning.

PART THREE: 1942

TWENTY-FOUR

GAS RATIONING for 17 eastern states was officially instituted on May 15, 1942. Gas deliveries to stations had been restricted since April. People quickly realized that having money didn't mean the gas stations had gas to give them. It was easy for someone to use all their gas rations before the end of the month. The speed limit was reduced to 35mph to conserve gas, and stop lights were turned off so they couldn't be identified from the air. Every intersection became a 4-way stop. Sonny adapted to the change quickly. He took the train from Melrose to North Station in Boston, where he cleaned railroad cars and had free access to travel by rail.

Sugar, butter, meat, canned goods, and nylon stockings were also rationed. Every family member had a ration card. Ration book applications had been posted in every newspaper, and Bertha had completed an application, had each person in the household sign it, and mailed them off. When the designated day arrived, she and Gran were in line at the Coolidge School to pick up their ration books from the school, where the superintendent and teachers were serving as the ration board. She suspected that was because they knew all the families in town and the number of children in each family. Bertha thought it was unreasonable to expect her to feed her family with the sugar coupons they provided. There were rumors that more food would soon be rationed.

The line was long and moved slowly because the process was new to everyone. Some people hadn't completed and mailed their forms, while others claimed books for family members who were no longer at home. Then, there were the people with hearing or vision issues. More than one person questioned how this could be happening in America.

"Well, well, Mrs. Macdonald. Picking up for the entire family, I see?" Mr. Holcomb passed by as she and Gran waited in line.

"And you are doing the same," Bertha replied.

"What with the gas rationing, my ability to sell on the road is greatly restricted," Mr. Holcomb huffed.

"I read about the problems traveling salesmen have with gas rationing," Bertha replied. This was the first time they had talked since the incident in March, and she was trying to keep her voice as even as possible.

"Have you heard back from the governor yet?" A voice in the line called out, followed by snickers and comments from others. The Governor was unwilling or unable to moderate a federal war-related decision.

"It's not fair. Some people seem to get more than their share of gas coupons," Mr. Holcomb continued. He was referring to Mac, who received gas coupons for all the travel he was doing for work, so she said nothing.

When she reached the front of the line in the school's large entry hall, tables ran the length of the hall, staffed with teachers. The superintendent walked behind them, answering any questions that arose. The first person took her name and address and pulled the family's forms. The forms were in good order and handed to the next person, who double-checked them and marked her off a list. Then, the forms were given to the following individual, who provided her with the sugar coupon books for the next six months, and so forth for each restricted item, except for tires and gasoline. The tire board was present in case any questions arose. Mac handled his gas rations through work.

"Mom, can I handle my ration coupons?" Ig asked.

"I guess you can handle all the coupons if you do all the shopping and cooking." She could see the wheels turning in Ig's head at the thought of shopping and cooking. Shopping wasn't so bad, but cooking would be a challenge.

"If there's one thing I know, I'm not a cook. But you had better make things I like," was Ig's final answer.

"What is it that you like?" Gran asked.

"Dessert," Ig responded.

"It's hard to put meat into dessert, although there is always mincemeat," Gran said with a twinkle in her eye.

Bertha watched Ig glance at his grandmother. Gran's quiet sarcasm wasn't lost on him anymore.

"It will be hard to make a dessert without sugar and butter," Bertha said. She had been reading the ration recipes in the paper and hoped they were better than they sounded.

"How will we feed Ginger if they stop making dog food in cans??" Ig had moved on from dessert to Ginger.

"We'll have to grind up our food for Ginger," Bertha replied.

"They're going to stop all canned food," Gran said. "That's why we have to work hard in the garden."

"They said I should give you my ration coupons when staying with you," Gran said, handing her ration coupons to Bertha.

"If I stay with Mabel, I'll have to give a change of address."

"Since the books are for six months, we can figure out what to do depending on where you are. We can always forward your coupons if they arrive here."

"You can't forward coupons. They said the address will be wrong, and they might get stolen," Ig said.

"You read all the ration coupon rules?" Bertha asked.

Ig shrugged and skipped ahead to greet his father. You're home early," Ig said.

"I need to drop off paperwork from the office to get a new gas sticker," Mac replied.

"That's one way to get you home for dinner," Bertha said.

"Would you like a ride? I parked in the back."

"I'll take a ride," Gran said.

"I'll put my books in the car and walk home with Mom," Ig said. He took Gran's arm to escort her to the car while Mac went inside to file his paperwork before the ration board closed at 5 pm.

Holcomb and Mac exited the building, and Bertha was waiting for Ig.

"It's not fair that you get an unlimited gas sticker. I'm going to complain about this. I need gas for work too," Holcomb stalked back into the ration board.

"Why don't you ride home with me. Holcomb said that a large group of traveling salesmen are planning to march on the ration board today," Mac suggested.

"That will be interesting to see," Bertha said as Mac steered her around the building to the parking lot.

TWENTY-FIVE

IN MID-MAY, Sonny received a call from Dole. They were set to go up, but was he still interested? He agreed to go and would get the time off. His boss would grumble but would rearrange the schedule once Sonny explained why he needed to go.

It was Saturday morning, and Sonny anticipated being the only one up, but when he came downstairs, he found his father at the dining room table reading the newspaper.

"What are you doing up so early?" Sonny asked.

"Would you like me to drive you up today?" Dad asked.

"I'm going with two of the Saugus guys, the brothers. Don't you have to work today?"

"I can take a day off here and there, you know. I'll drop you off in Saugus on my way," Dad said.

"OK, thanks. I'll call and let them know so they don't need to pick me up," Sonny said. When he returned to the dining room, his mother had served some eggs and bacon. Ginger stationed herself under his feet, hoping for handouts.

"I'm ready when you are," Dad said.

Sonny finished his breakfast and grabbed his skis, poles, boots, and extra clothing. There was still snow in the Tuck, but they would be climbing as well.

"So, Dad, what is it that you are working on?" Sonny asked as his father pulled out of the driveway and they headed for Saugus.

"It's a new factory in Beverly. They're creating oxidized metals of various sorts for scientists to use in experiments," Dad replied.

"What caught on fire?"

"The powdered uranium. Highly volatile stuff. We're working on the best way to keep it from igniting."

"What do scientists want to do with uranium?"

"To see if they can make a bomb," Dad replied.

"For the war?"

"If they figure it out, it will last forever, I think."

His father dropped him off, wished them well, and told them to be safe, then headed for Route 1 and the factory in Beverly.

In the car, he and the brothers also headed up Route 1. It was a beautiful, sunny Saturday morning.

"Sonny, have you joined up yet?" One of them asked.

"I'm on June 30," Sonny said. "Have you two joined up?"

"We'll be joining Hooker and Tiny in the 87th in a few weeks."

"That's where I want to be," Sonny replied.

"Looks like you'll get the recommendations you need after today."

"Have you ever done this before?"

"Once. It's hard work, but a good thing to do for the guys' families."

Sonny was worried about how he'd feel when he saw the bodies. They drove directly to the meeting point, where they joined Dole and the team. No skis were needed on this day. They used ropes and pitons to climb up to the crevasse. The sun reflecting off the remaining snow and bare rock kept him warm. As the guys said, it was hard, slow work.

Ted and Hank's bodies were no longer covered with snow, and the sun, wind, and cold had taken their toll. Their skin looked like leather. The crevasse was shaded, and it was gruesome work chipping the bodies out of the ice. Then, those handling the ropes wrapped them in tarpaulins and pulled them out of the crevasse as gently as possible.

Once the bodies were out of the crevasse and on the main slope, Sonny helped wrap the bodies and place them on stretchers. The team that had gone down into the crevasse was pulled up on the ropes. Once everyone was on the slope, Dole had them pause, take off their hats, and bow their heads while a brief prayer was said. Each of the men took a corner of one of the stretchers and carried the bodies down to the basin, where two hearses waited to take the boys home to their families.

Sonny and the Saugus boys headed to the farmhouse for the night. They would decompress, talk about Ted and Hank, and have some dinner before heading home to their families the following morning.

Sonny took Nancy out the following Saturday afternoon to pick a corsage for her prom and have dinner together.

"Sonny, after the prom, I want to see other people," Nancy said.

"I see," Sonny replied. He wasn't surprised. Their relationship had been rocky all spring.

"I want us to be friends and go out sometimes, but you'll be going off to war soon. I know you don't know when, but you will be, and I don't want to be tied to someone who leaves and might not come back."

"What are you going to do, date all the boys under 18?"

"Don't be ridiculous," Nancy replied.

TWENTY-SIX

IT WAS June 1942, and Ig's thoughts turned to summer while he pretended to do homework.

"Who was that?" Ig asked his mother as she hung up the phone.

"Johnny Wilson. Her mother is letting us use their cottage in Fieldston for a week?"

"A week." Ig could not believe what he was hearing. "That's not fair."

"It's wonderful of her to offer us some time there," Bertha replied.

"I wish Mabel hadn't sold her cottage. I'll miss our summers at that place," Gran said, sitting in her chair, knitting. Gran had joined the group at Hibernian Hall, which knitted items for sailors and soldiers. The hall was open 24 hours a day for anyone who wanted to knit. The yarn was donated and couldn't leave the building, but it prompted Gran to knit items for the family.

"So do I," Ig picked up the leash, and Ginger followed him to the back door. "It's awfully warm to be knitting."

"We'll need items in the winter, and I want to get a head start," Gran replied.

"Be back in time for dinner. Don't forget, you have homework to do," Bertha called after him.

"It doesn't matter, school'll be over soon."

"It does matter," Ig heard his mother say as the back screen door slammed shut.

Ig wanted to run, and Ginger was ready. He was about to finish 8th grade and would be a freshman in the Fall. Sonny was working and would probably be called up soon. Dad worked so many hours now that he rarely saw him, and Fieldston was gone, too, except for a week. Everything had changed.

Dinner was on the table when Ig returned, tired and hungry. Ginger ravenously finished her bowl of food and then slunk under the dining room table, hoping for food scraps, where she quickly fell asleep.

"Nice of you to join us," Mac said.

"You're home early again," Ig replied. "I thought we'd be eating later."

"Anything you want to talk about?" Mac asked.

"Nah. Have a date with Nancy tonight?" Ig asked Sonny.

"Yeah, squirt, I do. We're picking out a corsage for her prom."

"I don't know what this world is coming to," Ig replied.

"Jesus Christ, kid, you're 13," Sonny said. "What do you have to complain about?"

"No swearing at the table, and please don't talk with your mouth full," Bertha said.

"Fieldston for a week. What am I supposed to do if we don't go to the beach?"

"You can help your mother with the garden," Mac replied.

"You could get a job," Sonny said.

Ig sighed. No one understood how his life was changing. "Can I get a rifle? I want to join the rifle club in the Fall."

"We'll be going to Maine for a few days," Mac said. "To see your grandmother's grave. We'll talk about it then."

"That reminds me, Rollie and Betty are getting married soon," Sonny said.

"How long have you known?" Bertha said. "I haven't heard anything."

"Rollie called last night. I'm going to be a groomsman," Sonny said. "That's two this summer."

"Seems like short notice," Bertha said.

"Another wedding will be nice," Gran said.

"Is she pregnant?" Ig asked. "I told you everything is changing."

"Ig, eat your vegetables," Bertha said.

"I'm starting on a new project tomorrow," Mac said.

"That's wonderful. Does it mean more or less driving?" Bertha asked.

"More, maybe. I don't know yet," Mac replied.

"See, everything's changing," Ig said. "How are we going to get Grannie Macdonald's body home?"

"Not in the car with us," Sonny replied.

The new project, the weddings, and getting Grannie Macdonald's body disinterred and moved to Cambridge added to the usual dinner conversation of local boys being called up for active duty, war reports in the newspaper, local gossip, and the latest news from England. Ig considered all his father's questions and arguments for the long drive to Brownville Junction.

TWENTY-SEVEN

WITH METAL Hydrides on a sound footing, at least as far as vacuum valves and the process whereby the valves were needed to create and compress the powdered uranium were concerned, Mac was asked to take on a new project. Ramsdell had broader drafting responsibilities for the new factory and worked with the engineers, the Army, and senior management on the ongoing problems with the quality of the source product being provided to Metal Hydrides to create the uranium powder. The scientists at Columbia University and the University of Chicago were disappointed in the output. Still, they were the first to identify the problems they were encountering with the impurities in the uranium sources, rather than with the work being done by Stone and Webster Engineering.

Mac considered these thoughts as he headed into the office for a meeting on the train in June, 1942. Information on new projects had become more need-to-know than ever, so he had no inkling of this next project. There was a lot of activity with Army engineers and scientists, and the senior team traveled more than they could remember traveling in the recent past. As an inspecting engineer, he needed to convey information to senior staff at times, sometimes in person, but most often through reports. He found that he was writing his reports and handing them in, but he would receive responses a week or more after submitting them. Something was different, but with the war moving along quickly.

At the Malden stop, Betty asked to join him. As the crowd passed, he stood to let her into the seat near the window. He wanted to keep the aisle seat so he could grab his bag and head for the door before the train stopped at North Station. Seeing Mrs. Holcomb, he tipped his hat to her. She turned to her friend and pointedly ignored him. The blackout event still hung over them. And the gas rationing only added to the feelings. He was still standing when the train pulled away, and he almost lost his balance. He wasn't sure who was driving the trains these days. Their movements were jerky.

"How's the job going, Betty?" Mac asked.

"My boss thinks I'm doing a good job."

"I hear a but?" Mac asked.

"I can't believe that some people don't do any work, and they don't get into trouble."

"Is that so?" Ramsdell asked, looking over the top of the paper.

"There's this one woman at work who doesn't do anything. And she gets away with it all the time."

"That happens sometimes." Mac noticed they had the full attention of the commuters in the seats around them.

"It's so frustrating and unfair. I was supposed to have the day off, but I've been called to cover for her."

"Life isn't fair," Ramsdell said, sitting across from Betty and Mac. "As I keep telling Mac."

"How's your grandfather?" Mac asked, ignoring Ramsdell.

"Granddad talks about how he trained you to be the engineer you are today. He's driving Dad crazy," Betty replied, a shy smile curling her lips.

"He trained me well. I'll call and see how he's doing."

"He'd like that. He has lots of opinions to share," Betty replied.

Mac and Ramsdell packed their newspapers and headed for the train door as the train slowed to pull into Boston's North Station to get ahead of the slow-moving crowd. Mac needed to get to the meeting.

———

Once they were inside the Franklin Street building, Mac and Ramsdell separated. Ramsdell went to his desk, and Mac headed for the large conference room on the 8th floor for the meeting. As he approached the conference room, he noticed the door was closed, and one of the security guards had a clipboard and a list. He got in line behind several others, had his name checked off, and entered the room.

He was stunned to discover Dr. Vannevar Bush, his math instructor at Tufts and now and eminent college president, an Army officer with the rank of colonel based on the markings on his uniform, and what appeared to be several scientists as well as Dr. Argensinger, Stone and Webster Engineerings president, Mr. Hartridge, a senior engineer Mac had not previously worked with. Millie sat at one end of the room, taking notes during the meeting. She glanced at Mac, then back at her pad, adding the names of those entering the meeting. He had been told not to say anything to anyone about the meeting, and he was beginning to understand the reasons why; this was an impressive group of people. Mac, several men, and one woman who had just entered the room took seats, not at the table, which was already full, but in the chairs lined up against the wall.

After everyone was settled, Mr. Argensinger thanked everyone for coming and turned the meeting over to Dr. Bush. Dr. Bush explained the role of the Office of Scientific Research and Development, referred to as OSRD, and the S-1 committee working on various ways to harness the energy of uranium as a part of the war effort. The senior military officer was Colonel Kenneth Nichols, assigned to a new group called the Manhattan Engineering District (MED), and the senior scientist was Dr. Harold Urey from Columbia University, an expert on deuterium.

The conversation then turned to why they were all here: the process of using heavy water to create plutonium. It was a project they called P-9, which was a much better title than the deliberately misnamed 'trialloy' project at Metal Hydrides, Mac thought. The meeting provided a wealth of information and required him to research uranium, deuterium, heavy water, hydrogen, and the uranium fission process. Stone and Webster Engineering was the Architect and Engineering Manager for the expansion of a facility in Trail, British Columbia, and would oversee the work of Consolidated Mining & Smelting Company, the facility owner; E.B. Badger & Sons Engineering, who would be working on the 'exchange unit' for the hydrogen exchange process, using the water of the Columbia River and the hydrogen already in production at that plant. E.I. Dupont was working on similar processes at three plants in the

United States, at Morgantown, West Virginia, Wabash, Indiana, and in Alabama in a town Mac had never heard of, Sylacauga. This was a large project, much larger than Metal Hydrides, and Mac wasn't sure exactly why he was there, but everyone was told they would learn their specific assignments over the next week.

As the meeting broke up, Mac stepped aside to let others out of the room when he heard his name called.

"Mac, it's good to see you after all these years," Dr. Bush said, smiling and shaking his hand. "I was happy to see your name on the list."

"Thank you, Dr. Bush, it's good to see my old math instructor."

"Please, don't call me old, it will make my bones creak." This comment produced a laugh from all those still in the room.

"So that's how you two know one another," Mr. Hartridge said. "I understand that you were a 2-year man at Tufts Engineering."

"And he spent what would have been his junior year as a drafting instructor," Dr. Bush said.

"Why not continue classes?" Mr. Hartridge asked.

"I had my papers to join the navy on November 19, 1918. When the war ended, I was no longer needed. Most of us who called up didn't take classes, knowing we would never finish the semester. I agreed to teach drafting until I left, and since I didn't leave, I continued as an instructor."

"Why not rejoin and finish the four years?" Mr. Hartridge wanted to know more about Mac than was in his file.

"My father had died, and funds were tight with just my mother and me, so working made sense. French and Stewart continued to use my surveying skills."

"And let's not forget how skilled you are with a slide rule. I've met few people as skilled, except for Enrico Fermi," Dr. Bush replied, causing Dr. Urey to smile.

"Stop by my office after lunch, we'll talk more," Mr. Hartridge said. Mac nodded and left the room. Whatever the test was, he felt he had passed, with the help of Dr. Bush.

TWENTY-EIGHT

BERTHA CONTACTED the agency after Mrs. Brown left. Several women came in to help and then left when they got factory jobs or their families moved for work. Then Shillie, a young Black girl, came in to do laundry and house cleaning twice a week. Shillie talked constantly, complaining about her mother, her boyfriend, and anything else that came to mind.

One afternoon, she found Ig at the bottom of the stairs, waiting for Shillie to come down so he could drop his things off in his room. Shillie was throwing herself down the stairs, then going back up and repeating the same actions. When she asked what was wrong, Shillie looked at her with surprise and said that if she didn't know why she was doing this, she would wonder about her.

Bertha knew precisely what she was doing. Women have been doing similar things to get rid of an unwanted pregnancy forever. Ig, though, was fascinated by the whole drama. A drama that she didn't need with a 13-year-old boy to learn about or repeat at school: Shillie would never be like Mrs. Brown, but she was some help, and Bertha hesitated to report her to the agency. She and Mac discussed how best to handle her, and Bertha found that sitting down with her and discussing appropriate behavior, as well as what she should and shouldn't say in front of Ig, helped. It wasn't perfect, but nothing is these days.

TWENTY-NINE

IG AND Bertha spent the first week of August at Fieldston. Mabel and Gran joined them for the week while Sonny took the train down a few times after work and spent the night so he could spend a morning at the beach with Nancy, whose parents had rented a cottage for the month.

"Hey, Mom," Ig called out as he ran up the stairs to the cottage, opened the screen door, and let it slam behind him, ignoring his mother's pleas not to slam the door so much.

"You let the door slam again," Bertha said.

"Sorry. I saw Nancy kissing Pete by the pier." Ig said, stopping to catch his breath.

"And?" Mac said. He gave Ig a look over the newspaper.

"I didn't know you were here," Ig said.

"No one notices me around here," Mac said. Even Ginger ignored him if there was a chance to run around.

"What should I tell Sonny?"

"Nothing if I were you," Bertha said.

"Why not?" Ig contemplated his parents' lack of concern about this turn of events.

"What purpose would it serve?"

"You're answering a question with a question," Ig replied.

"I'd rather Sonny figure out the kind of girl Nancy is on his own," Bertha said.

"You already knew?" Ig asked.

"Nancy enjoys attention. She isn't one to wait around for Sonny or anyone else to find time for her," Mac said.

"But what about Sonny? Shouldn't he know?"

Nancy was betraying Sonny, and Ig thought no one cared. For once, he felt bad for his older brother.

"Sonny should be here soon. Why don't you and he walk along the beach when he gets here?" Mac said.

"Ok," Ig said hesitantly.

"Hey, squirt, where are you heading?" Sonny called to Ig as he walked towards the cottage, still dressed in grease-filled work clothes.

"Stop calling me squirt," Ig yelled at his brother. "I'm taking a walk on the beach before dinner, want to join me?"

"Why not? I can change later. What's for dinner?"

"It's Saturday, and Dad's here, so franks," Ig replied.

They both heard their mother say they should be back in half an hour if they wanted to eat.

Ig walked towards where he had seen Nancy kissing Pete. They found Nancy kissing a boy by the pier. The good news was that it wasn't their cousin Pete. The bad news was that she was kissing another boy.

"What are you doing?" Sonny asked, hands on hips, red-faced, as he confronted Nancy.

Nancy took Sonny's arm, said she was happy to see him, and walked to the cottage her parents rented as the boy ran off. Ig watched her kiss Sonny at the door and heard him say 'girls' while shaking his head as they headed to their cottage. He'd have to ask Dad if this was normal. He didn't think so.

THIRTY

MAC FOUND the work on the P-9 project to be challenging, and he enjoyed a good challenge. In the two months since the large meeting about the project, Mac was assigned to work with E.B. Badger Engineering on the cooling exchange towers for the Trail facility. E. B. Badger's skills lay in their experience with distillation processes, similar to what they were working on, and their manufacturing facility, which was able to produce the tower heads out of copper. Badger had started in the copper manufacturing business just after the Civil War.

Mac spent much of his time working out of the Badger facility in South Boston, working on the engineering plans for Trail and testing out the best way to form the tower heads. He'd been assigned to assess Badger's work and capabilities and reported each week that they were excelling at it, so much so that they had too much work with other contracts coming in. He spent so much time at Badger that he was only at his desk on Saturdays to write reports. He would have written the reports at home, to keep this project as secret as possible, but there were restrictions on taking work home, so he had to do the work on nights and Saturdays. He rarely saw Ramsdell anymore; he spent most of his time with new hires, many of whom had recently graduated from engineering schools. Bertha, Sonny, and Ig always wondered what he was doing, and he couldn't talk much about this project at home. He told them about working with copper and how impressed he was with Badger, but not about the project's goals.

On a Saturday in late August, Mac arrived early to pack up his desk and move to a new building. He'd been called into a meeting as soon as he arrived, and now he was packing up as quietly as possible amid a busy morning.

"Betty, I hear you're moving to a new office. What gives?" He watched the statuesque Dotty saunter over as Betty packed a few things into a box. Dotty's nails, hair, skin, and figure were perfect, designed to attract attention. She used her wiles with men to get out of as much work as possible, and to find a husband rich enough to take care of her in the manner she wanted to be taken care of. Knowing who she had latched onto at work, Mac doubted her choice of a married man to be wise.

"I'm moving to a new project," Betty replied, as she continued packing.

"I have no idea what they will do around here without you. You'll still be doing the Friday paychecks, won't you?" Mac enjoyed the growing look of concern on Dotty's face.

"Probably, but not for this group."

"Who's going to handle it for this group?"

"Hey Dotty, it's about time you started doing your work and stopped taking credit for what Betty does," said Ed, the young office clerk. It was an open office space, and everyone knew everyone else's business.

"I do my fair share of work around here," Dotty replied. Laughter came from every corner. She spun around to identify those mocking her, but everyone's head was down, busily focused on work, and no one looked her in the eye. Mac stepped back into his office so she wouldn't latch onto him.

"Dotty, you can handle the payroll, can't you?" Amos Bronson, the senior office manager, came to the door of his office, which overlooked the clerks, secretaries, and bookkeepers.

"Of course I can, Mr. Bronson." Dotty's tone suggested she was being unfairly maligned. "But I don't understand why Betty can't finish up before she leaves. She's much more up to speed on the hours and expenses for this week. I have plans for lunch."

"Since Betty is no longer a part of this office, you may want to get on this before it interrupts your lunch." Mr. Bronson looked at his watch.

"Well, of all...," Dotty's voice trailed off. Mr. Bronson was not smiling as he closed his office door.

"Thank you, Dotty. I'm sure we can count on you," Ed taunted.

Dotty turned and glared at the mockers, but once again, they were busily working and ignoring her.

"When did they tell you about this new project?" Dotty turned back to Betty.

"When I came in this morning," Betty said.

"Hey, Betty, we're all excited for you," Ed yelled. Others stood and clapped as she walked out of the office for the last time.

"You'll stop by for a drink after work, won't you?" Another one of the guys in the office called out.

"Can't tonight. I'm meeting my boyfriend for dinner," Betty replied.

The office cheered. Betty headed for the elevator, and Dotty returned to her desk. Mac spent more time packing and waited until most of the office had left for lunch before heading to the new location.

———

After lunch, Mac arrived at the new location. He stepped off the elevator on the eighth floor of the large, nondescript Devonshire Street building and looked down the long, narrow corridor of closed office doors with frosted glass windows. He could be on any floor in any building in any city across America. Office buildings in the movies looked like this. Stone and Webster had emptied this floor of its previous tenants. Maintenance men scraped the names of the former tenants off the frosted half-glass doors. They turned to look at him and then continued with their work.

Mac thought that the frosty-pebbled glass on each door would filter light from the hallway, making it hard to see inside from the hallway, but you could never see who or what was inside. His directions instructed him to walk to the end, turn right, and enter the office at the end of that hallway. He heard the elevator door open behind him and turned to see a tall, good-looking man in a suit step off the other elevator. The heat and humidity of early September hadn't yet ruined his suit's crisp, clean lines. The man was fit and trim enough to be an army officer. The Army Corps of Engineers was officially in charge of the new project, and the Manhattan Engineering District had recently decided to establish a Boston office.

"You must be the new Army Corps man who's going to run the office," Mac said.

The man turned to him in surprise, then smiled and introduced himself as Captain James Hanson. Mac introduced himself and realized that Captain Hanson seemed to know his name, which made sense. Hanson most likely had a file on everyone working on the project.

At over six feet, with blond hair and a disarming smile, this man exuded quiet authority. As they walked down the hall, Hanson opened the doors and checked out the empty offices that needed furniture, phones, and people. The elevator opened, and two men stepped off with a rack of telephones to be installed. They pulled out the plans, reviewed the locations of the phone installations, and got to work. It wouldn't be long before this floor and several others would bustle with activity and people.

At the last office at the end of the hallway, they saw shadows moving behind the door. At least someone else was here. Entering the office, Helen Ryerson, the office manager assigned by Stone and Webster, stood talking with a short, fireplug of a man with thick, iron-gray hair that Mac knew to be Wally Reynolds, one of the engineers from the University of California.

"Miss Ryerson?"

"Good morning. Helen, please. Should I call you Captain or...?" she trailed off, not knowing what the other option would be.

"Jim, when we're alone, and Captain Hanson when we're with others, will do."

"Very good," Helen replied, turning to the plans she had laid out on a desk. "Mac, good to see you again."

"Good to see you, Helen. Captain, they have given you one of the best," Mac said. A smile tugged at Mac's lips. This guy was in over his head, and it would be a while before he felt comfortable in this new place, creating a new office for a project no one could discuss with staff he knew little about.

"Good to know. Will anyone else be joining us today?" Hanson asked.

"Betty, here, will be our payroll clerk," Helen replied, turning to Betty. "A typist and a stenographer will be arriving either today or first thing

Monday morning. I've heard that a local secretarial school will send over a student to be a receptionist starting Monday, but that hasn't been confirmed yet."

Betty stood beside a desk since no chair had been delivered yet, and shook hands with Captain Hanson.

"Good," Hanson replied.

"What's going on here?" Hanson asked, looking at the plans that Helen had laid out on several desks.

"I took the liberty of deciding the desk layout for the reception area. Here are some quick drawings I put together to show where everything should be," Helen replied.

Hanson nodded.

"You'll have the largest office." She pointed to a door at the back of the receptionist area that lined up directly with the door he used to enter the suite. Other office doors were to the left and right along the back wall, leaving the reception area with little natural light.

"Thank you," Hanson said. Helen opened the door to show him the office.

"Wally, good to see you," Mac said as he shook hands with Wally Reynolds. They had gotten to know each other on a previous project. "When did you arrive?"

"I've been popping in and out of Boston for a few months now."

"Where are you staying?" Mac couldn't ask what project he was working on, so he asked the first thing that popped into his mind.

"All the project apartments are in the same building." That's interesting, Mac thought.

One of the telephone guys cleared his throat.

"Right, let me show you where the phones will go," Helen said, stepping back into the main office space. She took charge of the phone installations.

"Hanson, this is Donald Macdonald, one of the guys I'd like to recommend for my project."

"Great. What are you working on now?" Hanson asked.

"That's something I'm not supposed to talk about," Mac replied. "I've been told to report here today."

"Right. Why don't the three of us step into my office?" Hanson said. Hanson's office had a battered desk, a couple of nearly empty filing cabinets, a swiveling desk chair, and two wooden chairs for guests that filled his new office. Large and functional, but not particularly impressive or comfortable, with a view of a brick wall. The building next door was so close he could reach out and touch it through the open window. He suspected that there would be no sun most of the day due to the proximity of the building next door, but maybe there would be occasional sun rays.

"Metal Hydrides or Trail?" Hanson asked once the door was closed.

"Trail," Mac replied.

"Oh crap, I thought you were on Metal Hydrides and I could easily pull you off," Wally said. "He can have the office next to mine."

Hanson nodded.

"Will you be here for a while?" Hanson asked. "I'd like to catch up with you and the other engineers on the Trail project."

"I'll get my office set up. Let me know when you would like to meet."

"What have you got?" Hanson asked Wally.

"I've made some picks for the Stone and Webster engineers I'd like to see working on my project." Wally nodded toward the file folder sitting on Hanson's desk.

"Any concerns?" Hanson asked.

"Stone and Webster are strongly suggesting some folks I'm not sure about. I'm looking for seasoned professionals who can work effectively with vendors, communicate in their language, and consider their suggestions, like Mac here. They're pushing young guys. Maybe smart but still wet behind the ears."

"They are our partners. We may have to consider some of their suggestions," Hanson replied.

"The vendors are the most important part of the project. They know more than we do. We need problem solvers, not go-getters looking to make a reputation."

"Good points. I'll look these over and get back to you."

"When?"

"As soon as I figure out what's what and who's who."

"Can we talk first thing Monday?"

"Of course. What time?"

"I'll ask Helen to set up a time. Helen and I need to set up my schedule. Mac, do you know anything about a visit to Metal Hydrides on Monday?"

"I'm only lightly associated with that project right now, but Dr. Alexander likes to meet on Mondays; he tends to have lots of ideas on weekends."

"I've heard he's erratic," Hanson said.

"And brilliant," Mac replied. "I suspect that Dr. Chipman from MIT and Captain Ruhoff will be there."

"Thank you, that's helpful. I'll reach out to Ruhoff."

"Would you ask Helen to step in when you leave?" Hanson said. Mac nodded, knowing he'd been dismissed.

Mac picked up his things and followed Wally down the hall. Wally pointed out the small office next to his. Mac put his things down, closed the door, and pulled out some reports to work on. A phone had been installed, and he called Bertha to tell her he didn't know when he'd be home and gave her his new telephone number.

THIRTY-ONE

SUMMER FLEW by faster than Ig thought was possible. They had only a week at Fieldston rather than their usual month, but with many of his friends around all summer and the garden, he kept busy. His height hid the fact that he was 13 while most freshmen were 14. He joined the crowd of students entering the school, checked the board for his homeroom. He noticed a tall young man he had never seen before looking over everyone's heads to find his homeroom.

"Can I help you?" Ig asked.

"Do you know where Room 208 is?"

"Sure, follow me, I'm going to the same room. By the way, my name's Doug," Ig said.

"I'm Alan. Good to meet you."

"New in Melrose?"

"Yeah. Dad's overseas so Mom and I are staying with my grandfather."

"What branch?"

"Army."

"Did he serve in the last war?"

"Yep."

"My Dad wants to serve, but his projects keep him working. Where are you from?"

"Springvale, Maine."

"My grandmother was from Brownville Junction."

"Big train town."

"Why didn't you stay in Maine?" asked Ig.

"Granddad's a colonel and got called to work out of Boston. He needed a housekeeper and thought Mom would have time to fill in. What about you?"

"I've lived in Melrose most of my life. My Dad's an engineer in Boston."

"Where does your Dad work?"

"Stone and Webster."

"They're a big firm," Alan seemed impressed.

"They seem to be getting bigger," Ig said.

They took seats in Room 208. The teacher slammed a wooden pointer on a wooden desk to call the room to order. She rearranged them all according to height, leaving Alan and Ig at the back. She didn't say it, but they all knew it was easier for her to see what everyone was doing when the shortest was in the front and the tallest in the back.

The teacher handed each of them their class schedule, ran through roll call, and told them what was expected of high school students. The day was a blur of following his schedule from room to room. After the last class bell, Ig headed to a rifle club meeting, the one thing he'd been looking forward to all day. He had wanted to learn about rifles all summer, and he was surprised to see Alan there, too.

THIRTY-TWO

SONNY SPENT the summer of 1942 working, wondering when he might be called up to serve, and when he was called up to serve, what branch he wanted to join. He spent a few days and nights at the cottage in Fieldston, and the whole kissing incident with Nancy had him wondering, again, what she wanted. He saw her at both the weddings he ushered. They chatted pleasantly, danced, and then joined their respective crowds. The weddings were already tense since both grooms left for the service soon after. He dated several other women and generally had a great time, but still wondered about her.

When he registered for his classes in the spring, he thought he'd be there the whole semester. When he registered for the selective service in late June, he still thought he'd complete the entire fall semester. When he started classes in September, he and most of his classmates were waiting for their draft notice. Everyone had a reason for joining the Navy, Army, or Marines. For him, it was a choice between the ski troops with Hooker, Tiny, and the guys from Saugus, or the air corps and learning to fly like Web and Charlie. He never considered the Navy, even though Dad was a Navy man through and through.

Now his thoughts had shifted from if to when his notice would arrive, and if he should join up now or wait for his draft notice. In early October 1942, he knew it was time to discuss dropping out of school, withdrawing for the semester so his dad would receive some of the tuition money back, and working until he left. He picked a Saturday night to tell his parents about his plans because Dad would be home. Dad was working crazy hours these days, but he tended to be home on Saturday nights for his favorite dinner of franks, baked beans, and brown bread. Dad's support was critical because he knew his mother would be emotional, and if it were she and he having this conversation, everything would go downhill. Ig, on the other hand, was all for war and destruction. That kid worried him sometimes.

"Mom, Dad, I have something I need to talk about," Sonny said, clearing his throat and looking at his parents at the dinner table.

"This sounds important," Mac said. Dad's seriousness made Sonny feel more nervous but also hopeful.

"Maybe I should leave," Mabel said. Mabel had arrived in the afternoon, planned to have dinner with them, spend the night, and take Gran back to Hudson for a few months, or as long as Mabel and Gran lasted before Gran asked to come back. Gran wanted to see her newborn great-grandson, Mabel's third grandchild.

"Please stay," Sonny said. "What I have to say is for everyone to hear." And he could use all the moral support he could get.

"This should be good," Ig said, grinning from ear to ear. "Maybe it will be as good as stealing the train bell."

Sonny flushed bright red. Mac put his hand on Ig's shoulder, "Let's hear what Sonny has to say."

"As you know, I will be called up soon. I want to withdraw from school and enlist in the mountain troops now."

He watched his parents exchange a look.

"Withdrawing from classes is a good plan," Mac said. "You aren't as focused on school as you should be while you wait to be called up."

Sonny wanted to argue with his father on this point, but knew it was useless. He wasn't focused on his studies, and he tended to blow off studying for work.

"You don't think he'll finish the semester? That he'll leave before Christmas?" Bertha asked, looking at Mac. Her voice was quiet, quieter than Sonny could ever remember. He realized that his mother had been dreading this moment.

"I don't." Mac turned to Sonny. "Why the mountain troops?"

He explained his reasons for the ski troops and that his second choice was the Army Air Corps.

"Aren't there special requirements for the ski troops? I've seen something in the papers," Bertha said.

"You need three letters of recommendation," Sonny replied. "One needs to be from the National Ski Patrol."

"Do you think you can meet the requirements? Isn't there a skiing test of some sort?" Mac asked.

"Just the recommendations, which I have Hooker and Web, that shows I have some skill." Sonny saw his mother wince and realized he had resorted to sarcasm with his father, not the first time. His face started to flush red.

"Sorry, Dad. Of course, you want to know what's required," Sonny said.

"It's not a criticism," his father replied quietly. "You did that ski patrol work in May, can anyone give you a recommendation for that?"

"I don't know," Sonny said. "Minnie can't do it for a variety of reasons, and the others have left already."

"Why not cousin Phil? He's in the ski patrol," Mabel said.

"Who?" Sonny responded, watching his mother glare at her older sister.

"Phil Robertson. He's up at Cranmore, I believe. You should write him."

Sonny was surprised to learn he had a cousin who skied, let alone one in the Ski Patrol who worked at Cranmore. He wondered why he had never heard of this cousin.

"So, what does this mean for when you…" His mother let the question hang.

"My understanding is that if you enlist, you can list a preference, but if you wait until you are drafted, you can hand in all your paperwork," Mac said.

"Where did you hear that?" Sonny asked.

"From one of the Army Corps guys at work," Mac replied.

Sonny took a deep breath, ready to argue, but took a moment to consider the pros and cons. Dad said withdrawing was okay, even though they might lose some tuition money. If he waited to be drafted, he might have had more control over where he ended up, which was good. He was eager to go now, to get the next step.

"According to some of the stuff I read in the paper, the war could be over by the time you get called up," Ig said. The conversation at the table paused. "Of course, other stuff in the paper says the Nazis will be bombing us by then."

"Your youngest child seems well-informed," Mac told Bertha.

"It's in the newspapers and on the radio," Ig replied, indignant.

"Would it be that much longer if you wait?" Bertha asked.

Ig's comments aside, the war would last some time. Waiting a month or two wouldn't mean that much in the overall scheme, and it seemed as if it would make his mother happy.

"What's the rush? You've already registered. Now it's waiting for the letter telling you where and when to report," Dad said. "You can work more and save some money."

"You make some good points. I'll withdraw from school on Monday morning. And I'll work more hours to sock away some money before I go. If I wait for the letter, I'll have time to write this cousin, who I'm just learning about, and ask for a recommendation." He thought he saw tears in his mother's eyes.

"It will be fine, you know," Mac said quietly. "There are other plans in play to end the war."

"So you keep saying," his mother replied. He wondered at his father's statements about other projects and wondered if that was true. And if it was true, what were those projects?

Sonny withdrew from school on Monday morning, and in the afternoon, he told his boss he could pick up more hours. His boss, desperate for replacements for the men getting called up, put him to work immediately. Working kept him busy, but he was tired. The money he didn't spend on himself and dating, he handed over to his mother to put into a joint bank account, for the future. If something happened to him, his mother would have access to the account.

In November, he received a letter instructing him to report to Melrose City Hall in early March 1943, noting that a second letter would follow with more details. He also received a recommendation from Phil Robertson, the cousin he didn't know he had. Aunt Mabel explained the relationship, but it seemed complicated in such a large, extended family, so he decided not to worry about it. His path was set, as much as any path could be set in this ever-changing world.

THIRTY-THREE

BERTHA WALKED down the hill to the Cedar Grove stop and flagged the train, determined to get to the club ladies' meeting on time. Shillie had not shown up today, calling to say she had a new job, so Bertha had spent time getting the house organized, walking the dog, and catching up before leaving. She boarded the train and was barely up the steps before the train took off, causing her to stumble into the nearest seat. The conductor looked at his watch and, by way of apology, said there was a schedule to keep; they needed to make way for freight trains, and the engineer did not want to be sidetracked.

Getting off at North Station, she looked around to see if Sonny might be in sight, but he wasn't, so she crossed the street and boarded the trolley that would take her to Brookline. Once on the trolley, her thoughts turned to Johnny Tremain, the book they were discussing. Ig said that it didn't seem like a book an adult woman would read, no matter how exciting it was for him, and having read it, she agreed. The story presented Revolutionary Boston well, and she knew several members would adore this book for its locale and colonial heritage, as well as its portrayal of a world at war. But she wanted something with substance. Pulling the chain for her stop, she got off and walked a few blocks to the Pierce home.

"Bert, you look a bit flustered," Gladys Pierce said, greeting her at the door and directing Bertha to the front room where several of the group gathered.

"I took the train and then the trolley," Bertha replied.

"What a silly thing to do," Alice said. "I had Frank drive me today."

"Mac's traveling for work," Bert replied.

"Why not buy another car? You can always get what you need for a little more money. I can refer you to Frank's contact. These restrictions and rationing are ridiculous."

"You think it's important to have luxuries while our boys serve overseas," said Millie, the mother of a navy man.

"We can do without for a while. We're made of sterner stuff," Johnny said. She had driven from Somerville with the car her extended family shared.

"Isn't that like you two, always defending the rules," Alice replied.

A heated discussion about whether it was ethical or fair to buy restricted items on the black market showed how each of her friends felt about it. She was not surprised that Millie and Johnny sided with adhering to the restrictions, while Alice felt that restrictions were for others.

"Taking the train and the trolley was not the end of the world," Bertha said. "It gave me time to think about this book."

"Ladies, I think we should settle in and discuss Johnny Tremain," Gladys said, smoothing over the discussion. "Please help yourself, the food has been laid out in the dining room."

Bertha gathered tea and cake and joined Alice on the couch. Some had enjoyed the book, while others complained that it was intended for teenagers. Several thought the experiences were more suitable for someone much older than the hero of the story. Others didn't like the way the hero defied authority, and a few pointed out that the Revolutionary War was all about defying authority and the established order.

War was a challenging subject for many members of this group. She knew that soon, too soon, she would be among those with a son in the service. Bertha feared Sonny would discover some young woman of questionable morals and get into trouble. Mac was too free with his descriptions of women of loose morals around Scollay Square.

The group took a short break to refill their teacups and cake plates. Cake was a rare commodity, and she knew several members had brought cakes to today's meeting. They were all learning to bake without much sugar. Most of them anyway. She hadn't had time to bake, and carrying items on the train and trolley had seemed complicated. She would be hosting in November and will have items ready.

"A penny for your thoughts?" Johnny asked.

"A book about war is popular now that we are in a war, but I want something more literary next time," Bertha replied.

"War is a popular topic now," Johnny said, patting Bertha's arm. "How's Mac?"

"Busy, working all the time."

"What is he working on these days?" Gladys asked.

"War-related projects," Bertha replied.

"Stone and Webster seems to be into everything these days."

"No one works that hard. I bet he's seeing someone on the side," Alice said. "Frank is home for dinner every night."

"So, how is Ig doing?" Johnny asked.

"Can you believe he'll be 14 in a few months? I want to give him a good swift kick in the ass," Bertha replied.

"I think we can agree to leave the vulgarities at home, where they belong," Alice said.

Bertha bristled at the rebuke. She was starting to dislike Alice, which would be unfortunate after all these years.

"Ladies, please, we are here to support one another," Gladys said. "Our next book is The Fountainhead by Ayn Rand, and we will meet at Mrs. Macdonald's home in Melrose."

Edith announced that she had already read it and started to highlight the story's finer points until it was pointed out that the group's one rule was not to provide the book plot before the meeting.

"Given how the world has gotten so crazy, who knows where we will all be in a month?" Ethel replied.

"Let's assume we will have the opportunity to gather again," Johnny said.

Gladys reminded them that anyone who wanted to stay could help roll bandages for the Red Cross.

"This war is invading every part of our lives, and I have too much to do to spend my time on rolling bandages." Alice picked up her bag and headed for the door. Gladys was quick on her feet and opened the door for Alice and those who followed.

"Rolling bandages is fine with me," Millie said.

Bertha was getting quite good at rolling bandages. She, Johnny, Millie, Edith, and Ethel stayed.

THIRTY-FOUR

MAC SPENT more time at Badger's facility in South Boston than in his new office. The cooling towers they were developing required a lot of time and testing. At the same time, a group at the University of Chicago was working on creating plutonium using beryllium rods. While he didn't know if this was viable for creating plutonium on a large scale, he was curious to see how this would work.

He arrived early on Saturday morning, checked in on the first floor, and headed for the elevators, as the stairs were now locked to control access and provide additional security. As the elevator doors were about to close, Helen joined him.

"Aren't you a sight for sore eyes?" Mac said.

"It's strange seeing you in daylight, rather than when you skulk in after dark," Helen replied. "I saw you on Hanson's calendar today."

"Why a meeting?" Mac asked.

"To introduce everyone to the new Assistant Area Engineer starting today. I'm not sure why Hanson wants to meet with you, but Wally has been after him about you."

"This office seems to grow by the hour. Have you met him?"

"Not yet. He's arriving this morning."

"This should be interesting." Mac wondered what the expansion of the Army Corps of Engineers meant for the project he was working on and all the projects that Stone and Webster Engineering were working on. Rumors swirled around about the number and size of the projects, and the number of vendors under contract was growing rapidly. He and his team needed to discuss adding a subcontractor to assist Badger with the numerous parts for the cooling towers. A short, dark-haired man in an army uniform was waiting.

As they stepped off the elevator, they checked in with the security man in the floors lobby. Around-the-clock security was on every floor now.

"I'm Lieutenant Elmont Salvaggio, call me Monty." The man shook hands with Helen and Mac. "Any idea where I should go?"

"Why don't you follow me, lieutenant. We are expecting you today." Helen headed down the hall, followed by Monty and Mac.

Entering the Army Corps office at the end of the hall, they found Capt. Hanson, Betty, a receptionist, and several typists already at work.

"Monty, good to see you," Hanson shook hands with the young lieutenant. "No uniforms in the office for this one. We'll need to get that changed before the meeting."

"Good to know," Monty replied.

"Betty, please help Lt. Salvaggio find a suit. Anything they may have on the ready-to-wear rack," Helen said.

"What if I find something that needs a little tailoring?" Salvaggio asked.

"Once you know where the stores are, feel free to buy anything you like. They're usually open late on Mondays and Thursdays," Helen replied.

"I guess we should shop before the lunch crowd arrives," Betty said as she pinned her hat on and headed out the door, Salvaggio in tow.

"Would you pick up sandwiches and coffee on your way back? Here's some cash, and be sure to get a receipt," Helen said, handing some cash to Betty. The receptionist let Helen know she had a phone call.

"Any idea where we should put our things?" One of the three draftsmen came in the door as Betty and Monty left.

"Your drafting room is down the hall. I'll show you where," Helen replied as she hung up the phone.

"I'll show them where to go," Mac said.

"Thanks, Mac," Helen replied. Then she turned to Hanson and said, "The law firm on 10 is ready to meet with us now."

"Who's that?" Jeff asked. They were looking at the gray-haired woman seated at one of the drafting desks.

"A secretary shouldn't be at a drafting desk," Mutt said loudly.

"Keep your comments to yourselves," Mac said. He ignored the snicker from Jeff. "Sara, how wonderful to see you. I'm glad you're joining us. I'd like you to meet three of the draftsmen who will be working with you."

"Mac, it's been too long," Sara said with a smile, shaking Mac's hand. "How's Bertha?"

"She's well. Sorry to hear about Harry."

"It's what happens with an older man and a young wife. I'm glad to be back, if only for the duration."

"Gentlemen, Mrs. Olson will supervise your work," Hanson said, having followed them into the drafting room. Sara, Mac, the meeting will be in about an hour. Sorry for the delay."

The three young draftsmen were at a loss for words. Several more people arrived with their boxes in hand, bewildered and excited to start work on a project they knew little about. Among the group, Mac noticed a pregnant woman carrying a box. Louise was an excellent draftsman and had been requested for this project for as long as she could work.

"May I help you with that?" Mac asked as he took the box from her.

"Thanks, Mac," she smiled at him as the two young men gaped at her stomach.

"I cannot work with a pregnant woman."

"You can leave." Captain Hanson was still by the door.

"You can't do that!"

"I can."

This silenced most of the muttering.

"Let me introduce myself, I'm Captain Hanson. This project is being conducted under the Army Corps of Engineers and the Office of Scientific Research and Development. Stone and Webster Engineering is our partner. My team and I have reviewed and approved each of you for this project." Captain Hanson's emphasis on the phrase 'each of you' was not lost on the group. "These projects are for the war effort, and they are top secret. I expect everyone to work together to accomplish our goals and bring our boys home."

A rah, rah was heard in the back.

"Mrs. Olson has more skill and experience than most of you, and she will be your supervisor," Captain Hanson said as he strode through the group and took the arm of the mouthy young man, steering him into an office. The elevator opened, and several men arrived with furniture.

"If everyone would follow me, we could look at these two rooms and think about the best way to set up tables and desks," Sara said to the group. They followed her as she walked them through the rooms she had selected, their windows, light, and space. The spaces quickly became a buzz of activity as draftsmen and women selected their spots and placed furniture.

Mac was enjoying the energy of the project and the dynamic of all these transitions. It was good to be productive, like in the old days before the depression, and be a part of something no one had ever done. He hoped all these efforts would result in something that would end the war. Sonny would be leaving in four months, and as much as Sonny wanted to serve, he hoped the war would be over before anything happened to him.

He noticed two draftsmen hovered near the door, looking unsure whether to stay or to go.

"You two are draftsmen?" Helen, who had joined them, asked. The tall one ignored her, but the short one responded.

"Yes, ma'am. We've been sent over," said the short one.

"The guy in the uniform, who's he?" Asked the tall, snotty one who initially ignored her.

"He's one of the Army engineers," Mac replied.

"You've got to be kidding me," the snotty one said. "The Army is heading up this project? Now we're all doomed."

Hanson looked the two young draftsmen up and down.

"I'm the senior army officer. Sara, will you select spaces for these two, ah, gentlemen? Preferably as far from this office as possible." Both young men visibly cringed.

"Of course," Sara replied.

"Captain, it's time for us to head upstairs," Helen said, waiting for Hanson in the hallway. The two of them headed down the hall towards the elevator.

"I'm going back to the office and find out what's going on," the tall, snotty one said, loud enough for everyone to hear.

"If you do, don't bother coming back."

"You can't do that."

"I can and I will," Hanson replied as the elevator doors closed.

"Can he fire us?"

"It's not something I'm willing to test," Mac replied.

MacHe headed to his office to work on reports. When Hanson returned, closer to noon than an hour later, he called Mac, Wally, and Sara to the main office. They arrived to find that several other engineers, including Ramsdell, had arrived.

Hanson introduced them to Lt. Salvaggio, now dressed in a suit, who was the Assistant Acting Area Engineer for the Manhattan Engineering District in Boston, the office overseeing their projects, and a Sgt. Houston was introduced as one of the officers overseeing security. Background checks would be conducted on all individuals working in the office, regardless of their role. Afterwards, everyone returned to work. Mac and Ramsdell nodded to one another, but could no longer chat about their projects.

THIRTY-FIVE

As DECEMBER rolled around, Ig's thoughts turned to Christmas and the Rumor Clinic that appeared on one Sunday a month in the Boston Herald. The column had started in March as a way to put fact to some rather fanciful rumors. He was waiting patiently for the newspaper to come his way. He needed to verify an answer to one of the rumor clinic's questions before heading off to church with Mom. His friends Al and Milt challenged him, and they had money riding on the answer.

Mac was reading the Boston Herald at the dining room table. The paper sections were folded pristinely and hung over the back of the dining room chair beside him. The family rule was that no section could be read until he had read it, or if you did, it had to be returned to its proper spot, properly folded, with no wrinkles or folds that weren't there originally.

"What is it, Ig?" Mac asked.

"I need to read the Rumor Clinic before Sunday school."

"Why?" Mac seemed truly curious.

"We're going to talk about it, and I want to know what's in there," Ig replied.

"I get the section first after Dad, you know the rules," Sonny said.

Ig stuck his tongue out at his brother. He wanted to read one section. It wasn't fair that he had to go to church when Dad and Sonny stayed home.

To combat misinformation, the Herald had assembled an editorial board comprising doctors, nurses, social workers, and a representative from Harvard to research the rumors and report their findings to readers. The guys at Sunday school debated the rumors and used the Rumor Clinic to fuel their arguments.

"I think we can let Ig read the column before he goes to church," Mac said, handing the front section to Ig.

"No fair," Sonny said, trying to grab the section from Ig.

"What's not fair?" Bertha asked, placing a breakfast plate in front of each of them.

"How the paper is best read," Mac said, swatting Sonny's hand away.

"I have to go to work, so I should get to read the paper first," Sonny said.

Ig scanned the article on war rumors as quickly as he could.

"Ig, why don't you read the Rumor Clinic to us so we all know what's going on?" Gran said.

"Then Sonny won't need to take that section with him and read it on the train," Bertha said.

Ig raced through the Rumor Clinic before handing it back to his father. "It's the one about perms making women's heads explode."

"Funny, I've had several perms and kept my head," Gran replied with a mischievous smile. Ig glanced at his grandmother, unsure whether she was making fun of him or not.

"Why do you need to know so badly?" Bertha asked.

"We have a bet going and I want to win, then I won't owe Al and Milt any more money," Ig replied, eating everything on his plate.

"More money?" Bertha asked. "How much are you betting?"

"Not much, but I hate to lose," Ig replied.

"I'm impressed, I didn't think you had it in you," Sonny said. "I'm off. I'll call if I'm going to be late."

"You need to talk to your son about betting," Bertha told Mac.

It was looking like a dull Christmas. There were no lights on the Christmas trees and no colored lights lined Main Street to signify the season. Sonny was preparing to leave, and Dad was never home.

A few days later, Bertha reminded them that the Club Ladies would be at the house on Saturday for lunch and their meeting. Mac and Sonny will be working. Ig decides it would be best to spend Saturday at Alan's house rather than be fawned over by the ladies, and Bertha agreed.

"Will there be any leftovers for dinner?" Ig asked.

"Most likely," Bertha replied.

"It won't be franks and beans," Mac said.

"That's ok," Sonny said.

"Well, I guess I'd better finish that awful book before Saturday," Gran said.

"I thought it was awful," Ig replied. "I like the one you're going to suggest for next time. It was a lot more fun."

"You've read Frenchman's Creek?" Bertha asked.

"Yeah, it was around, so I picked it up," Ig replied. "I like that it's about another time and place. I think it will fall somewhere between Johnny Tremain and The Fountainhead."

Ig smiled at his mother. He liked reading the books and giving his reviews.

"I guess I'll have to pick books for Christmas that will appeal to both of you," Mac said. Sonny laughed so hard that milk came out of his nose.

PART FOUR: 1943

THIRTY-SIX

MAC WALKED the mile from North Station to the office in a sharp February wind that whipped his black coat with the fur collar around him. It's the coat he usually wore to keep warm at job sites in the winter, but today the wind off the water of Boston Harbor seemed to filter through his bones. When possible, he left the car at home for Sonny to prepare for his departure in March.

"Hey Mac, what are you doing in here today?" asked the tall draftsman Mac had taken to referring to as Mutt, the tall character from the Mutt and Jeff cartoon. He thought of the shorter draftsman as Jeff. Both had been assigned to Sara Olson and were drafting the plans for the cooling towers for the P-9 project. He referred to the project by the names used in his reports and on the procurement requests he provided to the expediting office. "We thought you were traveling."

Mac had deliberately arrived early, hoping to sneak into his office unnoticed. This morning, he had a meeting with Hanson, followed by a meeting in the large conference room on the 10th floor.

"I got a last-minute call about being in the office today. What are you doing here so early?"

"We have this unreasonable schedule for completing the drafting plans. The plans that someone keeps changing," Mutt said. Mac tried to hide the smile that was threatening to erupt on his lips.

"You know, since I'm in the office, I might have to review the plans after they're all done."

"I know. I should learn to keep my mouth shut."

They rode up the elevator, checked in with the porter at the 7th-floor security desk, and headed down the hall. He paused at the door to the room shared by Sara Olson, Mutt, Jeff, and a few other draftsmen, all in the office early and working hard.

"Good morning, all. Sara, would you join me in my office?" It sounded like a question. It was a request. Sara smiled, said good morning, and followed Mac to his office. Sara caught him up on the status of the drafts and expected completion date, should there be no major changes. No new staff had been assigned to them, although she was hoping to get at least one more draftsman to replace Louise.

"Wasn't she in the office last week?" Mac asked.

"She worked until lunch on Friday when she wasn't feeling well. Her mother picked her up. She gave birth to a baby girl on Saturday. She says she's coming back after six weeks. We'll see," Sara said.

"We can certainly use her," Mac said.

"Yes, but this work schedule is rough on us, let alone a new mother." The current work schedule was 7 days a week, 12 hours a day, or 84 hours a week. "And Jim wants to see you before your meeting upstairs."

"Great, I'll give him a call."

Jim, an engineer working on the cooling tower project, appeared at his office door almost before he hung up the phone. E.B. Badger couldn't keep up with the production and testing of the large valve screws needed for each cooling tower. They requested to subcontract to a vendor just down the street. Mac agreed that they should proceed with this arrangement. Badger had taken on some work for the electromagnetic project and likely more as well. He thanked Jim for the report, gathered the details that both Sara and Jim had provided, and headed to his meeting with Hanson.

When he stopped at the door to the ample office space, he was surprised to see the number of new people at work reporting on the number of hires each week, the number of blueprints and drawings completed, and reports produced. Each month, the Army Corps noted the need for more staff to churn out blueprints faster. He greeted the girls sitting out front, catching Betty's eye as she discussed something with Salvaggio. Betty seemed to be doing well. Hanson stepped out of his office with a quizzical look on his face.

"Mac, walk with me to the elevator. I want to chat with you briefly before today's meetings."

"Meetings? I thought it was just one?"

"It's turned into a conference on all the projects."

"How does that work?"

"I guess we'll see." They were in the elevator lobby waiting for the up elevator.

They spoke quietly, "You know why we're here today?" Hanson asked Mac.

"I was told to be prepared to answer questions on Badger and the cooling towers."

"Right. General Groves, Colonel Nichols, Dr. Urey, and Dr. Lawrence are here, along with several others. I'll be at the table, and you will be along the wall with the Stone and Webster team. Wally will be sitting with Dr. Lawrence's team. He may have lots to say about staffing for the electromagnetic project."

"Very good," Mac said, unsure why Hanson went into so much detail.

They haven't had a chance to tell you yet, but at the meeting, they will discuss the War Production Board and the engineers exempted from the draft. You are one of the engineers being given an exemption."

"Do you know that I've already had my Navy physical?"

"Yes, we do know,"

Mac pondered this turn of events. He had expected to be drafted for his skills, and the Navy was his service of choice, the service he was about to enter as a draftsman when World War I ended.

They were both checked in at the security desk and headed for the large conference room on the 10th floor, the floor where Hanson had evicted the law firm. The story added to Hanson's reputation as a masterful negotiator. He wondered if that's why Hanson was telling him this news rather than Stone and Webster.

"Can I appeal this decision?" Mac asked.

"No," Hanson replied.

They entered the conference room and took their seats. The meeting lasted the whole day, and each project provided an update. Mac heard about the War Production Board, and his name was mentioned as one of those approved to stay with the project. He was glad to hear that Jim, the engineer he chatted with this morning, was also on the list, as were Mutt and Jeff. He glanced at Richard Batch, the Stone and Webster senior engineer with whom he interacted the most. Richard nodded briefly. He wondered if it was better to have heard this news from Hanson, with whom he was less likely to argue.

When his turn arrived, he updated the group on his part of the work regarding the cooling towers and the need to find a subcontractor to help Badger, who was overwhelmed with work. Dr. Urey agreed that it was imperative to move forward with this to keep the project on track. They wanted to be in production in October, but no later than December. Dr. Urey invited him to join them on the next trip to Trail, British Columbia, to review the site and work to date. Mac glanced at Batch, who nodded and agreed to join the team.

Mac wasn't asked to leave, so he stayed to hear about progress on the Y-12 project, the electromagnetic separation of uranium, at Clinton Engineering Works in Tennessee. Stenographers came and went throughout the day, changing for each new topic. Millie was one of those who arrived, took notes, and left. He imagined that this would allow notes on each topic to be typed up and ready for review by the end of the meeting day.

The progress on the pile method for plutonium separation, the S-10 project, at the Chicago Metallurgical Labs in Chicago, was the next meeting. Richard Batch noted that this work would be moving to the Clinton Engineering Works, as a workers' protest had halted construction at the proposed facility outside of Chicago. An update was provided on the latest uranium separation method, gaseous diffusion, which was being proposed and was now known as the K-25 project. This method was less developed than electromagnetic separation but had the potential to be more accurate. He hadn't been to the Clinton Engineering Works yet, but it sounded like it would be a much larger place than described.

Ramsdell and Dr. Chipman from MIT arrived to give the Metal Hydrides update. Dr. Chipman agreed to take over reviewing and ordering each product requested, using students in his labs to test the products. He would work with Stone and Webster and the Army Corps Area Engineer office to ship the products to the Metallurgical Lab in Chicago, the Clinton Engineering labs in Knoxville, Tennessee, and to Santa Fe, New Mexico for the scientists at Los Alamos, a new location that Mac took note of, and several smaller offices across the US and Canada. Stone and Webster determined how the packages should be shipped, each package's priority security designation, and recorded all shipments, all with the review and approval of the Army Corps of Engineers.

Hanson was the last to speak. He updated everyone on the progress in hiring draftsmen, engineers, and support staff. Stone and Webster were roundly critiqued for not hiring fast enough to meet the project's needs and for accepting non-Manhattan Engineering District projects. Mac felt Batch tense up, but defended the speed at which they were moving on all these requested items.

When the meeting finally broke up at 5 pm, Mac was stiff from sitting all day. He had been privy to so much information, and wondered if this was to keep him from protesting the decision to keep him on the project and away from the war. Bertha would be happy. She didn't want her son and her husband both in danger.

THIRTY-SEVEN

SONNY REPORTED to City Hall at 6:40 am on Thursday, March 18, 1943, as the letter instructed. He told his mother not to worry about breakfast. He would be too wired to eat, and they would most likely have something on the way to Fort Devens. His mother said she'd make some sandwiches and leave them in the icebox for him to take. His father surprised everyone by arriving home at 9 pm the night before, with Gran in tow, having picked her up in Hudson.

His plan to slip out unnoticed was foiled when he found his family waiting for him at the breakfast table. In a rare departure from their usual breakfast routine, his mother had prepared a full meal of eggs, bacon, toast, and coffee, using up more rations than they could afford to do so. His father, preoccupied with the paper, was distracted. Ig cleared his throat. Gran, sipping her tea in silence, and Ginger, their loyal companion, added to the somber atmosphere. His mother's teary-eyed expression mirrored his own, making the impending separation all the more real.

"Why don't I drive you to City Hall this morning? Then I'll drop Ig off and be on my way," his dad said, unable to focus on the paper.

"When will you be back?" His mother asked his father.

"I'll call and let you know when I know more," his father said.

Sonny put his bag in the back seat and got into the car with Dad and Ig. His mother came out of the back door and handed him the sandwiches he had forgotten in the icebox. Gran, smaller, thinner, and frailer each time he saw her, smiled and waved at him from the porch with Ginger at her side. He wondered if he would see Gran again. Nancy ran down the street and kissed him while Ginger growled. Then Dad pulled away and made the short drive to City Hall. He jumped out of the car, grabbed his bag, waved and said 'see you soon', bounded up the stairs and into the City Hall. If he looked back, he knew he'd cry.

Sonny joined the other inductees gathered in the City Hall auditorium. They were sworn in and herded out to the bus to take them to Ft. Devens in Ayer, MA, to be processed, whatever that meant, undergo physicals, receive their uniforms, request the branch of service they were interested in joining, and receive their next assignment or location. He had hoped they would take the train, but the trains were used to their maximum, so they took the gas-guzzling bus. Some guys were excited, others were nervous, and several looked like they would throw up. Saying goodbye was one thing; saying hello to life as a recruit was something else altogether.

The bus ride was too familiar, and his thoughts drifted to Nancy. They had been inseparable through his senior year in high school, but she ran hot and cold once he graduated and started working. She didn't seem to land on anyone else for long, and they always seemed to make up after one of her 'adventures.' He couldn't figure her out. They had both been relieved when she wasn't pregnant; at least, he thought both were relieved. He would have married her, but they decided waiting was better. She seemed more worldly now that she had graduated and was taking a year off before college to work. The pull to marry didn't seem as vital for them as for his friends Betty and Elliot, who had one child. He wondered if he could marry someone who did not seem as loyal to each other as Betty and Elliot.

At Ft. Devens, they got off the bus, lined up for check-in, and then marched to lunch in the mess hall. He wasn't sure what they were being served, but it was warmish. He had eaten sandwiches on the bus. After lunch, they were assigned to barracks and bunks, performed some basic drills in their civilian clothes, and then had dinner. All the guys he had left Melrose with were assigned to the same barracks. Lights out was at 9 pm. Everyone was too wound up to sleep, and the talking and joking continued for a long time. Reveille sounded at 5:00 am, and most of the guys, Sonny included, rolled over and put pillows over their heads.

"Get your asses out of bed. You think the Krauts are waiting for you to get out of bed before they attack."

A sneering sergeant ripped the blanket off his warm body. "On the parade ground in 5 minutes."

Sonny dressed and headed out the door to the parade ground. He missed having a morning shower. It took them a while to figure out how to line up in an orderly fashion while sergeants and corporals yelled things like "This isn't a drill," which it was, and they'd "be dead now if they were overseas," which was true.

Then, they were marched off to breakfast in the mess hall. They stood in line for food. Then, they lined up for their medical exam. Those who passed the medical exam lined up for inoculations. After that they lined up to receive their uniforms. They were issued ODs, nice olive drab wool uniforms for dress and civvies, and loose-fitting working clothes. He liked the look of the ODs, but the civvies were much more comfortable. If the uniform didn't fit, they were given a chit with the date and time they were to visit the tailor. His clothes were several sizes too large, and he had an appointment for several days later. A chit was also issued for any missing gear. Finally, they were given a chit with the date and time to meet and discuss their preferred branch of service. He had his paperwork ready.

While they waited, they were assigned duties around the camp. Some were assigned to clean the grounds, walking and picking up anything they saw. Others were assigned to kitchen patrol, which everyone referred to as KP. His first assignment was picking up butts. He had his tailor appointment the morning he was assigned to KP, so the next guy in line replaced him.

At his preferred service branch appointment, Sonny presented his three letters of recommendation for the mountain troops. His papers were reviewed, and he was told they would be considered. Then, there was more cleaning and more drills, this time in civvies. One morning at the mess, an officer arrived and informed him that he was leaving. He and twelve others were taken into town and put on a regular train. The first guy in line was given their tickets and sealed orders. He handed the tickets to the guys but held onto the orders, which were to be handed, unopened, to an officer once they reached Pando, Colorado. None of them had ever heard of Pando. It didn't take long for the group to convince the guy with the orders to open them up. They were relieved to see that they were headed to the mountain troops.

It took three days and various train transfers to reach their destination. Troop trains were given priority, but they were not on a troop train; they were recruits on a passenger train. They transferred to a small train in Denver that chugged up the mountains. They were let out at the end of the line in Pando, three small buildings next to the railroad tracks. The altitude sign said they were at 9,000 feet. Sonny looked around, breathed deeply, and wondered if he would need oxygen at this altitude. A bus chugged up, opened the door, and they shuffled on. The door closed, and they headed out across a brown, flat valley with mountains, or at least hills, surrounding them with a few short pines here and there. The road was rough, and the sounds of construction became louder and louder. They passed an area of huts surrounded by a fence topped with barbed wire that the driver said was the POW camp. The valley ahead was laid out in a grid, barracks to the right of the road, and a fieldhouse, officers' quarters, a PX, hospital, and other buildings to the left. Soldiers marching in formation with wooden sticks rather than rifles were on the road while the POWs and other construction crews were at work on more barracks. Smoke curled up out of the chimneys of the completed barracks and hovered over the camp like a cloud. They had arrived at Camp Hale for mountain troop training.

THIRTY-EIGHT

IN THE crisp March of 1943, a few days after Sonny's departure, Mac told Ig he wanted to have a serious conversation after supper. His somber demeanor sparked a sense of unease in Ig, who couldn't fathom what they would discuss. Perhaps it was a discussion about his behavior, or maybe it was about Sonny.

Once they were in his home office, Dad said, "I want to talk to you about a job at my office."

"I'm only 14, you know."

"I know exactly how old you are." Dad was dressed in his dress shirt and suit pants but had removed his jacket and tie.

"What kind of job?"

"They're looking for messengers, and they specifically want to hire employees' children," Dad revealed. "Keep as much information as possible about this project contained."

The prospect of this job, at the tender age of 14, piqued Ig's interest. The monotony of school was wearying, and the idea of a new adventure was enticing. Dad explained that this was a top-secret project, a detail that only heightened his curiosity. The promise of a paycheck sealed the deal.

There was a cursory interview. The messengers were all children of those working on the Manhattan Project, so the fact that he was 14 and this was his first job didn't deter them from hiring him as a messenger carrying plans from one Stone and Webster office to another, with a security guard following him. The reason they didn't have the security guards carry plans was because they felt the security guards should continue to know as little as possible about the project.

Ig was surprised to see that the messengers were a mix of 15 girls and five guys. They trained on how to take the most circuitous routes from one building to another, through alleys where cars couldn't follow. They were told never to stop to help anyone asking directions, even though many people in Boston didn't know where they were going. Armed security guards accompanied them and monitored the crowds for anyone attempting to steal the plans. Ig couldn't understand why anyone would want to steal plans.

Ig worked one or two afternoons after school and all day on Saturdays. Dad usually met up with him at the end of the day on Saturdays when he was in the office. Otherwise, Ig took the train to North Station, walked to the office, and reversed the route at the end of his shift.

THIRTY-NINE

MAC WALKED from 161 Devonshire to the security office at 72 Franklin Street, as the letter directed. It was a walk of no more than 500 feet, but it seemed farther as the wind whipped his overcoat and the icy March air chapped his face. Would winter never end? He checked in on the 5th floor and was directed to Room 36. Outside Room 36, he was met by another security officer who took the memo he received, scanned a list of names, checked off names, and told him to take a seat. The memo was not returned to him.

Mac joined a group of people, mostly men, with a few women, sitting in a corner. He recognized a chemist, several engineers, a clerk, a stenographer, and a porter. They had all received a security clearance letter.

"You know why we're here, don't you? It's because they don't want us to talk about the project. As if something like this could be kept a secret," scoffed the tall, middle-aged man in a nice suit with his overcoat folded in his lap.

Everyone looked at him. One spoke up. "This isn't the place to talk."

Everyone nodded in agreement except the agitator.

"Do they think we'll give away secrets to the Germans?" Sarcasm dripped from him like honey dripping from a spoon. "The Germans have Heisenberg; we have Oppenheimer, Lawrence, Urey, and some refugees. I think we can learn from them."

Everyone was silent for a moment.

"It's for the war effort, you know," one man said, and others nodded.

"The war is just an avenue for this invention. I, for one, want full credit for my work. No one is going to take credit for what I invent," the agitator said vehemently. "How long do they think they can keep this a secret?"

"I've heard they will have a patent office at every major location," another said.

"I've heard that too," chimed in a third voice.

"I haven't seen a patent officer yet. And I'm working here every day," the agitator said.

"And what is it that you are doing?" Mac asked. He couldn't help himself. He recognized this man and hoped never to work with him.

"Wouldn't you want to know?" the agitator responded.

"Don't you think it would be best not to talk?" asked the chemist. "You might endanger others."

"You think there are spies in our midst?" the agitator scoffed.

"Yes," Mac replied.

"I've heard that there will be more security."

"Wouldn't spies have accents or something? And how would they get here?" This was from one of the younger people in the room, although Mac suspected they were drawing out this man's prejudices.

"I have an accent," a young man from England said.

"But it's not German or Italian," he replied.

"How do you know? I may have gone to school in England."

There was some silence after this comment. Engineers were familiar with industrial spies, often encountering engineers from competing companies at conferences. It was easy to sit in a bar or a hotel and chat about new and fascinating work. A spy who knew what he was doing might fool them.

"Don't be ridiculous. Wouldn't your credentials bear out where you went to school? Where are your licenses from?"

"Maybe. Or maybe I made those up. Who's going to check with someone in England?"

"Mac, didn't your son get called up recently?" asked one of the women.

"He's looking to get into the ski troops.

"He's at Tufts?"

"He withdrew. He knew he was leaving in February or March."

"Ladies and gentlemen, you don't know enough about this group to talk about what you know." Lieutenant Salvaggio said from the doorway to the conference room. "Loose lips sink ships. We want to protect our sailors and soldiers."

Everyone sat up straighter as Salvaggio reviewed a clipboard.

"Mr. Macdonald, would you please join us?" He was polite, but it wasn't a request.

When Mac entered the room, he noted that Hanson, the new security guy, Houston, Betty, and Salvaggio were there. A man he had never seen before, in a spiffy uniform, was also present. The first few questions were perfunctory, and Mac suspected they must be the same for everyone: name, title, address, phone number, and role on the project. After that, the questions became specific, and the final question was a supposed indiscretion. He had been reported for providing more detail than necessary to a vendor. The information he provided could be passed to agents monitoring Americans' progress.

Mac deftly demonstrated that using the specifications and a description of what they were ultimately looking for allowed for a greater understanding of what he was asking the vendors to accomplish, especially given the quick turnaround. He noted that the testing and inspection process would identify anything that did not meet their requirements, but several rounds of testing and inspection would further delay the project.

"An excellent summary," the man in the spiffy uniform said. "I suggest that future conversations occur where you won't be overheard."

"While optimal, it isn't always practical. We are meeting where the product is being molded to compare the specification and the product."

The man noted that the need for secrecy competed with the need for speed in production and training on something that had never been done at such a large scale; however, secrecy was also essential. Then he nodded to Hanson, and the interview ended; Mac was dismissed. He headed back to the waiting area to gather his coat.

He overheard the agitator telling everyone that he had been discussing ways to separate uranium with everyone at a bar more than once.

Salvaggio called him next. Mac suspected they were taking this man to keep him from telling this room full of folks more. As he headed down the hall, Mac heard him tell Salvaggio this interview was a charade. He didn't think much of the United States staying ahead of the Germans, Italians, Russians, or the Japanese. Mac felt sure that this man had no intention of keeping any information to himself.

FORTY

IG WAS excited to be hired as a messenger but quickly found the job tedious. All the messengers sat together at a table, waiting for a slip telling them where to pick up plans and, when they picked up the plans, walking to the office, getting the slip signed, walking to the delivery spot, getting the slip signed again, and then returning to the messenger office, and turning in their slip. Through each step, security officers escorted them. Since he was still in training, another messenger accompanied him as well.

The messengers conversed with one another, but none of the staff had time to chat, including the security officers, who were more interested in discussing matters with their colleagues. The most exciting part was walking through the rabbit warren of alleys between buildings around Franklin, Federal, and Devonshire Streets.

On a rainy Saturday in April, Ig was paired with Sally, a pretty, headstrong 15-year-old. The two of them decided to see if they could fool the security guards by hiding some of the plans under their clothes when no one was looking, taking them home, showing them off to their friends at school, and then returning them. Plans were always getting misplaced, and the messengers would be sent on a hunt to track them down. Would taking them be so hard? On Saturday, the agents were sluggish. Hungover is what they heard.

A slip arrived for two messengers. Ig and Sally waited for the security guard. They walked over to the pick-up point, found the assigned plans, checked the destination on the slip, walked the plans to their destination, checked in at the front desk, took the elevator to the office, and checked in with the guard on the floor. While their security guard chatted with the floor's security guard, they went down the hall and turned the corner.

Ig stuffed the folded plans in his pants, and Sally tucked them into the back of her skirt. Their coats hid any bulkiness. They delivered the plans, met the security guard at the elevator, and returned their slips to the messenger's office to wait for their next assignment.

Once he and Sally were alone, they packed the plans in their bags and took out their homework. They were both engrossed in their homework when two security guards arrived and told them to bring their coats and bags and follow the guards. When they arrived in the conference room, a security officer named Houston and Sally's father were waiting for them. Sara Olson arrived while the security officer went through each of their book bags, ignoring Ig and Sally's protests, and pulled out the purloined plans.

The engineers who had received the plans noticed missing pages and alerted the security office. After that, they tracked down the two who had picked up and delivered the plans, called Sally's father, and tried to call Ig's father, but learned he was out of town. They then brought them up to the conference room. Their brilliant plan had fooled no one. Ig hoped that Sally would admit that this was her idea, but she did not, so Ig told them it was his idea and was fired immediately.

Sara said that Ig was heading home immediately, and the two left, against the wishes of Houston, who seemed to want to say something more to Ig.

"Ready for a ride home?" Sara said as they left the building. Not trusting his voice, he nodded his head.

"What possessed you to do that?" Sara asked Ig once they were in the car.

"We wanted to show the plans to our friends. We figured no one would notice and we'd return them on Monday."

"Wouldn't the security guards know?"

"He stopped to talk to the guard on the floor, and we continued down the hall. When we were out of his sight, it was easy."

Sara nodded, then changed the subject and asked Ig how his classes were going. Ig was excited to tell her about his classes, new friends, and the rifle club. Ig was finishing up with his stories as they pulled into the driveway. His mother was waiting at the back door.

His mother came out to meet them and told Ig his father was on the phone, waiting to talk to him. Given the lump in his throat, Ig wasn't sure he could swallow, but he nodded, and they got out of the car.

"Don't ever do that again," Mac told Ig over the phone.

"I'm so sorry," Ig replied, near tears.

"Don't be sorry, be smart next time. Don't ever think you aren't being watched at this job."

"But they fired me."

"Of course they did. I wasn't there to defend you. They'll hire you again. We're going to wait until you are a little older."

"OK," Ig was hesitant. "But they didn't fire Sally, and she didn't admit it was her idea."

"Is that why you told them it was your idea?"

"How did you know?"

"I've talked with Houston and Sally's father." Ig thought it was pretty amazing since he hadn't left the office long ago.

"You and Sally pointed out a problem with the messenger and security guard system that they won't soon forget, and which I'll remind them when I'm back. And you learned that someone who leads you into trouble will save themselves first."

"I guess," Ig replied, a little confused. He had done something wrong, but Dad acted like it was a lesson.

"Don't guess, be sure of yourself and your actions. And don't be so noble next time."

"OK. Will you be home soon?"

"In a week or so," Mac said. Then he said he had to deal with a problem there and would call again tomorrow night.

FORTY-ONE

SONNY FOUND life at Camp Hale was basic training for the first nine weeks, mixed with mountain and ski training. Hooker, Tiny, and Sonny were among the fourteen guys from Melrose. The Camp Hale newspaper said Melrose had the most 10th-division men per capita, which made sense. Some he knew by name and others by sight.

Four of the Saugus crowd were here too, including the Kasabuski brothers, who were in the 87th regiment with Hooker and Tiny. He and most of the others were in the 86th regiment. There was a shortage of rifles and skis, so they practiced with wooden replicas and took turns skiing with what was available. The camp had German prisoners of war and some WAACs. Everyone rotated guard duty for the Germans and the WAACs. They were given clubs when guarding the Germans and rifles when they guarded the WAACs.

The barracks were long, wooden structures with coal-fired stoves at their center for heating. Smoke rose from the barracks chimneys and hung over the camp like a cloud. Because the camp was at 10,000 feet with mountains all around, the cloud of smoke never left. Everyone coughed, and many ended up in the infirmary with pneumonia.

Sonny wrote home about all the camp activities, the people he met, where they went, and what they did. Leadville, the nearest town, was off-limits, but Denver was open, and there were guys with cars. He had gas coupons from his dad, so he had regular rides into Denver until the 87th took over one hotel one weekend and the 86th, another, and they rappelled up and down the hotel walls. It was a lot of fun, but it did not endear them to the hotel owners, other guests, or their commanding officers. After that, passes to Denver were rare, but Leadville opened up.

By June, they had completed basic training, skied once or twice before the snow disappeared, and participated in simulations of throwing grenades and fighting as if in action. He wrote one letter to the family each Sunday, responding to the letters he had received from Mom, Dad, Gran, and Ig. Dad told him never to mention the coupons in his letters. He asked Mom for food and hoped she would get some to him soon. Ig wanted insignia, but the 10th was too new to have any, plus they kept threatening to disband the unit.

He also wrote to each of his friends, but not as regularly. Most of his friends were serving in one branch or another. Gert regularly wrote updates on their babies and life in Melrose. She was living with her in-laws while Elliot was overseas. Nancy wrote infrequently with updates on people he didn't know and, eventually, said she was too busy to write. He suspected that was her 'Dear John' letter. It had been a year since their 'conversation' about seeing other people, and he suspected that as long as he bought her things, she would stay with him. Once he was out of sight, she moved on.

FORTY-TWO

THE WEATHER in Boston in early May was moderate, and Mac walked from North Station to his office on Devonshire Street in his suit coat. It felt nice not to wear his overcoat. In Trail, it was so cold that he had to wear his overcoat every day. He felt lighter than he had in days. He entered the Devonshire Street building, took the elevator to the 7th floor, and checked in with the porter at the security desk. Walking down the hall, he noted that the project staff was expanding rapidly, and he hardly knew anyone he passed. He aimed to speak with Hanson before heading to his office and another long meeting. He had called from Trail, but he and Hanson had never been able to connect. He was still upset about Ig's firing, and he had heard that he would be picking up some work for the electromagnetic project. He had buttonholed Batch while they were both in Trail.

Opening the office door, he noted that Hanson's door was closed, Helen was not at her desk, and Betty was working with another staff person. He closed the door behind him and strode to Hanson's office. Salvaggio stepped out of his office and opened his mouth to say something. Mac opened Hanson's door and faced Hanson, Helen, Wally, and Dr. Lawrence. All conversation stopped.

"We need to talk," Mac said.

"Mac, I'm sorry we didn't connect by phone. We are talking about the needs of Dr. Lawrence's project," Hanson said.

"I want to talk before today's meeting," Mac said.

"Is there a problem?" Dr. Lawrence asked. He was courteous and smiling. Salvaggio entered the office behind Mac and closed the door.

"My son was fired while I was away. Since he was hired because I'm working on these projects, I want to know why no one called me to let me know what was happening. Why did I hear it from my wife and son?"

Hanson cleared his throat. "I didn't hear about the incident until after your son admitted guilt and was fired by Houston. While I'm not laying blame on your son or on Houston, I want to be clear on the sequence of events."

"I understand this is not the first time the young woman involved has encouraged another messenger to help her borrow plans."

"We have learned that is true. She has been talked to, and if it's alright with you, we will rehire your son," Hanson said.

Houston had slipped into the office and cleared his throat. He was about to speak when Mac spoke.

"While I appreciate the offer, it won't be happening now," Mac said. "What I want to know is why Sally is still here?"

There was silence for a few moments.

"At this time, we are working to control the situation. As you know, the young woman is also the child of an engineer and was hired similarly to your son. I can't speak to why she is still here, but I can tell you that this will never happen again. This is the only response you are going to get."

Hanson was firm, and Mac didn't like it. He knew who Sally's father was and that her father provided his daughter a degree of protection not afforded Ig. It wasn't fair to Ig to return under a cloud.

"We'll see you at the meeting," Dr. Lawrence said as he and Wally stepped out of the office.

"Is there a reason you said this in front of Dr. Lawrence?" Hanson asked.

"I was going to say it no matter who was here," Mac replied, turning and walking out of the office before Hanson could reply.

Mac entered his long, narrow office, which had a window to one side, a desk facing the door, a credenza behind him, two chairs in front of the desk for visitors, and a few extra chairs along the wall in case there were more than two visitors. A large calendar hung on the wall above the credenza, designed to draw the eye of anyone who entered away from the papers and plans on the desktop. Today was another big meeting with visitors from various projects and locations, and he needed to review each of the projects he was working on before today's meeting. He now had a solid team, and given all the restraints and complaints, they were getting closer to the final product designs.

After meeting with Sara for an update on drafting and Jim for an update on E.B. Badger's work, Mac felt ready for the meeting. He walked down the hall, checked out with the porter, and joined a large group heading up to the 10th floor for the meeting. No one on the elevator spoke, waiting to enter the conference room for introductions or small talk.

The folks filled every chair in the room, including those set up along the wall. Mac took his seat with the Stone and Webster team. Hanson was at the head of the table with General Groves and Colonel Nichols for the Manhattan Engineering District, and General Sherman, overseeing everything taking place in the Boston area. Regarding the various scientists sitting at the table, some he knew and some he had yet to meet. Dr. Urey was there, and they nodded to one another. They had spent time together at Trail, BC, on the cooling towers for the P-9 Project.

Hanson provided updates on the status of hiring draftsmen, and it was noted that they had a full complement of 746, a large number by any estimation. However, it was also stated that the hiring process had taken longer than expected. This was followed by a security report detailing the number of security and background checks conducted, as well as whether anyone had been fired or removed for failing to pass the security review. Then the report to the War Production Board was given, noting who had been exempted from the draft and whose drafts had been delayed. He was disappointed to hear Jim's name mentioned as one of those delayed another month, but not exempted. Helen was taking notes for these updates and was replaced by another stenographer for the next part of the meeting.

Hanson cleared his throat to get everyone's attention as they prepared to go through updates on the various projects that Stone and Webster Engineering was working on.

"There are some role updates I want to make the group aware of; First, Donald Macdonald has agreed to become our valve man. He will be the Resident Inspector at Chapman Valve for work on the Y-12 and S-10 projects at Clinton Engineering Works. He will continue working with E.B. Badger on the P-9 project while it continues construction. The P-9 project will be in production by late October or early November this year."

Mac nodded to the various people in the room who congratulated him. Several people clapped Dr. Urey on the back and congratulated him on a job well done. Dr. Urey remarked that he was only as good as those working with him.

Ramsdell and Dr. Chipman provided an update on the Metal Hydrides project, which was now producing good-quality powdered uranium due to the receipt of purer uranium. After their updates, Ramsdell and Dr. Chipman departed.

Dr. Lawrence and Wally gave updates on the Y-12, or Electromagnetic separation project. Mac reported on the work with Chapman Valve and E.B. Badger. Although Wally Reynolds had not secured Mac solely for the calutron cubicles, he was pleased to have Mac working with these vendors. Mac was happy to work with vendors he had a history with and to focus on valve design, drafting, and testing the various unique valves developed with Chapman Valve in Pittsfield, MA, as well as E.B. Badger and S.D. Hicks in Boston.

The goal of the Y-12 project was to expand the calutrons developed at the University of California at Berkeley Radiation Lab into a system capable of producing as much fissionable material as possible, which meant sufficient quantities for a bomb that could potentially end the war. Electromagnetic separation was a known effective method, while the other techniques, including gaseous diffusion (referred to as K-25) and the pile method for creating plutonium (known as S-10), were still in the testing phase for large-scale production. Mac also worked on valve requirements for the design of the town of the secret city known as Clinton Engineering Works, built near Knoxville, Tennessee, now sometimes referred to as Oak Ridge.

At the end of the electromagnetic separation discussion, it was noted that all drafting plans needed to be completed by July 16, 1943. A short 8 weeks away. The tension in the room was palpable.

FORTY-THREE

WITH GRAN and Ig's help, Bertha resurrected their garden in the spring of 1943. They had done well the previous year, and she had canned food for the winter. This year, the focus was on tomatoes, beans, carrots, parsnips, and peas, the most popular vegetables with the family, which could be preserved for the winter. She had kept seeds from last year's tomatoes, beans, and peas. She could trade her award-winning tomato seeds for carrot and turnip starts. She would attempt some squashes for the fall. Her family tolerated squash, and they were a crop that could be stored in the cellar for several months, so long as the mice and mold didn't get to them.

Ig ate foods like turnips and parsnips without complaint, which surprised her. While she could trade or donate food her family didn't want, growing what they would eat in their limited space was preferable.

On a rare day home, Mac, with help from Ig, rigged a fence of chicken wire on wooden stakes around the garden to protect the food from predators. The metal scraps Mac had used the previous year had been confiscated without warning, leaving the garden unprotected. She had complained to anyone who would listen that it was impossible to keep a garden when the tools used to protect it were suddenly removed, but her complaints were brushed aside. So this year, it was wooden stakes and chicken wire from Uncle Owen and Aunt Beatrice.

She thought rabbits would be the most significant garden pests. Wild dogs, often abandoned pets, roamed in packs, destroying unprotected gardens around town. In contrast, rabbits were captured, skinned, and eaten. She had added her voice to the uproar over the wild packs of dogs at the last Alderman's meeting, discussing whether or not to tie up all dogs to reduce the damage to gardens. Still, the dog-leashing proposal did not pass, and dogs continued to destroy gardens. She kept Ginger leashed in the yard for her safety and as a warning system in case a pack attacked her garden.

FORTY-FOUR

THE CLOUD of smoke still hung over the camp. Guys went to sick call with what seemed like a cold and were sent to the infirmary with bronchitis, or worse, pneumonia. Sonny had recovered from a cold in April and made sure to get out of the barracks and away from those who were sick as frequently as possible. When he had time, he went skiing.

He thought that once the snow melted, the colds, bronchitis, and pneumonia would clear up, but spring made things worse. One night, he found himself struggling to breathe, so he went outside, wrapped himself in his blankets, and spent the night watching the sky and the trains moving across the mountains around the camp. In the morning, he fainted at reveille. A detail brought him to the hospital, where the doctor said he should have gone on sick call sooner. He'd have responded, but it was hard to be sarcastic through a fit of coughing.

They put him in bed and started him on sulfa drugs. The first week was a blur, but he managed to write a letter home. The following week, he felt better, so he decided to go to the latrine alone. He was tired of having two nurses or a nurse, and an orderly took him to the latrine. An orderly was sent to find him when he was missing at bed check. They suspected he had gone out to watch the trains, but when he didn't return and couldn't find him, they tried the latrine. He didn't remember being carried back to his bunk.

He wrote his parents about his infirmary adventures and how he had narrowly avoided being sent to the Denver hospital. He thought he would give his parents a good laugh, but they called the camp as soon as they got his letter to make sure he was alive. It was another three weeks before he was discharged. They didn't want any repeat customers. Some of the guys who arrived at the hospital when he did were still there. One or two had been sent to the Denver Hospital, which meant they were out of the 10th and would either be discharged or sent to another unit. He felt lucky to have avoided that fate.

Arriving back at his barracks in late July, he was told to pack up his things and report to his new regiment. They had created a new regiment, the 85th, and he had been assigned to Company E. He arrived to find some of his old unit in the new unit, while others were assigned to different units. His mail had already been forwarded, and he sat on his bunk to read it. Maybe he shouldn't have told them how ill he was at home because they were all worried, even Gran. Mom was having dreams about his death. Jeez, she could carry on.

The Commanding Officer, Lt. Archibald Dolliver, of his new unit was a young, hotshot college grad who, at least, knew something about skiing and mountain climbing. This unit was at half-strength. The remaining members were coming from a disbanded truck convoy from Texas. Sonny volunteered to accompany the trucks, helping the recruits understand how they would fit into the mountain troops. Sonny was shocked; none of the truck drivers knew how to ski, most had never been on a mountain, and some had never seen a mountain.

All the truck drivers resented being demoted back to private and sent to this new outfit, where their driving skills were no longer needed. Sonny complained to Dolliver that he had joined the mountain troops, not the transportation corps, and that this half-assed outfit didn't seem to be focused on skiing or mountaineering if they were bringing in truckers from Texas and South Carolina. Older members who had had to produce the three letters of recommendation cheered him on. Dollie, as they called him, took it well and explained that they had run out of guys to make a whole regiment, so they were taking what they could get.

Sonny decided to apply to transfer to the Air Corps. Transfers were now open, so he wrote home about being discharged from the hospital, his new situation, the new unit information, and how he needed his birth certificate to complete the transfer. He asked his parents to send his birth certificate and other documents as soon as possible.

"Hey, kid, I've been sent to check on you," Tiny said.

"Check on me?" Sonny asked.

"Yeah, I got a letter from home saying that you'd been in the camp hospital and that your mother was having weird dreams about you."

"My mother is being dramatic," Sonny said. "I shouldn't have told them how I was found passed out in the latrine."

"Probably not," Tiny replied. "Anyway, there's a rumor going around that your father is having an affair. He didn't make it home to the dinner party."

"Dad is the last person who would have an affair. I bet he's been working too hard. He's on some top-secret project."

"That's what I hear. I just thought I'd let you know what the gossip is before I head out."

"Head out?"

"The 87th is heading out on a mission."

"Where to?"

"Can't say."

"Got it. See you when you get back, unless I've transferred by then."

"Where are you applying to transfer?"

"Air corps."

"Me too," Tiny said. "Maybe I'll see you there."

FORTY-FIVE

BERTHA GRITTED her teeth and focused on her knitting. How dare he say no to a Sunday drive! He had the sticker and the coupons, but he was saying that pleasure driving was restricted, and his sticker was for work. She knew all of these things, but she had been looking forward to a drive all week.

His no-show at the party had upset her, and the rumors that he was having an affair were more upsetting. Some of their friends were so catty, and he was so blasé about the whole thing. He had laughed at what Alice and Frank had said as if it were nothing. It was not nothing. She couldn't do much about what people thought or said, but she hoped to spend some time with Mac to discuss what was happening.

"I can't believe this."

"It's fine, dear," Mac replied, continuing to read the paper.

"No, it's not fine."

"If we took a drive and someone reported what we were doing, would that endanger your job?" Bertha asked. Her voice got louder. Ig looked up from his homework. Gran took a seat next to Ig at the dining room table.

Mac winced, his worry evident. "Yes," he said.

"Why?"

"Because having the gas coupons is a privilege that isn't available to many. The projects I'm working on are top-secret. If we drive around showing off, it will draw attention to me. If someone looks closely, they will notice that I work at Stone and Webster Engineering. If they look closely at what Stone and Webster are doing, they will see a lot of Army Corps of Engineers activity. One thing would lead to another. Details about these projects can be used against us in this war."

Bertha broke down in tears. Gran patted Bertha's back, trying to comfort her. Mac, with a sigh, folded his paper and got up. Ig and Ginger followed him, leaving the women to their moment.

FORTY-SIX

SONNY STOOD at mail call, hoping for a package from home. Resentment rose as other soldiers' names were called and packages of homemade food were handed out. All he kept getting were letters. The letters were fine. The letters were fun and full of information, although his parents kept asking the same questions, which was a little confusing since he'd already answered them. It was as if they didn't talk to each other. And they believed his statements that the Army food was good. The Army told him to say those things, but he hoped they would catch on with the menu he had sent.

He knew his resentment was irrational, but he couldn't help himself. He'd spent five weeks in sick bay, and all he wanted was some food from home. His name was called, and it was letters again. He got some joshing from the boys about the number of letters. He'd have to write his mother again and remind her to send anything they could eat. He wondered what she could be doing with all her time at home.

When he opened the letter, gas coupons floated out onto the ground. Everyone stood still while he picked them up. A quick scan of the letter from Dad told him to use the coupons as he saw fit. He would send more as soon as possible—the perks of working on this project.

"Who wants to drive to Denver this weekend?" he asked. Everyone with a car was now his best friend.

FORTY-SEVEN

THEIR ANNUAL dinner party was usually held in early August, near their anniversary. Still, this year, it would be in July, allowing Ig, Gran, and her to visit her sister Sue outside Rochester, New York, this August. Bertha had sent out the invitations and received the responses. With rationing, she was struggling to come up with a menu. She reviewed grocery store ads and considered what was in the garden. There was some late lettuce, early tomatoes, carrots from the garden, and peas she had canned in May. She would look for a recipe to make Swiss Chard palatable. Cheese was restricted, but she could find some for an appetizer. Potatoes were a must. She'd have to see what they had at the store. Meat or fish. She considered using the black market for meat, something many women she knew had done. She also knew all the reasons not to do this. Since local fish and seafood weren't rationed or restricted, she would have fish and seafood rather than chicken and beef. There were many things to make for dessert with local strawberries and rhubarb, which reminded her to make some desserts for Sonny to put in a package from home. He was clambering for things now that he was out of the hospital. She felt prepared for the challenge of creating a viable dinner party even with the restrictions.

Flipping through the paper, she noticed an ad with a picture of Helen Hayes pouring grease from a pan into a tin can with the help of a handsome young sailor. Did Helen Hayes do her own cooking? She would bet the answer was no. She didn't need an ad telling her she needed to do more to bring the boys home safely. She saved grease, maybe not all of it, but enough to keep the committee happy, and hid some for her use. She cleaned all the tin cans, removed the tops and bottoms, laid them flat, tied them together, and left them out to be collected. She made sure that no light shone out of the windows at night.

She grew and preserved vegetables for winter, managed the shopping and ration coupons, figured out when she could get sugar, coffee, and meat, which were never available at the same time, and cooked all the meals. Now that Shillie had taken a factory job, she cleaned the house, and she walked Ginger. Her only help was her mother and Ig. Then there were letters to the boys serving overseas, both those she knew and those she didn't. Keeping up with letters to Mabel now in California, Sue in New York, and Arlene in Chicago. She knitted hats with the Red Cross to be sent overseas to the boys serving, nurses, or the doughnut girls on the front lines.

Most of all, she cared for her mother, whose heart was failing. Lately, Gran had been taking dinner in her room, as the stairs were too much to manage more than once a day. She had called their doctor, but there wasn't much he could do unless Gran agreed to see him. After the party, she would discuss visiting the doctor with Gran. The nights when her mother coughed and needed help sitting up to breathe were the worst. Now Ginger needed surgery for a stomach tumor. She wondered if having a job outside the house would be easier, but who would care for Mac, Ig, Gran, and Ginger?

Ig had taken over jobs that used to be handled by Mac and Sonny, such as shoveling coal into the basement, walking Ginger, and helping weed the garden. Because he was growing so fast, Ig needed new clothes, but finding new clothing was difficult, and used clothing was nearly impossible to find.

She should also add some wine. Wine was plentiful and not rationed or restricted. She didn't imbibe herself, but she knew that many of their friends did, and she wanted this to be a fun event.

Why didn't she have a lovely boy in a sailor's uniform helping her like Helen Hayes?

FORTY-EIGHT

IT WAS a cool July morning when Mac pulled out of the driveway, heading to Springfield for the week. For once, he was alone in the car, which was a treat in these days of gas rationing and a luxury since he didn't need to talk about problems with the project, debate the pros and cons of different sets of actions, or force himself to get to know someone new. Most of the guys had traveled on Sunday to ensure they got a hotel room for the week, but he had chosen to spend Sunday with Bertha, Ig, and Ginger and finish his weekly letter to Sonny. He knew he should feel guilty about wasting gas rations, but he didn't. He planned to leave on Friday night or no later than Saturday morning to return for the party. He might cut it close, but he planned to arrive in time to eat or at the latest for dessert.

He marveled at how much had changed in the last 18 months. The time before the war, before gas rationing, before sugar and rubber rationing, before working seven days a week, twelve hours a day. He appreciated that Bertha and Ig worked hard in the garden, with Gran pitching in where she could without any other help now that Mrs. Brown had moved with her husband and family, working at the Quincy shipyard. Their youngest was doing well at Howard, and he had been happy to have the young man work on the project over the summer. Shillie was in a factory somewhere and occasionally threatened to come back to help out. He breathed a sigh of relief that Shillie's plans never panned out. Ig was enjoying the summer and would be heading to upstate New York with Bertha and Gran in August.

Sonny's attitude, expressed in his letters, was that this war was one long training regimen, and he was there to tell everyone what they were doing wrong. Sonny wanted specialized mountain training, but now he was stuck while training, and the army's needs constantly changed. He could not tell Sonny that; his information came from his army contacts, which he couldn't tell anyone about. He wanted Sonny to take his training seriously. He sometimes feared Sonny's hot head would get him shot on the first day of battle.

The further he traveled from home, the more his thoughts turned towards his role as Resident Inspector at Chapman Valve. After much persuasion, the electromagnetic team got him onto their project. Working with E.B. Badger had been a breeze compared to the problems he was encountering with the work being requested of him. He enjoyed the challenge of building something new that had never been tried before, but was worried that the contract specified the valves be delivered in working order to Oak Ridge in September. It was early July, and he had yet to test a fully functioning valve with a fully functioning cubicle. This week, with luck, they would test and ship valves that met the specifications for the cubicle operators to separate uranium into two parts, harnessing the energy of U-238 in a manner that contained the radiation.

—

It was Friday, July 16, at 7 p.m. when Mac finally left the Chapman Valve factory in Springfield, hoping he would make it home to say good night to everyone at their dinner party. It had been a long week of round after round of changes and testing. They then reviewed the results of the changes with folks from the University of California, the Army engineers, General Electric, Westinghouse, and Chapman Valve, followed by more refinements and testing. They were getting closer with each refinement, but the General Electric folks threatened to stop all work until the plans were finalized, so he had stayed. He hadn't slept much and struggled to keep his eyes open as he drove.

The project's needs were necessary for his family, his country, and, most importantly, for getting the boys home. When a local cop woke him at a stop sign in Concord, he knew he would never make it home. The officer allowed him to make a call from the police station, as all phone calls were blocked until 10 pm, except at the station itself. When the call finally went through, Bertha answered. He could hear everyone talking and laughing gaily in the background. She handed the phone to Ig without saying a word. Ig told him that dinner had been a success, that everyone missed him, and that those still there yelled hello in the background. Then the line went dead. Tears welled in Mac's eyes.

The police officer told him he needed to rest and arranged for Mac to get a room at the local boarding house for the night. When Mac protested, the officer said his other option was to spend the night in the jail cell. The police officer drove Mac to the boarding house in Mac's car, introduced him to the landlady, handed the car keys, and ensured he made it to his room. There would be no sneaking out to get home. Someday, he would be able to tell everyone what he was doing. Someday, they would rub their noses in the real story, but not now.

———

On the Monday morning after his failed late night drive home, and dealing with Bertha regarding the missed dinner party, Mac was in a meeting in the 10th-floor conference room of the Devonshire Street building with several Stone and Webster engineers, Captain Hanson, Lt. Ruhoff, the officer who had worked with him on the Metal Hydrides project, Reynolds, and a scientist from Berkeley, contemplating a problem with the cubicles and race tracks, when he noticed that Hanson and Wally were looking at him expectantly.

"Who will be going?" Mac had heard enough of the conversation to know it was about a trip.

"All of us here at the table will be going along with several of the security team," Hanson replied. "We'll travel by train, per usual."

Mac quickly calculated how long the train trip might last, taking into account the troop transports, siding, and schedule interruptions. "And you can't tell anyone where you're going."

"What do you mean by 'anyone'?" Mac asked, emphasizing the word 'anyone.' Bertha was exasperated by all the secrecy and the growing stack of items he couldn't discuss.

"Not your wife, children, friends, or co-workers," Hanson said.

Mac told them his wife was taking their younger son and her mother to visit her older sister, Sue, and Sue's family in upstate New York, the first week of August. Given her heart condition, this would be his mother-in-law's last trip. His absence would be less noticeable, and it would look like they were on vacation together.

"Mac, any work updates?" Wally asked.

"Of course," Mac replied. He presented his updates on the valve work, and there were a few comments and questions. Then they moved on to the next update. As they were leaving the meeting, Hanson asked Mac to stay behind a moment to chat.

"You've been doing a great job getting Chapman organized and the drafting plans on track and submitted on time. We have many concerns about how all of this will turn out, and one thing we haven't had to worry about is you."

"Thank you, although I feel this is leading to a new assignment," Mac replied. Reynolds and two senior Stone and Webster men had also stayed behind.

"We would like you to take on a new opportunity," Hanson said. There was a pause while they gauged Mac's reaction. Mac nodded.

"The good news is it will be a desk job, so less driving." Hanson continued.

"What are the responsibilities?"

"To review all the plans that the draughtsmen produce and compare those to the specifications."

"For which part of the process?" Mac asked, trying to keep the surprise out of his voice. This would be a tremendous job.

"All of them."

"That's quite a job," Mac said. "I'll have to think about it."

"We can assign you to any role," the senior S&W engineer said.

"Yes, and I can refuse any role," Mac snapped. He didn't like the implied control.

"The job we are proposing is important. We hope you will consider this favorably," Hanson said, emphasizing 'we' to everyone in the room. "It's important to have someone of your caliber overseeing all the plans. Let's take a break for lunch and reconvene here in an hour," Hanson said, "It's been a long morning." Reynolds took Mac to lunch and discussed the pros and cons of the new role.

"You will have sole control of the drafting review teams."

"Do I have a chance to think about this?"

"This is more or less a courtesy conversation. When we return, you'll hear more from the S&W and Army Corps folks."

"Who's going to take over Chapman and Badger?"

"We have some new resident inspectors coming on board."

"Anyone I know?"

"Please don't worry about them; you've got things moving in the right direction." Mac was worried, but he was also relieved. He believed in the project and wanted to bring the boys home, but this was the largest and most exciting project he had ever encountered, and he was enjoying the challenge. He would be foolish not to take this new role.

"Who'll be on this new team?"

"We have those two draftsmen you started with; they have turned out to be good team players."

"Mutt and Jeff are learning from their mistakes and are willing to take on more responsibility. They are smart but still wet behind the ears," Mac replied.

"Got it, so that's a no. Would you consider them for assistants?"

"If I can have Sara Olson."

"Sara Olson is yours. Although that's unofficial at the moment."

"Then, yes, I'd take Mutt and Jeff as seniors. They can oversee newer draftsmen on specific projects."

Mac thought about all of this while they ate. After lunch, they returned to the conference room to continue the meeting.

"While the pay structure is set for this project, we have some leeway, and your salary will reflect your new role," Hanson said.

"Thank you," Mac said.

"There will be daily, weekly, and monthly reports. We won't be able to assign you a dedicated stenographer immediately."

"So long as I can draw from the stenography pool, that should be fine."

"Of course." Using the pool was the next best alternative to having a dedicated stenographer and would give him time to assess good candidates.

"I guess asking for Helen is out of the question?"

"Most definitely," Hanson replied. "She'll be coming with me to my next assignment."

Mac looked at Hanson with surprise.

"I'll be setting up an office at the Clinton Engineering Works."

"Congratulations," Mac said. "What about Salvaggio?"

"He'll be staying here as the Assistant. A new Area Engineer will be arriving soon."

FORTY-NINE

BERTHA POOLED the ration coupons, checked out the new recipes, and gathered all the ingredients to make the hermits, cookies, and cake that Sonny kept asking for in his letters, which she wanted to send off before leaving for New York. And had done so without resorting to the black market or special favors. She had visions of Mr. Holcomb swooping down and wagging his finger at her. Being removed as an air raid warden had made that man the self-appointed judge of everything related to rationing. He had now singled out every neighbor for something, except for the Gilchrists, who were too old, he said.

She sifted flour, baking soda, cinnamon, ginger, and cloves for the hermits. She creamed the butter and sugar, added the egg and molasses, then added the dry ingredients, and finished by stirring in the raisins and dried cranberries. Cranberries were in abundance this year. She formed them into logs on the baking sheet and placed them in the oven. Her mother was at the kitchen table setting the egg timer.

While the hermits baked, she moved on to fruit cake, which would hold its shape and last a long time before going bad. She didn't hear the timer go off and was surprised when her mother reminded her to take the hermits out of the oven. While the hermits cooled, she popped the fruit cake in the oven. Then she began with the cranberry marmalade, followed by the cookies. The cranberry marmalade was a new recipe, and she hoped Sonny liked it as much as Ig.

The scarf she had around her head kept the sweat from her eyes, but sweat rolled down her back. Ig came in the back door. His nose must have smelled the hermits from down the street. He made a beeline and had one of the bars in his mouth before she could slap his hand and remind him that this was for Sonny and his army buddies. Ig rolled his eyes, moving to the living room and the radio. That would keep him occupied.

The next day, with the cooled and wrapped food, Bertha stood patiently beside her mother in the small post office. Everyone had something to mail to locations no one had ever heard of, and the rules and regulations for mailing food were changing constantly. She wondered how the clerks could keep up.

"Are you alright standing here? We can go, and I can come back later," Bertha asked her mother, who seemed to be wobbling.

"You know, I could sit down. Why don't I go outside and sit on the bench and wait for you?" Her mother patted her arm, but it felt like she needed to hold on to steady herself. Bertha put her hand under her mother's arm and steadied her as they left the line. Gran had avoided seeing the doctor, but Bertha felt it was time to see what was happening.

"Mrs. Mac," a voice called to her as she stepped out of line. "I'll mail your package for you. Why don't you get a table at the coffee shop across the street, and I'll join you. It will be nice to have a seat waiting for me."

"Gertie, I didn't see you standing there."

"It's hard to see anyone in this line, even me." Gertie, obviously pregnant now, took her packages, and Bertha took her mother's arm. "I'll be along as soon as I'm done here."

A cup of tea before the walk home would do them both a world of good. Catching up with Gertie would add some new gossip to her next letter to Sonny.

FIFTY

MAC CONSIDERED how to tell Bertha about the new role. How would he explain that he was no longer traveling, based in Boston, and working more hours? The Holcombs insisted that Betty was the mystery woman trying to break up his marriage. When he told Betty, she laughed. Several neighbors said it must be Mrs. Holcomb. Others surmised it was someone in Springfield. Alice had written to Sonny to see what he knew, creating more drama. Sonny had laughed, too. He loved their friends, but they were awful gossips. Johnny was the exception. Tears rolled down her face because she laughed so hard at the thought that he had strayed.

"Bert, I never wanted to miss our dinner party."

"Then why didn't you tell me you might not make it home?" Bertha asked. "I would have scheduled it for another date."

"I thought I'd be there for the end of the party. If we rescheduled, there's no guarantee I wouldn't be held up again."

"Now everyone is wondering about us. Will there be other times like this?"

"Probably," Mac replied.

Bertha continued to check clothes for any needed mending.

"I know my work is taking up more time, and I'm often not home. My work is constantly changing and will change again in September. It's going to take up more time, but I won't be driving as much."

"It has nothing to do with any woman you are having an affair with?"

"Why would I have an affair with another woman when I have you to come home to?"

"That's hard to say. You don't come home that often." A smile tugged at Bertha's lips.

Mac paused.

"Are you saying you'll work day and night while I'm gone?" Bertha took a seat next to Mac on their bed.

"Yes. I'll be in Tennessee checking out a new place being built."

"A factory?"

"A couple of factories and some housing," Mac replied. It was more information than he should have shared. "Not that you can tell anyone."

"I'll ask the club ladies to stop by with a casserole and make sure you're eating properly."

"No, that will be too obvious." Mac replied, patting his stomach. "I seem to be gaining weight without hardly trying."

"Maybe a walk at lunchtime will do you good."

"Not a bad idea," Mac replied. "I'll let you know if I have heatstroke in this weather."

"You might consider taking off your jacket."

"Heaven forbid, I can't have anyone see me less than properly dressed."

Bertha rolled her eyes. "Now I know what to put on your gravestone. He died with his suit on."

Mac laughed, then turned more serious. "If anyone asks, you should say I'm visiting Spencerport with you."

"You want me to lie?"

"I want you to tell a story that points away from where I am."

"What happens if you get home before me?"

"I'll say that I had to get back to work. Is Sue excited for your visit?"

"She's all in a tizzy. Which means she's excited and worried."

"Why?"

"Her boys have all been drafted and are leaving home soon. Winifred joined the WAACs and plans to see the world. Eleanor is getting married again."

"How long has she been widowed?"

"Since Corregidor. Sue says the guy she's marrying is as old as her father, maybe older, and once married, they are heading to Michigan."

"That will be hard. I bet Sue and Alfred have come to rely on their oldest being home," Mac said. "Do you have your return tickets?"

"I'm keeping it open-ended. Gran wants to attend Eleanor's wedding and see her latest great-grandchildren."

"Are you sure it's wise not to have return tickets? Train travel is changing rapidly."

"We'll be fine."

Ig popped his head in and announced that he was all packed.

"What do you mean you're all packed?" Bertha asked.

"I've packed what I need."

"So you have enough pants, shirts, socks, underwear, and a coat for the cold nights? And a sweater for chilly days?

"It's August. What do I need those things for?"

"It can be cold at night up there," Mac said.

"How do you know?" Ig said.

"We stopped there on our way back from Chicago," Mac replied. "We went to Niagara Falls, too."

"How old was I?"

"You know full well you were eight," Bertha said.

"Oh, yeah. I guess I remember."

"If you removed any clothes from your brother's closet, return them."

"Ah, Mom, his clothes fit me better, he'll never know."

"He'll know as soon as he comes home on furlough."

"All his clothes will be clean and hanging up in his closet when he gets here."

"Is that because I'll clean and hang them?"

Ig shrugged.

"Maybe I can find him something that fits while I'm in New York?" Bertha mused.

"I wonder where that kid's head is sometimes?" Mac mused.

FIFTY-ONE

SONNY JUMPED off the top bunk and started rifling through the letters he'd received from home. He put them in postmark date order, and then he referred to the letter he held in his hand. He had a bemused look on his face, wondering why his father kept asking him about the same letter over and over again. He didn't have anything with that date on it, and he didn't have one from Dad telling him all about the new project.

"Macdonald, what the hell are you doing?" Lt. Travis stood at the end of his bed, hands on his hips, staring at the open trunk.

"Sir," Sonny stood at attention and saluted.

"At ease." Sonny relaxed his stance.

"My Dad keeps asking me about a letter he sent, but I know I've never received it. It's funny he keeps asking about this one letter." Sonny's concern was contagious, and Trav soon looked at all the postmarks.

"Maybe your dad made a mistake. Maybe the letter was never sent?"

"It's not the first time he's written about it," Sonny replied.

"Was there money inside?" The most common question asked is when a letter goes missing.

"I don't think so."

"What does he say?"

"He says it's all about the new project he's working on."

"What's the new project?"

"I don't know. I don't have the letter."

"You were in sick bay for quite a while. Did it arrive then?"

"He says it was dated before I went in."

"Have you checked with the sick bay? Or with the mail clerk?"

"Sure, but I'll check again."

"It could have gotten lost in the mail."

"Maybe."

"Tell him you'll keep looking. It's all you can do. It's time for lunch." Trav left, and Sonny put the letters away. Walking towards the mess hall, he noticed Trav chatting with several officers and the officers' mess tent. He wondered if the letter had been censored. Dad said everything was hush-hush, and Ig had been fired for borrowing plans. Maybe Sonny should have kept the question of the missing letter to himself. Maybe he was overthinking this whole thing.

FIFTY-TWO

IG WOULD have enjoyed staying home with Dad and Ginger, but Dad had to travel for work, and they weren't supposed to tell anyone. He had had to stop himself several times from saying that out loud. It had been a rough summer for Dad, and it didn't look like it would let up soon. Ginger was at a camp in Vermont with Johnny Wilson and her family since the Wilson family cottage at Brant Rock had been commandeered for housing. Plus, they were taking the train the whole way, which was the best way to travel, and he could brag to Sonny about the long train ride in his next letter. No one loved trains more than Sonny, but he and Dad were close seconds.

Dad drove them to the station that Friday morning in August. He went over the route again as if they didn't have the whole thing memorized already: North Station to Springfield, Springfield to Albany, then switching trains to Rochester, New York. From Rochester, they would catch a local bus to Spencerport. It was nice to know that he was worried about the three of them, even if Mom rolled her eyes.

Due to delays, they spent a half-day in Albany. He wandered around the station, watching the trains and the people coming and going. There were lots of goodbyes, kisses, white handkerchiefs, tears, young people expressing undying love, older people looking resigned, and babies being passed around. It was like a movie. A serviceman whistled at Mom.

George was waiting for them at the Rochester station. He had Ig sit up front and said he was planning to put Ig to work on the farm, hauling hay for the cows and cleaning up muck. He could get as dirty as he wanted, and Mom couldn't complain. Ig grinned, and his mother chuckled.

They settled in at the farm, and Ig learned about haying, handling horses and wagons, mucking out stables, and milking cows. Lois, the cousin closest to him in age, enjoyed anything mechanical, wore dungarees and overalls, and loved to get her hands dirty. Ig adored her.

"Hey, kid, do you want to see what I can do with my motorcycle?" Les asked. He kept referring to Ig as a kid, and Ig adored his daredevil cousin.

"With luck, he'll fall and hurt himself before he gets to basic," George said. They were heading to basic training in the Fall.

"If you kill yourself, all the more dinner for us," Lois said. Ig's grin ran from ear to ear.

Les started his motorcycle, revving the engine for effect. Once he was going fast enough, he stood on the seat and let go of the handlebars. They waited to see him fall, but all they saw was the dust the motorcycle kicked up on the old dirt road.

"Damn, he's good," Ig said.

"Don't let your mother hear you swear like that," George Jr. said.

"She'll be upset and tell me you are a bad influence," Ig said. George laughed at this.

After dinner, they would sit around and chat. Gran told her grandchildren and great-grandchildren how she had been born in Plymouth, England, and lived there until she was ten, how her older brother had fallen out of a tree and broken his neck. After that, her father decided to move the family to Nova Scotia for a fresh start. Her mother died, and her father remarried and had more children. She was sent to Boston to be a maid and ended up meeting Gramps, getting married, and having children, which is how they all got to be. He'd heard it before, but the cousins ate it all up.

"Did you have lots of family in England?" Lois asked.

"Indeed. I had lots of cousins around. It seemed like every other person around was my cousin. My father wanted to make it on his own in Canada."

"We don't talk about the past here. The past doesn't put food on the table. But you can tell these kids about their ancestors," Uncle Alfred said to Gran.

Gran told them about the many Nichols cousins still in England. She told them how her mother and sisters had married and moved around the British Empire. One moved to Australia, one to India, one married a sea captain and went to sea, one married into a titled family and lived in a big house, and her mother went to Canada.

"I remember the aunt who went to sea. They used to visit Boston and bring us things from all over the world," Sue said.

Mom looked at her sister inquisitively.

"You're too young to remember them. I think you were a baby the last time I saw them," Sue continued.

And then Gran talked about Charles Church, where she had been baptized, and how the Germans had flattened it in the Plymouth Blitz.

Les said he'd been accepted into the flying school, which they all knew, but he couldn't help but bring it up again. He promised to take care of those guys.

"My brother wants to be a flyer," Ig said.

"No, he doesn't. He's in the mountain troops, where he wants to be," his mother said.

"Then why does he want to transfer?" Ig asked, but the conversation had already moved on.

Ig enjoyed the banter at the dinner table and afterwards. The evening Winifred announced that she had received her letter from the WAACs and would be leaving by the end of the week, Aunt Sue put her head in her hands at the dinner table while Uncle Alfred stared at his daughter, his face turning red.

"Where will you go?" Gran asked.

"I don't know yet, but I think it will be a marvelous way to see the world," Winifred responded brightly.

"I think you're brave," Ig said. "I want to be in the war."

"And what about your job? You have a perfectly good job with Eastman Kodak. What will happen to that?" Uncle George spit out the words.

"They told me my job will be there when I return," Winifred replied. She ignored Les, nudging her in the ribs.

"We'll see," her father said. "Promises were made to be broken."

The phone rang, and Lois jumped up from the table to answer it.

"It's for you, Aunt Bert, it's Uncle Don. Then he wants to talk to Ma."

His mother looked surprised. "I hardly ever hear from him; when I do, it's usually a letter." She sat on the front hall telephone table and picked up the phone.

"The trip was fine. Ig's learning how the farm works," Mom said. "We're having dinner."

Another pause.

"She got her WAAC assignment."

Pause.

"We were about to hear that part."

Another pause.

"She's enjoying her grandchildren and being the center of attention."

Pause.

"You haven't seen her for a while. She tires easily."

Pause.

"A discussion for another day."

Pause

"Getting home is complicated."

Pause

"I'm going back into town tomorrow to see what I can do."

Mom put the phone down, returned to the table, and told Sue that Don wanted to chat with her.

"I can't talk to him. I'm too distraught." Aunt Sue still had her head on the table.

"Get off your duff and talk to your baby brother," Uncle Alfred growled from his end of the table. Aunt Sue immediately got up. When she returned, she looked brighter but said only that Uncle Don had something to do. Ig wondered if Uncle Don had a say in what Winifred would be doing? Mom said he worked in the White House thanks to his high school classmate, Missy Lehand.

FIFTY-THREE

THE DAY after he dropped Bertha, Ig, and Gran at the train station, Mac boarded the train to Knoxville with a large group of engineers and scientists. They had a car reserved just for them. They were encouraged to keep the shades drawn day and night so no one could see them, but it meant he couldn't see where they were. What was the point of taking the train if you couldn't see anything?

They weren't allowed off at any stops, and grumblings were heard up and down the car. Mac used the train time to write reports, which was harder than expected, as the train stopped and started frequently. They had been told several secretaries and typists were in the Knoxville offices, and he hoped he could get these reports typed up there. Or maybe, if there were nothing to do, he would type them up himself. He thought he could accomplish more in the Boston Office and wasn't sure why it was imperative to visit Knoxville, but he kept that thought to himself. Their car was shunted to sidings during the day so they could sit and swelter in the stifling car, and during the night, they moved along in a herky-jerky movement, making it hard to sleep or write. A trip that should have taken less than 24 hours took them four days.

Mac took in the large railroad yard in Knoxville as they got off the train car carrying their luggage, walked up to Gay Street, and then continued down Gay Street to the Andrew Johnson Hotel, which served as the Project's headquarters while the Clinton Engineering Works was under construction. They checked into the hotel and had some dinner. Housing in Oak Ridge that had been completed, and the guest house was reserved for important visitors; he and most of the group he was with were not classified as important.

After breakfast, they traveled from Knoxville to Oak Ridge on the Oak Ridge Highway. Mac would have preferred to take the train, but even here, the train line was reserved for freight cars. Nevertheless, his first view of Oak Ridge was stunning. The hills and gullies had been cleared of all trees. On a rise was the administration building, dubbed the Castle, given its prominence on the hill overlooking housing both east and west sides of the building. Housing consisted of small homes, dormitories, hutments, and trailers. Everything was occupied as soon as it was put up.

After a stop at the Castle for each of them to gather their IDs and drop off reports with the typing pool, Mac joined the engineers and scientists at the Y-12 complex. Each valley between the mountain ridges held a different project facility. Y-12, S-10, and K-25 were kept separate so that any unexpected event at one facility would be less likely to affect another. An extensive bus system connecting each facility to the main townsite was underway. Riding over the dirt, pothole-filled roads was spine-jarring.

Mac was invited to this visit because of the Y-12 building, racetracks, and chemical buildings. The racetracks and cubicles were ready for some initial testing. Given the number of problems the team discovered over the next three days as they completed several tests and ran through the steps an operator would need to follow to separate uranium, testing was followed by two full days of discussions, recommendations, and plans. They agreed that a training schedule was imperative for those operating the calutron cubicles. They were targeting young, single women for this role, assuming they would follow directions and sit for 8-hour shifts with these machines. By the time they left Knoxville, Mac was happy he had come.

FIFTY-FOUR

Dear Folks,

Dad, thanks for the clippings. Be sure to send all the sports scores, not just baseball and football. What's going on with hockey? OK, they may not have too much going on right now but I bet there are some practice scores that you can find. Please save all the Train Magazines. I'll want to look over all of them when I get home. I want you to keep every edition possible. Did I tell you about the 2624 engine I saw the other day? Two engines were pulling 27 cars across the mountains. We were out on problems and I could see them much closer than I would from camp.

I'm sending you the menu from our 'rations' when we're out on problems for an extended period. These are good and I'm thinking I'd like these when I'm not in the army. Mom, please send food.

Love,
Sonny

FIFTY-FIVE

MAC READ through the letter from Sonny a second time. He hadn't had time to get to the newsstand and buy the latest Trains and Ski magazines. He had less and less time each day to read the newspapers and was woefully ignorant of the latest sports scores. Was the ration thing real? Or was that something the army had the boys writing home? He suspected the latter. He regretted what he was about to do, but couldn't see any other way.

"Sir?" A young man, whom he recognized as one of the new staff members in the public relations office, was at his door. It was hard to believe they now had two people checking every newspaper for articles related to or inferring anything about the project.

"Come in and close the door. I'd like you to do something for me," Mac said.

"Of course, sir, that's what we're here for."

"I would like you to pull some clippings for my son. Sports scores and items about trains will be good, plus things that someone your age would find interesting."

"I can do that. Would you like me to send them directly?"

"Yes. I'll draft a quick note that you can include with the clippings," Mac said. He quickly scribbled a note and handed it to the young man along with Sonny's address.

"Which reminds me, if you are out at a newsstand, would you pick up the latest Trains magazine?" Mac pulled out his wallet and handed over a few dollars for the magazine. "Include the magazine along with the clippings."

"Of course."

Would Sonny know the difference between what he sent and what this young man would send? It would be better if he read the newspapers and clipped the articles, but it was best to keep sending Sonny mail, no matter who sent it. Then he got back to work.

With Bertha, Ig, and Gran on their trip to Rochester, Mac checked the mail each day. He was also responsible for his own meals. He'd run through all the food Bertha had left him. On his way home, he drove to the lobster shop to get anything they might still have left. He lucked out with some fish and chips and decided to take the food to eat at home while he worked on reports. It was a hot night, and he had his jacket, vest, and tie off and loosened his tie. Driving up Franklin Street, he found the street closed by a group of youths playing games or yelling for some reason. Frustrated, he was about to beep his horn when a gunshot rang out. The young people scattered, all except one lying in the road. Then he saw Elaine and Mr. Chaplow run out of their building and into the street. There were screams and then another gunshot, this one into the air.

Getting out of his car, Mac joined the throng gathering around Maggie [SP3] Chaplow lying in the street. A police siren sounded, and several people beeped their horns. Mr. Chaplow was lying on the ground next to his 14-year-old daughter and wouldn't move. The man who had shot the gun, wearing a police auxiliary insignia on his hat, sat on the curb. Elaine was trying to pull her father up and out of the way. Mac helped keep people away until the ambulance could take her to the hospital. Then he drove Elaine and Mr. Chaplow to the hospital and left them. His dinner was cold but he was no longer hungry so he let Ginger have her fill.

A few days later, he came home to a letter from Sonny indicating that he wondered what was going on. It was as if his father hadn't read what he was sending. The clippings were from Chicago and Denver. he was surprised to receive a letter wondering why his father had sent him sports clippings about Chicago and Denver teams he knew nothing about. The articles had nothing to do with anything of interest to him. Sonny had bets with the boys from Saugus, so anything from Melrose and Saugus, particularly anything that made Melrose look good, and all the Tufts news was important.

Mac was embarrassed and angry at how the clippings had been sent, how the local authorities were sweeping Maggie [SP4] Chaplow's death under the rug, stating that the group in the streets was a danger to the auxiliary police officer, and that Bertha couldn't get home. He decided then and there that he needed to attend to some matters immediately. He put a leash on Ginger and walked to Franklin Street to talk to the Chaplows.

The following morning, he stopped at the Public Relations office. He found that the young man he had talked with a week ago was gone, but that a lovely young man named Miles was willing to help. He was surprised, then bemused. He and Miles reviewed the Boston, Melrose, and Saugus papers to understand what he would like to send to his son. Miles said he'd gather clippings for Mac to review and approve by lunchtime. Mac thanked Miles and headed to his office to find Millie inviting him to join her for a lunchtime jaunt to Somerville. The reason surprised him, and he was happy to join her.

FIFTY-SIX

BERTHA REGRETTED not getting return train tickets. The train agent apologized every time she visited him, but all trains were reserved for troop and freight transport. After ten days of asking, he asked her if her travel was necessary. She hesitated the first time, but after that, she told him she would not stay in Spencerport forever, as she had a home, a husband, a dog, and a son who needed to return to school.

She had expected to be seen off at the train station by George and Les, but instead, they were seeing the two young men off to basic training on a troop train. She saw Winifred off to Washington, DC, to start her new job—one that had priority train status. They waved Evelyn and her new husband off on their drive to Michigan. The smaller the farmhouse got, the more ready she was to get home.

Every morning, she walked to the main road to take the bus or catch a ride with one of the other farmers heading into Rochester. She would chat with the train agent, have coffee and toast, and then head back the same way. Once, she hitched a ride on the back of a hay wagon.

With phone calls restricted until 10 pm on a good day and denied most of the time, it took her several days to reach Mac and ask him to look into the train situation on his end. She could hear Ginger in the background. Johnny had been called home and had returned Ginger. She asked if there was any way he could drive to Spencerport, pick them up, and drive them home. Under normal circumstances, he would, but he couldn't miss deadlines and meetings. He could drive them home if she found a way to get to Springfield.

Once she procured tickets to Springfield, things moved along quickly. Ig was not concerned about starting school on Tuesday morning and would have preferred to stay on the farm longer. Sue cried when she heard they were leaving. Bertha had cooked and cleaned so Sue and Gran could spend time together, and Sue would miss her help. Bertha doubted Gran and Sue would see one another again. Gran had no more travel left in her, and Sue rarely left the farm. Alfred and Lois dropped them off at the train station, complaining about how much time he was taking away from the farm during harvest, and stating he sure could use Ig to help. She and Ig could have walked to the bus, but Gran was feeling weak and lightheaded. She finally reached Mac early Wednesday morning, before the sun was up, as they were about to board the Rochester to Albany train. Mac sounded relieved and would meet them in Springfield, come hell or high water, and get them home.

They spent a night and a day resting at a hotel in Albany. Late Thursday, they boarded the night train, which stopped at every street corner between Albany and Springfield as far as she could see. They arrived in Springfield very early Friday morning. A message from Mac was at the Springfield train station with reservation information for the hotel until he could pick them up on Sunday. When they arrived at the hotel, there was only one room for the three of them. Bertha inquired about a cot for Ig, but the hotel was all out of cots, so Ig slept on the floor.

Mac arrived on Sunday evening and said he would be working all week. Mac was able to secure another hotel room. Bertha and her mother stayed in the same hotel room, and Ig joined his father. Bertha felt guilty because the four had two rooms while whole families stayed in one room while waiting to meet up with a loved one passing through on their way overseas. Gran spent her time in bed, exhausted from the trip to Rochester. She agreed to see the doctor on their return. She talked about how nice it was to see Sue and her grandchildren, at least the ones still at home, and to attend Eleanor's wedding.

While she spent time with Gran, Ig read books, walked around Springfield, and kept himself occupied. She shopped for clothes for Ig and canning jars for herself. As soon as she returned, there would be tomatoes and vegetables to harvest and store for winter. When they left late Friday afternoon, the car was packed full of luggage, new items, and the four of them.

Mac waited until they were driving home to share all the news. Johnny had married an army officer whom she had met at the Vermont camp. They decided to marry before school started and did so at Somerville City Hall. It was very short notice, but Mac took a lunch hour, and he and Millie joined the brief ceremony. Johnny's mother had a small reception with Johnny's family, several teachers, and Millie, Gladys, Edith, Ethel, Alice, and Frank attended.

"She's 47 years old. What is she doing marrying on such short notice? They couldn't wait until I got back?" Bertha was indignant.

"What I learned at the reception is that Frank had left Alice for his secretary, who then dumped Frank for a soldier heading overseas, and Alice took Frank back."

"We always thought something was going on with Frank," Bertha said. She heard her mother chuckle in the back seat. Ig was riveted to the gossip.

"More than we ever thought," Mac said. "And there's one more thing."

"What?"

"Elaine Chaplow has moved in and she's been taking care of the house, Ginger, and the garden."

"What about her father?" Are you and she having an affair?" Bertha asked.

Mac grinned. "Not at all. Her father has also been staying with us. He was admitted to the state hospital in Greenfield, and I dropped him off on my way to Springfield."

Then he told them that Elaine's younger sister, Maggie, a classmate of Ig's, had been killed when an auxiliary police officer shot into a crowd of young people on Franklin Street. He witnessed the event and was angry at how it was handled. Elaine's mother had died a few years ago, and Elaine's father broke down. Mac had stepped in, offered them a home, and arranged help for Mr. Chaplow, feeling that Elaine would have a safe place to live and help Bertha. They arrived home to find Elaine and Ginger sitting on the porch.

FIFTY-SEVEN

Dear Folks,

So I'll start in the order that I received letters from you. Mom, I got your letter first. Thanks for the treats. The guys have now been paid back for all the food they shared with me. The fruit cake was delicious, and it was all gone by the time I made it back to the barracks. Of course, we're all together for mail calls, so it's easy to see who got food from home and hit them up for it. Passing around the cake helped me hide the hermits, at least until I got back to the barracks. The rule never to be broken is that anything in your locker is out of bounds. I'll share them, of course, after I've had some myself. The cranberry marmalade is my favorite. I've never had it before and didn't know what to expect. As it turns out, I like the tanginess and the fact that it's not too sweet. Feel free to send more.

Now for Ig. It's about time you wrote. I'll get you some insignia as soon as it's available. What you saw in the paper isn't exactly what the insignia will look like. So tell me, why do you want a machete? I can probably get one, but they aren't easy to find. And if I sent one and it got through the mail without being censored, I'm still not sure what you would do with it. Cut some tall grass? Defend the home front?

Are you still riding horses? I never could get the hang of that myself. I'm glad you enjoy it; it could be a great hobby.

Dad, thanks for the clips and magazines. You're improving, but you could still do better.

Love, Sonny

Bertha wondered why Sonny was saying the clippings were improving.

"Ig, what is it that you want with a machete?" Bertha asked at dinner that evening. She'd have to ask him about the clippings when he returned from his current trip.

"To help with weeding and stuff in the garden," Ig replied.

"Anything else?"

"Well, if we're invaded, it would be a great weapon. I can defend you and the house with it and my rifle." His passion for weapons and anything military was working overtime. She would add the machete to the list of things to discuss with Mac.

FIFTY-EIGHT

MAC UNLOCKED his office door, put his briefcase down, and picked up the phone to dial the steno pool when he saw a secretary standing in the doorway. He had never seen her before, but she seemed to have something urgent to tell him. He nodded, and she stepped in and closed the door behind her. He initially requested 9 a.m., but when the secretary shook her head, he changed it to 1 p.m.

"You're wanted in the conference room," she said once he hung up.

"Any idea what for?"

"Damned if I know," she replied. "Sorry. I started this week, and I'm still trying to understand what we do here."

Mac smiled as she turned pink. "Who are you working for?"

"You."

"What's your name?" Mac asked.

"Florence," she said, putting out her hand to shake Mac's. "Nice to meet you, Mr. Macdonald."

"Likewise," Mac said, shaking Florence's hand. Florence was tall, probably about 6 feet in heels, and towered over everyone, including him. He doubted she was 20 yet, and she was a bit gangly. Hopefully, she'd be around for a while. He suspected she would reveal her last name when she had calmed down.

"There are two draftsmen very anxious to talk to you. You have 10 minutes before you need to head upstairs."

"Thank god you're here," Mutt said, slipping behind Florence and walking into his office. "We've been working on these plans all week based on the updated information you sent, and we need your advice."

Jeff unrolled plans on Mac's drafting table, and the three huddled together to review the issue. The two men quickly explained the problem.

Mac asked a few questions and provided a suggestion, which they agreed to try. It was an interesting problem in determining the best way to represent the work he was doing on valves and pressure in the drafting plans in a manner that would make sense.

"Where's Mrs. Olson?" Mac asked as Jeff rolled up the plans and put them in a tube. Security protocol required they be kept rolled when transported, even though they were going only two doors down the hall.

"We think she's in the conference room," Mutt said. "A meeting's been going on since we got here."

"Any idea what it's about?" Mac asked.

"Hard to tell, they aren't yelling," Mutt and Jeff returned to their office.

Mac nodded as he stood up, straightened his vest, and put on his jacket. He always felt more professional when appropriately dressed. He was taken more seriously when professionally dressed. As he passed Florence's desk, he asked her to remind him to call Bertha.

Mac knocked but did not wait for a response before entering. A group of engineers and managers from Stone and Webster, along with some Army personnel he did not know, the new Area Engineer, Salvaggio, and Sara Olson, were gathered around the table.

"Mac, it's good to see you. We thought you'd be here earlier," the senior engineer said, glancing at his watch.

"I got back late last night," Mac explained. "I didn't know about any meeting this morning."

"We have been discussing a new role we'd like to have you accept."

"What is the role?"

He would be responsible for overseeing the construction and shipment of the Calutron cubicles to Oak Ridge, managing the necessary vendors, and coordinating the shipping process using specially designed train cars for transportation. He would continue to oversee the draftsmen's work, but Sara would take the lead on day-to-day oversight. They assured him he would be paid more money. And, like before, they weren't asking; they were being courteous.

Mac nodded at Sara and smiled. She was the best choice, but a woman, no matter how skilled, wasn't always accepted in a lead role. The meeting continued, with a variety of reassignments discussed. When it was concluded, Mac asked Sara to join him in his office to review the reports that were now her responsibility.

"Congratulations on your new role," Sara said, once the door was closed behind them.

"Thanks," Mac said. "How do you feel about all these changes?"

"It's nice to be recognized, but I hope I become invisible to them soon. How do you feel?"

"Like you, excited to be asked, but…"

"There's always a but, isn't there?" A wry smile appeared on Sara's face.

"We're being propelled forward so fast, something will fall through the cracks, and we won't know until it happens. It's nice to be recognized, but also to settle in and know all the ins and outs of what I'm doing. I'm hoping to settle into this new job for a while. Now that we have this out of the way, I'd like to ask Florence in to take notes while we review the reports you'll be doing starting this week."

Sara nodded, and Florence stepped in with a steno pad to take notes. They ignored the phone ringing to get through the reports in one sitting. When the phone started to ring for the fifth time, Mac began to worry. The next time the phone rang, he picked up.

The person at the other end of the line asked how this could have happened and why no one in the office was aware of what was going on. And in case he didn't understand, the man repeated himself at the top of his lungs. The man was angry, but Mac was unsure why he had been called. Sara and Florence both stood when Salvaggio and Grant from Procurement entered his office.

"Everything was packed on the freight car, the car was attached to the freight train, and it passed all the checkpoints. We have confirmation right here," Grant said, waving the paper confirmation at them as if it explained everything.

"Someone may have tampered with our shipments." Lt. Houston, the security officer, stepped in as somber as usual. He had also had a promotion.

Over the phone, the man asked Mac if he was listening and what he would do about this. Mac said he needed to investigate and would call the man back in an hour. He scribbled the man's phone number on a piece of paper and handed it to Florence. The man said he expected Mac to pass the problem on rather than call back and slammed the phone down. Mac placed the phone down and turned to Florence.

"Call this number and get the name of the man on the line, his role, and if he calms down enough, see if you can find out what he is concerned about," Mac said.

"Yes, sir," Florence said, looking a bit nervous.

"You'll do fine. He wants someone to listen to him, and in listening, you'll learn a lot. Don't hang up to answer any other line, no matter who tells you." Mac gave Florence a reassuring smile, and she stepped out, looking less than reassured.

"Gentlemen, what is the problem, and why are you bringing it to me?"

"You're now overseeing traffic, and we're getting calls from Oak Ridge that the product being shipped isn't arriving. This latest shipment has AAA government status," Grant said, pausing to catch his breath. "That means it's supposed to go through without any problems."

Mac knew what AAA government status meant for shipping; he'd used it when appropriate to ship products to British Columbia.

"Grant, double-check that the freight car was added to the train?" Mac asked. "I know you have the receipt, but we need eyes on the track to make sure it wasn't shunted on a siding and left behind."

"But...," Grant started, then stopped. "Yes, sir."

Grant stepped out of his office and headed to a phone.

"If someone tampered with our shipment, they could be on to where and how we are managing our shipping and therefore onto what we are building and where we are building the components," Houston said.

"You mean spies?" Mac asked.

"Yes," Houston replied.

"How could an entire rail car go missing?" Salvaggio asked.

"It's hard to hide an entire rail car. Especially one this size and shape," Mac said, referencing the shipping confirmation weight and specially designed freight car.

Florence stepped into his office. "That was faster than I expected. You wouldn't believe what this man says."

Florence was cut off by two of the senior engineers.

Mac's phone rang, and the conversation quieted. Florence looked at Mac. Mac nodded, and Florence answered.

"Yes, sir, he's right here. I'll put you right through," Florence said. She put the call on hold and mouthed, "Colonel Nichols." Houston shut the door so that they would have privacy.

"Macdonald here."

"Mac, Nichols here. Are you alone?"

"Salvaggio and Houston are with me," Mac replied.

"Good. Anyone else?"

"Several folks are in the outer office with Florence."

"Send them back to their offices, would you? It would be nice to have folks at their desks to answer their phones."

"Of course, we'll send everyone back to their office now." Houston nodded and stepped into the outer office, telling everyone to return to their desks and to answer any call that came in. He asked Florence to join them to take notes.

"Any ideas where the shipment might be?"

"Not yet. Everything I have in hand says that the shipment went out as scheduled."

"You're sure?"

"Yes, I'm sure. We followed the correct procedure. It's all supposed to be in Knoxville."

"So right now, there is no reason to believe there is any error on the production and shipping part of this process?"

"That's correct," Mac replied. Salvaggio and Houston nodded in agreement.

"You have confirmations in hand?"

"Yes, literally in my hand."

"Understood. You're to be informed of any schedule changes, is that correct?"

Mac hesitated before he replied. "Yes, that's correct."

"Why the hesitation?" Nichols was firm and direct.

"I've had this assignment for less than an hour," Mac replied.

"Right. You just returned. And you heard nothing about this shipment?"

"Correct."

"What happens now?"

General Groves's second in command, Colonel Nichols, was keeping his cool, but he was worried. Mac was concerned, too.

"We have people double-checking all messages, and security has sent a couple of men to the train office to review and confirm any issues or changes. We have someone going to the train yard to make sure nothing is sitting on the tracks."

"Good plan to send someone to the train depot. Not one of the draftsmen, I hope. They have other work to do."

"No, sir. I believe we're sending a junior procurement clerk," Mac quickly scribbled a note to Houston, who said he would immediately get a security man down there.

"Then what?"

"Sir, I think you should talk to this man," Florence said.

"I will talk to him in due course," Mac replied, putting his hand over the receiver so Colonel Nichols didn't hear. Then he turned his attention back to the phone.

"There is a man who called this morning, yelling at me to do something and do it immediately. If I'm not mistaken, he was calling from what sounded like a train depot. My secretary has more details. May I call you back after we have sorted out all the wrinkles?"

"I want an update every half-hour," Nichols said.

While Mac couldn't blame him for being angry, he needed to figure out where this top-secret security shipment had gone.

FIFTY-NINE

SONNY WAS getting ready for his first two-week furlough—two weeks at home visiting his friends who were home, seeing Gertie, who had just given birth to a girl. Hopefully, he'd see Nancy, who had been writing him again a lot lately. He wasn't sure what was happening with her, and he wasn't ready to put her photo back above his bed, but he was curious to find out. Ginger was a far more dependable pinup. His parents still hadn't sent his birth certificate, so he needed to find it so he could complete his transfer application. It didn't seem like the army wanted to create mountain troops, given how they acted. He'd tried his best to be home for his birthday on Halloween, but at least he was heading home. The two weeks at home flew by, and he was back at camp before he knew it. Walking up Camp Hale's main street, his duffle over his shoulder, Sonny heard a jeep horn and moved aside to let it by. The jeep stopped and Sonny looked over to see Tiny and Hooker.

"Hey, you're back from Kiska. How was it?"

"Not much we can say," Tiny replied.

"Drop off your bag and meet us at the PX," Hooker said.

"Yes, sir, Sergeant Major," Sonny saluted, as Hooker rolled his eyes and pulled away.

Sonny dropped his duffle, changed into fatigues, told Dollie he was back, and headed for the PX. His next duty roster assignment was guarding the German POWs that night, so he had some time to shoot the breeze. He found Hooker holding court, telling all the guys surrounding him that they should not apply for transfers. The army may be trying to figure out what to do with the mountain troops, and some senior army brass might not like such a specialized unit, such as the 10th, and might not know what to do with it. However, they worked hard to get here, so they shouldn't give up yet. Sonny nodded, as he knew he should, but kept quiet. It was hard being a mouthy, contradictory kid around Hooker, who knew him too well. When the group started to break up, Sonny sought out Tiny.

"What will you do?" Sonny asked.

"Apply for the transfer. Seems foolish not to," Tiny replied.

"Same here. There are all kinds of rumors about Kiska, and no one's talking.

"That's because we fought in the fog and dark, and we probably shot more at each other than the enemy."

"Hooker seems to have come out of it well?"

"He knows how to manage the men."

Sonny returned to his barracks and submitted his application for transfer to Trav, who reviewed it and sent it up the chain. They heard nothing until early December, when it was announced that all transfers were pulled back. They were gearing up for winter training, followed by something they called the D-Series.

SIXTY

WHAT HAD looked like a typical day in the office after another trip to Oak Ridge now had Mac looking at a train schedule while cradling the phone on his right shoulder, listening to a project team leader tell him that the items that he had been assured had been shipped hadn't arrived.

"Is there someone here that you talked to before about shipments?" Mac asked.

"Am I not supposed to ask you?" the team leader asked.

"I'm asking you because this is my first day in this role, and I'm wondering who handled these questions previously," Mac replied.

"We called one of the executive secretaries in Boston, and she relayed the message to management, and then they had someone in procurement or expediting do some research and get back to us. We've never had the sense that nothing could be found."

"Thank you for clarifying this. Are there any other orders that are missing?" Mac asked.

"There are several more we're expecting, but we've been told there might be a delay on those."

"Who told you that?"

"A construction manager here in Oak Ridge."

He told the man on the phone that he would get back to him in an hour, if not sooner, and then hung up. Everything he had in front of him indicated that the items had been packed on the train car and sent to their destination by the approved freight mapping protocols. If it were a train problem, they could fix it. It would be uncomfortable for whoever had overlooked the government shipping priority, but that could be resolved. If an unknown party or parties had taken the items, that would be another problem. One reason for the secrecy was to prevent anyone from learning about their progress in making a bomb. The other was to make sure no one delayed their progress.

Florence knocked on Mac's door with a nervous-looking young man behind her. Mac waved the young man into the office. Salvaggio and Houston were still in his office.

"I know I'm not supposed to know anything, but I was delivering some plans to an engineer today, and he was complaining about a call he had from someone in Knoxville. He said the man kept yelling something about train cars and cleaning up. Not that I overhear much, you know, and people don't talk much, but things get around."

"Which engineer?" Salvaggio asked.

"What's your name?" Mac smiled in an attempt to relax the young messenger.

"Daniel, sir. I don't want to get fired, I need this job," the young man said.

"You won't be fired, I'll make sure of that."

"Thanks, sir. I need to get back to work."

"Why did you come to me with this?"

"He said the man on the phone was yelling your name and complaining about no one calling him back." The young man named the engineer, and Houston was on his feet and out of the office, almost knocking over Florence. Mac said that he would find him if he needed any more information. The young man smiled nervously and left.

"Florence, see if you could get anyone from the Knoxville train yard on the line?"

"Of course, sir," Florence said.

"Has anyone at Oak Ridge checked with the Knoxville yard to see if they have any problems? That happened with those shipments to Detroit."

"I thought we cleared up the priority shipping codes," Salvaggio said. "Let me check."

Mac phoned Colonel Nichols directly and said he felt they were narrowing down the problem. He'd call again in an hour.

Nichols disconnected, and Mac let out a sigh. He had hoped that the Oak Ridge team would check with Knoxville, but it looked like it was up to him.

"I have someone from the Knoxville train yard on the line. He says he's been trying to get some attention all day. And these gentlemen are here to see you." There were several senior Stone and Webster men in the outer office.

A stream of swear words came over the line. "You would think that someone with enough awareness of the priority designation would know these things are sitting here."

"What do you mean? What have you got there?"

"Jesus Aloysius Christ. Haven't you been listening? I have 645 freight cars here, and I can't accept another one until somebody takes care of this."

"Whose are they?"

"They are all for that place I'm not supposed to know anything about," the man said, followed by more swear words.

"To be clear, you have 645 freight cars, all addressed for the Clinton Engineer Works, sitting in the yard?" Mac repeated what he was hearing so that the senior team in his office understood what was going on.

"Now you're getting it."

"Thank you for explaining." Mac was looking at the senior engineers who were about to leave his office. "Can I reach you at this number in an hour or so?"

"I ain't going nowhere, but these cars had better be." The man slammed down the phone.

"We will confer upstairs in the 10th-floor conference room. Please join us as soon as you can," said one of the senior engineers.

Mac saw that Miles was standing outside his office with Florence, holding a folder of clippings.

"I wanted to get these to you while you're in the office," Miles said. "Do you need any help?"

"We need coverage on the phones, particularly if someone has to come and get me," Mac checked his watch; it was 5 pm. "Can we have more than one telephone operator stay? And can we let the operators know that if anyone calls about train shipments, have the call transferred here?"

"I'll make sure we get that message to the phone operators. We'll keep some security men on too." Houston stepped out of the office.

"They're waiting for you," Salvaggio said.

Mac told Florence that it would most likely be a late night, and he'd appreciate her staying to answer the phones. Florence smiled and said she had already called her mother to say she would be late. She'd also called to arrange for a messenger to be dedicated to them. Miles agreed to stay late and help with any phone calls.

All talking subsided when Mac stepped into the conference room. They had Colonel Nichols and Houston in Oak Ridge on the phone, waiting for the report.

"From what I've learned today, there are 645 freight cars destined for the Clinton Engineer Works sitting in the Knoxville railyard."

"Yes, we decided that construction needed to be prioritized. We can't keep assigning construction workers to unload rail cars," said one of the senior management team. "We're behind on completing houses for workers. And if we don't have housing, how can anyone work in the factories?"

Colonel Nichols spoke before anyone else could respond. "While construction is important, keeping that many freight cars in the yard is dangerous. The materials could be damaged by the sun and heat, and are susceptible to being spotted from the air."

"Anyone walking or driving by, or living in the neighborhood, can also see the backup. That railyard is in downtown Knoxville." The implication was clear to all; some could identify such a large grouping of railcars and wonder where they were going and how to let the enemy know where they were building.

It was midnight before they confirmed that every available person at Oak Ridge would be deployed to unload all the cars and distribute the materials appropriately. Nichols was informed and said he would spend the night ensuring that unloading was handled. It was agreed that all workers in Oak Ridge, no matter their role, would work at identifying shipments and unloading cars.

Colonel Nichols hadn't yelled at anyone, at least not yet, but he clarified that he wanted to know how and who had determined that secure, priority items could be left in Knoxville. He also wanted written procedures for how transports were to be handled and prioritized, which were to be on his desk by noon the next day.

While senior management stayed in the conference room, Mac called the Knoxville rail yard manager. He owed the man a call after ignoring him most of the day. After many phone calls and discussions, it was 3 am when they felt they had a good enough handle on what had transpired and what the new transport policy would look like.

It had been a long day, and everyone would be back at their desks by 8 am. Security details took Mac, Florence, and Miles home. Mac sensed a budding romance, and as happy as he was for them, any sniff of two office people having a romantic attachment meant one of them would have to leave, and he knew that would mean Florence. He'd talk with her in the morning.

SIXTY-ONE

IT WAS close to midnight when she heard Mac in the kitchen. Putting on her dressing gown, Bertha went quietly downstairs to not wake Ig, Sonny, or Elaine. Gran had decided to spend time with Mabel, avoiding the issue of visiting the doctor. She found Mac rummaging through the icebox, looking for something to eat. She put a sandwich she had made for Sonny to take on the train in the morning on the table, gathered some silverware and a glass for the milk he'd already taken out of the icebox, and started drinking from the bottle. A moment later, she added the empty bottle to the container by the back door for the milkman to replace in the morning. She didn't know what this family would do if milk were rationed, a constant worry in the face of scarcity.

His work schedule had always been erratic when he was working on a project, but now it was even more unpredictable. Before he began this war work, he would tell stories about the people he worked with and the amusing or foolish things they said or did. She always knew what he was working on. He couldn't and didn't talk about the new project, at least not yet, he said. She filled him in on the day and what the boys were up to while he ate at the small table in the kitchen. He would quiz the boys on what she told him in the morning while she made breakfast.

She put the dishes in the sink to wash in the morning. She missed Mrs. Brown. On her way upstairs, she checked the thermostat to make sure it was set to 55 degrees, as per the latest directions on conserving heating oil. Mac was snoring when she got back into bed. He hadn't bothered to take his clothes off.

SIXTY-TWO

IG WAS standing by a food table, hoping no one noticed him eating as much as possible. Given all the war news and disruptions, the 1943 Christmas party at Mt. Hood was surprisingly boisterous. But it was Christmas, the season to greet friends, have drinks, dance, and make merry while they could. And they did. The buffet was smaller than they used to have, but alcohol and dancing were plentiful. He wore the only suit jacket that fit him, the sleeves showing more than just the cuffs. And he was always hungry now. Mrs. Brown would be laughing if she saw him eating everything. The lights were turned down, and blackout shades blocked all the windows. There was no fire in the fireplace this year, all wood being hoarded by those who needed to heat their homes and stoves. And there were no lights downtown or on their Christmas tree.

It had been two years since Pearl Harbor, and men and boys were still heading off for training. The papers were filled with news about the Germans bombing London with V-1 rockets, the Soviets were having success against the Germans while the Greeks were not, and Jews were being rounded up everywhere. Some stories were front-page headlines, while stories about Jews were buried deeper in the paper with smaller headlines and shorter columns. Americans were fighting in Europe and the South Pacific. Sonny might join the air corps if the army continued to be undecided about what to do with the Mountain Division.

Sonny and Dad weren't there; it was just him and Mom. Mom was talking to all her old friends. One friend of Sonny's was in an army unit shipping supplies and was home for Christmas. Other friends and neighbors were heading overseas; some had served, were home, or would never return.

Gertie handed Ig the baby when the band struck up some lively dance music, and danced with Jinx, Web's sister, who was home from college. There were so few men that most women danced together. Thankfully, neither had asked him to dance.

He saw old Mrs. Hooker wave him over to her table. "Take a seat, it's been so long since I held a baby." Mom had explained that Mrs. Hooker had had both of her children later in life, at nearly 40, which sometimes happened. "Now, why don't you get me a plate of food?"

"Of course," Ig said.

"Make sure you add some of your mother's stewed tomatoes. She does such a good job with those."

I'm glad you like them, Ig thought. He filled a plate with the food that had been brought in by the guests and returned to the table, where he put it in front of Mrs. Hooker, who was now bouncing the baby on her knee.

"Tell me, Ig, what are you reading these days?"

"What makes you think I'm reading anything?" Ig asked.

"You're always reading something, just like your mother."

Ig bristled, but Mrs. Hooker was right. He loved reading. "The Robe," he said.

"That's interesting."

"I guess. It's melodramatic in some parts."

"Very astute. Tell your mother I enjoyed the book, too."

Gertie and Jinx grabbed him and got him dancing. Sonny would be jealous when he wrote him about dancing with Jinx.

PART FIVE: 1944

SIXTY-THREE

FOR THE first time, Sonny was not home to celebrate Christmas with the family. He spoke with everyone on Christmas Day, telling them about the nice, candlelit dinner they had been served on Christmas Eve, and how everyone was out skiing or running into Leadville, now that Leadville, the closest town to Camp Hale, had opened to the 10th. He went to a Christmas dance there. What he didn't tell his parents and Ig was that the town had been closed off to them because of the whorehouses. He was pretty sure some of the women at the dance came from the whorehouses, but they looked nice and knew how to dance.

He signed up for guard duty on New Year's Eve. All the guys wanted to go to Denver, Leadville, or ski, but he decided to have the evening to himself with the dog and his rifle. He spent the night watching the sky and the trains passing through the mountains above camp. The dog was a good companion, no Ginger, but a good companion.

He and Tiny were surprised when all transfers out of the 10th, which didn't seem to be heading in the direction of training mountain troops, were canceled in December. He told his parents about his new friends, Georgie, Jack, Joey, and Eddie. Georgie from Roxbury was a great skier. Jack was from New Hampshire and loved pranks, drinking, dancing, having a good time, and skiing. Joey had been born in Italy and arrived on Staten Island without knowing much English but had been a fast learner. He was the youngest of the group, at 18, and played poker like a pro. His favorite was Eddie, a cowboy from Nevada who signed up to be a truck driver. When they no longer needed truck drivers, he was assigned to the 10th. Eddie had never skied, loved to gamble, wanted to get home to his ponies and girlfriend, and had no idea how he ended up in the ski troops.

After Christmas, they were assigned two weeks of solving problems as if they were at war, using cross-country skis or snowshoes. Sonny, Georgie, Joey, and Jack chose skis, while Eddie, who had never skied before arriving at Camp Hale, chose snowshoes. Most of the disbanded truck drivers had a choice of learning to ski or snowshoe.

They returned to camp for a short break before heading out for the D-Series. They had been hearing about the D-Series for a couple of months. The D-Series consisted of five weeks of training and simulated battles in small, platoon-sized groups of 10 or 12 men.

They left camp with full packs that weighed ninety pounds and held all the food, clothes, and gear available during these maneuvers. They lived as if they were in battle, digging in for the night where they were told, eating cold rations when they couldn't have a fire, taking off wet clothes so they didn't freeze in their sleeping bags, and working as units alternately as allied or enemy patrols attacking one another. During the skirmishes, they shot at one another with no bullets, winning or surrendering based on how many men were considered killed or wounded.

While in the mountains, the weather turned bitterly cold, as low as -30 at night. Men who didn't take the D-Series seriously headed for Leadville, thinking no one would look for them. MPs rounded them up, returned to camp, lectured them, and sent them to their units. If they were caught AWOL a second time, they would be out of the 10th.

Sonny stuck with the series. He decided to know his limits in the mountains if he couldn't transfer out. Of all the skirmishes they were either in or observed, the funniest was a skirmish between two platoons led by two brothers, both sergeants, one commanding a patrol and the other commanding an enemy patrol, meeting in battle. While all the men of the enemy patrol surrendered when caught, the enemy patrol sergeant refused to surrender or admit surrender to his brother. A fight ensued between the two brothers, who decided to end the disagreement with a fist fight while all the men under them bet on which one would win. Eddie made a killing on that one.

After two weeks in the field in extremely cold weather, they headed back to Camp Hale for a brief respite to gather fresh rations (fresh meaning not yet consumed since there was nothing fresh about rations), collect some clean, dry clothes, particularly dry socks, and have one decent meal.

Eddie had never been in such cold for such a long period, had held out pretty well for two weeks, but Sonny, Georgie, Joey, and Jack had to help him get into camp. His feet were a mass of blisters. They took him directly to the medical area, where the nurses and doctors peeled his socks from his swollen, frostbitten feet, removing the blistered skin that was attached to them. They had never seen anything quite like it and hoped never to see anything like this again. Eddie was admitted to the hospital.

After a night in their barracks, they headed back out again without Eddie. The following two weeks were just as brutal as the first two—a blur of skirmishes and problems, sleeping under the stars, and eating cold rations. Sonny visited Eddie during his next rotation through camp, and things did not look good. Every time the doctors healed one set of blisters, another set would pop up. Sonny didn't realize the tips of his ears had been frostbitten until he sat with Eddie, and they itched and peeled. The doctors said he'd be fine, gave him some salve to protect them, and sent him on his way.

The final week or so, Sonny kept his ears covered. They itched, but they were healing. The weather wasn't as cold, and knowing it was the last week made it easier to endure. When he returned to camp, the doctors were ready to send Eddie to Denver, where he would most likely be discharged or sent to another unit. Eddie's feet were improving, and, in the end, they kept him as a study to observe how his healing progressed.

Leaving the camp hospital, Sonny ran into Tiny and Hooker. Hooker had accepted a posting to Officer Candidate School and would be heading out the next day. Many guys who went to OCS ended up back in camp when they failed one portion or another. Sonny suspected that Hooker would return as one of their officers, and Tiny agreed. Hooker said you never know when they might see one another again.

SIXTY-FOUR

"MOM, MY rubbers won't fit," Ig yelled up the stairs. Ig and Mac were getting ready for the day, and it was mix of rain, sleet and snow on this miserable February morning.

"See if you can trade for larger ones at school," Bertha replied. She was getting her mother up and settled into a chair for the doctor, who would arrive soon. Gran had returned to stay with them when Mabel decided to head to California and live with her daughter and son-in-law while he was posted to the South Pacific. It wasn't permanent, but Gran decided she wasn't ready for that kind of travel.

"I don't think anyone's feet are getting smaller."

"Maybe someone dropped off larger rubbers."

"You mean someone who died? That's awful."

"Or was recently deployed," Bertha yelled down.

The rubber shortage meant that no new rubbers were being made. Everyone was supposed to drop off unused rubbers at the schools so no pair gathered dust.

"My birthday is coming," Ig yelled out hopefully.

"That doesn't mean new rubbers are being made."

"It's not fair," Ig replied.

"Ig can wear my rubbers. I'll take the car and drive to work," Mac said, handing his rubbers to Ig.

"You'll ruin your shoes. If you give Ig your rubbers, who's to say there will be any shoes for sale when the pair you are wearing are ruined," Bertha said,

"My birthday's coming up too. I'll figure something out."

"Maybe they have something available wherever it is you travel to," Bertha said, pouring hot water into the tea kettle to take up to her mother. Mac and Ig had had cereal. "I can't decide if it's worth the expense to buy those girdles at Collette's," Bertha said while she waited for the tea to steep.

"Buy them. I doubt you'll find girdles again for a few years," Mac replied.

"If the war ends, I'll feel silly for spending so much money."

"What will you do when you need a new girdle and rubber is still rationed?"

"You're sure the war won't end soon?"

"Yes. Please pick them up today. If it makes you feel better, they can be my birthday gift to you." Mac had neglected to get anything for her birthday the week before.

"How romantic," Bertha replied.

"The romance of practicality," Mac replied.

"I asked Sonny about the girdles in the last letter I sent," Bertha said. Mac gave her a funny look.

"Can't wait to see what he has to say about girdles," Ig said, rolling his eyes.

"You never know, what they have at the PX is amazing."

"Buy them, don't wait for Sonny to figure out what you are asking him," Mac growled.

Ig said goodbye, grabbed his lunch, and followed his father out to the car. The doctor pulled up as Mac and Ig pulled out of the driveway.

SIXTY-FIVE

MAC WAS in Oak Ridge to help with issues with the racetracks. After several months of addressing the coil issues, everyone thought all the issues had been resolved but they were wrong. Now they had gunk in the racetracks and didn't know what was causing it or how to get rid of it. Gunk was the only word that could describe the material left over after the separation that clogged the racetracks and shut them down.

They hoped to send enough of a U-235 sample to Los Alamos soon, but the racetracks failed to function as expected while dealing with various problems cropping up along with the Y-12 buildings. Slowly but surely, they were moving forward more than they were retreating. Testing and retesting to ensure everything worked as expected was challenging when you didn't know what to expect. And as frustrated as he was, he enjoyed the challenge.

The cooling towers and the vacuum system for the cubicles and racetracks utilized his skills as a draftsman, inspector, and problem-solver in dealing with vendors, engineering staff, and scientists to obtain the necessary product for the project. He, Larry, and several others were finishing the latest gunk cleaning on the racetracks.

"Mac, glad we found you. We showed some of these blueprints to that young scientist from Los Alamos, and he asked a question about the valves we want to run by you." Three of the senior Stone and Webster engineers had a sheaf of blueprints in their hands.

"Young scientist? You mean the young fool they've sent to lecture us about uranium safety?" Larry asked.

"Larry, please, we'd like to talk to Mac about valves," one of the Stone and Webster engineers said.

Larry shrugged, and Mac joined them at a table where the plans could be laid out. They showed Mac the pages they had asked Feynman to look at and pointed out the valves he had questioned. Mac looked at the plans he had reviewed and approved and at the three men huddled around the table. Larry wandered over to hear the conversation. Mac indicated that the plans looked fine to him.

"Are you sure? We should seriously look at these valves, their pressure volumes, and anything else that might indicate a problem."

"One of the few things I know is that those valves are indicated correctly on the plans, built, tested, and functioning as expected."

"Well, he is a scientist. Maybe there's some small tweak he can suggest."

"What is his experience with valves and with reading blueprints? Has he had a chance to look at the valves in production?"

"He's 25 and hasn't quite finished his coursework at Princeton," Larry said. "I've heard he likes to break into filing cabinets."

"He's a scientist, and you are engineers. Show some respect for your betters," one of the senior engineers sputtered.

"I'm more than happy to chat with this young man and identify any questions he may have," Dr. Ernest Lawrence said. He had overheard the conversation and decided to join in.

"Dr. Lawrence, surely this young man has experience and is questioning something perfectly appropriate."

"Feynman is a brilliant theoretical physicist, but Larry here is right; he is young and likes to pull pranks. Mac here is perfectly correct in asking about his experience with blueprints and valves. I want to get Mac and Larry back on my problem, if you don't mind. Let's discuss this over dinner before tonight's lecture."

The senior engineers nodded, gathered the plans, and left Dr. Lawrence, Mac, and Larry to work.

"Jesus, now we have to hear about what we already know from a 25-year-old know-it-all prankster? We have more important things to do," Larry said.

"A reminder about safety can never go amiss," Mac replied. "Or so they keep saying." Mac was irritated.

At dinner that evening, they learned that Feynman had never looked at the blueprints before and felt he should question something rather than say he had no idea what they were all about. Mac smiled. No one had oriented him to the plans, assuming he was familiar with all the references. He wasn't sure he would have done any better if he had faced the same questions and plans without knowing more than the information. That said, Feynman was young and way too cocky.

Dr. Lawrence explained that at Los Alamos, they challenged the young, new guys with questions and assessed them on quick responses regardless of knowledge. Mac had used that method himself, but having kids had taught him to know when one was lying or pretending to know more than they did.

The lecture was on safety procedures that they already knew about. Still, due to a lack of communication between teams, some radioactive uranium had been left unclaimed out in the open. That caused many problems, and procedures were implemented so that that never happened again. Later that night, Feynman did the thing he was famous for, breaking into locked filing cabinets to show he could. While it was somewhat childish, it also taught them that safety should never be taken for granted. He was on his way back to Los Alamos before his prank was discovered.

SIXTY-SIX

WHEN THE school nurse entered the room, Ig was at the lab bench, focused on the day's chemistry experiment. She was a retired nurse who agreed to return when all the school nurses in town joined up. One of her jobs was pulling students out of class and sending them home because a brother or father had died or was missing in action. The tension level among the students rose. Everyone had someone doing war work somewhere. She nodded to the instructor and asked Ig to follow her and bring his books. Ig could feel the students exhale as his tension level rose, knowing she wasn't there for one of them today.

She escorted Ig to her office, told him to go home, pick up the car, pick up the bag his mother had packed, and meet his mother at the hospital. His grandmother was doing ok, she said, but would be staying at the hospital. His mother had gone along in the ambulance with his grandmother, who would be staying at the hospital, and his mother needed a ride home. He wasn't old enough to drive, but that didn't matter these days. Anyone 15 or older could get a special wartime driving permit, and he would be 15 in a couple of weeks. The phone rang again. There was no secretary today, so the nurse was covering the calls. Ig was dismissed as she handled the next issue.

Ig walked home, grabbed Gran's overnight bag in the front hall, put Ginger in the car, and headed for Malden Hospital. Ginger loved riding with her head out the window any time of year and didn't care about the temperature or the wind. At the hospital, he told Ginger to wait in the car while he headed into the hospital to see Gran and gather his mother. Ginger, as always, knew exactly what he said.

He was directed to Gran's room and found his mother sitting by her bed. Gran looked so small lying in the hospital bed, eyes closed, with the blanket up to her neck. He knew that he and his mother couldn't handle much more of this in-and-out-and-home-again routine. His mother wasn't sleeping, but she didn't want to put Gran in the nursing home. He thought it was time. They both needed some sleep. He'd have to enlist Dad in this discussion if Dad were home again soon.

SIXTY-SEVEN

THE D-SERIES was completed in March, and they returned to camp for a few weeks before the flu outbreak. The coal-burning heaters in the barracks weren't helping anyone with congestion, so they were ordered to sleep outside for a few nights. Sleeping under the stars, in manageable weather, was a treat after sleeping in the cold and ice during the series. Sonny had complained about being forced outside because he didn't have the flu, and why should he have to sleep next to someone who was sick, but he enjoyed sleeping outside so much that now, they were back in their barracks, he couldn't sleep.

He slipped quietly out of bed, dressed, and padded across the barracks floor in stocking feet. The various snores from the 20 or so men blocked out any sound he was making. He was going to the latrine if anyone asked, but he didn't expect anyone to ask.

Standing on the dirt path between barracks, he watched the trains traveling across the high slope above Camp Hale. The view of the massive engines pulling the cars across the mountain range was a beautiful sight. He'd write home about the trains for Dad and Ig. He was worried about Gran being in the hospital again. The horizon was getting lighter, and reveille would sound soon. The rumor he had heard was that some new training was planned, and it had nothing to do with mountains or skiing.

"Taking in the sights, Mac?"

Eddie's voice surprised him. How good a soldier would he have been if he had been distracted by trains and had never heard the enemy behind him? If it had been the enemy, would he be dead now? Was he overthinking this whole thing?

"More or less."

"If we were in action…"

Sonny finished the sentence, "I'd be dead now."

"Something like that."

"I doubt either one of us would take a saunter to the latrine or be watching trains at dawn if we were in combat."

"True. The train looks beautiful in the morning light."

"Trains look beautiful anytime," Sonny replied.

"So you've said." Sonny turned and saw the twinkle in Eddie's eyes.

"I talk about trains a lot."

"Only when you're not talking about beer, poker, or girls," Eddie replied. "Or that damn ugly dog of yours."

"Ginny is beautiful. It doesn't show in the photos."

"So you say."

"I miss her the most."

"Unconditional love?"

Sonny laughed. He and Eddie stood with their backs to the barracks as they watched the train travel across the mountains as the sun rose. Another barracks mate wandered out, stopping to watch the train move along the ridge.

"Great view," Sonny said quietly. "Good thing we don't have a gun on you."

"What the hell!" He headed off towards the latrine.

"You've heard the latest poop?" Eddie asked.

"We're heading out somewhere? We've been hearing that for months. You're a corporal. Do you have any idea where we are headed?"

"Texas."

"Texas, what the hell for?"

"We'll learn to work with mules and cross rivers."

"Mules!" They had mule handlers in camp for that, so why would they need to handle mules?

"In the mountains, we'll need mules to haul stuff where Weasels and trucks can't go."

Eddie was a good, honest man who listened, followed instructions, helped others when needed, asked questions, and had won the trust of the men and the officers, who had promoted him to corporal. His western drawl and easy-going, aw-shucks manner made him seem not too bright, but Eddie used those mannerisms to his advantage. Sonny was a sharpshooter who could hit targets when stationary or skiing, a better-than-average skier in a field of the world's best skiers, outspoken, critical, and prone to running off at the mouth. He was a PFC and the assistant squad leader, with no ambitions beyond that.

"What's going to happen to our mules? Wonder if we can teach them to ski?" Sonny mused.

"We won't be shipping our mules overseas. We'll use ones that are already there if we need them."

"Another day, another dollar," Sonny said.

"You have some funny sayings there, easterner," Eddie replied, smiling.

"Learned them all from my dad," Sonny replied.

"Uh huh, and where did he learn them from?"

"His dad."

"Do you like him?"

Sonny laughed. "My Dad is full of advice, not all of it useful, and some of it downright useless."

"You sure?"

"He told me that not every girlfriend would work out, and he was right. 'Course, I don't know how he would know. He and Mom have known each other since high school."

"He never had another girlfriend?"

"Maybe. Mom had a boyfriend, so I think he had a girlfriend, but it's hard to say. Dad sometimes jokes that he rescued Mom from a broken heart."

"Huh."

"What does your mom say about your dad?" Sonny asked.

"He was a boy heading off to war that she hardly knew. Then I came along."

"Never came back?"

"Not so as I know. He may have died over there."

"Man, that's awful. Can't you find out what happened from records or something?"

"I'm not sure I know his name."

"It's not King?"

"I don't think so."

The train caboose was disappearing behind the mountain. The bugler sounded reveille. Rustling noises could be heard from the barracks.

"Think we'll get home for Christmas this year?" Sonny asked Eddie.

"Don't know. Take whatever leave you're offered. I, for one, plan to marry my girlfriend the next time I'm home," Eddie said

When Eddie headed out on furlough a few days later, after being promoted to sergeant and receiving the Good Conduct Medal, he told Sonny that he planned to return as a married man. When Eddie returned, he said he had found that his girlfriend had married someone else, a boy who had come home on leave the week before. He walked his mother down the aisle as she married a local man she had known since Eddie was a young boy. He was surprised that neither his girlfriend nor his mother had written him about these changes.

A few weeks later, Sonny headed home to Melrose for his furlough. He had no plans to marry anyone. His mother was worried about Elaine, and Sonny's interactions with her were filled with empathy and concern. He wanted to make sure she had some fun. Elaine invited him to a dance, and he escorted her in his dress uniform.

He was waiting for Elaine by the punch bowl when he heard Nancy.

"Aren't you handsome in your dress uniform?" Nancy said. She put her arm on his and smiled up at him. He was so surprised that he almost spit out his drink.

"Thank you," he said.

"What, no kiss?" Nancy raised her face for a kiss.

"Would you like me to find another way home?" Elaine asked.

"No, no. I'm your escort for the evening," Sonny put his arm out for her to take, noting the storm cloud on Nancy's face with satisfaction. She had written to him sporadically, and when he wondered what she was doing, she complained that he didn't understand how busy she was with her college classes. Others who wrote him said she was busy with her social life. He suspected one of those two was true.

"Well, I never," she said, hands on hips.

"That's not what I've heard," Elaine replied, the first smile he'd seen on her face since he'd been home.

SIXTY-EIGHT

MAC JOINED the family for dinner as much as possible while Sonny was home on furlough. After Sonny and Elaine headed out to a dance, Mac and Ig finished washing and drying the dinner dishes. Elaine took over the dishes when she was home, but worked many evenings. This was a rare night out for her.

"Ig, can I talk to you for a moment?" Mac said.

"Sure, Dad. Is it about school?"

"Not exactly." Mac finished drying his hands and took a seat at the kitchen table. Bert was muttering as they heard the radio dial being turned from station to station. She was looking for music while she read her group's next novel selection, and everywhere it was news. Not that there was anything wrong with the news, but everyone needed the occasional break from the latest on the war. Bert had spent part of the day with Gran and the doctor at the local hospital. In the end, they kept Gran for observation.

"I've recommended you for a summer job," Mac said.

"What job?"

"Messenger at the office."

"They said they'd never hire me again."

"Never listen to anyone who says they'll never hire you again. This time, there is no borrowing files for any reason."

"Dad, I'm 15."

"When you were 14, what happened?"

"An older woman influenced me." Ig looked at his father. "The job seemed liked fun, but I was bored."

"This is a vital project. It will help our soldiers and those at home."

"You mean Sonny, right?"

"Sonny is one of many. You and your mother could be affected too if bombs were dropped on us or enemy soldiers landed here."

"I know that."

Mac changed tack. "I worry that soldiers like Sonny might be fighting too long. The more they fight, the more opportunity they have to be killed or wounded. This project is helping to end the war."

"I understand."

"You'll report Monday morning after the last day of school."

"You already told them I'd do it?" Ig asked.

"I did. Do you have any homework to finish?"

"Yes, I have a paper to write."

"Go ahead. I'll finish drying the pots and pans."

"You can let them drain," Bertha stood at the kitchen door.

Ig passed his mother, picked up his papers on the dining room table, and headed into the living room to sit with Ginger while he worked.

"He's going to do it?" Bertha sat at the kitchen table with Mac.

"He'll have to sign an agreement this time."

"Is it too much responsibility?"

"Possibly. But there aren't enough people to do this job."

"Garniss Market wants to know if he can deliver groceries," Bertha said.

"Having two summer jobs will keep him busy."

"He won't have much fun."

"Maybe he can spend the summer on the farm when this war is over."

Bertha sighed. "I never thought I'd live to say this, but I hope Ig won't look back and wonder why he didn't have fun summers."

"Different times."

"Bobby Bruce would be old enough to enlist now?"

"I think about him a lot these days."

"He was such a sweet boy."

"He'll always be our sweet little boy." Mac took Bert's hands in his. They pressed their foreheads together.

"I wonder if he'd have been more of a problem than these two."

"Oh, I doubt that he could be more trouble."

They laughed while Mac dried the pots and pans, and Bertha put them away.

SIXTY-NINE

IG LOOKED at himself in the full-length mirror in his parent's bedroom. He was wearing gray flannel trousers, a white shirt, a blue tie, and a jacket for his first day on the job. His mother had pieced together this outfit from Sonny's closet, a church clothes jumble and donations from cousins, and then had lengthened sleeves and let out the cuffs so the pants covered his ankles.

Hearing his mother yell that the train would be here soon, he took one last look at himself and then bounded down the stairs. His mother checked him out, brushed some imaginary lint off his shoulder, asked him if he had enough money for the train ticket, pressed a few dollars into his hand along with some lunch, and shooed him out the door.

He ran to the train station, waving to the conductor about to close the doors. Schedules were tight, and the trains adhered to their schedules. Jumping into the nearest car, he took a seat for the 10-minute ride to North Station. He sat next to a man with the latest edition of the paper, which included more information on the D-Day invasion of Normandy. If the man put the paper down, he'd grab it to read, but the man took it with him as he exited the train. Then he hoofed it down Canal Street, past Haymarket Station, where he grabbed a paper on the run, throwing a nickel, which the kid selling the paper caught like a pro. He continued down Congress Street, then left onto Devonshire Street, crossed over to Franklin Street, and entered the office building lobby. He nodded to the old man at the desk, who would otherwise be retired, he suspected. The man checked his name off, handed him a badge, and nodded to one of the two men sitting by the elevator.

The elevators were manned, and the stairs were locked, so guests had to be checked in and escorted to their floor. When the elevator operator punched the button for the correct floor, he wondered if the man memorized the visitor list each morning. His escort exited the elevator on the eighth floor, escorted him down the hallway, and knocked on an unmarked office door. When the voice on the other side invited them in, the man opened the door. Ig stepped through, and the door closed.

"It's nice to meet you, Douglas. I've heard good things about you from your father." The man behind the desk was in his twenties, wearing a suit but carrying himself with a military posture.

"Thank you. It's nice to meet you as well, sir," Ig replied, taking the chair indicated.

"Some ground rules. Call me Lt. Makepeace when we are in front of others, but feel free to call me Mark when we're alone."

"Um, ok."

"If you have any questions, ask. I may yell, but I'd rather we cleared the air than have something go wrong."

"Of course."

"As a messenger, you'll take items from one office to another, or you'll be sent out to pick things up and bring them here."

"Yes, sir. Plans, right?"

"Sometimes. Sometimes, messages; other times, it may be documents in a locked briefcase. A security guard will accompany you and will have the key to the handcuffs that will be secured to your wrist when you carry the briefcase."

"Handcuffs?"

"Yes, for secure items. Sometimes, you'll be asked to wait for a signature, other times, it will be a drop-off. Of course, there will always be something to sign. Let's take a walk." Makepeace led Ig down the hall to another unmarked office with frosted glass. Inside was a large table with chairs occupied by a few young men. The room had a few separate desks with typewriters.

"Is typing involved?"

"Only when needed."

Ig nodded. He didn't know what that meant, but nodding seemed appropriate.

"This is where you'll report each day. When you receive an assignment, follow through as directed. No funny business."

"Yes, sir," Ig replied.

"The official start time each day is 8 am. There will be things to do if you arrive early. Each morning, you'll punch your timecard and take your seat. Be sure it's your timecard. If you punch someone else's timecard, they'll get paid instead of you. Now there's some paperwork for you to fill out," Makepeace said, handing Ig a file folder with an application to complete. A woman entered the room and gave each of the young men an assignment, and they put on their coats and left.

Ig completed all the forms using the typewriter. It's a good thing he had a pen on him since there didn't seem to be any in the room for him to sign each form. He didn't dare open a desk drawer in case that was the wrong thing to do. He'd have to remember to bring a pen every day. He closed the folder and waited. Was he supposed to get up and turn the paperwork in? If so, where was he supposed to go? It didn't seem like opening every door on the floor was a good idea.

A woman entered the room, took the file, and left as silently as she arrived. Soon after, Makepeace returned, escorting another young man into the office and handing Ig his first assignment. A security guard with a rifle met him in the hallway and followed him through his assignment. By the end of the day, he was a pro. When he left, the old man at the front desk nodded and said, "See you tomorrow."

Ig nodded and headed out to the street. I have a new job, Ig thought to himself. Then wondered what he would be paid for this job. No one had said, and he hadn't asked. The train was crowded with folks heading home from work, and today, he was one of them. He couldn't wait to tell the guys. He could only tell them he had a job, not what he did. He settled in to read the latest updates to the D-Day invasion.

SEVENTY

MAC HAD a decision to make. At this time in his career and the Manhattan Project, it was an important decision, probably the most critical decision of his career, and he wanted to make the right move. In the past, he and Bertha would talk this over, consider the pros and cons, and make a decision that served them and their family. This time, he had no one to talk it over with because he couldn't tell Bertha what he was doing or what the change might mean, other than one option had him traveling more, and the other would be similar to what he'd been doing his entire working career.

Stone and Webster Engineering's development role in Boston ended as operations for the town of Oak Ridge and the Y-12 facility shifted to the Tennessee Eastman Corporation in Oak Ridge. Ending was the wrong word to use since nothing was ending, everything was shifting. Shifting locations and shifting roles.

Stone and Webster Engineering talked about different roles he could take on for non-Manhattan Project work they had in the pipeline, and there was a lot of work to be done. Sara Olson would stay in Boston, as would most of the engineers and draftsmen he had worked with and managed for almost two years. He had no worries that he could spend the rest of his working life with Stone and Webster Engineering and work on challenging and rewarding work.

On the other hand, the Tennessee Eastman Corporation, which had had representatives in the offices down the hall, had approached him about joining the team at Oak Ridge. If he chose that option, it would be a change of employers, a move to a secret city that included his wife and son. It would be dicey to move Gran at this point. She had weak and strong periods with her heart condition, and now she was strong. If Gran stayed behind, there would be no family member to take care of her, and if she moved to a secret city, she would have Bertha, but no family members could visit her. Would she survive a move to California to stay with Bertha's brother or with Mabel?

E.B. Badger had offered a third option: to join their team permanently. The hydrogen cooling towers were up and producing plutonium that was being sent to Los Alamos. Their work on the copper spanner and valves for the S-10 project was being finalized. That job would involve Stone and Webster, Oak Ridge, and Los Alamos, and had the advantage of being local. He liked working with E.B. Badger, but he wasn't sure what their business model was for the post-war period since almost all their projects centered around Stone and Webster and the Manhattan Project.

He finished his report, locked his office door, handed it to Florence to type up, saying he'd look it over in the morning, and suggested she leave when she was done. Ig had the car to deliver groceries after work tonight, and walking to the train to clear his head would do some good.

"Penny for your thoughts." He looked up from his seat on the train to see Betty, looking happy and smart in a suit and pumps. The suit wasn't new, but who had new clothes these days?

"What a sight for sore eyes," Mac said, standing up to allow her to sit by the window. "What are you doing here so early? Did they let you go?"

"You know they would never let me go. I'm too valuable."

"Or you know too much."

They laughed at this. They were both valuable to this project.

"Gramps is doing poorly, and I want to see him again while he recognizes me. I got a weekend pass." Betty had moved to Oak Ridge in June.

"Please give your parents my best. How's your brother Al?"

"He's still in the South Pacific. He won't make it home to see Gramps."

"Does Gramps still remember me?"

"I don't think so, he hasn't mentioned you in a while."

"I thought you had travel restrictions?"

"Like you, I get some special privileges."

"Shh, don't say that too loud. You never know who's listening."

"Believe me, I'm reminded of that every day. Have you made a decision yet?"

"Have you been sent to influence me?'"

"Partly. Gramps is dying, and they make special exceptions for the death of family members."

They chatted cryptically, so no one knew what they were talking about. Posters and signs about keeping secrets everywhere, including on every train car, reinforced the need to be circumspect.

"Well, well, look who's here. I hope Mrs. Macdonald knows what's going on."

"She will, once I get home," Mac replied to Mrs. Holcomb.

Mrs. Holcomb had made it her mission to speak to Mac every time they were on the train together, which wasn't frequent but enough to be irritating. In retrospect, he preferred it when Mrs. Holcomb had ignored them.

"I feel like it's been a while since I've seen you on the train." Mrs. Holcomb took the seat across from Mac and Betty, leaving her friends to continue to the next car.

"Schedules, you know, what with the war and all. Lovely to see you again, Mrs. Holcomb. This is my stop. My Dad should be waiting for me." Betty got up at the Malden Station stop, gathering her coat and bag. She had blossomed from the shy young girl who turned red at any attention to a confident, self-assured professional woman.

"My grandfather isn't doing well so we're taking turns spending the night with him," Betty replied.

"That's too bad. And how's the boyfriend?"

Betty's face darkened briefly before she recovered, and her smile returned. "He's in France." She waved as the crowd swept everyone towards the doors in their rush to get home.

"Tell Gramps I'm thinking of him," Mac shouted to Betty.

"Give my regards to Mrs. Mac." And Betty was soon out of their sight.

"That was a little strange, wasn't it?" Mrs. Holcomb asked.

"Why is that?" Mac replied, organizing and folding his paper. It was two short stops until they both got off at Oak Grove.

"She's so vague about her boyfriend but she's wearing a ring."

"He died at Omaha Beach."

"And she's still wearing his ring?" Mrs. Holcomb asked, leaning forward a little to imply they were sharing a confidence and that Mrs. Holcomb could be trusted. "Don't you think that's a bit unusual?"

"It's only been two months. Less than that since she received the news." He'd seen so many people act perfectly normally, or as generally as anyone could these days, and then be unable to deal with the death of a loved one, especially a death so far away. Maybe the ring helped Betty to remember him. It didn't stop anyone from asking her out when she was in Oak Ridge.

"I see."

I wonder what you do see, Mac thought to himself. "How's Jimmy doing?" Mac asked. The Holcombs' son was in the Navy and assigned stateside in an office outside New Orleans.

"He calls every Sunday."

"That's nice. I wish Sonny could call every week."

"I know I'm lucky to have Jimmy assigned stateside and not overseas. Sonny may go overseas to fight. The Ramsdells are going through hell with one son lost on D-Day and the other married in California before heading overseas, and now they have a grandchild on the way and haven't yet met the daughter-in-law. The Gilchrists' daughter joined the Red Cross without asking her parents for permission, and she's in France somewhere on the front lines. But all I have is Jimmy and Mr. Holcomb, and I want someone to understand what it's like for me."

The train pulled into the Cedar Grove station, and Mrs. Holcomb left without looking back. Mac had more than one thing to chat with Bertha about tonight. When he arrived home, the car was in the driveway, so he asked Bertha and Ig to join him for dinner. They would drive to Revere Beach and have seafood by the seaside, and Ig could deliver groceries after dinner. Once they got back, he would take Ginger for a walk.

Mac explained the overall situation to Bertha and Ig without giving too much detail about his role or what the super-secret project does. Bertha was not excited about moving to Oak Ridge or continuing to travel. She didn't understand why he would leave Stone and Webster Engineering. And how would Sonny be able to visit when he was on furlough, or should he not be overseas? It was a good question that he would address when he had more information. Ig was excited to move but wanted to finish high school in Melrose.

SEVENTY-ONE

IG RETURNED from a messenger run and sat at the messenger table, sweat sticking his shirt to his back, his hair soaked. He had no idea how Dad wore a jacket and vest every day, no matter the weather. The next job was dropped in the basket on the table by Sally, now the messenger coordinator, and he picked it up. He and Sally nodded but never spoke. This slip said to report to the security office, which usually meant the next delivery would be by car, a nice reprieve from walking in the hot sun that reflected heat off the building and made it feel even hotter.

"Where are we going?" Ig asked the security officer.

"Springfield," the man replied, handcuffing Ig to a briefcase.

Ig looked from the man to the briefcase. He had never made such a long run and had never been handcuffed to a briefcase before. The sweat that had soaked his shirt now felt cold.

Two security guards armed with rifles escorted him to a car waiting outside. One guard sat in the front seat and the other in the back seat.

"Great day for a drive," the driver said, smiling at Ig. The guards said nothing.

"I guess," Ig replied, the handcuff chafing his wrist. "Better than walking."

They made good time to Springfield, exceeding the 35 mph speed limit that most people had to follow. The driver spent the entire ride checking the rearview mirror and the large side view mirrors to see if they were being followed. Another team had been followed to Springfield, so there was no reason why it couldn't happen to them.

"Mind if I check out the rifle?" Ig asked the guard next to him. "I'm in the rifle club at school." The guard didn't reply. He'd love to use the skills he was learning in the rifle club, but they weren't going to arm a 15-year-old messenger.

The driver pulled into a large factory building surrounded by a metal fence topped with barbed wire after showing papers to the guard at the factory gate. Once admitted, the guards told Ig to get out of the car and escorted him to the front door. Inside, Ig handed the delivery slip to the guard at the front desk. The man made a phone call and, after a wait that seemed like an eternity, a man with a key arrived, unlocked the briefcase, and took the briefcase through the secure door into what he assumed was the factory. The three of them waited. When the briefcase was returned, Dad was with the man with the briefcase. He was allowed to step aside to have a quick conversation with Dad.

"How's your mother?"

"Angry still, but she's calming down a little, I think," Ig replied.

"Good. I'll see you this weekend." Then Dad disappeared through the door.

The briefcase was reattached to his arm. He was handed the signed slip, and his two guards escorted him back to the car. They returned to the Boston office, handed in his slip, had the briefcase removed from his arm, and returned to the messenger office. He checked himself out and drove the car home, ready for some dinner before beginning his grocery deliveries.

"Take Ginger for a run. When you get back I'll have a sandwich waiting for you," his mother said.

"We're having sandwiches for dinner?"

"You are. The market called and wants you to start as soon as possible."

Ginger led them up and down the streets and around the houses in their neighborhood. The fresh breeze felt good. Ginger slowed, and he could take in the air, breathe deeply, and enjoy the moment. They made their way back to the house. His mother handed him a roast beef sandwich, the end of a roast she had been nursing all week.

"You should get those deliveries done," his mother said.

Ig nodded while he wolfed down the sandwich and a glass of milk. She had added butter, real butter, to it. He grabbed the keys. He drove down the street to the market and picked up the deliveries from Elaine. When he was done, he headed home again to find his mother was waiting for him at the kitchen table.

"Did you see your dad today?"

"No." It was a lie but if he said yes there would be too many questions.

"Any idea where he is?"

"Mom. You know I can't."

His mother shook her head and sighed. The tea kettle whistled, and Ig watched his mother rustle around, making tea and putting it on a tray to take to Gran.

"How's Gran?"

"She doesn't want to be a burden, but I don't know how long I can do this."

"I'll read to her while you rest. Have you found someone who can come in at night?"

"Nothing yet. The doctor is trying to line up a nursing student."

"Someone more dependable than Ruby?" The previous nursing student had run off to New York to marry her boyfriend one night and hadn't bothered to tell anyone, including her parents.

"I called Gert to see if she could fill in. She's pregnant and can't stay on her feet."

"What about the nursing home over on Oakland Street?"

"The doctor got me to agree to put her on the list."

"Good."

"I do wish I could keep her home but I can't keep doing this myself. And you can't keep filling in after work and grocery deliveries."

"Mom, we don't have a choice."

Bert nodded. She picked up the tray and headed up the stairs to see if her mother would drink tea and eat toast.

"Oh, and before I forget, Al called. He was wondering if you could play in a game this evening."

"I'll call Al and then be up."

"Don't your friends have jobs?" his mother asked as she headed up the back stairs.

"Of course they do."

Ig quickly called Al, got an update on the game they had lost, and headed up to read to Gran until she fell asleep. Ginger padded after him.

SEVENTY-TWO

MAC CONTEMPLATED the three roles offered to him over three weeks, never fully coming to a decision that favored one over another. Each role had merits and each role had faults. He and Bertha discussed what each job had to offer over dinner several times. He and Ig had discussed them in the car. One Sunday, he discussed the different roles with Sonny in a phone call. Everyone's favorite was E.B. Badger, and he agreed, but there was a "but" in the back of his mind.

"Hey, Mac, be in the conference room in 15 minutes," Salvaggio said as he poked his head into Mac's Boston office.

Mac muttered under his breath. He had been putting off the decision as long as possible. And he had reports to finish. He handed his edits to the report to Florence to type up and headed for the conference room. He was surprised to find not only Salvaggio and the Area Engineer Lord, along with Batch, the Stone and Webster representative at Oak Ridge, a representative from E.B. Badger, several Stone and Webster Engineering senior staff, Houston and another security officer, and two of the Tennessee Eastman Corporation staff that had been in Boston for more than a year and were now being relocated to Oak Ridge. Betty was taking notes of the meeting.

"We understand that we have asked you to decide your next role from among three very competitive offers," Salvaggio said. The new area engineer generally let Salvaggio speak as he had known the team the longest.

"Yes," Mac replied.

"Have you come to any conclusions?" asked Batch.

"I have been weighing each option, but I haven't come to a definitive answer," Mac replied.

"Stone and Webster has been your employer for almost six years now. I think your answer is obvious," a Stone and Webster senior engineer said.

No one spoke for a moment.

"We have another role for you to consider. We are creating a series of 11 field representative roles based in the hubs where multiple vendors are working on the current project. The field representatives will work for Tennessee Eastman and will be housed in the area they represent. The roles are for no more than 11 months. We would like you to consider the Boston area field representative role."

Mac nodded. While no one knew when the war would end, having an end date for a role would provide him flexibility to consider his post-war options. Given the work he had done so far and what he knew about separating uranium, he anticipated having many options open to him.

"Thanks for considering this role. Here's the description we've put together."

"Let me think about this," Mac said, skimming the role. "By the way, it says here that the field representative will always be accompanied by a security detail, except when I am in a secure area. How would that work when I'm at home?" Mac asked.

"Someone will be staying outside your home, or any other location you are at," Houston said. "In this case, someone on my staff or I will move closer to your home. If you accept the role, of course."

"Why more security?"

"You will be traveling to more vendors and will have plans on you for multiple parts of the project at any given time."

"This role allows me to stay in Boston. It involves more travel and security and involves working on requests for all parts of the project. Is there more project scope than I worked on previously?"

Everyone agreed with his assessment. If he took this role, and he suspected he would accept it, Bertha would not be happy with the security men outside the house when he was home. It would keep friends and neighbors away, as it was designed to do. Ig knew far too much, but the boy could keep a secret. Sonny knew even less, which was beneficial since he could barely keep a secret.

Everything he heard in Sonny's letters, from Lt. Houston, and the newspapers, indicated Sonny would be heading overseas soon. Sometimes, he spent more time with Houston than with his wife, another thing Bertha resented.

If not for Gran's health, he would encourage a move to Oak Ridge, but Gran needed attention, and Oak Ridge was not the place for an elderly woman. He'd known Gran since he was 16 and had watched her slow down and shrink over the past few years. Her mind was as sharp as ever, and she enjoyed a sip of 'medicine' every evening, which Bertha the teetotaler resented but which he enjoyed with her when he was home. From his perspective, keeping everyone in Melrose and traveling was the answer, for now. The good news was that Elaine was postponing school for another year while she made more money, kept tabs on her father, kept Bertha company, and helped with Gran.

SEVENTY-THREE

THE HOT, late August sun was beating down on them as the mules had kicked them around. The dust from the army cowboys driving cattle into camp choked and blinded them. The river crossing training was a relief from the sun, but the water was muddy and less than refreshing. They said that when it rained, the river would be better. It was nothing like snow and mountains with trains passing through. It was flat, dusty, hot, and full of bugs, mules, and a sense that no one knew what to do with the 10th. Rumors were rampant again that they would be sent to the jungles of the South Pacific after all their mountain training, be used to fill holes in existing units in France, or be heading to the Alps, to use the skills they trained for.

The watermelons lay ripe and ready in a field away, lying in the sun with light and dark green stripes. Other guys had visited and returned full of the delicious, sweet fruit, and they could see no reason why they shouldn't do the same on their afternoon off. They sauntered, their bodies more accustomed to the cold and high altitudes than the sea-level heat and humidity. The weathered farmer was sitting in a rocking chair on the porch of the old farmhouse.

"Howdy," he said as Sonny, Jack, and Georgie approached.

"Afternoon," Sonny replied.

"Come fer watermelon?"

"Yes, sir. We hear you have the best around."

"Only watermelon in the area," the farmer replied.

"I guess we wouldn't know. We haven't been here long."

"You the mountain boys from up north?"

"Yes, sir, we are," Georgie said politely. Georgie wouldn't look directly at the man. Sonny suspected because the old man looked like the land, his brown, wrinkled skin the color of dirt.

"Pick out one and sit awhile," the old man said.

"Thank you kindly," Sonny replied. "How much are they?"

"No charge."

"We have money and are happy to pay," Jack said. He seemed concerned that the old man was treating them too nicely.

"No charge," the old man said again. "Take as many as you like."

"How do you make money if you don't charge?"

"I make do," the old man said.

They hesitated a moment before heading into the field. The heat shimmered up off the land. to pick out watermelons, which sat on little hills of dirt. They perused the watermelons sitting on little hills of dirt, picked one each, and returned to the porch, where the old man nodded towards a knife on the table for them to use.

They spent a pleasant hour gorging on the red flesh, spitting seeds onto the ground off the porch, and chatting with the old man. He answered their questions in as few words as possible. When they were done with the watermelon, Jack noticed some cantaloupes. Seeing the boys eying the cantaloupes, he nodded, and they split one. The cantaloupe was golden, with no green showing at the rind. Sometimes, he wondered if he had ever tasted fruit before; it was so fresh, juicy, and ripe.

"That was a feast," Georgie said with satisfaction. "We must owe you something."

"No charge," the old man said.

"My mother would be very disappointed if I took something without paying," Jack said, squinting up at the old man, the sun in his eyes as soon as he was off the porch.

"You'll be overseas fighting soon."

"Do you know something we don't know?"

"Mebbe, mebbe not," the old man continued to rock.

"Look, I can't leave without paying you something," Sonny said.

The old man said nothing as Sonny placed a dollar bill on the table and put the knife handle over it to hold it down. Georgie and Jack added their dollars to the pile.

"I'll take it for your mama's sake." They heard the old man say as they walked back to their barracks.

SEVENTY-FOUR

THE DECISION to have some family pictures taken to send to Sonny and other family members was planned for this hot, humid August day. The papers said they were in the middle of a heatwave, one of the worst in recent memory. It had been going on for more than 10 days. Mom was angry that Dad had accepted a new job with the Tennessee Eastman Corporation without consulting her. Dad was angry that she didn't understand how important this project was to him, even though she wasn't sure what the project was. They had fought over the decision, and the remnants of their angry words hung in the air. She wanted him to stay closer to home, possibly on a less stressful project, and he wanted to see this project through to the end. Mom was in her chair, and Dad was in his chair, and they wouldn't look at one another. Ginger lay on the floor between them, patiently waiting, neither angry nor taking sides.

"I'm ready," Ig said.

"Oh good, you're wearing your brother's shirt," Gran said. "It looks nice on you."

"It shows how tall I'm getting," Ig replied.

"Those pants are above your ankle bones. Don't you have anything that fits?" Mac said.

"I'll see if I can let them out," Bertha said.

"Oh, hey, look, you're both speaking now," Ig said, smiling.

They both turned silent, acting like he was someone they had never seen before. Ig looked at Ginger, who turned her head and wouldn't look him in the eye. Her first loyalty was to Dad.

"Et Tu, Ginger?" Ig said. Ginger raised one eyebrow, but wouldn't look him in the eye.

Mom wore her flowered dress with freshly polished white shoes. Dad wore a white shirt, dark pants with suspenders running over the shoulders, and black shoes. His shirt was open at the collar, showing his white undershirt underneath, and no vest or jacket—a casual look on this hot, humid day. Gran, dressed in her best dress that fit her ever-thinner frame, was the photographer for the day. She added film to her camera.

The daily glass of Scotch the doctor prescribed Gran as her new 'medicine' seemed to be working. Gran seemed brighter and loved having a tipple. Mom tolerated alcohol in the house. Dad had a glass with her when he was home, which was most evenings now that he was home more until the new job started. Ig snuck a sip when Mom was out of the room. Most people told him it tasted awful, but he rather liked it.

Gran cleared her throat. His parents continued to ignore one another.

"You can sulk later," Gran said. "I may not be here much longer, and Sonny wants some family photos, so let's get this show on the road. You two sit on the sofa next to one another."

Mom and Dad followed Gran's command but refused to look at one another while she snapped a few photos.

"Gran, aren't you aggressive today?" Ig hadn't heard his grandmother speak sternly in a long time.

"I'm serious. I don't have much time," Gran said. "Outside, everyone." She took Ig's arm, and they walked through the dining room onto the side porch and around the garden to the shady part of the yard under the neighbor's trees. The sun hid behind the high, thin clouds. Mom and Dad arrived, with Ginger walking next to Dad. The changes and problems brought on by the war showed in Mom's white hair and Dad's increased weight, Ig thought.

Gran organized them, snapped a few pictures, and then rearranged them. Mom and Dad were clearly stiff and uncomfortable sitting next to each other. He had hoped they would relax. These pictures would last forever, or at least longer than this fight. Neither of them was willing to forgive or apologize. Mom didn't want Dad to take the job. He, not liking Mom's response, told her she had an easy life cleaning, cooking, and taking a week in Maine with her friends without a worry about him, working seven days a week, or Sonny getting ready to head overseas, or Ig working two jobs, or her mother in poor health. Mom responded that it appeared to her she was working more than two jobs, and he never told her what he was doing or where he was going. If nothing else, leaving everyone to fend for themselves pointed out just how much she was doing without anyone taking notice. That's when Dad started spending every evening with Gran, sipping scotch, making Mom even angrier.

"I'm done," Dad said when Gran said she wanted a few more pictures on the porch. He was sweating through his shirt as he stomped through the house to the front porch; Ginger followed. Mom retreated to the side porch, flushed and fanning herself.

"Gran, let's get a few pictures of you to send out," Ig said, taking the camera from his grandmother. She fussed and said there was no need for pictures of her, but he persisted and she agreed to a photo under the trees, by herself. He suspected that this would be the last picture of her that anyone would ever take.

Mom waved him away when he tried to take a photo of her, but patted the chair next to her so he could sit.

"Your father is still angry." It was more of a statement than a question.

"Yes," Ig replied. "I think you are too."

"I don't like this project, whatever it is, that your father is working on, and I don't like that he left Stone and Webster."

"I know," Ig replied. "Will you and Dad talk again before he leaves?"

"I don't know," Mom replied.

"I'm going to drop the film off to be developed. I have a few deliveries to make."

"That sounds nice. Would you drive Gran back to the rest home?"

"Of course. What are we having for dinner?"

"It's too hot to cook," Mom replied.

"Why don't I pick up something at the Lobster Pot on my way home?" Ig was always hungry, and if his parents didn't want to eat, all the more for him.

Then, he took some photos of Ginger and Dad on the front porch, Dad swishing flies away from him and Ginger. Sonny was always looking for pictures of Ginger.

"Your mother say anything?"

"No, not much," Ig replied. "I'll pick up some seafood after I drop Gran off and make my deliveries."

"She doesn't want to stay? Probably best," Dad said.

Gran's heart was erratic, the doctor had told them countless times. Ig wondered how much longer she could have these bursts of energy, followed by lying in bed to recover more often. And what would he do when she was no longer there?

SEVENTY-FIVE

MAC FLEW to Knoxville, Tennessee, on Tuesday, August 22, 1944, along with Lt. Houston. The project now allowed for travel by plane. They had previously been restricted to train travel. They were picked up at the airport and driven to Oak Ridge. He and the ten other procurement field representatives had their physicals and job orientation. Besides Boston, field representatives were in Pittsfield, Massachusetts, Newark, New Jersey, Rochester, New York, Pittsburgh, Pennsylvania, Chicago, Illinois, Nashville, Tennessee, Cincinnati, Ohio, Bristol, Tennessee, Detroit, Michigan, and Atlanta, Georgia. They all reported to the procurement office and all had security with them. Mac knew most of the others by name and had talked with several on the phone as they traded information when necessary.

Once his paperwork and medical exam with the Oak Ridge doctor were completed, the field representatives spent the rest of the week in meetings learning about their new roles and responsibilities. Houston returned to Boston on Thursday, while Mac and the other field representatives stayed on to learn about the new group purchasing system, expediting from the field rather than from the office, and understand what was expected of this group over the next few months. Working closely with Stone and Webster engineers was essential now that he was responsible for all the contracts, specifications, and parts for all the project-related work being built in the Boston area, not just the electromagnetic separation part of the project. Stone and Webster wasn't happy he had left and had thrown up one or two roadblocks, most of which were cleared up quickly with the help of Colonel Nichols.

He stayed in one of the dorms, a functional space with one bed, a dresser, a desk, a chair, and a shared bath in the hallway. Helen met him for breakfast most mornings, and he had dinner with Wally and Hanson several times. He saw Mrs. Brown's son, Howard, regularly. Howard had been hired to work on the project without finishing his degree. Howard lived in the 'colored' or negro village and they had their cafeterias and entertainment. Which meant they didn't intermingle socially. This separation made Mac uncomfortable, but he wasn't ready to start breaking the rules.

It was almost two weeks before Mac was able to return home. On Saturday morning, he was working in his office. Bertha and Ig were returning home by ferry from Provincetown to Boston, and he would pick them up in Boston, his attempt to make up for the fights they had had all through August. Ig would start school on Tuesday, and he wanted to be home to see him off to his first day as a high school junior.

For the first time in ages, he was engrossed in the family finances when he noticed the wind blowing leaves into spirals in the driveway as black clouds swiftly covered the sun. Ginger growled at the distant thunder. The radio broke into the music program with a report of a deadly storm, but the electricity of the storm turned the report into a crackling mess before the power shut off, ending the static.

He hoped the ferry had enough warning not to leave the dock. The ferry trip wasn't long, but a storm could make it a rough passage. He wondered if Sgt. Burns, the new security man who recently returned from overseas with one leg shorter than the other, was paying attention to the weather. He had learned how to get around well and was assigned to watch him today.

He ran outside to put away anything loose. The winds picked up the fencing around the garden and dropped it into the neighbor's yard. Ginger barked at him from the side porch. An uprooted tree flew over his head and landed on the power lines. He waved Sgt. Burns into the house. Burns hesitated, then exited the car, fighting the winds, head bent, limping across the street. Mac lowered his car windows to keep the windows from blowing out, grabbed Burns, and the two fought their way to the back door. Mac latched the screen door behind them.

Ginger was shaking in the living room. Mac picked her up and carried her upstairs, placing her in the bathtub and wrapping towels around her to calm her down. Despite the chaos of the storm, Mac remained calm and collected. He knew the importance of staying focused, especially in a crisis. "You should get out of those wet clothes," Mac said to Burns, his voice steady and composed. "And take them downstairs; don't leave them on the floor." His calm instructions helped maintain order amid the storm's aftermath.

Mac rubbed Ginger to slow her shaking. Burns had decided to stay in his office to keep an eye on the car. The power was out until the following afternoon. A fallen tree blocked the end of their driveway. Bertha and Ig spent the night at the ferry terminal, catching an early morning ferry and then the train, and arrived home in time for Sunday breakfast long after Burns had been replaced. With Bertha and Ig home safely, Mac took the opportunity to write a long letter to Sonny describing the storm.

SEVENTY-SIX

IN LATE August, the doctor was able to secure a bed for Gran at the local nursing home, and Gran agreed it was time for her to go. Mabel had helped to move Gran. After the move, Bertha decided not to worry about things she couldn't control. She couldn't stop what Mac was doing, make Sonny become someone he would never be, nor could she do the same with Ig. She wondered how the dynamic would have been if Bobby Bruce were alive. He'd be starting college now or, most likely, heading off to serve. Would he have been interested in engineering like his father, trains like Sonny, arts and literature like her, or history and science like Ig? Or would he be someone entirely different?

While she had decided not to worry, she was still angry with Mac. He was always working, never home, and she didn't like the security around this job or the fact that a security guard was outside every time he was home. She had long since given up trying to explain what he did to her family and friends, just that it was for the war. She found it strange that everyone, even Alice, accepted this.

With Gran settled, she decided that she and Ig would go to Provincetown for a week to take in the artists, writers, plays, and any other artistic event she could find. Provincetown could be reached by ferry from Boston, and it was walkable, so there was no need for a car. Ig needed a break, and he had a week between the end of his messenger job and the start of school. She told Garniss that they would have to do without him for grocery deliveries for a week. Mac said it was a communist town and that he would stay home. She said he would pick work over his family, again, and they had another tiff, but she wasn't going to let it ruin her week.

On the last Sunday morning in August, she and Ig packed, took the train to Boston and the ferry to Provincetown. She dragged Ig to artists' studios, chatting with the artists and those who used their vacation time to paint and write. They attended author readings, plays, and musical performances, some of which made no sense to her son. She could get used to this life.

"Mom, this is boring!" Ig broke through her reverie.

"Art and culture are good for you."

Ig groaned. "I would have preferred Maine."

"You wouldn't have liked it with all my adult friends."

"You mean you wouldn't have liked it because you didn't want me around."

Bertha paused. Ig thought she had excluded him when she needed a week to herself.

"There are things you do without me, don't you?"

"That's different."

"How is that different?"

Bertha could see that Ig had to think about that. "You went to an island for a week and left us at home to fend for ourselves."

"Yes, and I might do it again," Bertha said, a twinkle in her eyes.

She saw Ig looking at her quizzically. She could still keep him on his toes.

"Do you think Gran will be home again?"

"No. She's settled in and being cared for on a schedule that works for her."

"It must be hard getting old."

"I think so," Bertha replied. "Let's get you an ice cream, then check out the artists on the road out of town."

Ig groaned but followed her.

SEVENTY-SEVEN

"HEY, SONNY, that's a funny look on your face. Is it a Dear John letter?" Jack asked. "Or another letter from your dad?"

The guys laughed. Sonny rubbed his middle finger on the bridge of his nose and re-read the letter. Jack cleared his throat, and Sonny stopped gesturing. Everyone complained that Texas was hot and humid and had no mountains, and they were right. He was sweating just reading the letter.

The wording was a bit cryptic. His father wanted him to find Life magazine dated August 28, 1944, read an article on long-range airplanes, and then send him a letter when he was done. His father's letters fell into three categories. Full of clippings and not much else, long descriptions of some event, like the recent hurricane, during which his father was home, trying to soothe Ginny and keep the house in one piece. Or they were cryptic, like this one.

Eddie, recently promoted to sergeant, grabbed the letter. "Now, what have we here? A letter from home, I see. What could Mother and Dad be talking about this week that is getting so much of your attention? Are they sports scores you can use to bet with the Saugus boys? Or is it gossip from the neighborhood?"

Ed sat on Sonny's bunk while he read the letter. Then he asked if anyone had recent Life Magazines. Life Magazine was popular in camp because it had more pictures than words and short articles. One of the guys said they might have a copy at the canteen, and another said he saw one in the Company C barracks.

When nothing turned up in the barracks, they tried the canteen. At the canteen, they were directed to the camp library. At the library, they read the copy from cover to cover. A short, blunt article boldly stated the new

B-29 bombers could travel from China to Japan, drop their bombs on Tokyo, and return on one fuel tank. Was his father working on airplanes?

It left many open questions about what his father was doing that related to the article, and it took him a week to figure out how to respond to his father should his letter be censored. There were still the mules to deal with, river crossing training to complete, and his furlough to plan. There was gossip and gambling, the two most common activities in the barracks, and letters to write. Things were changing. The weather, the location, and the work. They were heading overseas. The only question was when. Everyone would have one more furlough.

Sonny composed a brief response, buried in a letter home, that answered several letters' worth of questions. He said that if it was the article, he thought it was, and had to do with whatever super-secret work his father was working on, his eldest son approved. The guys, who had all read the magazine cover to cover, approved the wording. Then he said he hoped Dad was around when he was home on furlough. He didn't say it might be the last time he was home because he suspected Dad knew that.

SEVENTY-EIGHT

As Mac got out of the car, Sgt. Burns said he would be nearby. It was nice of him to say it, but it wasn't necessary. Someone was always keeping an eye on him when he was home. Bertha complained about the constant monitoring. The Holcombs no longer gossiped about his whereabouts with a soldier in uniform sitting outside whenever he was home.

When he opened the back door, he was astounded to see every available surface covered with green and purple grapes in colanders, pots, and pans.

"Bert, you home?" Mac called out.

"On the porch," Bertha called back.

Mac found Bert with Elaine and Jeannette Ramsdell sorting grapes.

"Hi, Uncle Mac," Jeannette giggled. "What do you think?"

"Of what?" Mac said with a twinkle in his eye.

"All the grapes, silly," Jeannette replied. "Men," she said, looking at Bertha.

"I didn't expect you," Bertha said.

"I got back early and thought I'd join you for dinner," Mac said.

"Dinner's not here yet," Jeannette piped up.

"Oh, where is it?"

"The ladies are bringing it," Jeannette replied.

"How was the baseball game yesterday?" Mac asked.

"They're awful, Dad says," Jeannette piped in.

"Your father has a keen eye."

"That's true," Jeannette said.

"What's with all the grapes?" Mac finally asked.

"Uncle Owen had them delivered from his new property in Concord. Aunt Bea has more grapes than she can handle."

"Why us?"

"To see the look on your face," Bertha said, laughing.

Mac burst out laughing, and Elaine and Jeannette laughed, too. Bertha explained that she had called women from church and her social groups to bring sugar, wax, and canning jars for a jelly-making party and something to share for everyone's dinner.

Mac shook his head. Uncle Owen's appearances were always memorable.

"I'm staying overnight to help clean up," Jeannette said.

"That's nice," Mac replied. He knew Bertha would explain later, but he suspected it had to do with Ramsdell's younger son being shot down over Normandy and their new daughter-in-law, who had come to live with them, due to give birth. Under normal circumstances, he'd go across the street to talk to Ramsdell, but these weren't normal circumstances. Mac couldn't mingle with a Stone and Webster employee who was not a part of the project, or the lovely young man in the car would report on his movements. Bertha would send his sympathies once he was away from the house. She was the conduit for all his local news and gossip.

It wasn't long before the ladies arrived with their casseroles, canned vegetables, desserts, cane sugar, jars, and wax. Food was heated and served. Ladies washed and crushed the grapes, while others strained them and began cooking with sugar and honey. Mac was fascinated by the process and organization of these women. They served him dinner, which was much appreciated, and then he settled into his chair to read the paper.

Sgt. Burns stayed in the car and was brought a dinner plate. He was stunned at the number of people going in and out of the house. He would have raised the alarm if it were men, but since it was all women, and they brought him dinner, he decided to wait until Lt. Houston arrived to relieve him.

Houston wasn't happy to hear about all this activity but decided there was no way to address the situation without raising the alarm. He asked the young man to stay longer while he went to speak with Mac. When he entered the kitchen, Bertha nodded and yelled for Mac. While Mac and he retreated to Mac's office, the women continued their work well into the night.

SEVENTY-NINE

SONNY ARRANGED his furlough so he would be home for his 21st birthday, October 31, 1944. He treated himself to an unusual train ride via Brownville Junction, Maine, to visit his grandmother Macdonald's grave. It was an excuse to ride the train as long as possible. From Brownville Junction, he grabbed a night train to Boston. His first stop would be to see his father's face when he showed up at the office and met his secretary. From Boston's North Station, he walked to his father's office building on Devonshire Street. Dressed in ODs, he thought they would let him right into the building. His plans to meet his father's secretary were dashed when security, unimpressed with this young man in uniform, called his father's office and gathered from Florence that he was expected and would have to wait in the lobby until Mac was out of his meeting. Sonny chafed at the restrictions. He was about to give his father an earful when his father stepped off the elevator with a colonel, who hurried to a waiting car, and with General Paul Sherman, who was born in Melrose. He saluted, and the general saluted back, then shook his hand, saying he was honored to meet him.

"Ready for some lunch?" Mac asked Sonny.

"I'm ready to meet your cute secretary," Sonny said smiling.

"I don't think you have the security clearance for that," General Sherman replied, with a smile. "I need to return to the office."

Sonny watched the General and his father shake hands. The General appeared to know his father and what his father did.

"Sonny, be sure to contact me if you need anything," General Sherman said, shaking Sonny's hand. "No need to salute. Let's not draw too much attention."

The General strode down the street, turning heads as he went. Mac said he had just the place in mind for lunch. They headed down the street and around the corner, followed by a young, limping man dressed in a nondescript suit. Sonny assumed the man was security since his father never said a word. Mac opened the door at Brigham's Ice Cream shop, followed by Sonny and Burns. Burns sat at the counter while Sonny and Mac were shown to a booth.

"I have some questions about the article you had me read," Sonny said, after they ordered burgers and milkshakes. Dad was keeping interesting company.

"Let's talk about that at dinner," Mac said. "How's working with mules and fording rivers?"

Sonny told his father that he had finally gotten a mule to bend his leg, which was a significant accomplishment, and not one he wanted to have to do again. Another accomplishment was crossing a river with a pack on his back and holding his rifle over his head. He suspected no European river was as warm as the Colorado River near Camp Swift.

After lunch, Sonny grabbed the train to Cedar Park and walked up the hill, waving to everyone he saw. Taking the front steps two at a time, duffel bag over his shoulder, he opened the front door and announced that he was home. Ginger put her front paws on his shoulders and licked his face. Then jumped down and headed for the kitchen. He apologized to his mother for being late, and his mother said Florence, Dad's secretary, had called to let her know.

His plan to walk over to the nursing home to visit Gran was stalled when he fell asleep on the couch. His mother left him there, waking him when dinner guests arrived. Bertha had made a few calls and arranged a dinner party for his 21st birthday. He was now eligible to vote as well as fight.

Gertie was the first to arrive, with both children, including his month-old godson. He found it hard to believe that Web and Gertie were the parents of two children, and that he was a godfather. Charlie, also home on leave, arrived with Arnette. Elaine made it home from the store in time for dinner. Hooker, home on leave from Officer's Candidate

School, came with his mother. Ig was glad to see him and, for once, he approved of Ig wearing his clothes.

At the end of the evening, he kissed his mother goodnight and headed out with Hooker, Elaine, Charlie and Arnette. Hooker and Elaine brought him home and helped Bertha put him to bed.

After breakfast, he headed down the street and over four blocks to the nursing home. Mom must have called because Gran was sitting in a rocking chair on the front porch.

"You are a sight for sore eyes," Gran said.

"It's wonderful to see you," Sonny said, kissing his grandmother's cheek, tears in his eyes. Ig had noted that she seemed to be shrinking, and it was an apt description.

"So, where will you be sent?"

"Officially, we don't know. But they're bringing in officers who speak German and Italian, so we're guessing the Alps or the Apennines in Italy," Sonny said.

"So you will see a battle. Are you scared?"

"Yes, I am," Sonny replied.

"I wish I could say don't be, but I know that's not helpful or even something you can do. I will say that I hope to see you when this war's over."

"Gran, I hope I see you when the war's over too." He wanted to cry. It didn't seem like Gran would be here then, but she had survived a lot so far, so she might surprise him yet.

His two-week leave went by quickly. He spent time with Gran, with his godson, and with Ig. Charlie returned to the Air Corps soon after their dinner. He escorted Elaine wherever she needed to go. He hadn't seen Nancy once. She hadn't made the trip home from Mt. Holyoke, and he hadn't made it out to see her. Their courtship had been officially reduced to friends, and now no longer close friends.

On his last night, Dad arrived home for dinner, a rare surprise, and the two of them went for a walk, followed by a security man in a car.

"You asked me about the airplane article," Mac said.

"Yes. I was wondering why you wanted me to read that?"

"You wonder why I asked you to read an article about a new B-28 bomber with longer-range flying capability for use in the South Pacific?" His father's cryptic tone made Sonny pause and consider his response.

"Because you're working on a bomb that the plane will carry?"

There was a pause before Mac responded. "Yes."

"Is it a special bomb?"

"Let's hurry, we don't want Gran to finish her medicine without us," Mac said.

—

Sonny returned to Texas in late October with cookies and hermits from Mom and cash from Dad. Which of the two, food or money, would be more prized in the poker game? His mother thought he paid back the guys with the food he had eaten. He paid them back if they won and kept the food if they lost, just like everyone else. They looked forward to playing poker, enjoying homemade food, and drinking beer each week. Beer wasn't allowed in the barracks, only in the canteen, and poker playing wasn't allowed there, so they did their best to get beer into the barracks. That required some planning, which some officers agreed to, as it utilized their strategic skills.

"Think your luck will change tonight, Eddie?" Sonny looked at his friend.

"I can't lose so bad three times in a row," Eddie said. His Nevada drawl seemed more prominent in the Texas sun than it had ever sounded in the Colorado Rockies.

"Oh, I don't know about that," Joey said. Sonny was surprised at how much the young Italian kid could win. He was a shark and said that he picked it up in high school and on the streets of Staten Island. This made you wonder what went on in the NYC school system.

Joey had joined them straight from Staten Island High School, where he and his family had landed after leaving Sicily. They surmised they would be sent to Italy based on the number of new guys who spoke Italian. Sonny, Georgie, and Jack missed the mountains while Eddie soaked up the sun and warmth of Texas. They weren't sure if Joey missed the mountains, but the kid had learned to ski, snowshoe, and mountain climb like a pro in a very short time.

"Why don't you hand him all your money? Losing hand after hand seems real painful," Jack said to Eddie, a grin on his handsome face as he collected his winnings from the round. Jack, a New Hampshire boy, and Georgie and Jonesy, another Melrose guy, rounded out the group. While some guys wouldn't play with a Jew, they were an open group, never asking anyone with money or food about religion or politics. As the night wore on, Eddie's luck changed, and he started making money, but Joey was persistent, and the game wasn't over yet.

Sonny was quiet that night. He and the new sergeant had had words. The new sergeant wanted to promote him to squad leader, and he had declined. He'd fight, but he wouldn't lead anyone into battle. Being an assistant squad leader was fine with him. The next thing he knew, he and Leo, one of the former truck drivers he barely knew, were learning how to handle a bazooka. He was angry at first; how dare they reassign him, but he liked Leo, quiet and practical, a strong counterpoint to Sonny's know-it-all demeanor, and they made a good bazooka team.

It wasn't long before Sonny folded and went over to the bunk to check on their adopted cat giving birth.

EIGHTY

MAC SPENT the first few months in his new job setting up contracts to ensure that all necessary parts for the operation of the electromagnetic separation (Y-12), the graphite process (X-10), and the gaseous diffusion process (K-25) were procured from the vendors he was assigned. The part of the job that took the most time and was the most stressful was assessing why the Y-12 facility wasn't working as well as expected. The gunk problem persisted until the scientists and engineers recognized that insufficient attention had been devoted to the chemical aspect of the process. Mac had been at the meeting where Dr. Lawrence finally had to admit that what could be handled in the smaller 184" calutron constructed on the grounds of the University of California, Berkeley campus, and the larger size, which they were operating in much larger sizes at Oak Ridge, had lacked the attention needed in the chemical processing portion of the process. No one was happy about this, but Mac felt somewhat justified in having defended the valves being produced by EB Badger and Chapman. He imagined that Wally and Dr. Lawrence may have been dragged, kicking and screaming, to that conclusion.

Mac was spending time at Oak Ridge and in Boston. The most challenging part of the job turned out to be expediting from the field. The traffic department was no longer in Boston, and each field representative had to arrange shipping from the facility to the final destination. They each had a secretary, and Florence had become a wonder at freight schedules, but it was overwhelming. He made it clear that the need for an assistant was evident, as had every other field representative, but they were stalling, thinking they could put this off until the bombs were dropped or the contract ended in July 1945.

In Oak Ridge, the output of highly enriched uranium by the cubicle operators was increasing now that the chemical refinements were implemented. In November, the cubicle operators successfully sent 40 grams of highly enriched uranium to Los Alamos, anticipating that this output would be doubled in December. The electromagnetic separation process, initially selected because it had been proven to be effective, was finally producing enough uranium to demonstrate progress. The anticipation was that they should have enough highly enriched uranium by July 1 to fuel the gun-type bomb.

The second bomb, which would utilize plutonium, was receiving significantly more attention from the scientists at Los Alamos, as it was an implosion bomb employing a highly complex structure that required precise components, including explosive lenses manufactured to exact specifications, and the final specifications had not yet been determined. Still, the Hanford, Washington, facility and the S-10 site at Oak Ridge were not producing plutonium. The plutonium produced at Trail, British Columbia, using the heavy water and hydrogen method, was being used in these tests.

Mac was contemplating all of these problems and solutions after a long day of one-hour meetings on each topic as he avoided getting caught in the mud that was called a street in Oak Ridge. His goal was to get something to eat at the cafeteria before settling in for a night of reading and writing reports.

"Heading over to the cafeteria?" Hanson asked, startling Mac.

"Yes, as a matter of fact, I am. Want to join me?"

"Thanks, I will. It's been a while since we've had a chance to chat."

Mac laughed. He suspected Hanson had more than a chat in mind.

After getting their food and finding a relatively empty table, Hanson started the conversation.

"You must feel vindicated on the valve process now that they have addressed the chemical inadequacies?"

"Vindicated, huh. Were you wondering how I would react?" Mac had handled all the inquiries and testing required of the valves developed and used in the Y-12 uranium process. He had made clear, in his quiet yet authoritative manner, that the problem was not with the valves or the cubicles.

"I wondered what you would say at the meeting today, but you said nothing, so I thought I'd ask you myself."

"That's nice of you to ask. I thought it was about time the scientists started listening to the engineers rather than blaming us for problems," Mac said.

Hanson nodded.

"I liked that the 'dumb' women hired to operate the calutrons beat the physics students in the cubicle test. Showed that training can beat brains most days," Mac grinned as he said this. It's not that he thought women were better, but they were trained to follow directions and identify problems, while the physics students were taught to think outside the box.

"I'm sure that has nothing to do with the training materials you helped put together," Hanson said.

"Of course," Mac said with a smile.

"I also want to talk to you about the steel casing for the uranium bomb. We're going to build that here in Oak Ridge, and when you're available, we would like to consult with you on the thickness of steel being used."

"Will there be some testing?"

"No. There isn't enough enriched uranium to test with. They'll be using a gun-type mechanism, which has been well tested in the past, so there's confidence that it will be successful."

Mac couldn't do anything but agree. The fact that they approached him was a sign that they had already decided he would help.

"And the last thing is a warning on what you write to your son. Everything is scrutinized."

"Anything in particular?" Mac asked.

"The drowning over at the Tennessee Army base," Hanson said.

"That's someone Sonny knows."

"Like I said, be careful. We know the boy's father has worked on at least one project contract."

"Sure, but it was a drowning during a river crossing lesson. Something Sonny doesn't think he'll ever need. You never know what training you may need."

"Just be careful what you write," Hanson said.

EIGHTY-ONE

ON DECEMBER 21st, the 85th and the 87th regiments boarded the train and headed East, arriving at Camp Patrick Henry in Virginia, a much larger camp than Swift or Hale on Christmas Eve. They settled into their barracks, their temporary home until they shipped out. He could call home and was surprised when Dad answered the phone. Dad said he'd heard they were headed to Italy, which matched what most of the guys thought. He used to discount everything Dad said, but he'd been right enough times, and now he believed his father had accurate information. Ig was disappointed that he wouldn't be able to visit the camp. Shaky of voice and short of breath, Gran wished him a Merry Christmas. He didn't think he would be emotional but wanted to cry. Mom wished him a Merry Christmas. He hung up before they heard him cry.

On Christmas Day, they were served a turkey dinner with all the trimmings, one of his best dinners in a long time. Some guys said it felt like the last supper, but he was sure he wouldn't eat this well again. Then they were told to write letters home, telling their families they wouldn't write again until they got the okay from their company commanders. Then, it was final preparations. During his free time, he caught up on recent movies at one of the camp's three movie theatres. It was cheaper than poker and took his mind off all the speculation about what was next.

EIGHTY-TWO

BERTHA LOOKED forward to catching up with her old friends at the Christmas party. Since the grape night, as she fondly called it, and Sonny's furlough, she had been seeing more and more of the 10th Mountain parents' group and less of her Melrose friends and the club ladies.

Mrs. Rosenstein, Georgie's mother, had contacted all the parents of the 10th men in the Boston area to meet and share information and gossip they gleaned from their sons' letters. She looked forward to her time with this group, with whom she had more in common than her old friends. She talked with Johnny on the phone regularly but hadn't attended a club ladies' meeting since their trip to Cliff Island in August.

The Mt. Hood clubhouse had a fire in the fireplace, white tablecloths on the tables, potluck dishes laid out, music, and dancing. There was mistletoe at the door, and Mac kissed her when they stopped underneath to survey the room. She blushed and laughed. Then he had Ig take the casserole to the kitchen and spun her around the dance floor with their coats still on. She couldn't remember the last time she had danced or that Mac had kissed her in public.

Ig was now over 6 feet tall, taller than his father or brother, and at 15, going on 16, he noticed girls, and girls noticed him, and he spent the night dancing and eating. A letter from Sonny stated that he was on the East Coast, but he couldn't reveal his exact location. She shivered when she saw the stamp on this letter stating that a censor had read and approved it. This was real.

Bertha put her worries about Sonny aside as she caught up with the Tousleys, the Benedicts, the McWades, Mrs. Hooker, and all their old friends from Hillside Avenue and Rowe Street. She didn't notice Mac drinking more than his usual single glass of wine until Mr. T pointed it out. He has been hopping from table to table, chatting, imbibing, laughing, and having a good time. He swung Jinx Benedict, Web's younger sister, around the floor. When Jinx sat down, Gertie handed her the baby, and he took her for a spin.

Early Sunday morning, Bertha heard Mac groaning from the bathroom.

"I feel awful."

Bertha laughed.

"Stop, my head hurts when you laugh."

Ginger walked over to him, sniffed, and left the bathroom. In all their years together, she had rarely seen Mac incapacitated by drink.

PART SIX: 1945

EIGHTY-THREE

ON WEDNESDAY, January 3, they boarded the USS West Point, the world's largest cruise ship repurposed as a troop ship. On January 4, they headed down the Potomac and out to sea. Once they were at sea, they learned that their first stop would be Naples, Italy. It was good to have their assumptions confirmed.

The rough, rolling seas caused by storms slowed their trip across the Atlantic. So many men around him suffered from seasickness that Sonny joined those who weren't ill. They spent their days on deck, away from the smells and sounds of the sick men or in the mess hall. They discussed how they would handle the ship should they be asked and tried talking their way into the women's quarters. They were persistent, but the guards were firm. The women had their dining area and deck, so the chance of running into any of them was null and void, and the guards kept them at bay.

After eight rough days at sea, their ship stopped off the island of Capri. They didn't disembark, so Capri looked like a rocky, forbidding place. Not the romantic place Dad thought it should be. He hoped it wouldn't break the old man's heart when he wrote about Capri in his letter.

On Saturday, January 13, the ship docked in Naples. The men were given a few hours of free time. Many guys stuck close to the waterfront, meeting women and handing out cigarettes. He and a couple of others decided to climb Mt. Vesuvius. The climb relieved his excess energy. Sitting on the side of the mountain, contemplating the landscape, he was glad he'd climbed. Now, he'd seen Naples, Capri, and Mt. Vesuvius, all things to write home about.

Returning to the ship, they gathered their things for a nighttime trip on LCIs, short for Landing Craft Infantry, hugging the coast north to

Livorno. LCIs, bare boats with thin hulls and benches for seating, had been built to land men on beaches. He stayed on deck, which was fortunate because the diesel lines had been cut, and several of the guys below deck were covered in diesel, including Leo. Landing in Livorno after what seemed like an interminable amount of time, they marched past the Leaning Tower of Pisa to the staging area. He had always figured the Leaning Tower was a hoax, but it was real. He'd have to add this to his letter.

The 85th and the 87th had traveled on the same ship to Naples, while the 86th had shipped out earlier. They were reunited at the staging area, where they were issued mountain gear and supplies. The air was electric with the anticipation and dread of battle. They bivouacked and were issued more clothing, including mountain jackets and crampons; Sonny and Leo were issued a bazooka, Sonny was issued an M-1 rifle, and Leo a Browning Automatic Rifle, and ammunition, along with C and K rations, canteen, etc. The skis had arrived, but no poles. Snowshoes weren't good in the hilly terrain, but the crampons gripped in ice and rock. Advance parties were sent out to reconnoiter positions held by the 86th. Motor officers and mechanics were assigned throughout the unit.

While at the staging area, local families were paid to put the men in their homes. The family he stayed with had a daughter his age, homely as hell but very popular. The first night, he found that she and several of her friends were teaching Italian to soldiers. Since almost all the women they had met so far were willing to do anything, the teaching was a surprise. The family's 3-year-old son finished everyone's wine, even his father's, at dinner if you didn't drink fast enough. He laughed along with everyone else; who was he to be critical, but he told his parents he was surprised someone this young could drink so much.

Letters from home were distributed, and Sonny decided to read his before attending a dance hosted by the local families. He was surprised to find his mother writing about how wonderful Mrs. Rosenfield was. Before he wrote home, he tracked down Georgie to verify that his mother was running a 10th Mountain family group in Boston, and Georgie confirmed this.

He tried the new vMail process for his first letter home, which was designed to expedite delivery . They would take a picture of his and others' letters, put it on microfilm, send it to the US, print it out, and mail it. To be sure, he wrote a regular letter to Ig, asked him to write back, and let him know if the vMail letter arrived.

After several days at the staging area, they were trucked to their first post. His company, E, of the 85th Mountain Regiment, was in the 2nd Battalion. They set up their command post near Gavinana and patrolled the roads for enemy activity. Their orders were for reconnaissance only, no engagement unless the enemy made the first move. On his first patrol, Sonny, Leo, and eight others came across a series of abandoned buildings near the supply depot that were slowly being occupied. They had seen a young chaplain, a priest, winding through the small groups of men as they gathered their belongings and chatted with each other. When he reached their group, he said he knew they were new to the area and would soon be heading into battle. Anyone who wanted to chat before heading out was welcome to join him at the last building on the left.

"Thank you, Father. Some of us might take you up on your offer," Sonny said.

"I think I will," Georgie said.

The chaplain nodded, and they watched him walk to the last of the abandoned buildings. At the doorway, the chaplain stopped briefly, a fleeting look of surprise on his face as the front of the building erupted, and the priest was gone. They looked on in shock as groups of men rushed forward, saying they had gotten all the landmines left behind.

Two days later, E Company was set up near Campo Tizzoro, and on January 23, Sonny and Leo were part of a 12-man patrol on the road nearby. They were an observation patrol, so they had their rifles but no bazooka, looking for signs of enemy activity. Heading up a steep, rocky gulley to an abandoned farmhouse, they could hear cries coming from what sounded like a young girl. They split up and slowly approached the building, guns ready, not assuming that only one person was there. When they reached the front of the building, three Germans rushed out of the back and up the gully. Lying near the cold hearth, on her side, was a young girl, curled up on her side, moaning and unaware of them.

While Georgie and Jack checked the outside for any more Krauts, Sonny scanned the inside. Leo turned the girl onto her back, and she cried out but didn't open her eyes. She was a tiny thing, no more than 13 or 14, with a huge stomach. She cried out again, and the baby arrived on the dirt floor, squirming and crying. The girl was now quiet, barely breathing. Leo tied off the umbilical cord with the cord from his mountain jacket. Sonny made sure the baby was wrapped up tightly in a field coat he pulled from his pack. While Georgie, Jack, and the others stayed at the farmhouse, Leo and Sonny carried their bundles downhill to the medics. The medics took her and the baby to a cot and wrapped them both in blankets. Sonny grabbed his field coat, and Leo his mountain coat, and they headed back out to join Jack, Georgie, their corporal, and several others who had remained huddled inside the farmhouse waiting for the Krauts to return. When Sonny and Leo returned, they continued patrolling up the gulley. The mud of the gulley mixed with and darkened the blood on their coats.

They continued patrolling for four more days, sleeping in their bags, eating rations, and observing enemy movements, all while reporting back. On Saturday, January 27, a fresh patrol relieved them and sent them back to resupply, after which they headed out on patrols again.

EIGHTY-FOUR

"HOW MANY jobs do you have?" Larry asked. Larry was a skilled engineer, but when he was bored and stressed, he often found himself engaging in gossip.

It was February, and Mac had been in Oak Ridge more than he'd been home since Christmas. Mac put down his pencil, turned over the papers he was working on, and put both arms on his desk on top of the documents.

"You're not talking," Larry said. He had been sitting on the corner of Mac's desk, spinning a top, but now he stood, put the top down, and looked around the room.

"We can't talk about what I'm working on. What's going on?"

"I'm on the second shift tonight. Cubicles," Larry replied.

"And the young lady you've been helping. Is she not on tonight?"

"They said you were observant," Larry replied.

"She seems like a nice young woman," Mac said.

"She's sick. Been sick all week."

"Has she been checked out?" The risk of radiation poisoning was constant.

"Yes, they say it's the flu."

"Why don't you visit her and see if she needs anything."

"You know I can't go into the women's dorm."

"You're not supposed to ask me questions, but that hasn't stopped you."

"True," Larry shrugged.

"Sometimes in this life, you have to try until you get your hand slapped."

"Maybe." Larry had picked up the top and started to spin it again. "How old are your kids?"

"They're 21 and about to turn 16 in a week."

"They outgrew the top?"

"It was the favorite toy of my other son, who died young."

Larry was taken by surprise. "I'm sorry. I had no idea."

"Things happen, and we have no control over them."

"Do you miss him?"

"Every day."

"What about the other two?" Larry had his hands in his pockets and rocked back and forth. Mac wasn't sure what Larry was looking for.

"One is overseas in the army, and the other is dying to get into the fight."

"Are you worried?"

"Always. I don't think boys like them, or you, should ever look down the barrel of a gun held by someone who has been told to kill them. There's no guarantee that any of us will survive to see tomorrow."

"But what if they do the same to someone else?"

"It's happened to lots of our soldiers, kill or be killed. Not everyone will come out of this the person we were when we started."

"But few of us deserve to die."

"I wish it were less complicated. There is no perfect answer."

Larry spun the top several times, then put it down, and stood with his hands in his pockets.

"If I were your son, would you tell me to visit the girl?"

"It's better to go after the girl than wait around to see if she'll chase you. If I had waited for my wife to chase me she would be married to someone else today."

"My parents would be upset if they knew. She's not very educated, you know," said Larry.

"How much education do they think a girl you bring home should have?"

"A college education and her parents should have lots of money."

"Do you have someone to go home to?"

"Not since my girl up and married a guy who was home on leave."

"Why do you think she did that?" asked Mac.

"She understands what he does. She has no idea what I do and why I'm never home. What about your son? If he brought some girl home he met overseas?"

"If he loved her, I would be happy."

"What about your wife?"

"Bert wouldn't like someone she doesn't know marrying one of her boys."

The corners of Larry's lips twitched.

"So you think I should pursue her."

"What's the worst that could happen?"

"She might like me, and we might get married and have some kids."

Mac laughed. "Would that be so bad?"

EIGHTY-FIVE

ON MONDAY, February 5, they were sent to the back to resupply and take showers. It had been two grueling weeks of climbing, listening, reporting back, and heading out again. They ate cold C-rations and slept whenever they could, which wasn't often. At the resupply posting, they had K-rations. Not much better, but it was warm. A shower felt almost foreign at this point, but they enjoyed getting out of their dirty gear, washing themselves and their clothes, and being able to sleep in a tent.

They were encouraged to write letters home telling everyone they were doing well and that everything was just fine. While 'just fine' could be interpreted in many ways, it was the most they could say. They couldn't say where they were or what they were doing. Officers would review all the letters before being mailed. The officers walked around with letters that needed to be read stuck in their jacket pockets and any other location they could find, so it was hard to tell when their letters might get home. Sonny didn't sleep as well as he thought he would, but it felt good to take a shower, have some warm food, and read mail from home, well from Ig. He had no mail from his parents or friends.

Every unit had a mail clerk, and Leo was their mail clerk. He would distribute mail when he next saw the recipient. He, too, stuck mail in any pocket he could find, trying to keep it safe. Sonny wondered at this less-than-efficient mail system.

Two days later, they were back and patrolling. Any Krauts they saw could be taken as prisoners. Some patrols had taken in prisoners without much resistance. The 87th regiment, stationed further towards the front, was seeing action. The plans for the first battle with the enemy were underway, and the Italian Pack group joined them with their mules.

Some deserters arrived with a couple of partisans and were sent to the rear for interrogation. By Valentine's Day, most activity was geared toward the battle. They worked on small unit problems, and all equipment was checked out, including the bazookas. Any remaining mountain equipment was distributed, and they packed everything they didn't need to be put into storage.

The plans for their first battle were laid out to the men, who knew they were serious when General Hays came and talked to them. The 85th spearheaded the attack on Mt. della Torraccia, with the 87th to the left and the 86th to the right. The flanking action of the other two regiments was meant to distract the Krauts from what the 85th was doing, climbing the nearly unscalable wall to surprise the enemy. They climbed with bayonets and grenades. All other guns, weapons, and ammo were left behind lest someone was tempted to shoot and alert the enemy. Their weapons and ammo would be trucked up once they had pushed the enemy back. They were all nervous, and waiting at the bottom wasn't doing anything for their nerves.

They started to scale the wall before sunrise when there was just enough light to see. They waited, tense and silent, to climb the wall, making as little noise as possible. When they were over the top, they huddled in small groups or were cut down as mortar fire fell all around them. It never stopped, and the smoke from the mortar mixed with the morning fog made it hard to see. As the light brightened, Sonny, Leo, Georgie, and Jack stumbled over a lieutenant clutching his stomach, his jacket thrown open and his shirt burned away, his intestines hanging out. The officer pleaded with them to run him through with a bayonet. Huddled around him, not one of them was ready to kill. The officer said there was no hope that he wanted to be put out of his pain. He was loud and they did their best to muffle his sound. Sonny crouched and went through the mortar smoke to find a medic. The medics returned with Sonny, put a cloth soaked in water into the lieutenant's mouth, and carried him back to the ropes. As the smoke briefly cleared, they watched as they tied him up with this jacket covering his abdomen, and rappelled him down. Sonny, Leo, Georgie, Joey, and Jack joined others who had survived the first wave and moved forward, crouching in the early morning fog, bayonets in hand, mortars and shells falling around them.

They continued to the meetup point to collect their equipment, rifles, and ammo. The mules were loaded up with more supplies. Colonel Barlow took the lead, telling the men to move forward. When the Colonel looked back to see how many of Company E remained, he was surprised and told them to go back and get the laggards. Sonny watched as Leo and Jack were sent back, returning white-faced, to tell the colonel that the men were dead or wounded. The colonel yelled that all those men couldn't be dead. They must be cowards pretending to be dead. Leo and Jack turned back again while Sonny, Joey, Georgie, and the other crack riflemen were firing against counterattacks.

When Leo and Jack returned, they told the colonel that they checked several bodies and watched the wounded being taken back on stretchers. The men on the field were dead or too injured to move forward. When the colonel turned, yelling that they were all liars protecting their platoon mates, the usually quiet, thoughtful Leo got in the colonel's face, yelling that the men were dead, nothing and no one was going to help them now, and he, for one, would not be going back to somehow make dead men come to life. At that moment, one of the AP photographers snapped a photo of Leo and the Colonel. Sonny and Jack grabbed Leo while several officers calmed the colonel.

Their next mission was to take Mt. Della Torracia. They moved slowly, taking enemy fire and repelling counterattacks that came in waves. Trav led Company E as they pushed forward, supported by air, mortar, and units to the left and right, continuing the attack to take Mt. Della Torracia and hold it until expended.

When they experienced heavy machine gun and artillery fire and requested to withdraw behind the ridge for the night they were told to dig in, hold their positions, and call in for counterfire. In the early morning hours, Company E jumped off to take the objective they had failed to take the night before and completed their assignment easily but were soon forced back. When Colonel Barlow was called back to regimental command, his Lt. Colonel reported that the 2nd battalion was now down 400 men and needed replacements, guns, ammo, and water. He was told to hold his position, and supplies would be sent forward.

They continued moving forward for three days. On the morning of February 25, six days after scaling the wall and taking Mt. della Torracia, they were sent back to Campo Tissoro to shower and resupply. A Red Cross donut truck pulled into camp to provide coffee, donuts, cigarettes and news.

"You, the Macdonald kid from Melrose," the young woman serving coffee asked as Sonny's turn to order brought him to the front of the line.

"Yeah, who's asking?"

"I'm Debbie Bankart from Melrose. Tiny says to write your mother, she's worried about you," Debbie replied.

"How's Tiny?" Sonny asked.

"Fine, the last time I saw him," Debbie replied.

"Where are you from?"

"Lynn. When you write, tell your mother you met me and have her call my parents."

Sonny agreed to do so and wondered at his mother's network. Taking his coffee, donut, and cigarettes, he sat down to write his mother a letter, mentioning his meeting with Debbie.

"Do you know who she is?" Leo asked.

"She's a skier," Sonny replied.

"You never saw the recruiting movie she made for the 10th?"

"No, did you?"

"Yeah, they showed it to us just before they moved us to the 10th."

They headed back up to the front and were finally relieved on February 28, by the Brazilian Expeditionary Force. Company E and the rest of the 2nd Battalion wanted to take their dead off the field, but were told their dead were lying in a minefield, and had to be left in place. Sonny, not religious, silently said a prayer for the men he once stood and fought with before they returned to Campo Tissoro for rest.

EIGHTY-SIX

MAC ARRIVED at his Boston office early on a Friday morning in February. It was still dark outside, but the lights were on, and people were busy. The office was smaller now that the primary operations had relocated to Oak Ridge. However, procurement was still managed out of Boston, and the Army Corps of Engineers maintained a presence, including a full security detail.

Mac entered his office, keeping the door ajar so he could see Florence when she arrived and Miles when he came with the recent clippings. He wanted to see everything Miles had found about the 10th's assault on Riva Ridge in Italy. He also wanted to see everything that Miles had on the latest B-29 raids on Japan and the destruction of Dresden, Germany. It was hard to keep up with all the news. He'd just returned from an agonizing trip to New York, where he discussed the changes to parts needed for the K-25 plant at Oak Ridge, which was going online as he sat at his desk. Houston had accompanied him, as he usually did, and they had spent most of their time talking about the Italian campaign since they couldn't talk about anything work-related on the train.

"You're a sight for sore eyes," Florence slipped into his office, coat and galoshes still on. "Miles will be here in a few minutes."

"Are you two traveling to work together?" Mac asked, then took back the comment. "Don't answer that. I don't want to know."

"We wouldn't want you blabbing to Houston about anything other than that we ran into each other on the elevator."

"Thank you. It's best I don't know," Mac replied with a smile. "We have some things to review."

"Yes," Florence replied. "Have they agreed to find you an assistant yet?"

"In principle, but they don't have an actual person yet."

"One step forward...," Florence said. "Let me get my things off and grab a steno book."

Florence and Mac spent the morning working on a series of memos that he needed to send. He also handed her reports he had written while on the road to be typed up.

Miles arrived with a folder full of clippings. Some for him to send to Sonny, although he had no idea where Sonny was or if he would ever get mail, as well as the clippings he had requested. It was encouraging to see that the modified B-29s were finally able to hit more than a few targets on their runs from China to Japan, as they relied on those planes to drop the bombs.

When he and Miles were finished, Florence let him know that Mr. Wayman from procurement wanted to see him. He walked across the hall to Hugh's office to see what he wanted. He found Houston in the office too. Hugh showed him two resumes for assistant and Mac picked the one who had grown up in Springfield. They were both 22 and both were about to graduate from MIT, so the fact that one was local seemed to make the most sense.

EIGHTY-SEVEN

ON MARCH 2, they returned to the front and bivouacked just south of Mt. Castello. On March 5, Company E started across the ridge to Tora and was halted by enemy fire up the hill. As they backtracked down the draw, Lt. Burton was killed by enemy machine gun fire. The machine gun was wiped out, and Company E moved up the hill to their next objective. There was no time to mourn the loss; they would do that later. For now, they compartmentalized their work. Sonny and Leo found that they were using the bazooka constantly against an enemy who didn't want them to take this hill, shooting from the farmhouses at the top. As the afternoon sun dipped in the sky and the battle continued all around them, Lt. Travers had Sonny and Leo, with their bazooka, follow him around the ridge to the other side of a farmhouse.

On this side, there was tree coverage. Four Company E soldiers nodded at them and continued firing. Three Company E soldiers lay dead, including this patrol's bazooka team. Sonny and Leo put down their rifles, set up the bazooka, and aimed at the farmhouse. They adjusted their position to avoid a tree with gunfire all around. Sonny aimed the bazooka to attempt to do the most damage possible to the old stone farmhouse that had withstood everything they had thrown at it and signaled Leo to shoot. The shot took down the right front of the farmhouse. Travers yelled as the Germans in the farmhouse waved a white cloth tied to the end of the gun, stepped out, and put their weapons on the ground.

When Sonny heard movement from the bushes behind him, he made a guttural sound. Leo and Trav turned around to find several enemy soldiers climbing out of their foxhole, protected by trees and brush. As the Krauts raised their hands and threw their weapons on the ground,

Sonny grabbed his rifle and motioned them to move away from the brush. Trav kept his rifle trained on the Krauts at the farmhouse. While Jack and Joey followed Lt. Travers, Georgie joined Leo and Sonny, keeping their guns trained on the group Sonny had corralled. As Leo picked up his BAR, there was more rustling, and several more soldiers appeared through the brush, followed by more.

"What the hell," Sonny said.

"Mac, bring that group up here," Lt. Travers yelled.

As more men surrendered, it became apparent that the Krauts were in a trench of foxholes behind them the whole time. They formed a line and directed the Krauts up the hill to the farmhouse.

"What should we do with them?" Georgie asked.

"Coiro," Travers yelled at Joey. "Go down the line until you find someone with a clear line to call the Battalion command post."

Joey headed back to find anyone with a radio to communicate back to CP while they scanned the hills for snipers. This could be a trap. Everyone was jumpy, particularly since they were six men with little ammunition holding 40 Krauts, and trying to look like they knew what they are doing. When Joey returned, he let them know that they were instructed to keep the Krauts overnight, then march them to the CP in the morning. Travers looked around the farmhouse and discovered a potato cellar. "Sonny, use your German. Tell them to stay in the potato cellar."

Back when he had been cocky, Sonny had practiced his high school and College German on the guys. He stepped forward and told them they would stay in the potato cellar until sunrise. He tried not to look surprised when they followed his instructions. A couple of platoons that arrived after Joey made the call collected the German guns and gathered them into one pile, checking them for ammunition. All the guns were empty. Another platoon moved the Company E men to the side. One of the Krauts spoke to Sonny.

"What's he want, Sonny?" Travers asked.

"He wants to know if they can move their dead off the field."

"Tell him they can do that in the morning. Too dark now."

Sonny relayed the message. It was dark, and they could hear German 88s close by. None of the prisoners wanted to be shot by their own missiles, and most weren't happy with the answer.

"Lt, could I speak to you for a moment?" Eddie said to Travers. Travers nodded and followed Eddie, now a sergeant with a platoon of his own. The two returned to the group and set up a rotating guard schedule for the night. Sonny was sure that some of those who had surrendered could speak some English, so he indicated that conversation would be kept to a minimum.

The men grabbed some sleep when not on rotation and in the morning they shared some rations and cigarettes with the prisoners. Medics checked the presumed dead in the field to see if anyone had survived and needed attention. Communication lines had been reestablished during the night, and they received a call instructing them to escort the prisoners up the hill to the command post. Travers assigned Sonny and Leo to the task.

"Trav, you know we have no ammo," Leo said.

"You'll be fine. These bastards are starving, can't you tell."

"But we're still out of ammo," Leo said.

"Don't speak too loud; they might think you're scared of them."

"Ok, but. . ."

"No buts, just get going. Leave your bazooka here; it still has some ammo."

Jack stepped forward and took the bazooka.

Sonny wasn't sure this would work, but he pointed his gun and said they would head out. Leo grabbed their rucksacks and headed up the gulley to CP.

"Where should we put them?" Sonny asked the first officer he found.

"Jesus, we have no room. We're breaking down to move out. How many you got there?"

"35."

"Stay here. I need to check on this." The officer headed off to the large tent to confer with other officers.

Sonny, Leo, and the prisoners stood to one side as soldiers milled around.

"OK, you're going to divisional HQ down the road. Pick up ammo and head back up in any truck heading this way. We have five more prisoners to add to your group."

"You'll let Lt. Travers know?"

"Of course."

Sonny, Leo, and the 40 prisoners headed down the road. At division headquarters, they were instructed to proceed further down the road to Regimental Headquarters, which had the necessary resources to take the prisoners. It wasn't long before they reached Regimental HQ.

"You two are taking all the prisoners down to Division HQ."

"But what about our platoon? They're expecting us."

"As I said, head down this road, and you'll find Division HQ."

"Ah, sir, we don't have any rifle ammo."

"Don't tell them that."

They watched the back of the officer as he headed off to his next assignment.

"Is he nuts?" Leo asked.

"Of course, he's an officer."

Sonny spoke to them in his best German, which wasn't great, and told them they would be marching down the road in formation. One of the Germans repeated the orders to the men, who lined up as directed. Leo noticed one of the men reach under his jacket and pointed a BAR at the man, indicating that he should remove his hands slowly. Then he approached the man and patted him down while Sonny trained his rifle on them. Leo pulled out a gun, removed the ammo, and tossed it to one of the men milling outside the HQ tent.

They walked in single file, Leo in the front and Sonny bringing up the rear as men and vehicles passed them heading to the front. Partisans and locals lined the roadside. No words were spoken, but they seemed to say, 'Go ahead, stray off the path, we'll be waiting for you.' With partisans and soldiers on the road, they no longer felt overwhelmed. The sun was getting low as they reached Division HQ. They were relieved of the prisoners and sent to the mess tent for food.

They were surprised when General Hays entered the enlisted man's mess tent, stood, and saluted. They turned bright red when the General congratulated them on walking in with the largest number of prisoners. They stammered their thanks, unsure what to say, and got in line. It didn't matter what it was; it was hot, and they hadn't had hot food in days.

"Well, if it isn't the heroes of 85-E." Debbie Bankart, the Red Cross donut girl, joined them in the mess tent. "You guys are famous."

"Thanks," Sonny said. "Any donuts on your truck?"

"It's in for repairs, so no donuts, but here's some cigarettes for you." She handed them each two packs, a gold mine. "Don't spend it all in one place." She winked at them.

"Thanks," Leo said, stuffing the cigarettes into his pockets.

"Sorry about Hank Ramsdell. I heard he bought it on Omaha Beach," Debbie said.

"He was a good guy," Sonny replied. "I hear the Ramsdells are about to have a grandchild."

"That's great news," Debbie replied.

"There you are," an officer said to them in the mess tent. "The truck of ammo and a few replacements is ready to roll. There's mail on the truck, too."

"Replacements?" Leo and Sonny looked at one another in surprise. "Bazooka ammo, too?"

"Get out to the truck. They need you to back up the line."

Sonny and Leo grabbed their rifles and helmets, found the trucks, and jumped on board. The trek up the road was slower than if they had walked, but they weren't complaining.

"I was just about to report you two AWOL," Lt. Travers said. "Where have you been."

Between them, they told the story of their day delivering the prisoners, meeting General Hays, and returning with the ammo, mail, and a few replacements.

"I guess it's ok to tear up the paperwork," the clerk said. Then, he had the replacements follow him to get their assignments. Leo distributed mail to those near him, handed Lt. Travers the mail for those dead, and stuffed the rest in his pockets to distribute when he came across the recipient. Sonny distributed the cigarettes.

Back on the line, they spent the month holding their position and conducting reconnaissance patrols. There were skirmishes here and there, prisoners were captured, and partisans turned in prisoners. The German 88 mortars were constant, the sound becoming the backdrop of their days and nights. Trudging down the dusty road, exhausted from the blur of skirmishes and no sleep, Sonny, Leo, Georgie, Jack, and Joey barely flinched at the shell fire around them. When an 88 could be heard coming close to the two lines of men, they had no time to duck for cover. When the smoke cleared, Sonny saw all the guys standing still. The shell was a dud. It was their lucky day.

They checked farmhouses, all now abandoned, and made reports on any ammo they found to be picked up by the engineers. They set up ambush patrols to attempt to engage the enemy, but they didn't find many soldiers. Any they found, they took to headquarters for interrogation.

The men of Company E were sent to the rest area at Montecatini, an old spa town. When Sonny's turn came, he was in the group with Eddie. They took in a play with the British actress, Anabella, and saw the USO show with actual US girls and several comedians. They enjoyed a steak dinner at an authentic Italian restaurant, served by real Italian waiters. It was nice, but the food was GI food.

"Why do you keep rubbing your jaw? Everything ok?" Eddie asked.

"Sometimes I get sore when I chew too much. Must be from lack of chewing," Sonny said with a laugh.

On April 2, they were trucked back to the front, rested, showered, and entertained to the waiting war.

"Hey, you the Macdonald kid from Melrose," he heard a voice from behind him. "I have a bone to pick with you."

Sonny wanted to ignore whoever this was, but the voice was persistent. He and Georgie Rosenfield were waiting in line for some chow.

"Yeah, what makes you think I don't have a bone to pick with you."

"'Cause you don't know me. I'm Bob Lange, and I keep getting letters telling me I need to write home every week like you do."

"And what's wrong with that?" Georgie asked. "I write home whenever I can."

"That's a lot, can't you slow it down a bit. I'll never be able to keep up and you're making me look bad."

"Jeez, I'm trying to keep up with Georgie here; he writes home every day." Laughter rippled down the line.

"Both of you slow it up a bit. I need to look better to my Mom, and all she hears about is how often you two write home." Again, there was laughter. Some of the guys joked about what mother doesn't know won't hurt her. At least they were still here to write home.

EIGHTY-EIGHT

BERTHA YELLED for Ig to come down for dinner. When he finally drifted down the stairs, she took in the rash that had spread over his face, hands, and arms. She had seen scarlet fever too many times not to recognize the signs.

"How long have you been scratching?"

"Maybe since I got home," Ig replied.

She handed him two aspirin and a glass of water. "Take these and get back into bed."

"My throat hurts, I can't swallow," Ig said.

"Yes, you can; you'll feel better once you do," Bertha replied.

He choked on the aspirin and water, and she sent him back upstairs, telling him to take the calamine lotion from the bathroom and put it all over his body. She also reminded him to then put on his pajamas, and to leave his clothes on the floor. Ginger left her spot under the piano and followed Ig upstairs.

"I think I should head back now," Gran said to Bertha. "Looks like scarlet fever."

"You can't walk by yourself," Bertha said.

"I'm feeling pretty good."

"Why don't you have your medicine before you leave?" Bertha poured Gran a glass of scotch and had her sit at the dining room table. She knew her mother would savor it rather than rush through it and out the door. Her first call was to the doctor, who informed her that scarlet fever was spreading among the members of the rifle club and their families. Probably from the rifle club tournament they had participated in the previous weekend. The doctor was heading out on his evening visits and would add Ig to the list. He also suggested that everyone else leave the house. Bertha agreed and told him she wasn't sure how to get her mother home. The doctor said to keep her there until he arrived, and he would take her back to the nursing home.

Then she headed upstairs to check on Ig.

"You said to put calamine lotion all over," Ig replied through the bathroom door. She opened the bathroom door and found Ig sitting on the bathtub's edge, looking shaky. "Let's get you into your room and some pajamas."

Bertha helped him onto the bed, put on his clothes, and covered him with the blankets. She asked him if he could eat anything, and he shook his head no. Then she asked if he could have some soup, and he nodded yes.

Back downstairs, she called the store and asked Elaine to bring home any soups they had. Ig had scarlet fever and wouldn't be able to deliver groceries. Elaine told her not to worry, Mr. Garniss had hired some returning vets to deliver groceries, and she would be home with the soup.

Bertha told her mother to sip slowly. Help was on the way. Gran smiled. Next, she called Mac's office. After several rings, a secretary picked up. She explained the problem, and her call was put through to security.

"Mrs. Mac, Lou Houston here. It sounds like things are not going well," Lou said.

"No, they are not," Bertha replied. Houston always seemed to be a barrier between her and Mac.

"Has the doctor been there yet?"

Bertha saw car lights swing into the driveway through the dining room window. A car door slammed, and the doctor let himself in through the back door. He didn't bother to take off his overcoat and nodded at her as he walked to the front of the house and up the stairs.

"He just arrived. It appears that everyone in the rifle club has contracted the infection. Would you let Mac know and suggest he may not want to come home this weekend?"

"I'll let Mac know. You take care now." Houston hung up even before she could say 'thank you.'

"I do not like that man," Bertha said to no one in particular. She was going to follow the doctor up the stairs when Elaine arrived with the soup. She opened the can and poured it into a pan to warm while Elaine helped Gran with her coat. The doctor stopped in the kitchen. It was scarlet fever, and he had a limited supply of the new wonder drug, penicillin. He'd check in on Ig tomorrow and do his best to get more penicillin.

"Mrs. Robertson, let me give you a ride," the doctor said to Gran.

"That's ok, doctor, I can walk," Gran said.

"It's cold, dark, and sleeting out there. Who drove you over?"

"I walked over," Gran said.

"I'm glad you're feeling better. Maybe you can walk home on a nicer night," the doctor replied with kindness, making it sound like he was asking her permission. "You better eat some dinner, too, Mrs. Mac," he said as he escorted Gran to his car.

Bertha had some soup and then took a bowl of soup and some crackers to Ig on a tray. She didn't want to expose Elaine to scarlet fever. She woke him to eat, and he did a decent job finishing the soup. She brought the tray back down and washed the dishes, returning to Ig's room with a glass of water. She sat by his bed while Ginny jumped up and lay beside him. She put on her reading glasses and pulled out her knitting. Ig was old enough and strong enough to survive, but she and Ginny would watch him.

EIGHTY-NINE

THE DEATH of President Roosevelt and the installation of President Truman had stunned the world. Mac hoped it wasn't the start of something new, as they were close to finishing all their work on the bombs. He discovered he needn't have worried, General Groves and team had things well under control, including keeping President Truman on track, at least with the project.

Mac's new assistant, Saul, was a quick learner and had relieved a certain amount of pressure from Mac's everyday procurement life. After a week of Saul demanding attention and finding fault with everything Florence and he did, they found a way to work together. After two weeks, the three of them had settled into a routine, leaving Mac a little more time to work with the team on his latest assignment, the Little Boy uranium bomb casing.

Once the casing was complete and on its way to Tinian Island, he would feel a sense of relief. There was still work to be done, but they were closer to bringing the war to a close. Which was good, because the news on the 10th's activities in Italy was concerning. They received letters from Sonny sporadically, and the letters themselves said nothing. The army didn't want them learning anything from the actual soldiers, just the news reports. He was grateful that Miles was still in the office, pulling news stories for him to read. There was a knock on his door.

"Have a minute?" Houston said. He rarely asked.

"Of course," Mac said, turning papers on his desk over as Houston took a seat.

"Your wife just called…"

"Where's Florence? Why didn't she put Bert through?" Mac cut Houston off.

"She's stepped away for lunch or something. Maybe dinner. Anyway, Mrs. Mac wants to let you know that Ig has scarlet fever."

"Of all the things you might have said, I didn't expect this."

"I know, I thought it would be worse too," Houston replied. "Anyway, she wanted to know if you'd be home tonight. I said probably not. I don't think you should expose yourself."

Mac paused a moment and counted to ten so he didn't reach over and try to strangle Houston.

"If I were going to be exposed, it was when my middle boy had scarlet fever 15 years ago."

"Right, well, I don't think you should go home, but it's up to you."

"Yes, it is up to me and I'll be going home," Mac replied.

Houston opened his mouth as if to speak and then closed it, then said, "I'll arrange a car. How long do you think you'll be?"

"I need to call Bert, then chat with Florence and with Saul. About two hours."

Houston nodded and stepped out of Mac's office. Mac locked the papers he was working on in his office safe. He ensured that anything that needed to be burned was placed in the proper bin and had Florence notify the porter to collect the bin promptly. Then he sent Florence and Saul home to get some rest before they started again on Saturday morning.

NINETY

BACK ON the line in early April, Sonny was almost immune, walking by bodies without much thought or notice. He had seen more dead bodies, dead enemies, dead locals, and dead friends than he had any right to see. It was grueling, mind-numbing, and best not to think about too much. They were ordered to halt their advance at 1900 hours when a German counterattack commenced, and they successfully repulsed it. While the communications team fixed broken communication lines, engineers removed mines from the road. The weather turned cold, it snowed, and the Krauts were tough, as tough as nails as they defended their last bread route. More than half of Germany was occupied, and France was largely under German control. The best troops left in the Wehrmacht were protecting the food and supplies in the Po Valley, and these were the troops they were going up against.

On April 6, General Hays and Colonel Barlow gave commendations and decorations. Sonny and the team that captured 35 prisoners were commended for their actions. It was nice, but then they were back on the line. Sonny had been on the front lines for so long that he no longer remembered what it was like not being on the front lines.

On April 14, Company E jumped off just before 10 a.m. into a haze of dust provided by heavy artillery fire. They took their first hill in 30 minutes, taking enemy fire from the front and both flanks. Along the way, they captured five prisoners. The officers had them moving again, stopping and spreading out to exchange fire with the enemy. Sonny and Leo deployed their bazooka against another building. After the enemy surrendered, they moved down the hill and joined their unit to share some cigarettes before moving again.

"Sonny, Leo," Eddie barked at the two bazooka men. "You're with this team." Sonny and Leo gathered their things, nodded to the guys they would support, and followed along. He was happy to hear Eddie assign Joey to their platoon. That would keep the kid safer.

"Take care of the guys," Eddie yelled as they walked away. Sonny raised his rifle in an informal salute, then turned and smiled at his old friend.

The small platoons headed up the mountain by different paths, culminating, they hoped, with a meeting at the top. They were immune to the mortar fire all around them. They watched the guys who ducked and those who fell. Sonny and Leo crouched by a small tree as soon as rifle fire was heard. The tree provided some protection, allowing them to try to pinpoint where the shots were coming from. They used hand signals to set up the bazooka. They aimed for the area with the heaviest gunfire. The gunfire stopped, and the guys were able to move forward, and the medics moved in to handle the wounded.

Around 7 pm, they were ordered to the rear to be replaced by the 1st Battalion, who had been held in reserve. While heading back, they took more prisoners. Once they had a chance to settle down, Leo handed Joey a letter he had been carrying around. Joey opened and read the letter immediately. They never knew what the letter said because Joey jumped up, yelled, "What the hell?" and was shot in the head by a sniper. He fell on Leo, his blood and brains splattered Leo and the letter.

"Jesus Christ, Jesus Christ, I am no longer the mail clerk. Someone else can do it."

Sonny, sitting on the other side of Leo, yelled for a medic, but it was too late. Sonny, Georgie, and Jack moved Joey away from Leo. The letter Joey had opened was covered in his blood. Sonny heard himself volunteer to be the mail clerk.

During the night, new plans were made, and units were shifted. They were sent to their new location on the road towards Castel d'Aiano and replaced by the Brazil Expeditionary Forces. They moved so quickly that command posts were set up, and they soon moved again. As the day wore on, Sonny began to worry about Eddie.

"Anyone see Eddie around here?" he asked each group he passed. After each conversation, he became more concerned, and his stomach, already tied in knots, wasn't improving. Each group talked about the guys who had been killed. The survivors were beginning to feel guilty. Why were they here, and their friends were not? There was no logic to any of this. Joey, the small, wiry, and quick Italian kid who could dance like nobody's business, was gone. Jesus, he hoped nothing had happened to Eddie.

Shit, shit, shit, shit. This shouldn't be happening. Sonny sat on the ground, and a medic came by to check him out. Sonny told him that he'd not been feeling well. The medic gave him a canteen of water and told him to drink the whole thing. Sonny grumbled and swore but did as he was told. The water helped, and he found himself drifting in and out under the tree, thinking of summer in Massachusetts.

When Leo woke him, it was with news that Eddie had last been seen in a landmine area. Everyone was pretty sure he didn't make it, but it would be a while before they knew, since no one was picking up bodies in minefields. Sonny nodded and followed Leo to their next patrol.

Sonny woke up in a sweat in the back of the German truck they had found. He had no idea where he was or where they were headed. He hadn't had much food in the past few weeks. Rations were in short supply, and he hadn't been hungry. Every time he tried to chew, his teeth hurt. The guys joked that he had scurvy. A girl he'd whistled at in a town they passed through had slapped him in the face, and he'd almost fainted from the pain. This whole thing was fucked up. Too much death, too much sickness, too much poverty, too much pain.

"Yo, Mac you in there?" It was Lt. Travers. "We gotta switch to let some other guys ride."

Sonny turned his head and looked at Leo and Trav. He couldn't move his mouth to say anything. It was like his cheeks were filled with cotton.

"Jesus Christ, you look like you have mumps," Travers said. He sent Leo to find a medic. Leo returned with a nurse he had found tending some of the wounded by the side of the road. She climbed into the back of the truck and opened Sonny's mouth. Sonny screamed. A wave of nausea came over him, and he broke out in a sweat even though he felt cold. He needed to find some water. He just wanted to sleep. And maybe when he woke up, this would never have happened.

"You need to get him a doctor if you can find one. A dentist would be best. I'm going to give him morphine, but that's a bad infection; he needs penicillin," she said matter-of-factly as she injected the morphine near his jaw and wrote M on his forehead so he wasn't given a second shot too soon. If that happened, it would kill him. Sonny screamed again but soon closed his eyes. Leo and Trav looked at one another in surprise.

She jumped out of the truck. "I need to get back to the other wounded. If I see a doctor, I'll send him back here."

"We need to get some of guys some relief," Travers said.

"Unless you're carrying him, he's staying in the truck. Make sure he gets some water."

Travers explained the situation to those waiting to rest for a few miles. They saw the 'M' on his forehead and the swollen face and took their turns in the truck, doing their best to get him to drink.

When Sonny woke, he could hear 88s close by, too close for comfort. He pulled his rifle close and was out again. The guy peeled his fingers from the gun and laid it by his side.

The next time he woke, they had arrived at Battalion HQ, and Leo, Jack, Georgie, and other Company E men carried him from the truck to the medical tent under a tree. The dentist looked him over and gave him penicillin, saying to leave Sonny with him so he could keep an eye on any reactions to the morphine and penicillin. Sonny was soon out again. While Company E headed into the Po Valley, Sonny followed as a part of the medical convoy. The dentist monitored him, administering penicillin every day for seven days.

NINETY-ONE

IG'S RECOVERY had been miraculous, as far as Mac was concerned. The penicillin worked wonders. He observed Ig on the phone, chatting with Al about all the gory details of his illness. Mac was reading in his chair, and Bertha was setting the table when they saw the telegram messenger stopping at their house. Mac was out of his seat and heading for the front door as if shot from a cannon. Bertha and Ig followed. Mac's heart dropped as he took the telegram from the Army, and Bertha handed the messenger some change.

He ripped open the telegram and read it out loud. Several of the neighbors, including the Ramsdells, Gilchrists, and Holcombs, had seen the messenger and gathered on the sidewalk to hear the news. Burns was standing by his car, keeping an eye on the house.

Sonny was missing in action.

"It could be worse," Ramsdell said. "There's hope that he'll be found."

"I know, but there are pockets of resistance," Mac replied. The Ramsdells were still struggling with the loss of their oldest boy.

"We'll say a prayer for Sonny," Mr. Holcomb said.

Bertha went inside and picked up the phone.

"Who are you calling?" Mac asked, following her inside.

"Mrs. Rosie. She'll get the word out for everyone to write their sons and see if they heard or saw anything."

"I'll go into the office and see if I can get any information from the Army," Mac replied.

Mac noticed that Ig had not followed them inside. When he went back outside, Ig was sitting on the porch steps with Ginny's head in her lap. Mac squeezed his shoulder and took a seat next to him.

"Any number of things could have happened. It doesn't mean he's dead," Mac said, as much to Ig as to himself. Ig nodded.

"I should tell Al I won't be playing."

"You'll do no such thing," Bertha said. "There's nothing you can do by waiting around here."

Mac watched Ig as he reiterated Bertha's sentiment. "Your mother's right. A game will burn off some energy. I'll stop by on my way back from the office."

"That'll put the fear of God into the team," Ig said ruefully. "Last time you stopped by a game, you told us how bad we were. I think you yelled at all of us."

"Maybe I was a little harsh. I know you play for fun," Mac replied with a laugh. Sometimes he needed to blow off steam.

Ig nodded, looked at his parents, gathered his things, and headed out to join the guys.

Mac's face changed as soon as Ig was out of sight. He rarely cried, but this time, he couldn't help himself. It was too much. He was working so hard to bring the boys home, and he might not be able to get his son home. Bert put her head on his shoulder.

NINETY-TWO

SEVEN DAYS of penicillin and food had done wonders, and Sonny rejoined his group at the Villafranca Airport on April 26. From there, they boarded trucks to Lake Garda. They got off the truck in the town of Garda around 8 pm and proceeded on foot along the lake to Assenza. When they woke in the morning, they could see the Alps rising from the shores of Lake Garda. The 10th had pushed the Germans across the valley and back into the mountains ahead of all other divisions.

On April 28, the 85th moved forward to spearhead the division's attack when the Germans blew up one of the tunnels on the eastern shore of Lake Garda, disrupting their advance. Stubborn German resistance stopped their advance for two days while an enemy horse-drawn convoy was observed heading into the mountains on the lake's western coast. Artillery and air support attacked the convoy, while the 2nd Battalion remained in Malcesine.

On April 28, Mussolini and his mistress were killed in Milan by partisans. On April 29, one unit was sent across Lake Garda to seize Mussolini's villa and office. On April 30, a small group from Company E was sent to a house in the hills of Villa Gruber to investigate a report of Germans in the area. Sonny and Leo traveled with the bazooka. At the Villa, some partisans turned over nine German prisoners they had been holding in the Villa's basement. Hitler and his mistress committed suicide on April 30.

The 85th regiment was held in reserve in Malcesine and billeted in the many empty summer homes nearby. They took time to rest, clean up, and clean their rifles.

Georgie opened the letter from his mother. More than a little perplexed, he left the poker game, saying he needed to find Macdonald.

They razzed him, but they could see the concern on his face, so they let him grab his money and pull out. He walked around the different groupings of tents and men until he found Sonny outside his tent, smoking a cigar with Jack.

"What is it, Rosie?" Sonny asked.

"I have a letter from my mother ..."

"That's nice. Did they all get together again?"

"She says your parents received a telegram saying that you were missing in action and asked me to write back and tell them what happened."

"Is this a joke? What did they pay you to find me and say that?"

Georgie handed Sonny the letter to read. Sonny's brain was filled with images of his parents and Ig and the waves at the beach at Brandt's Rock. Why was that the first thing that came to mind?

"Who reported us as missing in action?" Sonny asked.

"You were reported, not us," Georgie replied, sitting on the ground next to Sonny.

"Jesus H. Christ in a rain barrel!" One of his father's favorite sayings. "I was on sick call."

Sonny strode over to the officer in charge at the E-Company command tent to give him a piece of his mind. He was yelling even before he reached the tent. He and the officer went back and forth about how to report him as missing in a telegram to his parents, when in fact he'd been with the unit the whole time.

Just as angry, the officer in charge yelled back. It would have turned into a fistfight if Georgie, Leo, and Jack hadn't stepped between them and made sure they remained separated.

"When you were released at the airport, did you check in?" the Captain asked.

"No. When I returned, we were on the move and kept moving. Everyone saw me."

"My mother dated the letter April 25 and says the telegram is dated April 25," Georgie said, looking at the letter again.

The guy with the clipboard called Battalion HQ and requested a review of the daily reports for the past two weeks to see if PFC Macdonald had been reported as unknown. He held on while the clerk checked the reports. PFC Macdonald had been reported as unknown on April 19. That report wasn't changed, so on April 25, the telegram was sent.

The Battalion commander took the phone from the clerk and asked to speak to PFC Macdonald. Sonny was handed the phone. The commander didn't apologize but said he had authorized a telegram indicating the misreporting. He would arrange for Sonny to call home in the next few days.

Sonny returned the phone to the officer in charge, who listened and nodded. Sonny stood back and apologized; his temper had gotten the better of him.

Leo, Jack, and Georgie followed Sonny to his tent.

"Your parents must be devastated," Georgie said.

"I hope no one told Gran," Sonny replied. "She's so frail."

"It seems like she's hanging in there," Jack said. "Be thankful you're alive; at least your parents aren't receiving a telegram that says you're dead, or learning that you're in a hospital with wounds so severe they can't be described, or that you've been sent for observation and are no longer competent."

Sonny nodded. All of these had happened to someone in the unit and could have happened to any one of them. Under the circumstances, the best outcome is that he's been found alive and unharmed.

A jeep pulled up as they were talking, and Tiny jumped out. He stopped short when Sonny stood up to hug his old friend.

"I got a letter from my parents asking me to find out what happened," Tiny said, tears beginning to form in his eyes. "I didn't expect to have you greet me. What the hell happened?"

"They let you take a jeep?"

"I'm at HQ now."

"Well, hell," Sonny said. "I had an infection in my jaw. I was put on a truck and given morphine and penicillin and traveled with the medics until they released me."

"How did they send a telegram to your parents?"

Sonny, Georgie, Jack, and Leo told Tiny a jumbled story, and he took in as much as he could before saying he had to head back with the jeep. As soon as Tiny left, Debbie arrived in the Red Cross truck, checking on a letter she had received from her mother. She was relieved to see him alive and well.

Jesus Christ, his mother had found a network where so many people were looking for him. He immediately wrote a letter home, explaining that he was okay, but it was a misreport. However, because all letters were censored, he couldn't say more, but he hoped to talk to them soon.

NINETY-THREE

THE NEWS about Sonny missing in action shocked everyone. Ig's friends, Al and Milt, kept telling him how anxious they were that he wasn't more upset, that he was always in motion, delivering groceries, taking care of Ginger, at a rifle club event where he was the field manager, or helping his mother and grandmother. Ig took it all in, but wanted to be busy, always moving. If he stopped, he might cry. According to the newspapers and everyone they knew, the war in Europe was on the verge of ending. It wouldn't be fair for Sonny to die now.

"Hey Ig, are you up for playing today?" Al caught up with him in the hall between classes. "A baseball game will take your mind off everything for a few hours."

"Sure, when are we playing?" Ig responded.

"Meet at the field at about 1 pm tomorrow. Milt's making calls to find a bunch of guys to play against us."

"Will the high school game be done by then?" Ig asked.

"Yep, they're playing this morning."

"Oh, shit," Ig said.

"Don't let your mother hear you. She'll wash your mouth out with soap."

"Ginger's been sick again. I'm supposed to take him to the vet this morning." No one stopped him from leaving school. He took the car home to gather Ginger and Elaine, who was not working for once. It was a quick appointment. He dropped Elaine at the nursing home and Ginger at home.

At 1 pm, the teams were gathered at the baseball field across from the high school, when Ig came running with his glove and bat.

"Hey, what gives, man? I thought you couldn't make it."

"I came to play ball. The vet appointment was quick and Ginger's back home with Mom," Ig said.

"OK, girls. You got us here. Are we going to play or what?" One of the guys from Wakefield called out.

"I see they got a team together," Ig said.

"Let's cream them," Milt replied.

The baseball field was next to a pond and a brook, so the field frequently flooded. While the rain had made the field soggy, it had not flooded, and both sides agreed it was good enough to play on. They tossed a coin to see who would start at bat. By the top of the fifth inning, they were covered in mud. Sliding into a base was the norm, whether you intended to or not. The game was good for a few laughs, attracting a small crowd of friends, neighbors, girlfriends, and folks wanting to see the idiots play in a muddy field.

"Ig." A voice called from the sidelines. They all turned to see Ig's Dad waving. Ig waved back, one foot on second base. Ig took the opportunity provided by the distraction to steal third base. A roar went up from the crowd. Ig made the turn and drove home. The catcher jumped up to grab the ball and slipped in the mud. Ig was home safe.

The game was called somewhere in the sixth inning when both teams were too muddy, waterlogged, and cold to continue. By this time, his mother, Elaine, and Ginger had joined his father, laughing while Ginger shied away from the muddy Ig.

"I came from the nursing home. Someone told her the news," Elaine said. They had done their best to keep the news about Sonny from Gran.

"I was going to stop by and tell her after the game," Bertha said, now very serious.

"News travels fast around here," Elaine said.

"Hey, Mr. Mac, thanks for not yelling at us today," Al said, greeting Ig's parents. "And for distracting everyone so Ig could steal home."

"No problem," Mac replied. "Happy to help where I can."

NINETY-FOUR

ON MAY 1, Company E was sent from Malcesine into the mountains to search houses for prisoners. They encountered many groups of partisans who reported that there were no Germans left in that area. On May 2, they were preparing to move into the mountains for another long, grueling operation against the German stronghold. There were also talks of a German surrender of all forces in Italy.

"No one's reporting any activity," the guy with the radio said.

"That's strange," Trav said.

"You should take this," the radio man said, handing the receiver to Trav. They heard him report no activity and then saw him nod a few times. Trav returned the receiver to the radioman and told him to broadcast the news for everyone to hear.

It was evening, and they listened to the surrender of the German forces in Italy. Cheers could be heard up and down the eastern shore of Lake Garda. Sonny and several of the men of Company E climbed the tower of the old building where they were being housed and rang the bell. The German General had requested to surrender directly to the 10th, stating they were the best and fiercest soldiers he had encountered. The sound of other bells being rung mixed with the noise of the cheers and shots being fired. It was good to release all this energy, but it was short-lived. Work was to be done; the war wasn't over, but they had tasted a victory.

On May 3, General Hays arrived in the early afternoon to thank the men and officers. It had been a spectacular but grueling drive out of the Apennines and across the Po Valley. The hostilities had ended, but the work of mopping up was just beginning.

"It looks like we're going to be taking prisoners. The Germans will be walking down the mountain."

"You're shittin' me. We should take them out and save ourselves the trouble."

"We will be taking 4,000 prisoners."

Trav told them that the prisoners would need to be processed, but for now, they were to accept their surrender, escort them to a holding area, and await further instructions.

"Jesus Christ, it's the corporal, and he's alive," someone yelled. The corporal had been taken prisoner on April 14 and was one of the many German prisoners released to return to their units. Men fit enough to serve were released from the hospital and joined their units. PX rations and beer were distributed to the men. Sonny started his turn as mail clerk and gathered all the mail to be distributed.

On May 4, all army units began to file into Malcesine. Everyone started regular drills, along with cleaning their equipment. All confiscated vehicles and transportation they had acquired for the trip across the Po Valley were turned over to the division ordinance officer.

They began to disarm and assemble the German Forces. Patrols were sent out to find stragglers, with German and Italian interpreters accompanying each patrol. Rumors of an unconditional surrender of all German forces were all they talked about, and late on May 7, the world heard of Germany's official surrender. While the world cheered, the men of the 10th wondered if they would go home or to the Pacific.

May 9 was designated an Allied National Holiday in commemoration of V-E Day. All training, except for necessary fatigue and guard details, was put aside, and activities such as swimming, boating, ball games, sightseeing, and relaxation were the order of the day.

After a short celebration, Sonny and some of the guys returned to the farmhouse where they were housed and sat in the kitchen talking about the guys who were no longer with them. They each had a bottle of wine or brandy that they finished.

Sonny opened a letter from his father asking him to find out what he could about Lt. Bill Callahan for his old friend, Mr. Callahan. Lt. Callahan had been in Company F. Sonny wondered if the letter had been sent before the misreporting about his being missing, but didn't hesitate to write back to let his father know that he'd find out what he could do once he got to Company F, which was protecting the German General's HQ while the prisoner processing was taking place.

NINETY-FIVE

THE WAR in Europe was officially over, and the baseball game rematch was set for Sunday afternoon. Ig was at bat and ready to hit the ball as hard and as far as he could. Not only was Sonny missing, his delivery job had been given to a returning soldier looking for work, and the rifle team was done for the season, having not made it beyond the semi-finals. He was too frustrated, confused, and angry to stay home and mope.

It was sunny and warm. The stands were filled. The ground was wet but not muddy. Elaine had stopped by on her way home from the market. She still had a cashier's job because she was supporting herself. Ig was ready for the pitch when he saw the telegram rider in the distance. The pitch whizzed by his ear, and the catcher yelled, 'strike,' but his eyes were on the telegram rider making the left turn onto Tremont Street. Everyone in the stands and players in the outfield turned to watch. Ig dropped the bat and started to run for home. Elaine followed him. He could hear yelling from the field. The telegram could have been for anyone, but he was sure it was headed for his house.

The telegram rider was tilting his cap to his mother as Ig took the front steps two at a time. The rider nodded at Ig as they passed on the stairs, picked up the bike leaning against the fence, and rode off.

"It's from the Army," his mother said, holding the unopened telegram.

"Open it," Ig said. Elaine joined them on the porch while neighbors watched from the sidewalk or in front of their houses.

"I don't know what it will say," His mother replied.

"Let me open it." Ig ripped open the telegram and scanned it.

"He's fine. It was a misreporting," Ig said, letting out his breath. His mother sat on the porch chair and put her head in her hands, sobbing.

"We need to tell Dad," Ig said. "You should call."

Bertha went inside, picked up the phone, and dialed the office. Florence answered, must have said that Mr. Macdonald wasn't able to come to the phone because his mother replied in her sternest tone that it was important, very important, too important to leave a message, and that she needed to speak to Mr. Macdonald or the security office immediately. Ig moved to stand next to her in the front hall. He heard several phone clicks followed by Lt. Houston's voice. His mother calmly and directly explained that she received a telegram. Sonny was not missing; it was misreported, and she would appreciate a call from her husband at the earliest possible opportunity. He heard Lt. Houston pause and then say he would get the message through quickly.

"How long do you think it will take?" His mother asked.

"Don't go far. I hope it will be within half an hour," Ig heard Houston reply.

Bertha waited by the phone. Ig went to the kitchen and found Elaine getting tea ready.

"I'm glad Sonny's ok," Elaine replied with a weak smile. "He's been so good to me since my sister and all. You should tell everyone outside."

Ig wanted to say something to Elaine, but he wasn't sure he had the right words. So he turned and headed for the front door, glancing at his mother as he passed her in the front hallway, waiting for the phone to ring.

Stepping onto the porch, he immediately had everyone's attention, including the baseball team, who must have followed them. He said that Sonny was okay. He was misreported as missing in action in the confusion surrounding the 10th's movements. The crowd cheered and clapped.

Mrs. Ramsdell, holding her newborn granddaughter, thanked Ig for the update. Then, she and the neighbors drifted back home while the two baseball teams headed back to the field. Ig heard the phone ring. He listened to his mother give his father the update. Dad was ecstatic.

Then she called Mrs. Rosie with the news. Mrs. Rosie would update the rest of the 10th families. She told Ig and Elaine to return to the game and take Ginger. She would walk over to the nursing home to spend time with Gran. She might not be the first person to tell Gran the good news, but she wanted to talk to her mother.

NINETY-SIX

MAC WAS at Oak Ridge when he learned that Sonny was safe. He felt his muscles relax for the first time in over a week. The worry of losing Sonny had kept him awake at night and occupied his thoughts during the day. The newspapers were filled with the exploits of the 10th, along with the death toll, which added to his fears. He got this news just as the news that the Germans in the Apennines had surrendered to General Hays. After the deaths of Mussolini and Hitler, victory in Europe was a given. It took a few more days, but on May 8, the Germans surrendered. The war's end in Europe seemed like good news, but there was still the war in the South Pacific, and that's where they wanted to send the 10th next. Mac decided to head home for the weekend. It wasn't on his schedule, but he wasn't worried.

"We need to get this show on the road. If you've forgotten your ID or your weekend pass, please exit now and arrange a ride with someone else. I want to get through the gate and on the road quickly," Larry yelled. "I don't want to get stuck behind the slow movers."

Mac dropped his suitcase into the trunk and climbed into the back seat. Four of them joined Larry in his car, heading for the Knoxville airport, making the back seat crowded.

"You know that the guards are doing their jobs," one of the guys said.

"Yeah, sure," Larry rolled his eyes. He was as ready to get out of here as any of them. This project was important, but they needed a break.

Larry was fast, but so were many others. The guards closed the gates between each car, checking all IDs and rifling through everything in the vehicle, including suitcases, before opening the gates to let a car through or turning a car back.

Larry prodded Mac to chat with the guards to see if they could pull ahead since they each had planes to catch. One guard checked Mac's ID's priority and agreed to call their car ahead. The guard scanned their IDs while Mac got back in the car. Larry pulled away so fast the door slammed shut more from the forward motion than from Mac closing the door himself.

"So, Mac, what exactly do you do? You always have the magic touch regarding the guards and administration." Larry looked at Mac in the rearview mirror.

"It's all in the way you present things," Mac said.

"You're full of crap," Larry replied.

Mac smiled, closed his eyes, and said nothing. He was tired, and his priority was getting to the Knoxville airport and getting on the plane. He hoped to have a couple of nights at home to rest and catch up on family news before returning.

NINETY-SEVEN

By the end of May, regular training, field exercises, shooting, and problems became their daily routine. Everyone had the choice of taking a short leave at Lake Maggiore or going to Venice; some of them took both leaves, but that required some haggling. Sonny chose Lake Maggiore for the swimming, something he did every day with the young women from Garda.

When he returned, the 2nd Battalion headed for the Austrian border, to keep the partisans from filling in the spaces the Germans had occupied for six years. There were no battles, just patrols, carrying arms, and encouraging the partisans to return to Yugoslavia.

Over time, Sonny managed the pain in his jaw with alcohol until that didn't work, and he was forced to line up for a sick call. He hoped they could give him penicillin and get rid of this infection. At sick call, the dentist examined his mouth, prescribed penicillin, and kept him for observation. He didn't want to tell anyone he was relieved, but said he was happy he wouldn't be returning to the castle to sleep on the damp floor in a sleeping bag. They took X-rays of Sonny's jaw when the swelling and infection went down.

"Sonny, the X-rays are back, and they don't look good," the dentist said.

"That sounds ominous."

"Your wisdom teeth are trying to come through but there's no room."

"How can I have new teeth when I'm 21?" Sonny asked. This was the same dentist who shot him up with penicillin, kept him in the hospital, and then sent him back to his unit.

"Your wisdom teeth usually come in about now. Yours are impacted and need to be removed."

"Impacted? Can't you pull them?"

"No, they're underneath your 12-year molars. They need to be cut out of your jaw."

"What?"

"The Evac Hospital has an oral surgeon who will do this."

"What if I say no?"

"The infection will get into your bloodstream and kill you."

Given all the things he survived, dying by infection seemed crazy. As he was thinking about this, Leo, Georgie, and Jack arrived with his bedroll and pack. They had packed him up and were there to send him off.

"Make sure no idiot sends a telegram home telling my parents I'm missing again," Sonny said.

"We'll do our best," Jack said with a laugh.

"Write a letter to your parents so they know where you're going," Georgie said. "I've written my mother in case anything happens."

"Where will you guys be when I get out?"

"Don't know. They're letting us do whatever we want. I'll probably never be here again, I'm going to the Riviera," Leo said.

"I'm going to Florence," Georgie said. Just then, a truck beeped the horn, and the driver yelled for Leo and Georgie. They waved back and got up to leave.

"Isn't that a truck full of dead soldiers?" Jack asked.

"Yeah, we're joining them on the way to the cemetery in Florence."

"What about you?"

"They're putting together a climbing school in Austria, that's where I'm heading."

Two orderlies arrived with a stretcher to take Sonny to the ambulance. The guys walked him to the ambulance, pretending he was getting special treatment. He would have smiled, but it hurt too much.

The trip to the Evac Hospital was bumpy and rough. He was triaged there and assigned to a bed in the pre-op ward. The doctors and the surgeon checked on him, and a nurse prepared him for surgery.

"Well, look who it is. Your problem is back with a capital B." The nurse was smiling.

"Have we met before?"

"I gave you morphine, what, two months ago? I'm surprised you lasted this long," she replied.

"They kept giving me penicillin," Sonny said.

"Probably cured you of everything you've ever had," she said.

He would have said something cute and flirtatious, but he was too sleepy. When he woke, the surgery was done, and he felt like his mouth was full of cotton, which it was. They told him it had been more challenging than they expected. His wisdom teeth were stuck in there. He had lots of stitches in his jaw, and they would keep him for a week to keep an eye on him and take the stitches out. He couldn't talk, so he nodded, and soon he was asleep again.

When he woke again, Tiny was sitting next to his bed.

"Don't talk. They say you can't talk much yet. I dropped in to see how you're doing," Tiny said.

Sonny nodded. They had removed the packing from his mouth, but his jaw felt frozen.

"Got a letter from your mother asking me to check on you. Looks like you've had quite a time."

Sonny tried to smile but ended up wincing.

"Guess I shouldn't make you laugh?" Tiny chuckled. "I'm on my way to ice climbing school in Austria. Now that it's all over, they think the Army might need to keep up with the alpine stuff."

Good idea, Sonny thought, but all he could do was nod.

"Your friend Lange will be there too."

Bob Lange, he thought. His mother wrote about Lange's parents. She'd become very friendly with them.

"Time for me to go. The transport is ready to leave. Write home and tell your mother how you're doing." Tiny said. "It's not like you have anything else to do while you wait."

Sonny rolled his eyes and Tiny laughed again.

NINETY-EIGHT

BERTHA WAS surprised to receive an invitation to a second Robertson wedding. Miriam's younger sister, Frances, who was barely 18, was getting married in a week. She called her cousin Daniel to say that she, Mac, and Ig would attend, but a trip to Worcester would be too much for Gran. She assured Dan that the penicillin had worked wonders, and Ig was recovered.

Frances had been Ig's favorite playmate when they all lived in Belmont. While Ig would have chosen to stay home and play baseball on a Saturday between the end of school and the start of his summer job, she told him he would attend the wedding. Ig had mixed feelings about this. He remembered Frances as the tomboy he played with, not a young woman. Mac's role was winding down, and he would start a new project in July or August after he finished training his replacement.

On Saturday morning, the three of them piled into the car and drove to Worcester. They greeted family members and watched as the bride walked down the aisle in a dark suit, adorned with a large spray of flowers on her lapel, a wrist corsage, and carrying a bouquet. Wedding dresses were challenging to find, and most women either wore a suit or made a dress if they could find any material. Frances and her beau decided to get married while he was home on leave, and her parents thought a church wedding would be more suitable than a civil ceremony.

Bertha enjoyed catching up with her cousins. Mac and Dan chatted about having sons in Italy. The war in Europe was over, but Sonny's unit had been chasing partisans into Yugoslavia. Dan's son, David, an army band musician, had witnessed enemy activity at the Italian front while playing for soldiers on leave and for visiting dignitaries. David and Sonny never saw one another.

Ig danced with Miriam and Frances, listening to them talk about each other and their new husbands. Miriam thought Frances was being a copycat and had married the first man who came along. Frances thought Miriam had pushed her husband into marriage against his will. He chatted with both men and felt his cousins had made interesting choices.

They each wrote Sonny wildly divergent descriptions of the wedding and reception, and he wasn't sure they had attended the same event, except they each said it was Frances' wedding.

NINETY-NINE

IT WAS hot and sticky in Oak Ridge on July 1, and he would be glad to get back home where the air might be just as warm, but it was a short drive to the ocean. His role with Tennessee Eastman was wrapping up, and he had several offers to consider next. The folks at Oak Ridge had asked him to join the permanent team. The University of California wanted him to join them and work on new projects, and Bertha wanted him to return to Stone and Webster Engineering. He had discussed the options with Bert and Ig before leaving, so they would have time to consider the possibilities. Bert was not ready to leave her mother, and Gran was still hanging on. Ig was excited about all the options.

He had sufficient knowledge of all the parts of the Y-12 complex to review and understand the final statements from all the prominent project vendors, including General Electric, Westinghouse, Chapman Valve, and even Stone and Webster, and either recommend approval of the final payments or request adjustments to the invoice to reflect the completed work. He spent his days reviewing the invoices and sending telexes to the Boston Office with either approval or a need for an adjustment. The procurement office, which had remained in Boston, would contact the vendor requesting more information or an adjustment. The project was winding down, and they wanted to wrap up as many loose ends as possible before the world became aware of the bombs.

"Mac, it's good to see you," Leo Szilard said. Leo was a scientist at Los Alamos who appeared in Oak Ridge on occasion, like almost all the scientists, looking for help or providing solutions to one problem or another.

"Great to see you, Leo. What are you doing here in the backwater?" Mac was surprised that one of the senior scientists was traveling with all the final plans in place.

"I'm checking in on some things. I'll be heading back today or tomorrow. I want to discuss a petition I'm putting together."

"Another petition?"

"Yes, I want to get this one on the President's desk. To ask him to consider not dropping the bomb on people, to use an uninhabited island to demonstrate the power of our creation."

"I thought they had already decided to drop the bomb on Japan." Mac knew that was the case. The Little Boy bomb casing was already at Tinian Island, and the final shipments of uranium and plutonium were being sent to Los Alamos the following day. He was traveling to Los Alamos in a few days to attend the Trinity test.

"Ah, so you've heard. I think there's still time to effect a change, to test and drop the bomb, just not on an inhabited city."

As much as Mac would like to see a last-minute change, he also wanted Sonny home. It was time to bring all the boys home. Leo was great to work with, but Mac wasn't inclined to have his name attached to a document going to President Truman.

"I'll get back to you. I want to think about it before I sign anything."

"Of course, we all have to make the decision that works best for us. As you know, I'm passionate about this. Oh, I'm glad to hear that your son is safe."

"Thanks. How did you know?"

"These things get around. We all like to gossip."

Mac chuckled. He had grown close to many of the scientists and engineers he had worked with over the past three years, and gossip was common.

"Think about it. I want to obtain all the signatures before the test next week. Will you be here?"

"Plan to be," Mac replied.

—

It was Sunday, July 8, he had wrapped up his assignment, packed his bags and was ready to join Larry and others in the convoy heading for the airport. Leo had been in touch more than once in the past week, and Mac had ultimately decided not to sign the petition. During the past week he'd had dinner with Helen and Hanson, breakfast with Howard Brown, met with Colonel Nichols, Ruhoff, Wally, and Dr. Lawrence, and seen Houston around.

They were part of the large convoy of trucks and vehicles taking the final shipment of uranium and plutonium to the Knoxville Airport. Of course everything was labeled to disguise what it was and where it was going. He knew that the flights were going to Texas and then being trucked to New Mexico.

Now that all the critical work was done, the project was shedding employees. He had used his free time this week to consider his next move and decided on the path of least resistance, return to Stone and Webster Engineering until a solid offer was made and he knew exactly what he would be doing. He wasn't comfortable with the offers that had vague references, such as staying at Oak Ridge to help out or go to California for unnamed testing. Bertha would be happy and who knew about Gran, who kept hanging on. He'd go home for a night or two, get his laundry done and then head to New Mexico for the bomb testing. Not his bomb, they were testing the plutonium bomb, but he wanted to be there.

"Hey, Mac, did Szilard find you?" Larry asked.

"Yep, he's persistent," Mac replied.

"It's not such a bad idea, you know?" one of the other guys said.

"I'm not sure I signed up to kill people," said another.

None of them had signed up to kill people. Creating the bomb had started as an experiment, a 'what if we could do this.' Building the machinery to separate uranium was an exercise, an experience. From a military perspective, it was a plan. If they could create a bomb and then use the bomb to end the war, they would use it. Even if it meant killing lots of civilians, how many people had been killed already? And how many more would be saved?

Since Leo asked about signing the petition, he had been struggling with his feelings on where to drop the bomb. They were going to drop the bomb, not on soldiers and not as a demonstration of power, but on cities. He wasn't sure there was any sense in protesting the dropping of the bomb because the decision had already been made.

He wanted the war to end as much as anyone, more so than some. Sonny was still in Italy, and Ig would soon be a high school senior. Once he turned 17 in February, he would want to enlist if the war was still being fought. He didn't need to lose another son, but that didn't mean he wanted to see someone else lose a son or their entire family.

"More of our boys will survive if we drop the bomb. I can't help but think that a test drop might be as effective as a drop on a city filled with innocent people," Mac replied.

"A lot of boys have already died," Larry said. "We're trying to stop more from dying."

ONE HUNDRED

TIRED AS he was, he wanted to keep an eye on his mother, who was waiting for a phone call from Dad. It sounded funny, even to his ears, but he didn't want to leave her alone. He had skipped today's baseball game and gone with Mom to church, then visited Gran before heading to work. He'd seen Lt. Houston at work but had heard nothing about his dad.

Ig turned on the radio to keep himself awake. Ginny pushed and kicked to get more comfortable beside him on the couch. The next thing he heard was a crash as the phone fell to the floor. He leaped off the couch and ran for the front hall. Mom, her head in her hands, was rocking back and forth at the telephone table.

"He's dead," was all she said.

He grabbed the phone. Had something happened to Sonny? Or cousin Les in the POW camp in Germany? One of Sonny's friends? Someone in the 10th? Maybe Tiny or Charlie? Or cousins George, John, and Rodger? or maybe Gran.

"Is this Douglas?" the unfamiliar voice on the other end asked.

"Yes, it is."

"Is your mother alright?"

"She's sitting down."

"Good. I'm sorry to say your father's dead."

Dad, his dad. Ginger had lost her best friend, and he and Mom were now on their own. It was incomprehensible.

"Are you sure?" Ig squeaked out.

There was a pause. "Yes."

"How?"

"You're working on the project?"

"Yes."

The man hesitated and then started talking about finding his father at the airport, already dead. They believed it was a heart attack. He'd seemed fine on Saturday. They had no idea what had happened.

"What time was he found?" Ig heard himself ask.

There was a long pause on the other end of the phone.

"About 5 pm."

"That's 5 hours ago."

"Mr. Hurst will be there in the morning. He'll have more information for you."

"Don't you know?" Ig yelled.

"It took them a while to alert us. It's Sunday night, and not many people were around."

That didn't make sense. The project ran 24 hours a day, seven days a week, and everyone lived in the city or nearby. There was always someone around. He felt his mother's cold fingers on his, taking the phone from him.

"Where is he now?" she asked.

Ig brought a dining room chair beside the telephone table, rubbing Ginger's ears absently. Ginger was sensitive to the tone of voice, anger, and even the general mood. She waited patiently, stoically, for the call to end.

He gathered that his father had been moved to a mortuary in Maryville, Tennessee. From there, they would send him home for burial. The funeral home in Melrose had been contacted, and a brief death notice had been sent to all the Boston papers. Mr. Hurst would arrive in the morning to help with the funeral planning. While planning first and telling them second sounded like the project, the fact that they did all this work before calling left him cold.

Ig, tears running down his cheeks, put his arms around his mother as she sat, head in hand, crying. They needed to make phone calls and start the information chain for family and friends, but right now, they could only cry.

ONE HUNDRED ONE

LARRY HAD them all in the car and was in line behind the convoy heading to the airport with the product to be shipped to Los Alamos. The final shipment was being trucked from Oak Ridge to Knoxville, then by plane to Texas, and then onto trucks from Texas to New Mexico.

Mac closed his eyes to try to catch some sleep. He hated slow traffic, always had. All those summers driving to Brant Rock and back in heavy traffic, and back and forth to various jobs, had taken all his travel patience.

His thoughts and heart turned to his boys, Sonny, Bobby Bruce, and Ig. In his mind, Bobby Bruce would always be the almost three-year-old in the knobby sweater he had been wearing when Mac had taken those last pictures of him one warm February day. He had been such a sweet, pretty boy. Would he have grown up to be the thoughtful, handsome young man his younger self promised to be? Sonny and Ig were both good kids, but they were young men on the journey to become the adults they would become. Bobby Bruce was forever young, with blond, curly hair like Bertha's and a sweet temperament. Those pictures were taken when he appeared to be on the mend after a bout of scarlet fever. A few days later, he died; a week before Ig's first birthday, he died. Bert made it to the funeral, but he had to put her in MacLean Hospital right after. In her grief, she had become a danger to herself, Sonny, and Ig—a horrible, horrible time.

"Mac, did you hear the question?" The guy next to Mac in the back seat said. "Mac, Mac, can you hear me?"

Mac turned his head slightly before he slumped down in his seat. He heard the young man with curly blond hair beside him.

"Is he asleep?" Larry asked.

He felt the young man shake him.

He loved Sonny and Ig with all his heart, but wouldn't characterize them as sweet-tempered. Sonny was a challenge on his best days, and now he was rugged, smart-mouthed, and at 21, had seen too much battle and death. He was ecstatic that Sonny was OK when so many friends would never come home. Had he been that obnoxious at that age? Probably.

Ig was too much like him; he was curious and intelligent. School came much easier to him than to Sonny. And he had too much responsibility for a 16-year-old, which was partially his fault.

Which reminded him that Gran was . . . What? He'd lost that train of thought. Someone was yelling. He tried to respond, but he couldn't get the words out. Pressure on his chest, he couldn't catch his breath. He wanted to open his eyes, but it was too hard. When he finally did, everything was blurry.

"Does he have a pulse?"

"Yep, but it's weak."

"Shit. What do we do?"

Larry stopped the car in the middle of the road, causing all the cars and trucks behind him to stop. The guys got out, all except the one cradling Mac's head in his arms. He heard more people outside the car talking rapidly but the buzzing in his ears made the words indistinguishable. He wanted to sit up. The pressure was cutting off his air. Faces became distinct and then blurry again. He could feel their hands holding him as his body squirmed. He recognized one of the security guys leaning in, checking on him.

"We can't go back. The convoy has to get to the airport."

"There are more doctors in Knoxville. Maybe we can get him to the hospital."

"OK, you guys will split off when we reach a passable road. We'll radio the others and let them know."

As the guys became blurrier, Mac focused on the young man cradling him, a smiling boy with curly blond hair. He imagined him in a sweater that was beginning to unravel at the neck, like in the last picture he took of Bobby Bruce. This boy was taller, wore a suit, and was older than 18; the age Bobby Bruce would be today. Funny, Bobby Bruce's 18th birthday was when he heard Sonny was alive. He closed his eyes. The warmth was calming.

ONE HUNDRED TWO

BERTHA, GINGER at her side, looked at the man standing next to Capt. Houston on her front porch. This man had dark hair with a smattering of gray and wore a suit rather than a uniform, but the way he stood and acted made her think he was military. He should be sweating on a hot summer day, but he was perfectly composed. On the other hand, she had swollen, red eyes and a puffy face. She hadn't slept much since the news arrived the night before and had been on the phone early and written notes to several people who were away for the summer, including Johnny.

"I assume you're the person they sent from the project." It was more of a statement than a question. She didn't doubt or question where he was from with Houston as the driver.

"I'm James Hurst. I'm sorry for your loss. We're all sorry to lose Mr. Macdonald."

"I don't know why they sent you. I'm capable of arranging his funeral," Bertha replied.

"You are more than capable. There are some specific requirements for this funeral due to the sensitivity of Mr. Macdonald's work. May I come in?"

Anger flared in Bertha, turning her face even redder. They would control his funeral in the same manner as his work life. Bertha stepped back to allow Hurst and Houston to come in. Ginger didn't move. Something was wrong here, and she would keep vigilant.

"Ginny, let the man through," Ig said, coming down the stairs, grabbing Ginny by her collar, and moving her away. Ginny looked up at Ig with sad eyes. "Good girl."

"Thank you," Hurst said. "You must be Douglas?

"Yes, I am," Ig replied.

"Why don't we sit?"

Bertha nodded. She wasn't sure what to make of this man. She and Ig took seats at the dining room table. Houston took a cup and stood while Hurst joined them at the table. "Mr. Hurst, what are you here to tell us?"

Mrs. Brown bustled out of the kitchen with a pot of coffee. She placed settings on the dining room table and poured coffee into four cups. Miraculously, Mrs. Brown had arrived that morning and made breakfast. Bertha would later learn that Mrs. Brown had seen the death notice in the paper early that morning. She had her husband drive her to Melrose and told him she'd be home when she was home. It had been almost three years, but Mrs. Brown bustled around as if she hadn't missed a day, bringing Bertha and Ig plates of eggs, toast, and bacon. Bertha would have to ask her where she found the bacon.

"Has the boy in the car had any breakfast?" Mrs. Brown asked Houston.

"No need to worry about him," Houston replied.

"That would be a no then. I'll take him some food. Someone should be gracious." Mrs. Brown left them in the dining room.

"My apologies for my directness." Hurst had been sent to handle this situation, smooth out her ruffled feathers, keep the funeral moving quickly, and keep the rules in place even when no one wanted rules. Between Sunday night and Monday morning, he had arranged a funeral home in Tennessee to take the body and prepare it for burial, arranged the funeral for Thursday. He had arranged for Reverend Wiley at The First Baptist Church and updated the death notices that would appear in all the Boston newspapers to provide the time of the service.

Hurst continued, saying that there would be no obituary in any Boston paper. They could have a small one in the local Melrose paper that could reference his wife and children, not his work. If she preferred, he would compose this for her.

"Do I have any say in this?"

"Given the sensitivity of his work, we'll discuss any requests, and see what can be done," Hurst replied.

Bertha wanted to scream and argue with this man. How could they obliterate Mac's life? She wanted to go out into the street and yell Look at me! I'm a widow, so look what they are making me do. But she knew that doing something like that would reflect on her, not them and their secrets.

"So you will arrange everything, and I'll pay for it," Bertha's anger rose to the surface.

"The project will cover the cost of the funeral and all attendance costs," Hurst said. Houston put down his coffee cup and followed Mrs. Brown to the car.

"I'd like my son to walk me down the aisle."

"Which son?"

"Sonny."

Bertha watched Mr. Hurst put down his pen and look at her thoughtfully.

"We would fly him home if we could. So far, the Army is still looking for him."

"Is he missing?" Bertha's heart beat faster. Fear flashed across her face. "Again?"

"As far as we know, he is perfectly fine, but he's not currently with his unit. The men have been given some free time to do whatever they want, and there's no information on what Sonny chose to do. If we don't find him by the end of today, I don't think we'll be able to get him home in time[SP7] ."

Bertha blinked back tears.

"It boils down to that Sonny won't be here, and Douglas cannot attend the funeral." Mr. Hurst was firm; his lips pressed together to form a thin line. His mannerisms did not reflect the pain and sadness in his eyes.

"But …," Ig didn't get very far.

"You know the rules," Hurst said, not unkindly.

"What in the world are you talking about?" Bertha said, her voice shaking. "This is his father."

"Project employees cannot attend the funeral."

"Are you out of your mind?" His mother's voice was cold, firm, and low. Something that would have chills running up and down Ig's spine, but she wasn't directing her comments to him.

"I know it's painful and doesn't make sense, but this is how it will be."

Bertha drummed her fingers on the table. Tears welled in Ig's eyes. Mac had clarified that the project took precedence, and his death didn't change that.

"How dare you say that it won't make much sense. It makes perfect sense. You are from the government, and the government is here to help me do what they want me to do."

Mr. Hurst cleared his throat. Bertha was angry, and she was furious with him.

"Mom, I think we have to go along with him," Ig jumped in.

Mrs. Brown bustled in with more coffee and cleared their plates. She didn't say anything but gave Hurst and Houston looks that said she wasn't happy with this conversation.

"Where's Mrs. R?" she asked Bertha.

"At the nursing home. I must go over and tell her before someone else does."

"I'd like to visit her too," Mrs. Brown said. "I'll walk over with you."

"She will be glad to see you."

"Is there anything else?" Hurst asked.

"I'd like to have him buried at Newton Cemetery. We're both going to be buried there."

"You have the deed?"

"Yes, I do."

"I'll need that to make the arrangements."

"What will we tell people about Douglas not being at the funeral?"

"I see in my notes that he had scarlet fever recently. We're going to say that he's had a relapse. I took the liberty of calling your doctor early this morning. He'll be here in a little while to confirm the diagnosis," Hurst said. He turned to Ig and told him to put on pajamas and get into bed.

"They gave him penicillin and he's been fine for nearly three months. Will anyone believe this?

"Will we be able to see him?" Ig asked.

Mr. Hurst hesitated. "A small group of family members may view the body."

The three of them sat at the dining room table in silence. Bertha knew that Ig would not see his father or attend the funeral.

"Now, Mrs. Macdonald, we must discuss some other details. Your uncle, Owen, will be here on Thursday for the funeral."

"What about Mabel and my brothers?"

"Mabel and Willis won't have time to get here from California. Don has work occupying him in Washington."

Bertha nodded, more tears rolling down her face and Ig placed his arm around her shoulder. Mr. Hurst moved on.

"Do you have anyone else we should check in on?"

"Will our family friends be able to attend?" Bertha asked. She wanted a fight but wasn't ready, and Mac would be upset with her if she caused a scene.

"Anyone not working on the project is welcome," Hurst replied.

"Who will escort me?" Bertha asked.

"Is there a friend of your older son who could escort you? Maybe someone in uniform?"

"There's Web," Ig said.

"No, dear, his hands. He can't hold anything yet."

Hurst thought about this for a moment. "If this young man can walk, I don't see why we can't have him be your escort."

Web would make a statement in uniform, with his hands bandaged and still healing.

"We'll call on him this afternoon. Douglas, I need you to change and get back into bed."

"I'm inside."

"Everyone will see the doctor arrive and leave. They can't see you dressed and at the dining room table."

Bertha followed Ig upstairs, waited as he changed, and got into bed. Mrs. Brown brought him a glass of water. The doctor arrived soon after and declared Ig to be in a relapse. He winked at Ig. He expressed his condolences to Bertha and said he would see her at the funeral.

Bertha escorted the doctor downstairs, making it look like Ig was seriously ill. He put on his hat and was out the back door before Mr. Hurst could say anything. Elaine arrived with a delivery of food and took Ginger for a walk. Bertha knew she would head for the nursing home. Her mother most likely had heard the news. Ginger reluctantly allowed herself to be led outside.

Next, they addressed what Bertha would wear. She had lost weight, and her old black dress was too large. Mr. Hurst assessed her size and made a phone call to have a couple of new black dresses delivered to the house. Against her will, she was impressed that Hurst could find a new dress and have it delivered with a simple phone call.

—

Bertha, dressed in black, with a black hat and small black veil, black stockings, and black shoes, a black purse in her black-gloved hands, sat on the edge of her bed, unable to go downstairs. Downstairs was the world without Mac. Upstairs, she could hope it was all a mistake. Her world forever changed; she viewed this world through the lens of permanent, irretrievable loss.

She listened to the sounds of quiet activity floating up the stairs. A car door opened and closed, followed by footsteps on the front steps. They weren't Mac's. It felt like she could hear everything that was happening. The front door had opened and closed, and the voices and activity shifted as the people downstairs left for the church. There were more footfalls on the stairs, and the screen door opened and closed again. Someone came upstairs, pausing at the bedroom door. Then, Uncle Owen sat on the edge of the bed next to her. He took her hand in his, and there were tears in his eyes.

"It's time, Bertie," he said.

Bertha nodded. She understood, but she wasn't ready to leave. It was safe here. She could be alone with her thoughts here. A hollow version of Mac would be at the church. Neither of her sons nor any of her siblings would be there. Tears spilled from her eyes.

"Your mother's in the car with Beatrice." Uncle Owen patted her hand.

"Is he still here?"

"Yes, he's running the show. He's arguing with Mrs. Brown in the kitchen."

"I'm glad she's here. She'll make sure everything runs smoothly." Bertha sighed. She was about to bury her husband, and there was no way to talk to Mac about it. Or, to persuade or convince someone that this was wrong, they had to take it back. It was going to happen.

"Is Ig downstairs?"

"Ig's been told to stay in bed, that he's too sick to get up."

"This whole thing is a godawful mess," Bertha said.

"I know." Uncle Owen's voice was quiet again, not showing an impatience to get moving.

"How long have you been here?" Bertha asked.

"A couple of hours now."

"I don't think I've thanked you yet."

"There's no need to thank me. It is the least I can do." Her mother's younger half-brother had always been kind. "Shall we go?"

Bertha stood, smoothed her dress, checked to make sure that she had everything, and walked to the door. She paused, then carefully stepped into the hallway. Owen followed silently. Ig was in the hallway, tears in his eyes as he wordlessly hugged his mother. Owen reassuringly placed a hand on Ig's shoulder and squeezed it. Ig smiled and quietly returned to his bedroom. To deny a 16-year-old boy the right to attend his own father's funeral was a horrific thing, but Mr. Hurst would brook no argument from anyone on this point.

Owen followed Bertha as she slowly made her way down the stairs. Hurst was at the bottom of the stairs, checking his watch. Ginger moved before Hurst to meet her, and Bertha stooped to hug the dog. Mrs. Brown hugged her.

"Will you be at the church?"

"Her youngest is on the project," Hurst said.

Bertha nodded. That was a surprising bit of news.

"I'll be here to make sure everything is ready, and Ig is fed," Mrs. Brown said, tears in her eyes. "Mr. Brown sends his condolences."

Uncle Owen escorted her out of the house, followed by Hurst. Bertha got into the car with Beatrice and Gran. Owen sat up front with the driver. Hurst closed the door and stood back.

"I don't know what this 'project' is all about, but to send this man to 'help' is, as far as I can see, not helpful."

It was a short drive from the house to the First Baptist Church on Main Street. She presented a calm, brave, almost friendly face to the friends and family gathered in the church for the service. Web, looking solemn, walked her down the aisle after Uncle Owen, Gran, and Beatrice were seated. Mr. Hurst kept a watchful eye from the back of the church.

Mac received a full sermon from Reverend Wiley, who did and said what he felt was right rather than follow the instructions to keep it short. He noted the absence of Mac's sons and discussed the toll this war took on so many families. Hurst was looking more stern than usual.

Uncle Owen stood and read the eulogy that Hurst had approved, talking about Mac, his family, and the need for family at these sad times. He noted that the family would not be gathering at the house after the funeral due to scarlet fever and that graveside services would follow at Newton Cemetery.

After everyone had spoken and the songs had been sung, the minister, followed by Bertha and Web, then Owen, Gran, and Beatrice, led the congregation out of the church. The casket was loaded into the hearse, then the flowers. Bertha greeted those who had attended the funeral and lingered to talk. She was gracious and kind and pointedly ignored Mr. Hurst's looking at his watch. Owen and Beatrice returned Gran to the nursing home. She had gotten through the funeral to the receiving line but would sleep for a week. She promised to take her mother to the cemetery at the first opportunity.

Bertha noticed Houston get out of a parked car. They exchanged subtle nods. He and Mac had spent much time together, but he, too, had been barred from the service. She had many questions for Houston and suspected she would never see him again. Hurst nodded to Houston, who returned to the car. When everyone had been moved to their cars, some to head home and others to join her at the cemetery, Web and Gertie led Bertha to the vehicle. She watched Houston's car pull away from the curb.

The hearse and the cars that followed did not stop for a prayer service at the chapel but continued to the back of the cemetery to the gravesite where Mac would be buried with Big Aunt Bertha. Bertha had been named after her aunt, who had never married. Reverend Wiley said a few words; there were flowers to be placed on the coffin, and those who came to the cemetery said their final goodbyes to Mac.

ONE HUNDRED THREE

SONNY STOOD in the chow line, waiting for his turn. It had been a long day delivering the company mail, and he didn't care what they served as long as it was hot. Ice climbing had brought his appetite back. His turn came, and he took whatever they served up. Rumors about whether they would be heading home or heading to the South Pacific were being traded like baseball cards. But what else would you do when all you had to do was wait?

"Hey, Sonny, I need to look better to my mom. All she hears from your mom is that you are such a good boy. I'll have to write and tell them what you're like," Bob Lange yelled. Laughter rippled through the line. Even Sonny smiled. Some guys joked about what mothers don't know won't hurt them. Others encouraged Lange to write home and tell everyone what Sonny, or any of them, was like. At least they were still here to write home.

He took a table with Jack and some others from the 85th. They were laughing and joking, hoping to organize a poker game. A game, good company, some treats from home, and a few beers were all he was looking for now.

The buzz of conversation in the tent changed. They looked around to see a Red Cross guy showing a telegram and looking for someone. They watched with curiosity to see where the Red Cross guy headed. The closer the Red Cross guy got, the quieter the tables got. When he passed a table, conversation picked up again. They wondered who it could be for and what it was about. It wasn't long before it became apparent that they were looking for him. It must be about Gran, he thought.

"Jeez, Macdonald, now it's telegrams. What will be next?" he heard Lange say, and he was dying to punch him out.

"Shut up, Lange. At least it's not for you," Jack said.

"Donald Macdonald Jr.?" the Red Cross man asked.

Sonny nodded. A lump in his throat. Some of the guys got up, and one or two others moved over to make room for the Red Cross guy.

"I have a telegram for you."

"Is it about my grandmother?"

"No, I'm afraid it's about your father."

"Dad?" Jesus, now what?

"I'm sorry to say he died on July 8."

"Died?! Where, how?" Tears popped into his eyes. "That's more than a week ago!"

"It says here it was at the Knoxville airport. I'm sorry, I don't have any more details. I'm sure a letter will arrive soon."

Sonny nodded. Words failed him, and with his throat closing, he found it was too hard to speak without revealing his emotions. Not another one, he thought. How could it be Dad?

Another rustle at the door to the mess tent caused them to look up. It was the chaplain.

"I have some letters I've been keeping for you," the chaplain briefly touched his shoulder. "My sincerest condolences. Come by the tent if you need anything." The chaplain was gone as quickly as he'd arrived. There were other letters and other bad news for him to deliver.

The letter from Elaine was lighter than his mother's, so he read that one first. It offered condolences on his father's death and his father's obituary from the Melrose Free Press.

Then he opened his mother's and parsed through the contents. It couldn't have been easy writing this to him. He got up from the table and headed to his barracks. He needed to write back to his mother and Ig. Lange and Jack followed him. They didn't want him to do anything foolish.

ONE HUNDRED FOUR

BERTHA TURNED over the paper with the figures she was working with to understand how she and Ig would survive without Mac's income and no pension. It was hard to focus on the income when she struggled with being angry at Mac for leaving and then mourning when she thought about how she would never see him again.

Mabel sat in the living room, reading the paper and listening to the news. She had arrived by train about two weeks after Mac's death. The failed attempt by plane had made her nervous about flying. She had told Willis to wait until Gran's funeral. The doctor anticipated Gran wouldn't be able to hold on much longer, but the doctor had been saying this for a year, and Gran seemed quite happy at the nursing home.

Mrs. Brown, who had continued to take care of her for the weeks after the funeral, came into the dining room with her bag over her arm.

"Well, Mrs. Mac, I'll be off. You'll be alright?" She had been a big help to Bertha's adjustment to her new life. Not that she had adjusted in such a short time, but she had at least come to an acceptance of how things were, much as she had accepted Mac's mysterious schedule, Sonny's army service in Italy, and Ig's secrecy.

"I'll be fine. My sister's here now, and Elaine and Ig are here," Bertha replied. "I hope you and your family have a wonderful vacation."

"We will. Even Howard will be able to join us," Mrs. Brown said. "Howard will forever be grateful for everything Mr. Mac did for him."

"I'm glad that Mr. Mac was able to help." Bertha had no idea what Mac had done for Howard beyond writing a recommendation for him, but Howard had benefited, and Mac had mentioned him a few times.

"Did you hear that?" Mabel said, turning up the radio. "They say they've dropped a bomb in Japan."

"Really?" Bertha replied.

"Listen," Mabel replied. With the volume turned up, they could hear the radio announcer say that a bomb, with the power of 20,000 pounds of TNT, had been dropped on Hiroshima earlier that morning, a port city in Japan.

"Where is Hiroshima?" Mabel asked.

"Ig will know," Mrs. Brown replied.

"He's at work," Bertha said. Ig had returned to work a week after his father's funeral. She wasn't sure what he felt about not being able to attend his father's funeral, but he needed to keep busy and be around people who had known him. She didn't have that option, and she sometimes resented the ease with which he fell in with those people.

The radio broadcast went on talking about this bomb, the super-secret project with Britain and Canada, as well as the construction of some secret cities to help build the bomb.

Mrs. Brown said she needed to catch the train, and Bertha thanked her again for all her help, asking her to keep in touch. Mabel answered the ringing telephone, and Bertha went to answer the ringing front doorbell. Bertha opened the screen to the front porch to find Mrs. Ramsdell carrying her granddaughter and Mr. Holcomb. Mabel announced that Willis was on the phone. Bertha greeted her neighbors, and Mabel nodded. As soon as she hung up, the phone rang again.

"Have you heard the radio reports?" Mrs. Ramsdell said. "The war's over, and the boys can come home. And Mr. Ramsdell can talk to you." Tears were streaming down Mrs. Ramsdell's face.

"I'm sure Gary will be heading home soon. How is your daughter-in-law?"

"She's at work, she'll be so relieved."

Bertha wondered if her daughter-in-law would be relieved. The war might be over, but Hank Ramsdell would never be coming home, and this little girl would never meet her uncle. Who knew what her father had seen in the South China Seas.

"Jimmy is fine, too," Mr. Holcomb said.

"I'm glad he's doing well. Of course, he never went overseas, so his danger was less," Mrs. Ramsdell said.

"There were dangers here, you know," Mr. Holcomb said defensively.

"I know." Bertha wanted to scream at this man who had spent so much time questioning everything Mac and Sonny did.

"Of course there were. Look what happened to Mac," Mabel said, stepping onto the porch. Mabel was intimidating at 6 feet tall in low heels, with a stern demeanor.

"Yes, of course. I mean, well, I want to say that I always knew Mac was working on something important," Mr. Holcomb stuttered.

The three women were at a loss for words. Mr. Holcomb had complained about Mac and his travels so long that no response immediately came to mind. The phone rang again.

"Where is Mrs. Brown? Shouldn't she be answering the phone?" Mr. Holcomb said.

"She's left for her vacation," Bertha said. Mrs. Brown would not be coming back, but Mr. Holcomb didn't need to know.

"I think you should answer it. Everyone will want to talk to you," Mabel said.

ONE HUNDRED FIVE

SONNY WAS stunned when the Red Cross and the chaplain told him it would take longer to apply for compassionate leave and wait for a response than to wait for the 10th to be sent home. It seemed ridiculous, but the company clerk said the same thing: waiting for a response with so much paperwork moving around was not recommended. Things were happening that had nothing to do with logic or order.

He wrote to his mother and Ig to tell them he would be home as soon as possible but didn't have a departure date. This was after writing home as soon as he received the news of his father's death. Then, he called home when the Red Cross could arrange the call. It wasn't a great connection, but he had heard their voices, and they had heard his.

As preparations were underway to send them home, they gathered in Florence, Italy. After checking in, they were given the job of burning the duffle bags and clothing of those who died and were buried at the Florence American Cemetery. A trench was dug and filled with gasoline, and they pulled the clothes from the duffle bag. The local Italians had been so long without that they risked being burned, diving and fighting for the clothes and the duffle bags. They even pulled half-burned clothes from the fire. They would see people cut a hole for the head and two holes for the arms and use the drawstring opening for the legs, creating a makeshift dress or top with the soldier's name stenciled on the back.

Officers ordered them to pull the clothing back, but they couldn't. In Yugoslavia, they donated their mules to the Yugoslavian government rather than destroy them as ordered. Why kill them when they could be used? Of course, those were the mules that hadn't been given to or taken by the local population. The people had not seen new clothing since before the war and the American clothes and duffle bags were made of solid, sturdy cloth that was hard to take back and burn. It would be a waste of something that could be used. When the army threw out food after a meal, the locals would take it to eat, no matter how bad. What appeared to be waste to the soldiers was manna to the locals.

On July 30, they were trucked from Florence to Naples, much as they had been sent from Naples to Florence six and a half months earlier, and put on a boat home. Sonny thought he was going to see Pompei for a second time, but in the end, that didn't happen. They boarded a ship and joined a large group of boats that crossed the Atlantic to New York. This time, there were no drills or army training. It was a pleasant ride home. Like all the guys, he traded stories of his exploits. Unlike many of them, he thought about his father. It was hard to believe he would never see his father again.

"Hey, did you hear that?" Georgie asked Sonny. They were relaxing on deck.

"What?" Sonny replied. He'd been reading a book he'd found—one of the cheap paperbacks they'd printed and distributed to soldiers.

"They'll play it again," Jack said.

"Sixteen hours ago, an American airplane dropped one bomb on Hiroshima, an important Japanese Army base. That bomb had more power than 20,000 tons of T.N.T. It had more than two thousand times the blast power of the British "Grand Slam," which is the largest bomb ever yet used in the history of warfare.

The Japanese began the war from the air at Pearl Harbor. They have been repaid many fold. And the end is not yet. With this bomb, we have now added a new and revolutionary increase in destruction to supplement the growing power of our armed forces. In their present form, these bombs are now in production, and even more powerful forms are in development.

It is an atomic bomb. It is a harnessing of the basic power of the universe. The force from which the sun draws its power has been loosed against those who brought war to the Far East."

It was President Truman's announcement to the world. The radio announcement continued to play, discussing this super-secret project, the secret cities, and the future of atomic power. Sonny listened to every word.

"Is that the project your dad worked on?"

"Yes," Sonny said. The tears in his eyes threatened to spill over onto the cheap paper in the book as he thought about his father telling him about B-29s and bombs.

When the Japanese didn't surrender, a second bomb was dropped on Nagasaki on August 9. Sonny spent as much time on deck as possible. Once they landed at Camp Shanks and were served a steak dinner, Sonny boarded a troop train for Boston. He had thirty days' leave before he was to report back, this time to Camp Carson in Colorado.

ONE HUNDRED SIX

IG, GINGER trailing behind him, trudged up the front stairs, after a long day of sorting and reviewing files, putting more documents in the to-be-incinerated than in the Trash bins. Between sorting assignments, he'd made deliveries to the senior army engineer and returned with stuff to be added to the bins. The Army engineers would be reassigned to new projects in a few weeks. In the car, between runs, he and Sgt. Burns heard the news that Emperor Hirohito had finally agreed to surrender. It was August 15, six days after the second bomb had been dropped.

He opened the screen door and heard Sonny, Mom, and Aunt Mabel yell, "Surprise." Ginger jumped up and down. His brother grabbed and hugged him, and he began to cry. He hadn't cried much since the call came through about Dad's death.

"Did you hear the news?" Ig asked.

"What?" Sonny said.

"The emperor agreed to surrender."

"Well, I guess the work Dad did was successful," Sonny said.

"Don't you talk about it," Bertha said. "I haven't cried since the funeral, and I won't start now." Ig could see tears in her eyes and the stunned look on Sonny's face.

Over the next few days, they discussed the war, Dad, the future, money, and how they would manage to survive. During the day, everything seemed normal. The first night, Ig found Sonny patrolling with Ig's rifle. Sonny pointed the gun at him when Ig asked him what he was doing. Sonny said he needed to keep the area safe.

Ig kept his worries about his brother's state of mind to himself and made coffee. When the coffee was ready, Ig found Sonny asleep at the dining room table. He took the gun and put it in his bedroom closet.

"What are you doing?" Ig asked Sonny, who was rummaging through his closet.

"I need the rifle," Sonny replied.

Ig was up early the next morning. While Sonny slept, he took his rifle ammo to Mr. Ramsdell and asked him to keep it hidden. Mr. Ramsdell looked concerned but agreed. After that, Sonny slept with the gun by his side, and Ig felt safer with no ammo in the house.

The doctor stopped by to chat with Sonny. He told Mom that Sonny needed some normalcy to start feeling secure. After a week, Sonny stopped patrolling at night and could sit still for more than a few minutes during the day.

ONE HUNDRED SEVEN

IG CAME downstairs to find Mom and Sonny having breakfast. The paper was hanging over the dining room chair as Dad preferred.

"You need to visit him," Bertha said to Sonny. "Mr. Callahan wants to know how his son died."

"I wrote Dad all the details."

"I'm not sure Dad and Mr. Callahan talked. He keeps calling. He wants to hear about it from you."

"Why do I need to relive something that's already happened?"

"He's an old friend of your father's, and he's been good to us since… last month." Bertha avoided saying the word funeral.

They had all seen the articles about the boys coming home from war and that they might be louder or quieter than they were before they left. They might have vivid dreams about the war. The newspaper descriptions made it sound better than it was. One minute, Sonny was laughing maniacally at the most mundane thing, and the next, he was yelling and swearing.

Mr. and Mrs. Callahan, who had lost their son while he was serving in the 10th in F-85, had reached out when Mac died, sending flowers and condolences, and attended the funeral.

Sonny nodded. "Ig, what are you doing today?"

"Working."

Sonny rolled his eyes. "Don't they know it's all over? The bombs work."

"Ig handles things better when he's occupied," Bertha said.

"Don't we all."

"Did you read the memos that Douglas brought home?" Bertha asked Sonny while Ig finished his breakfast.

No one had told her directly that Mac had been working on what they now called the Manhattan Project, but the two memos Ig had brought home, plus the book, called it the Manhattan Project. After all the secrecy, security, and the telegram from General Groves, she now knew what the super-secret project was called. It didn't make the horror of the bomb easier to handle.

"Are you supposed to bring things like that home?" Sonny asked Ig.

"I think they were supposed to be collected at work," Ig replied.

Bertha had been horrified when Ig had borrowed the plans, afraid he'd have a black mark on his future. Now, she was proud of him for taking the memos.

"How are negotiations going with Stone and Webster?"

"They're passing the buck around with Tennessee Eastman."

"Are you pressuring them?"

"Would you expect anything less from me?"

"Of course not." They both smiled at this. "I'm still stinging from the whole bell [SP9] incident."

"I got you off the hook, didn't I?"

"You interfered in our fun. No one knew it was us."

"Everyone knew it was you. If I hadn't arranged for the bell to be 'found,' You and Mildram would both have records now. The Boston & Maine has a long arm."

"I know. I worked for them."

"Is that something you might like to do again?"

"I'd love to. First, I have to get discharged, then finish college. After that, who knows?" Sonny shrugged. "I guess I can go see Callahan. He might not want all the real details."

Bertha felt grateful. [SP10]

"After you talk to him, you can pick up Johnny's nephew. Johnny and her family are looking forward to seeing you both."

"What about Ig?" Sonny's memory was like a sieve.

"I'm working. I'll take a ride into Boston with you."

Bertha had called Johnny's family, who were staying at Chatham on Cape Cod, to invite Sonny for a weekend. They had agreed that having

Sonny away for a weekend would be a relief. Bobby MacLean wanted to go, too, and Bertha thought that having 13-year-old Bobby in the car would encourage Sonny to drive carefully.

———

Sonny drove from Melrose to downtown Boston as if his foot were made of lead; his two speeds were fast or stopped. Given the current state of affairs, he doubted that there would be a new car in the family's future. He wished his mother would stop asking him about their finances. It was all too confusing. He wasn't sleeping, and eating was something he only did occasionally. He wasn't sure how to tell his mother he couldn't handle being home full-time. And he was sure he wouldn't be the man of the house, no matter what Mom thought. He needed to return and complete his term until he was demobilized, or demobbed as everyone referred to the effort to release soldiers from service based on the point system. Ig had a better handle on the bills and the money and knew how to balance a checkbook. Plus, Elaine got a discount at the Market. Elaine was putting off college until December, which was good for Mom.

He grabbed the first parking space he saw, pulling in front of someone who was going too slow. The driver honked and yelled, but he didn't care. He didn't hear much except the exploding in his head. Gunfire, shells, and mortar splattering the mud, blood, and guts all around were his constant companions.

Ig jumped out of the passenger seat and joined him on the sidewalk outside the Old Howard.

"Ever been inside?" Sonny asked.

"Yep," Ig replied.

"Fancy going in now?"

"I've got to get to work, and you should talk to Mr. Callahan before he calls Mom again."

"Dad caught me here once. We skipped school and came here to see strippers. When the lights came up, Dad saw us. It was like someone had called Dad and told him we were here. He lectured me about skipping school."

"I remember."

When Dad told Mom what he had done, he accused his dad of being there too. His mother hadn't batted an eye. He thought this revelation would turn his mother to his side but guessed wrong. Mom agreed with Dad, and he was grounded. That was the first time he realized that his mother knew about Dad's habits.

"I guess I'll go see Mr. Callahan."

"See you when you get back," Ig said, heading to work.

Mom was unhappy that her last picture of Dad was taken in his office and had a girlie calendar in the background. It was a pretty tame girlie calendar, and she didn't condemn Dad for it; she just lamented its presence.

Going into the Old Howard would be easier than talking to Mr. Callahan. If he skipped Callahan, Mom would get another call. He turned away from the Old Howard and headed up the hill.

"You must be Mr. Macdonald?" the pretty young secretary said. He hadn't even had a chance to say hello. "Mr. Callahan's been waiting for you. It's very nice of you to do this."

"That's Private Macdonald."

"Of course, my apologies."

"And you are?"

"Mrs. Right," she replied.

Of course, Sonny thought. He saw the wedding band on her finger and smiled as she came around the desk. That's probably spelled 'Wright,' but she looked right at him.

She opened one-half of the large, double wooden doors, announced him, then waved him in and closed the door behind him.

"Thank you for coming in to see me, Sonny." Mr. Callahan stood and shook his hand. Sonny could see that he'd been crying.

"Of course, Mr. Callahan."

"How's your mother doing?"

"Oh, you know, some days are better than others. She's, um, not like she was before."

"I can understand that. Neither Sally nor I are the way we were before."

"I understand you and my dad were friends," Sonny said.

"Yes, we were. We knew your mother too. We've been in touch off and on, oh, for 25 years. I got to know your dad when he was with French and Stewart. That was a long time ago."

"Back when he was a surveyor."

"That's right."

"I'm not sure that I remember you."

"You were pretty young the last time we met. It was around the time your brother died."

That comment made Sonny start. They never talked about Bobby Bruce. He'd forgotten that time as best as he could.

"Lots of people were coming and going then."

"Yes, your mother. She needed help, and she needed quiet. We helped where we could. We used to take Douglas occasionally to give him time to play with other kids."

"I see."

"Now that we have that out of the way, I want to talk to you about my Bill." Sonny could see the tears welling up in the man's eyes. "He was a good boy. I don't understand why he died?"

From what the guys in Company F had told him, Lt. Callahan had been a good egg if a little too sure that he was invincible. They all thought they were unstoppable in that first battle, and many of them had died. Sonny didn't remember meeting Lt. Callahan but had seen many officers, new and old, go down. Some were too aggressive, some were unlucky, and some were both. He was sure he should be dead now. Maybe he survived because his father died. He had no idea how these things worked. Was it karma or something like that? He'd have to think about that when he had a chance.

"It was all very fast, sir. My company, E, moved forward and captured one hill and one bunch of Krauts. His Company, F, was in reserve. Once we had captured that hill, Company F started to move forward. Another bunch of Krauts opened fire. He and a sergeant were in the lead, and they were hit. It all happened so fast."

"And you saw this happen?"

"I didn't know who he was at the time. My partner and I, bazooka men, were on the hill looking back when we heard shots."

"Do you know, did he suffer? I know they said it was instantaneous, but it's the army. Don't they always say it's instantaneous?"

"It was quick. I don't think he knew what happened."

Except that he did know, and it wasn't instantaneous. From his perch on the hill, he'd seen Lt. Callahan and the sergeant rise from the crouch and move forward. A sniper hit Lt. Callahan in the throat. Sonny had watched as his back arched, blood spurted out, and he struggled to breathe. Then he fell and clutched his throat. The sergeant took it in the thigh; it hit the artery, and he bled out before a medic could get there.

The hills were treacherous, steep, and rocky. That's why the Krauts had held out so long; they had the cover and the advantage of knowing the hills better than anyone except the locals and the partisans. Thank god they had had the partisans. And there were always more Krauts. It was slow going from hill to hill. You could never tell when they would surrender or when a sniper would shoot.

"My boy."

Sonny was roused from his reverie.

"If he'd held on a couple more weeks. He'd be home now."

Sonny wanted to say that that wasn't necessarily true. His son could have survived that battle and then stepped on a land mine, like Eddie, or been shot by a different sniper on a different hill. The more he thought about it, the more he felt the randomness of life and death. Anything could happen, and it usually did. Mr. Callahan didn't look like he could handle his dark philosophy.

"You never know what's going to happen."

"But you came home. I understand that you were missing in action for a while."

"Well, sir, that's a funny story. My wisdom teeth decided it was time to come in. They got infected, and I was given some morphine, thrown on a truck, and then kept in a hospital tent while they waited to see how the penicillin worked. When I returned to my unit, no one remembered they'd listed me as unknown. When a letter arrived asking one of my platoon mates what had happened to me, he was sitting near me, and that's how I found out I'd been reported missing. Funny because I was the mail clerk who handed him the letter."

Both Sonny and Mr. Callahan chuckled.

"Your father was distraught at the time," Mr. Callahan said.

"I'm glad he knew I was ok before, you know…"

ONE HUNDRED EIGHT

THE SIZE and heft of the package told Bertha it was a book. She wondered if Mac had ordered a book for her, possibly for their anniversary. She wasn't sure she wanted to open it. Maybe she would keep it forever wrapped, to wonder but not look.

"Aren't you going to open it?" Ig asked.

"Maybe I want to keep it a secret, a surprise, and open it when I'm ready. Maybe it's from your father?"

Ig picked up the package and looked it over, inspecting the return address, hefting it for weight, and looking at all sides. "I don't think it's from Dad. A bunch of guys at work got a similar package."

"What is it?"

"Maybe you should open it and find out," Ig replied.

"I'm with Ig; I think you should open it," Sonny said. He had returned from his conversation with Mr. Callahan and his weekend at the Cape.

"So you think it's something from his work?"

"Yeah, I think so," Ig replied.

"What are you waiting for," Sonny said. She could feel his anxiety, as if he wanted to take it out of her hands and rip it open.

She let it sit on her knees for a few minutes before opening it. And, indeed, it was a book, Atomic Energy for Military Purposes.

"Why in the world would I want to read this?"

"Is Dad's name in it?" Sonny asked.

"I doubt it. I hear it named the scientists, and only the senior ones at that. No engineers," Ig said, looking through the book. "Look, it's signed by General Groves, Enrico Fermi, Ernest Lawrence, and a bunch of others."

Bertha placed the book on the dining room table and headed to the kitchen to make dinner. Ginger followed her, loyal to the one who might feed her.

"I don't think she's very impressed," Sonny said.

"I guess not," Ig replied.

"You know them, right?"

"I've met some of them," Ig replied.

"Which ones did you meet?"

"I can't tell."

"Is the book true?"

"How would I know?"

"You know more than anyone else around here," Sonny replied, leafing through the book.

ONE HUNDRED NINE

THE FORMAL articles of the Japanese surrender were signed on board the USS Missouri on Sunday, September 2. When Ig started school a few days later, he had no interest in classes or the rifle club. He'd spent three years preparing to be an officer in the club and a rifleman if the war was still going on, and now he didn't care. He was staring out of the physics classroom while the teacher droned on. Every time his teachers talked, he heard the buzzing of bees inside his head.

After the teachers were informed about his father's death and his brother's return from the war, they took it easy on him—everyone except the Physics teacher. Mr. Hendricks did his best to keep Ig's attention in class. He knew Ig was smart and needed to become engaged in his own life again.

"Macdonald, stop daydreaming," Hendricks said from the front of the room. "Can you tell us what today's topic is?"

Ig didn't turn away from the window. The buzzing he heard wasn't bees, after all. I'm not daydreaming, he meant to say, at least not this time. It was a B-52, and it was it was descending too quickly. They had been identifying planes flying overhead for the past four years. He started high school learning to recognize a friend or enemy in the air. Identifying planes, tanks, jeeps, uniforms, emblems, and insignias became second nature to Ig. Other students were gathering at the window. The aircraft was flying low, very low, and heading for downtown Melrose. Hendricks joined them. The engine was on fire, and smoke streaked across the sky. It was too low to go over Mount Hood and land at Logan. Someone from the other side of the building ran in and said they had seen parachutes, so someone must have jumped. Then, the plane dipped from their site, followed by a loud sound.

"I think it hit Mt. Hood."

Ig looked at his teacher. The car keys in his pocket were itching to be used. The teacher nodded. Ig, Alan, and Milt raced across the street and jumped into the car. Ig followed the plume of smoke to Mt. Hood, rushing to the wreckage. It looked like the pilot had looked for an unpopulated area to crash land, and Mt. Hood served that purpose. The pilot was the only person on the plane; all the others had parachuted out. Ig focused on finding a small piece of metal. He needed that metal to remember the bombs and Dad. He'd make one of those arm bracelets in the school shop to remember those who died. He had all his brother's insignias but nothing for Dad.

The world was still adjusting to the war's end, and Ig was adjusting to the world without his father.

ONE HUNDRED TEN

BERTHA NOTICED how all the leaves were transformed into brilliant yellows, reds, and oranges on her walks back and forth to the nursing home in October. Gran could gaze at them as she lay in bed. Some days, she had enough energy to sit up, but she no longer had the strength to get out of bed. The doctor told Bertha it was time to prepare the rest of the family. Bertha and Mabel informed Sue, Willis, and Don that they should visit now or expect to attend her funeral. She did the same with Gran's half-siblings Owen, Wallace, and Maude, along with her 21 or so grandchildren, several of whom were now married with children of their own. She hoped that they would visit Gran or be present at the funeral. She was still upset with Aunt Maude for staying on the Cape instead of attending Mac's funeral.

Gran wanted her granddaughter, Mabel's daughter Marion, to write down her history. Neither Gran nor Mabel could figure out why it had to be Marion, but they did as their mother asked. The next day, Marion arrived with her two little boys. While she sat beside Gran, taking notes as Gran rambled between her childhood and married life, Sonny, Ig, and Ginger entertained the boys at the house. Sonny had returned to Camp Carson, and with nothing left for him to do, he had requested a furlough to spend time with his grandmother. The following day, Gran was gone.

———

Bertha stood at the back of the church. Gran's surviving children, many of her grandchildren, and two great-grandchildren had arrived for Gran's funeral. Being in the same church with the same minister as in July felt sad, yet satisfying. Her mother had stayed as long as she could, and Bertha was grateful for the time they had spent together over the last few years.

Sonny called General Sherman in Boston and requested an extension to his furlough for Gran's funeral. Bertha was happy to have him walk her down the aisle in his uniform. The point system kept him in the army, with little to do. Soldiers who were unmarried and without children were demobbed last. She thought he should petition for an early release since he was now the head of the household, but he declined. Aunt Maude decided Ig would escort her, and Owen thought it best not to argue.

After the service, everyone was invited to the downstairs hall for refreshments. Uncle Owen toasted Gran and Mac. All the neighbors, the doctor, and even the nursing home staff attended. The family, close friends, skiing, and 10th Mountain families returned to the house, where she had cake for Sonny's 22nd birthday. The air was cool, but the event spilled into the yard and driveway. Uncle Owen again toasted Mac, and she was unable to speak. He would have loved seeing everyone again.

ONE HUNDRED ELEVEN

DISGRUNTLED, SONNY got up early to catch the train back to Denver and Camp Carson. He couldn't believe they were making him return to wait for his points group to be discharged. He ran down Cedar Park; the conductor saw his uniform and signaled the engineer to wait. Hopping on, he found a seat. He was one of many soldiers on their way to Boston and then back. His three-year hitch was up in 2 months plus a few days, and now he wanted to be home, but he had committed to staying until he was discharged. As far as he could see, Mom and Ig were as damaged by the war as he was, and he wanted to be home to help, but applying for a bereavement discharge now might delay his discharge.

At North Station, he waved as he ran by the MP; his cousin, John, had been staying with them on weekends, so they had chatted the previous night over dinner. As Ig said, you never knew who would be at the breakfast table in the morning these days. He ran to South Station and stopped at Asa Osbourn's for skiing magazines to read on the long trip to Camp Carson. After buying the Ski Annual, he dashed to South Station and jumped on his train. What would they do if he were late? Put him in the stockade? It was all so silly. That's when he realized that he had forgotten to grab the sandwiches his mother made for him. He could hear her yelling at him from home. How could he be so forgetful? His forgetfulness was getting better. He'd write and apologize as soon as he got to camp.

ONE HUNDRED TWELVE

BERTHA TRUDGED up the street in the slush and snow, walking home from downtown in December. There were Christmas lights downtown this year, and on homes in the neighborhood. There were gifts to buy, and she felt lethargic. For the first time, she didn't know what the future promised. And there was no one there to tell her what would happen.

She stood in front of the home she and Mac had purchased seven years earlier. The home where they would see their boys off on their own, grow old together, and play with grandchildren. Six of them, counting Mac's mother and Gran, had moved in together. Now, she was contemplating selling the house and moving to an apartment in Somerville once Ig graduated in June. The house held too many memories.

She unlocked the back door and dropped her packages in the kitchen. After another successful stomach tumor removal, Ginny greeted her tail wagging. She was almost her old self again, but she wondered how many surgeries the dog could endure. Mabel was in Hudson with her children and grandchildren, and Elaine was visiting her aunt in New Hampshire for the holidays. Ig would be home from school soon.

The club ladies had a festive Christmas party planned, and she had no desire to attend. Johnny was concerned. Mabel had taken her to a doctor, who had written a prescription and suggested a hysterectomy. The minister chatted with her after every Sunday service. They were kind conversations, full of promise for the future, but the Reverend was too optimistic. Mrs. Rosie still checked in, although the 10th Mountain parents no longer met. She needed someone who knew how she felt right now.

Ig was grateful when she suggested that he not attend college right after graduation and take a year to figure things out. She sighed; she knew she needed to start thinking of Ig as Douglas. Funny how she didn't like the nickname Doug for Douglas, but she'd latched onto the short form of Ig for Ignatz.

Ginny barked and headed to the dining room. She followed to see if Ginny had had an accident. There, standing in the living room, grinning like an idiot, was Sonny. She let out a short cry, and they hugged. She smiled at Ig over Sonny's shoulder.

"What are you doing home?"

"Sonny came to the high school, and we came home to surprise you."

"You didn't say that you had received a furlough."

"They let us go 'cause they didn't know what to do with us. I'm supposed to return to Camp Campbell in Kentucky after the New Year."

"What do you mean supposed to?" Bertha was wiping tears from her eyes. "I don't know why you must wait for points to be demobbed. You've done enough."

Ig took the groceries into the kitchen to put away.

"No worries, I'll wait to be discharged from there like a good boy."

"Those are groceries for all of us, not for you to snack on," she called out as Ig headed for the kitchen.

"Mom, there's absolutely nothing here to snack on," came the reply.

"I guess he's not so picky anymore?" Sonny said.

"Now it's finding enough food to feed him."

This comment made Sonny smile, and then he and Bertha laughed. Their laughter became uncontrollable, and they had tears on their cheeks before long. "What's so funny?"

"You," Sonny said, looking at Ig. Ig had a handful of crackers.

"I don't think I'm that funny."

"You're eating anything you can get your hands on."

"There's not enough food to be picky."

This caused more laughter, and Ig started to laugh, too. Ginny was on her front paws, ready to pounce and play.

"If your father were here," Bertha said; tears continued to roll down her face, but she was no longer laughing.

They drove to Hudson on Christmas Day to spend time with Mabel, her children, and grandchildren. The excitement of young children brought Christmas magic. For a while, they didn't dwell too much on those missing.

PART SEVEN: SUMMER 1967

ONE HUNDRED THIRTEEN

THE ONE thing Ig regretted about buying this house was the acre of lawn. While the four kids had plenty of space to play, and Natalie had some flat land for gardening, he was sure mowing it would give him a heart attack one day. If there was one thing he feared, it was having a heart attack and dying unexpectedly, like his father. Natalie was not convinced that he needed a riding mower and suggested the exercise was good for him.

He lived a quiet life as an executive with the gas company in New Hampshire. Early in their married life, he and Natalie had decided to raise their children away from the hustle and bustle, as well as the temptations, of Boston. This job brought them to a town with a strong school system and closer to his mother, who had lived in New Hampshire with his stepfather, Fred, for the past 16 years.

Growing up in Melrose, they had a nice, small, flat yard that allowed them to create a victory garden during World War II. The thought of the war came unbidden. He kept it tucked away in a corner, alongside his memories of his father.

Now, his mother, brother, cousins, and some old friends were coming for a barbecue to remember Fred. Bertha had now outlived two husbands: their father, Mac, in 1945, and Fred in 1967. Sonny, his wife Pat, and their three kids were flying out from Colorado, and it would be the first time they had all been together, possibly since his brother's wedding fifteen years ago. It's funny how life got in the way of their being together.

He paused the lawn mower when he heard the phone ring through the open window. Everyone had their phones set to ring as loudly as possible so they could be heard while outside. If you listened closely enough, you could hear one side of the conversation, like a Bob Newhart routine.

When Natalie yelled out the window that the call was for him, he was relieved to take a break from mowing. Ig went inside, mopped his brow, and picked up the phone. "Douglas Macdonald."

The man introduced himself and explained that he was working on a book about the Manhattan Project and wanted to interview him about his and his father's roles in the project. Ig took the long phone cord that extended from the kitchen, through the dining room, to his home office, using his fingers to ensure the cord was uncurled and didn't rip the phone out of the wall, closing the door behind him. He had been sworn to secrecy. Everyone who had worked on it was sworn to secrecy both during the project and for the 11 years after the war when he worked for Stone and Webster Engineering on atomic-related projects.

He knew books were coming out left and right, but this conversation made his heart beat faster. More than an hour had passed when Natalie lightly knocked on the glass-paned door to get his attention. He shook his head and turned his back to her.

She had brought the three older kids in for lunch when he hung up the phone and stepped out of the office. He made a peanut butter sandwich and joined them at the table, laughing and joking. Then he led the eight-year-old and the six-year-old outside and showed them how to start a gas-powered lawn mower while the 10-year-old headed down the street to play with friends, and Natalie wrestled to get clothes on their 3-year-old.

Later that night, after the kids were in bed and he and Natalie had the living room to themselves, he turned up the TV volume so they could talk without being overheard.

"Did Arthur Gold say anything to you?" Ig asked Natalie.

"Just that he wanted to speak to you. Is he writing a book about you?" Natalie teased.

"Not exactly," he replied.

"Who is he writing about?"

He paused.

"What's he writing about?" Natalie asked.

"The Manhattan Project."

"Does he want to talk about your dad?"

"Someone gave him my name as a former messenger, and the son of a Manhattan Project engineer."

"I thought the records weren't public yet?"

"They aren't, not until 72 or 73. Whatever they consider 25 years after the project ended. That hasn't stopped the scientists and Groves from writing books."

"Did he interview you?"

"We talked about a few things. He's sending some questions and wants me to think about the answers before we talk. He's recording all the conversations. He doesn't know as much as he thinks he does."

"I see." Natalie continued with her knitting, frowning.

"Or I'm just kidding myself. He's sending along some questions, and then we'll chat. An envelope will arrive, and a few more phone calls. I told him to hang up if one of the kids answers. I don't want the kids writing anything down or yelling around the neighborhood."

"An envelope arrived late this afternoon. I put it on your desk."

As much as he wanted to find out how his father died, he wasn't at all sure of this. He and Natalie had been trained to be cautious and circumspect due to their work on atomic projects for Stone and Webster Engineering.

"You're worried?" Natalie asked quietly.

"I've spent so long keeping secrets. I don't know if or when I should give them up."

He entered the office on Sunday morning while Natalie took the children to church. The manila envelope had the University of California at Berkeley Physics Department logo and return address. It impressed him, but not as much as the author had hoped. He had mentioned working with graduate students on his research. He opened the envelope and pulled out the sheaf of papers. The first question asked for a description of typical family life before the war. Were things normal then? Or did they only think they were?

The scientists and engineers from Berkeley would know what his father had done, but would they have provided information to the author? Or had someone from Stone and Webster Engineering pointed the author to him? A lot of the people Dad had worked with were still at Stone and Webster Engineering.

He left the survey on the desk in the office and closed the door. His four children obeyed the rule about never entering the office if the door were shut, a small victory with four children under 10.

Ig walked down Boston's Devonshire Street, his ten-year-old in tow, checking out the buildings where he once worked for Stone and Webster. They were being demolished. He had time before picking up his mother at the airport on her return trip from visiting Fred's oldest daughter in Ohio.

He described the shortcuts he would take through alleys between buildings to deliver plans from one office to another. According to the signs and pictures on the fence, the alleys and smaller buildings were being torn down to make way for concrete and glass buildings that occupy an entire block. Dust filled the air and clung to their clothes.

"Ed, how are you?" he said to the older, heavy-set man in a wool suit that seemed incongruous on a hot summer day.

"Well, I'll be damned," Ed stopped and shook his hand. "What are you doing here?"

"Checking out the construction, telling my daughter here about being a messenger and carrying plans through the alleys."

"Those alleys are disappearing. The landscape is changing."

"So I see. I haven't been into the city in a while."

"Where are you working now?"

"At the gas company in Concord."

"Out in the boonies, huh?" Ed said. "They'd take you back in a heartbeat. We could use someone with your skills and knowledge."

"That's nice of you to say. I don't think going back would work for Natalie and I."

"You and Natalie are still married?"

"Is he talking about Mom?" his daughter asked.

The man blushed a little and pulled at his collar. They had both forgotten a child was listening.

"Sara Olson is retiring soon. She'd be thrilled to see you again," he said.

"I thought she would have retired already."

"She was needed, so she stayed."

He got the point. She was loyal, and he less so. They had paid for his college education, although not with the degree he wanted, and he had skipped out when he didn't like the direction they wanted him to take.

"Do you know how my father died?" he asked. It was on his mind, and now was as good a time as any.

The man paused, looked Ig up and down, then looked around at the people on the street.

"How do you think he died?"

Ig launched into three scenarios he had spent years mulling over. The first was that his father had a heart attack at the Knoxville, Tennessee, airport while waiting for a plane home and died there, which is the cause of death on his death certificate. The second was that he died at Oak Ridge, Tennessee, and rather than deal with the mess his death would cause, he was taken to the Knoxville airport and left to be found there. Not a pleasant thought but one he could see happening. The third scenario was that his father was traveling from Oak Ridge to Knoxville airport in the middle of a convoy of trucks escorting 'product' to Los Alamos. The transport's criticality, the road's narrowness, and the number of vehicles meant they could not turn back or leap forward. When he fell ill, they proceeded to the airport and dealt with him there.

"You're heading in the right direction on that. But this isn't the time or place for this discussion because you never know who's listening." The man nodded and looked around as if he was looking for someone.

"What do you mean? Security is long gone."

"Not with all the demolition and construction. They've had security personnel everywhere, looking for anything that might have been hidden or lost in the building. You know what I mean." The time he and another messenger tried to borrow some blueprints would follow him forever.

"I need to be getting on," Ed said. "Be sure to reach out to Sara."

Shaking his head, Ig watched Ed continue down Devonshire Street, blending into the crowd.

"What did your father do?"

"He inspected things, lots of things. Let's get some lunch before we pick up your grandmother."

He took his daughter to the Robin Hood diner, one of his and Natalie's favorite places in their working days. He put her on a stool at the counter and studied the menu while she spun around.

"Well, I figured I'd find you here."

He turned to find Sara Olson smiling down on him. "And this must be your oldest."

He introduced Sara to his daughter, then quickly placed an order to keep his daughter occupied while they chatted.

"I hear you're retiring," he said.

"Friday is my last day," Sara said.

"What will you do?"

"I'm spending a few months on the Cape with my niece. Then I want to travel."

"That sounds great."

"By the way, you scared the bejesus out of Ed. Be careful, things aren't as open as you may think."

"That seems strange."

"You've been away too long. There's always something going on with atomic energy."

"Is Houston around?"

"He's one of the folks checking us out. I was sorry to read your stepfather's obituary in the paper.

"Unlike my dad's."

Sonny arrived with his wife, Pat, and their three children, who were making their first-ever visit to New England and were staying with their mother at the farm in North Hampton that Bertha and Fred had purchased after selling the family home in Melrose.

As the six piled out of the car, he introduced Natalie and Pat. They had written to each other and spoken on the phone, but this was their first in-person meeting. Natalie and Pat corralled the kids in the backyard while he steered his mother and brother into the office. He told them about the phone call and the survey.

"You say he hasn't told you how they got your name?" Bertha asked.

"He hasn't answered that question directly," Doug replied.

"You should tear it up and throw it away," she said.

"We've always wanted to know what happened. Maybe this will get us some answers?" Sonny said.

"Don't be ridiculous. Security will be on us like flies in honey," Bertha said. She harbored a great deal of disdain for the security personnel who had monitored her and Mac for the last few years of his life. "I never want someone sitting in a car watching my comings and goings ever again."

"Some of these questions make me laugh," Sonny said.

"Like what?"

"What was life like before the war? You could write a whole book on that. Hey, remember when we took you skiing when you were like 10?"

"He was 11," Bertha said, suppressing a smile. Sonny had effectively distracted her.

"Why did you never go with us again?" Sonny asked.

"I was 11 and you were 17. The other guys were older than you. It was an eye-opening weekend."

"Why did you let us take him?" Sonny asked his mother.

"If I remember correctly, my father had died, Mac's mother had died, and Ig had no one to keep an eye on him while I spent the day with my friends. We decided his older brother could do it," Bertha said.

Ig laughed. At least they were reminiscing and not arguing.

"How did we find out that the war had started? Are they kidding? It was all around us," Bertha said, reviewing the questions.

"It's bringing back memories. Remember how Gran couldn't get over the bombing of Charles Church?"

"It was where she was baptized," Sonny said.

"And where her brother was buried," Ig said.

"What the hell! They want to know why it was important to bring the boys home? If Dad were here, he'd box their ears. I need a beer," Sonny said, heading to the kitchen.

"You don't need a beer," Bertha said, her lips pressed firmly. "I've seen you when you have too much beer."

Ig looked at Sonny quizzically but said nothing.

"Are you still reading that thing?" Sonny said, stepping back into the office with two beers, one for himself and one for Ig. Bertha rolled her eyes.

"It's a stupid question," Sonny said. "I'll tell you why because we were fighting and dying overseas. We saw things no 18-year-old should ever see."

"You were 21," Bertha said automatically.

"I saw things no 18 or 21-year-old should see."

While Sonny muttered and flipped the questionnaire pages, Bertha talked about the many sympathy cards she had received at Mac's death. Several mentioned how much he wanted to 'bring the boys home'.

"I don't think we should forget how deadly the war was," Sonny said.

"At least we don't have any children who are old enough to be drafted," Ig replied. Sonny's sons were 13 and 11, and Ig's sons were 6 and 3.

"You just wait. Some idiot will find a reason to draft our kids. Probably the girls, too."

Ig had listened to his brother's stories about the 10th Mountain Division in Italy after he was discharged, and they were both responsible for washing and drying the supper dishes when Bertha took in boarders to make ends meet. Stories that Sonny wouldn't share with their mother or anyone other than Tiny. Back then, he supported the household with his salary as a clerk at Stone and Webster, while Sonny used his VA benefits to complete his degree in English Literature at Tufts. Then, their mother remarried, sold the house, and moved.

"Are you sure you want to answer these questions?" Sonny asked after he finished reading.

"I don't know; that's why I wanted to show them to both of you," Ig replied.

"I say let sleeping dogs lie," Sonny replied. "No need to dredge up the past. It's not like the project treated us all that well."

"They paid for my degree," Ig replied.

"For accounting, you wanted to be an engineer," Sonny said. "Plus, they made you work full-time while you finished your degree. And then they sent you to California."

"Dad wanted to move to California after the war," Ig replied.

"That's enough," Bertha said. "It's time to join the party outside, not rehash things we can't change."

Early Monday morning, Ig took the survey to the office to shred. Perhaps one day he would reveal more information, but he wasn't ready to discuss his father or the most significant project ever conceived with this professor and his graduate assistants. As his mother said, they should look to the future, not the past.

* * *

10th Mountain Division battalion locations during the Spring Offensive – March 3-6, 1945

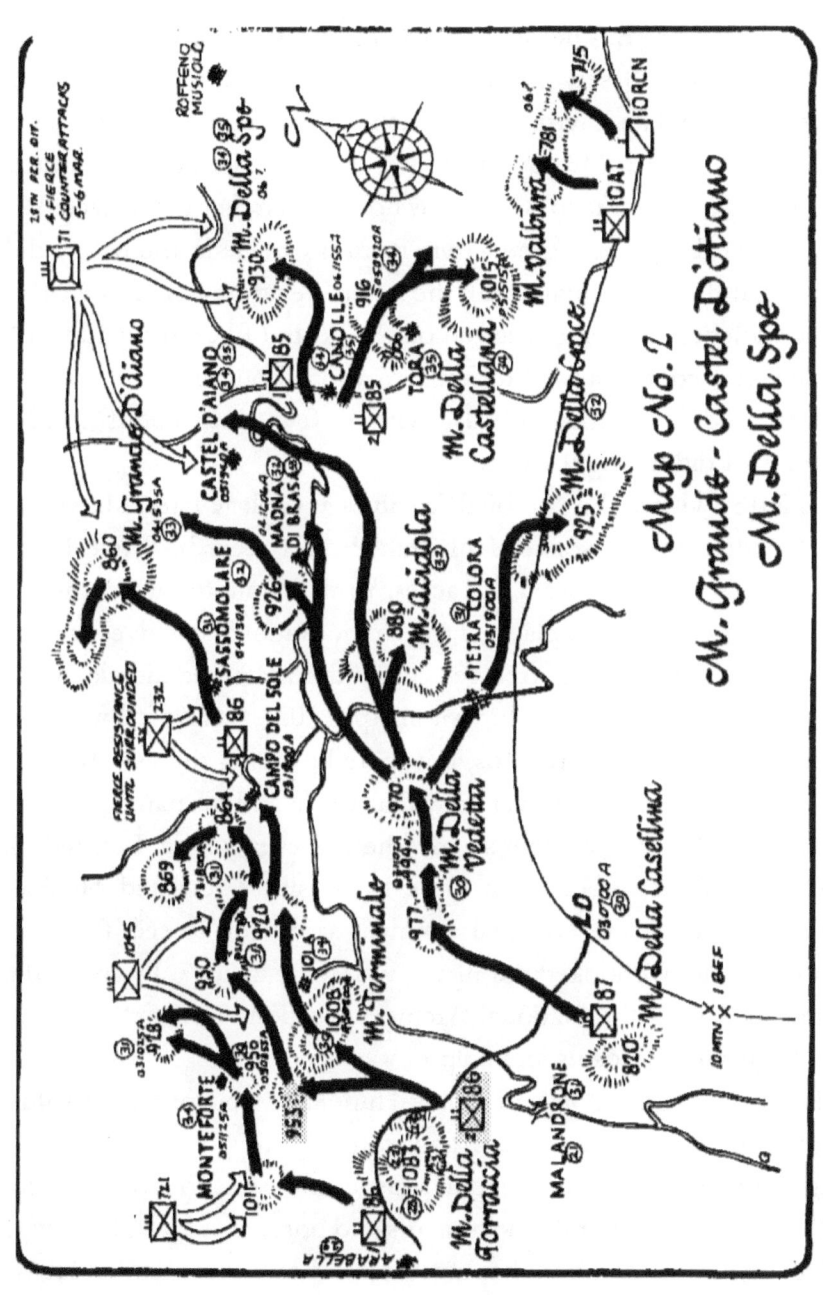

ACKNOWLEDGMENTS

IF YOU are reading this before you read the book, there are some spoilers here. This story is based on letters my uncle wrote home during his time in the 10th Mountain Division and which my grandmother kept in a green box until her death. My parents stored the green box in their attic and eventually gave it to me to store at my home when they downsized. While I knew that there were some letters from my uncle in the box, I didn't realize that the box contained all the letters he wrote home as well as all the condolence cards she received on the death of her husband in 1945. These letters contain a wealth of information about the family and what they were doing during WWII, with a few clues about what my grandfather did during the war.

In 2018 I visited the National Archives at College Park, Maryland, to see if I could review some Manhattan Project records. While I wasn't given access to secure files, I had access to all the photos and some plans. I followed this up with a planned trip to the National Archives at Atlanta in April 2020. When the Archives closed during the pandemic, my visit was put on hold. I was able to visit in April 2022, unsure if I would find his name in the written records, but there he was in the very first box I reviewed. I reviewed files every day that week, and his name popped up again on my last day where it seemed he was everywhere. I visited again in October 2022. In between these two visits, I revisited Manhattan Project records at the National Archives at Boston to see if there was anything I had overlooked during my visit there in 2017. I want to thank all the staff at all the National Archives locations I visited. They were unfailingly kind, gracious and helpful.

I want to thank Don and Emily Hunnicutt who provided valuable insights about the documents I had in hand during a visit to The Oak Ridge Heritage and Preservation Association (ORPHA) in October 2018. Don looked over the documents and noted that given his low Oak Ridge employee number, he must have been there early. He was. Through Don and Emily, I was able to meet Emily's father, Ed Westcott, the official photographer for the Manhattan Project in Oak Ridge during WWII.

The Voices of the Manhattan Project website hosts many interviews (https://ahf.nuclearmuseum.org/voices/) with those who worked on the Manhattan Project and this resource proved invaluable.

I want to thank Keli Schmid, 10th Mountain Division Archivist, Special Collections and Archives, Central Library, Denver Public Library for all her help accessing 10th Mountain Division information held in the Archives. I had done a short oral history on my uncle for an Oral History class at Northeastern University and that oral history is now at the Denver Public Library.

And the Melrose Public Library for assistance in accessing the Melrose Free Press, the newspaper of record in Melrose during the war years.

My siblings, Mary, Robert and John, and my cousins, Don, Rory, Alison and Crislynn, their spouses and children have received more information from me that they ever thought possible regarding our shared grandparents, the letters, and other random facts I picked up and passed on. They graciously answered any questions I posed. We are the grandchildren of Bertha and Mac, and the children of Ig and Sonny. And Bob MacLean who told me about his favorite "Uncle Mac".

I would never have gotten this far without the support and advice of my writer's group – the Jitterbugs – Cameron, Lisa, Amanda, Jane, Betsy and sometimes Louis. Seven years ago, we were a group of strangers who agreed to meet and talk about all things writing. Our group has become a community of friends, confidants, and supporters of our writing and life journeys.

My writing community among the Writer's in Residence at Follow Your Art in Melrose Massachusetts, is a diverse group of fiction, non-fiction, poetry and script writers who share a writing space and our knowledge of different topics through meetings and classes.

Through a member of my writing group, I found Steve Parolini, the Novel Doctor. I have deep appreciation and awe for this editor who took my manuscript for a developmental edit and set me on the right course. When the manuscript became a novel, he completed a line edit.

I was fortunate to put out a request to five different cover artists and found Peter Selig – cover designer extraordinaire. He took my words and created a visual book cover that blew me away.

And last, but most important, I want to thank my husband, Sean, who has lived with me through all the research, writing, angst, and joy of writing a novel based on letters and the random memories of stories I heard as a child growing up in a household that liked to keep secrets. He read and edited various versions of this book.

Please know that any and all errors and omissions are due to me and me alone. I have been fortunate to have had so much support in my journey and no one other than me is responsible for misinterpreting, misrepresenting or overlooking any details.

Anne E. Macdonald
Melrose, Massachusetts
August 2025

ABOUT THE AUTHOR

Anne E. Macdonald is the author of two mystery stories, DEADLINES ARE MURDER and WEDDINGS ARE MURDER, with the third, TRIALS ARE MURDER, in development. She writes more about the letters used in creating this story on her blog. She lives with her husband in Melrose, Massachusetts. Read more about the author at aemacdonald.com.